PRAISE FOR MARK T. SULLIVAN'S "HARD NEWS"

"HARD NEWS" is a great read. Mark Sullivan does an expert's job of taking you inside the newsroom and out on the story. He adds the right touches of cynicism, humor and mystery. His characters, from the dastardly to the noble, are genuine and great fun to follow through a story that never disappoints—unless you count how you wish it hadn't ended."

—Michael Connelly
Edgar-Award winning author of THE BLACK ICE

"Sullivan's *Post* newsroom pulsates with captivating weirdness.. . . [He] has created some memorable characters."

—Publishers Weekly

"Rings with authenticity."

—The Plain Dealer

"Sets a cracking pace."

—The Greenwich Times

"This one has all the elements of the best. Hard-hitting, tough and durable characters. Prime setting and a smashing conclusion."

—Kemper County Messenger

HARD
NEWS

Mark T. Sullivan

PINNACLE BOOKS
KENSINGTON PUBLISHING CORP.
http://www.pinnacle.books.com

PINNACLE BOOKS are published by

Kensington Publishing Corp.
850 Third Avenue
New York, NY 10022

First Pinnacle Printing: November, 1996

Printed in the United States of America
10 9 8 7 6 5 4 3 2 1

For my mother, who taught me to love to write, and my father, who taught me to love to laugh.

Acknowledgments

I am indebted to countless fellow journalism survivors for all the great stories, gossips, and intrigues that festered and warped in my mind over the years. Many of you don't know how much you helped. Special appreciation must go to my former partners David Hasymeyer, Rick Shaughnessy, and Joe Cantlupe, and my editor Todd Merriman, for teaching me much about the business of being an investigative reporter. And to cohorts Ann Krueger, Jeff Ristine, and Preston Turegano, for teaching me too much about the strange dynamics of newsroom politics.

I am indebted to fellow print reporters Tom Bowman, Jim Erickson, Brigid Schulte, Andrea Sand, and Jacqueline Swearingen, who suffered as readers and critics of the early drafts. Writers Damien Slattery, John Glionna, and Mel Allen offered advice and boosted my morale so many times I can't thank them enough.

Thanks also to my agent, Linda Chester, and her patient associate, Billie Fitzpatrick, who provided invaluable counsel in finishing the manuscript, and to Sarah Gallick, my editor.

But my undying gratitude upon the completion of this novel must go to two people: Kazuo Chiba, my Aikido sensei, who gave me the courage to walk away to follow my dream, and Betsy, my wife, who led the way.

Whenever I take up a newspaper and read it, I fancy I see ghosts creeping between the lines.

—Henrik Ibsen

Part 1

NO SACRED COWS

Self-Help . . .

T hey found her because of a personal improvement program.

Mick Hennessy, an out-of-work, overweight aerospace engineer, had spent the better part of the last six months watching half-hour television commercials posing as daytime talk shows. He could recite the scripts of every new infomercial touting the latest kitchen device, real estate recipe, or hair detangler.

Nothing had prompted him to open his wallet, however, until he'd gone channel surfing one day about two weeks prior to the discovery and seen the big toothsome smile and heard the velvety, supercharged voice. The product: a twenty-eight-day series of motivational audiotapes—only $149.95!—all produced by a smooth-talking, incredibly wealthy guy in his late twenties who flew his own helicopter back and forth between personal castles he'd had built in California and Arizona.

Mick was mesmerized. The gray flannel guru seemed to look right inside him, to tell him things that he instinctively knew but had never acted upon. If he bought the tapes, the man told him, Mick would learn to control his emotions, to improve his physical state, and to make his family love him. Mick would become more than the colossal flop he was now. Mick picked up the phone. He ordered the tapes. He listened to the voice every day.

Which was why Mick had suggested the late-afternoon desert hike with his adolescent son. A couple of hours of exercise and father-son bonding in the great out-of-doors. Physical, financial, and emotional well-being couldn't be far away.

Now, as they pulled off the highway sixty miles outside the city, his son, Tim, scrunched down in the front seat of the airconditioned car and scowled. The boy wanted to spend the afternoon in his darkened bedroom, rattling his brain with the heavy metal throb of Clinically Comatose, his favorite new band. The temperature outside hovered near one hundred. The manzanita and greasewood stood like stick matches waiting for friction.

"This is gonna be righteous," Tim groused. "We're going to fry out there. And as we die, we'll watch the vultures begin to circle. I hope you drop first."

"Shut up, Tim." Mick heard a voice in his head preach understanding. "We'll make it a short walk, okay?"

Tim groaned, but got out. He squinted at the landscape. He noticed a pile of massive rocks that jutted off the desert floor about a half mile in from the road. *Hey, good site for a black mass,* he thought. *Let's check it out.*

"Bouldering, Dad," Tim said. "We'll go bouldering. Saw it on ESPN."

Mick rubbed his gut uncertainly. Gripping scorched rocks wasn't what he had in mind. Honestly he'd rather be back in his Barcalounger seeing what Cher and Victoria Principal had cooked up for hair sheen. The voice again. This time it spoke soothingly about commitment and follow-through and how people could walk across red-hot coals barefoot if they set their minds to it.

Tim jogged off through the brush in black T-shirt, black jeans, and green high-topped sneakers. Mick wheezed and followed.

Tim made the rim of the boulder pile five minutes before his father. He examined the surface of the stones for runes or dried blood from animal sacrifice. Disappointed to find none, he climbed higher. There the rocks formed a ring. He came over the top and dropped into a broad, sand-filled circle. He stopped short.

"Totally cool!" he whispered.

She looked just like the cover art on the Clinically Comatose CD he'd bought the other day. She was blond. Her skin waxy. She was nude from the waist down. Her legs were splayed. She wore black stiletto heels. White cord stretched from her wrists to a pair of gnarled live oaks. One firm breast jutted from the torn black blouse. Fishnet stockings cinched her neck. Her bulging eyes seemed to study him. And what the hell was that coming out of her mouth? Silently Tim hoped they were bugs; his friends at school would lose it! He took two steps forward and frowned. Gravel?

Tim was trying to remember if he'd ever seen tiny stones shoved in the mouths of tied-up heavy metal babes on MTV when his father huffed and scrambled into the macabre scene.

Tim turned, beaming back at Mick's horrified expression. "Welcome to Satan's Lair, Dad. Bet that old self-help dude never talked about stuff like this!"

The Living Dead . . .

General assignment reporter Prentice LaFontaine figured he could go to his grave happy if he ever managed to unravel the intricate mystery that was *The Post*.

It troubled him constantly how the editorial staff, a dysfunctional pack of 175 neurotics, paranoids, egoists, eccentrics, and Ivy League graduates managed to put out a newspaper every day. He declined to consider his own status among the information freaks. He'd been at work nearly seven hours and had successfully avoided being given an assignment. There had been too many of his fellow workers to study today, too many gossip leads inside *The Post* to run down, too many power analyses to perform to risk being sent outside the confines of the newsroom.

Another hour and he was free. LaFontaine pretended to focus on the neon verbs, nouns, and adjectives glowing on his computer screen. Out of the corner of his eye he watched the city desk's editing drones continue their dizzying series of meetings, phone calls, and career-enhancing maneuvers. Four hours to deadline. The management spear-carriers of *The Post*'s hard news operation already had that glazed veneer about them. Their expressions reminded LaFontaine of a movie he'd once seen about machines taking over human bodies. *That's who they are,* he thought to himself; *they're the Stepford Editors!*

LaFontaine adjusted the cuff of his purple pinpoint cotton shirt, ran his fingers lightly over his newly coiffed hair, checked his waistline, then patted himself on the left hand in congratulation. Stepford Editors! The phrase was bound to annoy the powerful and delight the downtrodden.

He reached past his papier-mâché statues of Joe DiMaggio, Eddie Fisher, and Arthur Miller to adjust the cardboard sign taped to the edge of his desk. In bold red crayon it read: "ALL THE DIRT THAT'S FIT TO SPREAD." He smiled. He remained the undisputed champion. They didn't call him News for nothing.

"News! Where's that no-account McCarthy?" growled a gigantic black woman dressed in an orange-and-ebony batik jumpsuit.

LaFontaine shuddered. Caught by a Stepford Editor.

Only this one's eyes weren't glazed; they popped around inside her head like Ping-Pong balls.

"Ms. X-executive assistant city editor, do I look like poor Orpheus's keeper?" he replied in his deep Louisiana twang. "Probably at the night cops shop. It is four o'clock, isn't it?"

Her popping eyes slowed. Her lids drooped. Reporters like LaFontaine pissed Claudette Forbes off. Which wasn't unusual. The fact was that she had been pissed off since before Martin Luther King's assassination, at least since the Watts riots, maybe as far back as that white doctor's cold hand slapping her rump. So predictable were her daily fulminations that one day LaFontaine had compared her to the angry dead black nationalist and had given her the newsroom sobriquet of Claudette X. No one had the guts to call her that to her face. No one except News.

"There's been another body found in the desert," she said.

"So he'll actually get a byline," LaFontaine said. "Three months. It's about time."

"If we can find him," she said.

"Beep him," LaFontaine suggested.

"I have, three times."

"Then why bother me? Let me alone now, Ms. X. I'm busy, busy, busy."

"Not so fast," the editor said. "I want a follow-up interview to your development story."

"More drivel on that dreadful monstrosity?" he asked, affecting weariness. "It's only a construction project."

"Sloan Burkhardt's going to control twenty-two acres of downtown waterfront and to you it's only a construction project? You ever hear of urban renewal?"

"Such terms imply a greater good," News replied. "No such thing. With private development it's just one monument to ego replacing another."

Before Claudette X could respond, LaFontaine lowered his voice and whispered conspiratorially. "Speaking of edi-

fices to ego, I hear Neil Harpster's bought a new home up in
The Ranch and is shelling out thousands for landscaping,
including a greenhouse. Anything to add?"

Her shoulders—massive and round from her days as a
college shot-putter—tensed. "Prentice, you spent as much
time digging up news as you do gossip about this place,
you'd have won the prize by now."

"Heavens!" the general assignment reporter cried.
"News win the Pulitzer? And become as respected and insufferable as our great editor-in-chief, Connor Lawlor? I
think not, Ms. X."

Claudette X scowled. "I want you to arrange an interview ASAP," she ordered. "And if McCarthy calls in, tell
him to get out to the desert, pronto!"

News held his fist to his chest like a Roman centurion. "It
shall be done, my liege."

Claudette X bolted back toward the city desk. Grudg-
ingly, LaFontaine called Burkhardt's office. His secretary
told News that the developer had a late cancellation in his
schedule. He could see LaFontaine at six-thirty if it was convenient.

It wasn't convenient. It meant overtime, which News despised. But it was better than having to explain why he'd
passed up a follow-up interview. He told the secretary he'd
be there.

Which gave News an hour to waste. Not much time. But
at least he'd be able to take inventory of this afternoon's go-
ings-on. LaFontaine looked around. A warm prickly feeling
came over him. Even after nearly twenty years in the business, the buzz, the whine, the screech of news gathering still
managed to comfort and goad him.

Like *The Beacon*, its last remaining competitor, *The Post* occupied the entire twenty-first floor of a skyscraper, the base
of which filled a city block. Divided into five main sections—Sports, Features, Business, Copy, and, the last and
largest, City—to the uninitiated the newsroom more closely

resembled an orgy scene for pack rats than the nerve center of the city's second-largest circulation daily. Littered across desks were stacks of yellowed past editions, crinkled budget reports, forgotten indictments, unread press releases, unintelligible legal briefs, half-used white notebooks, and coffee cups sprouting mold; not to mention reams of wire copy, frayed police reports, transcripts of ancient court proceedings and the letters: letters from critical readers, letters from hateful readers, letters from bigoted readers, and—the letters LaFontaine respected most—missives from the truly deranged; they were the only ones who seemed to understand the world these days.

Amid this paper jungle telephones rang, computer keyboards snapped and clacked, editors swore and pounded their fists, reporters begged for stories, reporters begged off of stories. Reporter and editor alike peered over their shoulders to make sure no one with clout coveted their jobs. Clerks bustled with shopping carts filled with interoffice memos. Fax machines cawed with the latest spin of every public relations flack in the city trying to influence *The Post*'s current interpretation of truth, justice, and the American way.

LaFontaine peered over at a man in his fifties slouched before a computer terminal. A photograph of three monkeys was taped to the side of the machine. "HEARS ALL EVIL, SEES ALL EVIL, SPEAKS NO . . ." was scrawled underneath the photo in black Magic Marker. The man's complexion was sallow, his flesh spare, his knuckles bubbled with scabs. His brown hair hung crazily over his telephone headset. Behind his thick glasses, his eyes seemed to glow an unnatural red.

The Zombie was *The Post*'s obituary writer, had been for nearly twelve years, during which no one, not even LaFontaine, had heard him speak an intelligible sentence. How the Zombie managed to get accurate information from funeral homes, clergymen, and bereaved relatives—and then to fashion such beautiful, terse elegies to the dead—was one of the newspaper's many enigmas.

LaFontaine followed the Zombie's gaze to the series of glass-faced boxes that stretched along the north and south walls of the newsroom. The line of cubicles served as offices to *The Post*'s top editors. The majority of reporters referred to the giant aquariums and their occupants as the "Glassholes." News prided himself on his more sardonic appraisal. Long ago he'd named the offices "Lobotomy Lane," for they were inhabited by a dozen post operatives. How else could they have risen to power in such an insane business?

Following his daily routine, LaFontaine studied the configuration of Lobotomy Lane. He searched for clues to the shifting winds of influence. Some evidence was easily discerned. The raw power of each editor, for example, was determined by the proximity of his or her office to the northeastern and largest of the Glassholes, the one occupied by Connor Lawlor, *The Post*'s owner, publisher, and editor-in-chief.

News, however, based his analysis on more subtle manifestations of clout: whether an editor visited another Glasshole or was visited; whether an editor warranted copies of *The New York Times, The Wall Street Journal* and the *Los Angeles Times* each morning; who an editor lunched with and how often; whether an editor sat behind a desk during large meetings or sat in supplication before the real deal. This was the grist LaFontaine gathered, milled, and leavened with his own cynical critique. This was what made him the peerless gossip baker in the hot oven of the newsroom.

LaFontaine glanced again at the Zombie, the only person who studied Lobotomy Lane as much as he did. There he was, staring bullets at the offices. And what's this? He's breaking the tops off a bouquet of daffodils while he leers? That's a new twist.

What the Zombie must discern with such focus! Then again, LaFontaine thought, the Zombie didn't watch the

Glassholes for pleasure. LaFontaine's mind swirled with the Zombie's possible motives, almost all of them cast in shades of flesh and blood. He shuddered, then checked the time. Half an hour to go. Maybe he'd head to Burkhardt's office early. He tossed his notebook into his alligator-skinned briefcase and snapped it shut.

But before he left he sneaked a peek under his desk to see if it was big enough to conceal him should the Zombie's magenta eyes ever start to slap side to side like excited atoms before the Big Bang.

No Humans Involved . . .

An hour later, Gideon McCarthy angled his battered blue Toyota sedan past the fire truck mounted with a generator to run electricity out to the body. It would be dark soon. The portable lights would illuminate the crime scene. He parked beyond the medical examiner's blue van. Two uniformed officers drank coffee with the gurney men. A good sign: the body wasn't ready to be moved yet; the homicide detectives were still out there.

McCarthy prayed that the homicide cops—uncooperative and cocky as a rule—would be willing sources this evening. He desperately needed a good yarn. If he was ever to emerge from the black hole he'd dug for himself, he had to break stories, stories with weight, stories that would force the editors to put his name back in the paper. Three long months without a byline. To a daily reporter three months without a bylined story was worse than limbo—it was oblivion.

To make matters worse, he'd gotten here late. He'd heard the pages from Claudette X, but had been unable to return the call for nearly an hour. His car had been broken into for the third time this year and he'd been filling out police reports. *Maybe I'll get lucky and contract polio tomorrow,* he thought.

Time to work. McCarthy grabbed his tape recorder and notebook. He jogged to the end of the yellow tape line, then angled off through the brush.

Within fifty yards he gasped for air. He felt like hell and knew he appeared worse. He was barely thirty-five, but gray had vanquished brown in the battle for his hair color. Cocoons of pasty skin hung under his eyes, which were receding, liquid and ruddy. He told himself his physical ailments stemmed from the car crash two years ago. On the back wall, however, was the knowledge that mental scars often reveal themselves on the flesh.

Ten minutes later, after nearly breaking his ankle twice on exposed roots, he crawled up the embankment of a dry riverbed to encounter the singularly diminutive figure of Lt. Geribome Fisk.

"They're coming out of the frigging sand now!" the homicide detective screeched. Up the hill through the little detective's legs, McCarthy could make out the lower half of her body and the cords which linked her to the live oaks.

"I thought I told you to keep the media back on the road!" Fisk squealed at the cops who stood by as the evidence technicians photographed and combed the area.

One of the patrol officers, a beefy kid with an acne-scarred face, mumbled, "I sealed it off back there by the road, Lieutenant."

"Didn't work, did it, Officer?" Fisk demanded. He stood on his tiptoes, scowling up at the patrol cop. "As if it wasn't bad enough that flaky kid tried to scrawl a pentangle in the sand around the body, now we got two reporters on the crime scene."

"You want I should take them out of here, Lieutenant?"

"And hear them shriek about their rights? I can't take that tonight. Get him over there with *The Beacon* woman."

"C'mon, Fisko," McCarthy pleaded. "I'm on deadline here. What do we got? Is she part of the series?"

Fisk smiled sourly at the reporter. "What do you need to talk to me for, McCarthy? Why don't you just wait to see *The Beacon*'s early edition, copy down what she writes, and put your byline over it? That's your scam these days, isn't it?"

McCarthy took the taunt in stride. "That's what I've always admired about you, Fisko. You'd kick a man when he was down."

"Payback's a bitch," Fisk said.

"Look, when did I write that story? Eight years ago?"

"I got the memory of an elephant."

And the stature of a rat, McCarthy thought. But there was no use antagonizing a source he needed. "Fine, Lieutenant," he said. "I'll wait for your words of wisdom."

The acne-scarred patrol officer pointed a thick finger toward the portable lights. McCarthy shuffled off, scribbling a description of the scene in his notebook.

Fisk. The shortest cop he'd ever met. The most egotistical cop he'd ever met. The smartest cop he'd ever met. Over the years McCarthy had written a dozen or more articles about the detective's unconventional prowess. Fisk's first big case occurred when he worked vice. He'd gone undercover as a telephone repairman to break up a huge gambling operation in a condo overlooking the Sea View Race Track. Then he'd moved to narcotics and ran a famous investigation into a cocaine-trafficking ring run by a brilliant fifteen-year-old kid nicknamed Short Stuff Swain.

Fisk appeared destined for the top rungs of the force, maybe even Chief T. Lawrence Leslie's job one day. That was before the detective transferred into special investigations and was given his own car. The word McCarthy got back then was that Fisk worked less for the department than the chief. His job: to gather dirt for Leslie.

One day McCarthy found a big envelope in his mailbox. It was filled with photographs and detailed logs of Fisk's personal comings and goings in a city-owned Pontiac Grand Am. The detective claimed he never used the car off duty. McCarthy knew better. Among other things, Fisk had driven it all the way to Las Vegas with two of his civilian pals for a weekend of gambling, golf, and hookers over five-foot-ten.

A good story for McCarthy. A bad story for Fisk. Police Chief Leslie knew the effect of bad publicity. Leslie busted Fisk back to sergeant and transferred him to burglary. Fisk wallowed there for several years. Then he broke a massive ring that brought stolen cars into Mexico, a coup which prompted his transfer to homicide. When was that? Four years ago? At least that. And now Fisk was the supervising homicide investigator.

McCarthy's nuts were in a vise. No Fisk. No story.

McCarthy glanced up from his notebook to see a very good-looking woman in her late twenties scribbling in her own white notebook. She wore a white cotton blouse, khaki pants, and purple hiking boots. Braided dark hair hung over her left shoulder.

"You Karen Rivers?" he asked.

"Who's asking?" she replied, still writing.

"Gideon McCarthy. I work for *The Post.*"

She paused to consider him. "Thought you'd look different."

"How's that?"

Rivers stood. "Seedier perhaps."

McCarthy rubbed his jaw. So this is how it was now. "Well," he said. "At least you look like I'd imagined you would."

"How's that?"

"Like most *Beacon* reporters. Studious wannabes."

She sneered. "I'm no want to be, Mr. Has-Been. I already am. And I'm not long for this job."

"How unusual these days," he replied. "A young reporter who thinks she's ready to be a national correspondent after four months on the night cops beat."

"I've got a master's degree and did internships at the *Chicago Tribune*, *The Miami Herald*, and *The Oregonian*," she said, her arms crossed now.

"A master's degree in journalism!" McCarthy exclaimed. "Don't tell me now. I'll guess. Studied arrogance, a patina of cynicism, and the certainty that grunt journalism jobs are beneath you. Northwestern? No, Columbia, am I right?"

The Beacon reporter furiously twisted her braid between her fingers. "All they told me was you were a plagiarist. They forgot to mention A-1 asshole."

"It only comes out in the presence of special people."

"If you'd been at *The Beacon* and pulled that stunt, Harry Plake would have fired you on the spot."

McCarthy didn't answer. She was right. If it hadn't been for Connor Lawlor's kindness and the fact that *The Post* and *The Beacon* were embroiled in a vicious circulation war, he'd be flipping burgers in some hamburger stand right now. Or worse, sporting that gold coat for Century 21 Real Estate, practicing his double-pump handshake for newlywed couples trying to take that first step up the ladder of the American Dream.

From behind them Fisk said "You guys got two minutes. One ground rule. There are details about the killing I won't get into."

"So you think she is a serial victim?" McCarthy asked.

Fisk stuffed his hands in his pants pockets. "You can never be sure in these situations, but we're leaning in that direction."

"You have an ID?" Rivers asked.

"We can't make a positive until we check dental records."

"How was she killed?" McCarthy asked. "I mean, I could see she was tied up."

Fisk nodded. "Like the others: bound and strangled."

"Sexually abused?" Rivers asked.

"Doesn't appear so," the homicide detective said. "But that will have to wait for the medical examiner."

"So the other women have been sexually abused?" Rivers pressed.

"I didn't say that."

"Were they?" McCarthy demanded.

"I'm not saying one way or the other."

"What about the hikers who found her?" McCarthy asked.

"Shook up by the whole thing. Father and son. The dad wants their names kept out of it. I don't blame him."

Rivers said, "This is the sixth or seventh body you've found out here in the last year. Some people might think you're not doing enough to solve these murders."

"NHI," McCarthy said.

"No humans involved," Rivers said, nodding.

Even in the shadows thrown by the spotlights, they could see Fisk's face redden. "There's no NHI when I'm around! The victims have been transients, whores, addicts. They put themselves in jeopardy every day. But if you're saying we're ignoring these slayings because the victims are somehow unsavory, you're both out of line. We've got four detectives, including me, working this full-time."

That was news. McCarthy pounced on it. "A task force?"

"Formed last week," Fisk said. "Chief Lawrence is very concerned about the safety of women on the streets, *any woman on the streets.*"

The two reporters peppered the detective for several more minutes about the task force and the direction it would take. Then another homicide detective came up and whispered in Fisk's ear. Fisk made a windshield wiper motion with his hands. "That's it. Any other questions you can get me tomorrow or later at the office. Much later, I think."

Rivers turned and rushed off through the brush toward her car. McCarthy glanced down at his watch. Two hours until *The Post*'s final deadline. He had to move.

The little Dodge Omni emblazoned with *The Beacon*'s logo squealed a U-turn just as McCarthy reached the pavement. He watched Rivers go, annoyed that she'd been able to get to him like that. *My own fault,* McCarthy thought as he got in his car. *I created this hell, now I've got to figure out a way out of it.*

Two miles down the highway he noticed her car parked in front of an all-night convenience store. She stood at a pay phone. He watched her dial as he drove by. She shifted from one leg to the other, revealing the presence of a very fit fanny. For some reason that aggravated McCarthy even more.

The Dirty Details Count . . .

Meanwhile Prentice LaFontaine drove north on the freeway toward Sloan Burkhardt's office. He preferred stories about people, not buildings. But a dull chat with a real estate developer was as good as it got these days. Despite his disinterest, he intended to do his job well. He prided himself on being prepared. He always did his homework.

He knew, for example, that Burkhardt kept an office in a complex north of downtown, but that the developer did most of his work from a mansion in posh Mesquite Hills, about four miles up the road from The Ranch. He'd seen pictures of the estate in the local city magazine: white-washed adobe with trellised verandas, a black-bottomed pool, a helicopter pad, and a tennis court.

Not a bad spread for someone who went through a divorce five years ago, LaFontaine thought. Last week, when *News* got wind that Burkhardt might win the right to develop the waterfront, he had tried to read the details of the developer's divorce proceedings. The records were sealed. Not unusual. Rich people did it all the time. And by any estimation, Burkhardt was rich, perhaps not filthy wealthy, but $35 million will get you a sealed divorce record in any court in the land.

Still it was a shame. LaFontaine liked understanding the dirty details of people before dealing with them. It gave him leverage, insight into who they were, what they did, and why.

Hadn't he learned the value of such knowledge the hard way? *The Post* had hired LaFontaine off a Louisiana weekly, where he'd been allowed to review movies in addition to his routine hard news assignments. Movie critic was the job he'd coveted at *The Post*. Ed Tower, then an assistant managing editor, had told him he'd have to earn the movie critic slot. So LaFontaine spent ten years toiling for the city desk on beats he hated, but from which he learned much about urban mechanics and the human condition.

It was in the mid seventies, while covering superior court, that he found an obscure appendix to the divorce proceedings between Tower and his ex-wife, Patricia. There, in the back of a dusty volume, he discovered that Tower had once burned the back of his wife's leg with the tip of a cigar. LaFontaine kept a copy of the appendix in his private files. His mother had taught him long ago to protect himself by guarding his own skeletons and hoarding the mysterious bones of others. She'd employed the strategy to endure a rotten marriage to a grain dealer by clandestinely loving an attorney in Pontchatoula, Louisiana.

News had followed his mother's example to save himself from the beatings he'd received ever since his father saw he liked to look at the sweaty muscular backs of farm boys who unloaded rice at the family grain-trading business. One hot August Saturday afternoon when LaFontaine was seventeen, he'd wandered into the back of the grain warehouse. There on a pile of burlap rice sacks he'd seen his father's rump pumping between the legs of one of the young black women who helped run the office.

The boy instinctively understood that the bold declaration of discovery gelds the power of knowledge. Damaging gossip achieves potency through oblique suggestion; the idea being that the hint of the curtain about to be drawn back stirs more fear and passion than the secret squirming plainly in the light.

The next time his father raised his fist to him, LaFontaine sweetly asked whether his father thought young black girls considered the smell of burlap rice sacks an aphrodisiac? The hatred and trepidation that swept over his father was pure and plain. The paternal fist opened and fell limp to the waist. They rarely spoke again.

Since then LaFontaine had made it a habit to gather ammunition. Time and again, the dirty details had proved protective. Five years after discovering that Ed Tower had a thing for searing flesh, News was arrested for trying to pick up a vice cop posing as a marine in an area of the Alta Bay Park known as Vicious Queen's Circle.

Tower called LaFontaine into his office to fire him. News played his trump card. He talked about the evils a burning cigar can wreak on the delicate skin at the back of a female thigh.

LaFontaine kept his job. But Tower made sure he never became movie critic. News was kept on a short leash, at the beck and call of the city desk, no chance of becoming more than what he was, a reporter blackballed by an event that no one at the paper, with the probable exception of Lawlor and certainly McCarthy, ever knew occurred. And yet, the experience of reducing Tower to a mass of fear had created in LaFontaine an insatiable hunger for newsroom filth. He loved gossip more than his own sweet mother.

LaFontaine parked his car beside the glass building and thought of McCarthy. Unless his friend hustled a good story soon, he risked being canned even if *The Post* was short-handed in the final battles of a news war. LaFontaine forced himself to squelch these emotions. Nothing dulled a reporter's edge like pity.

Inside, the receptionist told LaFontaine he'd have to wait five minutes. He killed the time going over the details of the Cote D'Azure development. Prime downtown waterfront property. Two high-rise hotels, an office tower, a marina; a festival market and an arts center designed in a series of grand aquamarine glass tubes. Estimated cost: $225 million.

He opened the proposal's four-color map. A decent layout. Adequate pedestrian access. Sweeping waterfront views. The arts center aside, however, no better than what the other seven development teams proposed. Indeed, to LaFontaine's way of thinking, several of their designs had been much better than Burkhardt's.

"Mr. Burkhardt will see you now," the receptionist said, opening the door to the office beyond.

Sloan Burkhardt stood from behind his desk as the reporter entered. He was a pale, fit man in his late thirties. His hair was light brown, slicked back into a ponytail. He wore an expensively cut poplin suit, white shirt, and a tie of a blue circular pattern. Not the sort of man or dress LaFontaine found attractive. The developer crossed the carpet, touching his fingers to a large mole on his right upper lip before offering his hand. The developer's grip was limp, almost cold. He said: "I seldom grant interviews."

"You don't usually win the rights to develop one of the choicest waterfront properties in America."

Burkhardt's thin eyebrows arched. "Yes, well . . . Coffee?"

"Cream, no sugar," News drawled. "Unless you have some molasses? I adore café Creole."

Burkhardt winced. "I suspect that variation is not available, Mr. LaFountain."

"LaFontaine. There's an 'e' at the end."

Burkhardt seemed not to hear. He pressed an intercom button and asked for coffee, cream, no sugar. He looked at his hands. "Excuse me a moment, will you?"

The developer crossed to the far side of the room to a sink. It was the kind doctors have in their offices, with exaggerated faucet handles so users can turn the water on and off with their elbows. Burkhardt took off his coat, rolled up his sleeves, then washed his hands thoroughly. When he realized the reporter watched, he said: "I seem to have soiled my hands somewhere."

You fibbing ass, LaFontaine thought, *you're washing your hands because you find me dirty.* He decided to get the interview over as quickly as possible; he wanted to head out on the town and forget this insipid fool.

While the developer dried himself, LaFontaine glanced about the office. The furniture was contemporary white oak, the paintings on the walls modern and nondescript, the desk devoid of personal items. The only thing in the entire room that spoke to Burkhardt's personal life was a blown-up black-and-white photograph of the developer's late father, Coughlin, putting a shovel into some marshy ground. A sign behind the old man said "Alta Bay Development." The picture loomed on the wall over a white plastic model of the Cote D'Azure project.

LaFontaine pointed at the photograph. "I bet your father would be proud of you landing this deal."

The developer tossed a linen towel into a hamper. "Perhaps."

"No?"

"Father didn't like to be one-upped."

A tidy angle! News pulled out a notebook and wrote the quote down. "So you think your development will be more important than Alta Bay Park was to the city?"

"Infinitely."

"Many argue that if it wasn't for Alta Bay, the city wouldn't have its identity."

Burkhardt leaned forward with his hands on his desk. "You're the public Boswell. Define that identity."

"A mix of urbanity and beach, perhaps. A place where lawyers and bankers can surf before office hours."

Burkhardt smiled weakly. "A vague image at best."

"Brings in the tourists."

"So does Disney terrain," he replied. "And for those who reside here their entire lives, what do their epitaphs say: We lived in nice weather where we could ride floating planks of fiberglass?"

"People have lived for worse," LaFontaine offered.

Burkhardt crossed his arms. "I'll allow that for the 1960s, Alta Bay was somewhat visionary. It transformed five hundred acres of marshland into a wonderful urban water park. And I'll allow it gave what was a town masquerading as a city something to point to, but surely not the definitive backdrop a city so desperately requires."

News said, "Alta Bay also represented the end of Mayor Jennings."

"True enough," Burkhardt replied. "Before your editor there, what's his name? Lawlor? exposed the corruption, Jennings blocked Alta Bay. And I suppose by finally building it, my father put the nail in the old mayor's coffin. But that was thirty years ago. The population here has increased tenfold since then and even now there's nothing that says definitively that this is our city."

"You think the arts center will do that?"

"As much as the opera house in Sydney, Australia."

LaFontaine fought the urge to titter. "You actually believe that?"

The developer pursed his lips. "I believe the entire development will become the force that says this community is ready to be a twenty-first century city."

"Architecture can create civic attitude?"

"Desire is perhaps a better word than attitude," Burkhardt said. "I'm a student of desire, of dreams, of primal urges. Father said that one must understand what motivates people to influence change."

The receptionist entered and placed the coffee cups on the table. "Your dinner appointment has arrived, Mr. Burkhardt," she said.

"Are we almost finished?" the developer asked.

News looked at his list. He was just getting started. Straight to the tough questions. He tapped his pen on the pad. The tip broke, spattering his hand with ink. He rubbed it on the notebook, threw the busted pen in the wastepaper basket, then took another from his pocket. "Sorry. A couple of other areas I'd like to cover."

"You have five minutes."

"Several of the other developers who bid on the project think the selection process was unfair."

Burkhardt shrugged. "Sour grapes. Cote D'Azure was the best project. Period."

"By most estimates I've seen, the shipyard's land is worth a minimum $14 million. Under the deal the city gave you, you pay $4 million."

"This project is good for the city," Burkhardt said firmly. "As such, the city is a partner."

"What about the financing?"

"What about it?"

"The majority of it came from Bobby Carlton's bank."

"True," he said, shifting in his chair. "So?"

"So how do you swing a huge real estate loan from a bank under federal scrutiny at about the same time the bank's president dies?"

Burkhardt chuckled. "You're really perusing the chaff for a kernel, aren't you? You act as if such deals are consummated in a matter of days. We, and by that I mean myself and my partners, negotiated with Carlton Bank for eighteen months on Cote D'Azure."

Now Burkhardt turned serious. "Bobby Carlton's death was a shock for me, for this city. He had a deep understanding of where we were trying to take it with this project."

News scribbled all that down. "You've given a great deal of money to Mayor Portillo and members of the city council."

Burkhardt hesitated, then said: "I make political contributions to almost every candidate who supports economic development. It gives me access to defend my projects, nothing more. I declare it as the law requires."

With that the developer stood. "I hope you have a nice day, Mr. LaFountain."

"That's LaFontaine, Mr. Burkhardt," News said. He deliberately offered his ink-stained hand. "I'm sure we will be talking again as the project goes forward."

Burkhardt glanced at the proffered hand with distaste, then gingerly reached out and shook it. "I'm sure we will, *Mr. LaFontaine.*"

Fall from Grace . . .

It was past midnight now.

McCarthy had filed his story on the discovery of the body and driven north of the city to his house, dark and quiet now save for the breathing of the children. He stood in the hallway outside their rooms and listened to the little girl, Miriam, and the older boy, Carlos. Ordinarily their gentle night noises would calm him enough to sleep.

Tonight they did not help. He padded across the bare wood floor out into the living room of the single-story hacienda-style home. He got his father's trumpet from its stand. He went out through sliding glass doors to the deck. He slumped into a white wicker chair, barely aware of the brilliant stars and the rustling of the avocado trees.

He cradled the trumpet in his arms. He closed his eyes and let his thoughts wander back thirty years. McCarthy's mother cooked dinner while he played with his toys. Outside there was a hundred-acre avocado orchard. And down the hill a shed where his father kept the tractor, the sprayer, the ladders, and the other tools he used to eke out a living. From beyond the shed came the wilting sound of a muted trumpet echoing like a rumor retold.

His father had revered the land but loved the horn. Every evening after the day's work he would perch on the big rock at the edge of the canyon and play bebop to the sky. After an hour or so, the old man would return to the house, cradling the trumpet as McCarthy did now. He would rub his son's head, ignore his wife, who chastised him for wasting time, wash up, then polish the instrument before setting it on the stand.

McCarthy opened his eyes. How it had changed. His father died of a heart attack fifteen years ago. His mother sold all but twenty acres and the house to a developer for a minor fortune. Now she lived in Palm Desert, golfed and assured friends her late husband had been an investment banker, not an avocado grower with an affinity for jazz.

The developer had uprooted most of the orchard to build a residential paradise for the newly wealthy he called "The Ranch." Pink-roofed houses. Swimming pools. Tennis courts. Elaborate gardens.

McCarthy's remaining property included the old rock on the edge of the canyon where his father used to play. An Oklahoma natural gas millionaire had been after him to sell the acreage surrounding the rock, but McCarthy had steadfastly refused. It was on that rock that he'd asked Tina Rodriguez to marry him and allow him to be father to her two children. It was there she'd said yes.

McCarthy got up from the chair, opened the sliding glass doors, and reached inside for his stereo headphones. He flipped on Dizzy Gillespie and returned to his seat, the extension cord of the earphones playing out behind him. He waited until Gillespie's horn began, then gingerly pressed his father's trumpet to his lips. He fingered the valves in time with the music, but did not blow through the tube.

Three selections later McCarthy felt a tap on his shoulder. He started and tugged off the headphones. The woman was older than she looked. Her beautiful silver hair hung about her shoulders. She clutched a quilted black night robe about herself.

"Why you no play *la trompeta* for real no more?" she asked.

"Don't want to wake the kids."

"You no fool me. You no play even when they are up."

He pointed at the brass mouthpiece. "Since the accident, it hurts my lips to play."

She shook her head. "You know, I, too, love Tina more than myself. But *la vida*, she goes on. She has to."

McCarthy didn't say anything. Estelle was Tina's aunt. At times he couldn't bear to look at this woman. Tina had derived her dark grace from Estelle's family.

Estelle said, "What you want, to spend all day wearing black like me?"

"You loved Miguel Los Rochas."

"Like he squeezes my heart even now since forty years.

But, you know, this is something okay for a woman of my heritage: to ache my whole life for the boy who dies before he becomes the man. But not for you."

McCarthy hugged the trumpet to his chest. "I wasn't thinking about her so much tonight."

"You worried about Charley?"

"No." He was surprised to feel his throat tighten. "Yes."

Charley Owens. The children's natural father. Nearly five years after his divorce from Tina had been finalized, Charley Owens wanted the kids back. He'd asked to visit them. There was a court appearance the day after tomorrow. Owens was flying in from Santa Fe for the hearing.

"You're their father, Gideon," Estelle said.

"Charley has rights under the law that I don't," McCarthy said softly.

A small white terrier with a brown head trotted out on the porch and yapped. Estelle smiled. "Malice, he bite that Charley if he comes near Carlos and Miriam."

McCarthy nodded, rubbed the dog's head, and looked out toward his father's rock.

Estelle got up and patted him on the shoulder. "You sleep soon, huh?"

"With luck."

She rustled off into the house. He wondered if the scenes that raced through his mind every night about this time would ever stop replaying. McCarthy reached to the small blue medallion around his neck. Kokopelli, the Anasazi flute player. Tina had given it to him on his birthday.

The accident occurred two years ago last month, a week after his birthday. The police report said the driver of the car that hit them head-on was two and a half times over the alcohol limit. The impact flung McCarthy onto the dashboard, shattering every tooth in his mouth. It broke his jaw in three places. It snapped his right arm below the elbow. It sheared the steering column, which penetrated Tina's chest.

Tina knew she was dying. McCarthy held her hand

through the shards of the windshield while the firemen tried
to free her. She made him swear on Kokopelli, god of her
ancestors, that he would be a good father to her children.

The wind shifted, turning out of the desert. A Santa Ana.
Tomorrow the land would seethe again. The terrier
grimaced at the dust the wind churned.

McCarthy stirred, thinking about his promise. For eighteen months after the crash, he'd drifted through his job at
the paper, every story perfunctory, straight, unenlightened.
He worked because he had to. For the sake of the children.

Then the circulation war heated up between *The Post* and
The Beacon. By all accounts the city could support only one
paper. One would have to die, spilling hundreds of writers
and editors into the streets. The competition grew vicious.

McCarthy's fall from limbo into hell occurred on a Friday, the Friday before Memorial Day Weekend. Preceding
such weekends there are three simultaneous deadlines on
Friday evening: one for the Saturday edition, one for non-
breaking Sunday copy, and a third for holiday assignments.

The week before Memorial Day, McCarthy had covered
a prostitute named Carol Alice Gentry. Gentry testified
before a grand jury that patrol cops were coercing street
hookers for sex in return for protection. Ordinary stuff in
Southern California. But in a news war these brutal, ordinary stories were lobbed like mortar shells.

Grand jury proceedings are ordinarily secret. The fact
that Gentry was talking got out, however, and a media circus pitched its tent. McCarthy was *The Post*'s man in the
three-ring mob, writing and reporting on Gentry's allegations, snippets of which she made public after each session.
The first day she named two uniformed officers, one a pa-
trolman, one a supervising lieutenant, as having extorted
sex from her. The second day she threw a grenade into the

trenches, telling reporters that corruption went higher, much higher, than street cops.

The hooker wouldn't be more specific. She just rolled her eyes at their questions and said, "It will all come out in time." *The Beacon* and *The Post* played it page one. This was war, after all, with only one paper likely to survive, and nothing, absolutely nothing, sells papers like the foul whiff of scandal. Except, perhaps, the horoscopes.

On Thursday night Claudette X asked McCarthy to follow Gentry's allegations with a reaction piece for Saturday. That was on top of his news analysis assignment, slated for Sunday, which would review the implications of her testimony.

To make matters more complicated, the editor-in-chief himself had asked McCarthy to write a piece to be published on Memorial Day. It concerned the psychological trauma endured by families of soldiers who'd died in Vietnam. All three of McCarthy's articles were due at 5:00 P.M. Friday evening.

Professor J. D. Clapper, a veterans expert who'd spent five years studying the ancillary effects of combat fatigue, hated reporters. He refused to talk with McCarthy. The only writer he'd ever spoken to about his work toiled for an obscure academic journal called *Homecoming*. McCarthy read that piece, which quoted Clapper and a professor at the University of Virginia studying some of the same issues.

That Friday morning, as McCarthy attempted to deal with the backbreaking series of assignments, a California state social worker called. She told him that Charley Owens had filed papers to block his application to adopt Carlos and Miriam. He had to meet with her at five-thirty or risk losing the children.

McCarthy tried three times to get out of the Vietnam veterans' piece, but the editors were adamant. McCarthy went to Professor Clapper's office and home. Clapper had already left on vacation. University of Virginia Professor Lisa Kraul did not return repeated phone calls.

Dread underpins the worst of dreams. By two o'clock McCarthy knew he was in trouble. Panic set in after he wrote the analysis piece. He framed the Vietnam article from notes taken earlier from interviews with families found through a veterans support group. He left message after message with Professor Kraul's answering service.

At four-thirty, he thought of Carlos and Miriam. He thought of Charley Owens wanting custody. He thought of his promise to Tina. He thought of the thousands of stories he'd written over the years that had disappeared into the black hole of news with no comment from editors or readers.

He stared at the veterans' journal. Circulation 350. A pothole on the information highway. He opened his computer. He typed in altered versions of the quotes Professor Kraul had given the editor of *Homecoming*.

McCarthy opened his eyes. He sighed, remembering how Lawlor had summoned him to his office the Tuesday after Memorial Day.

"Sit down," the editor-in-chief had ordered. "I'll be a minute."

Lawlor's office occupied the northeasternmost corner of *The Post* newsroom. The floor was raised six inches above that of the other senior editors, a not-so-subtle reminder of who ran the show. McCarthy took one of the two red leather chairs before the great mahogany desk. He swallowed nervously as the editor tapped away at his keyboard.

As always McCarthy's attention was drawn to the three framed objects on the wall. A black-and-white newspaper photograph showed police officers leading a much younger, gaunter Lawlor from the county courthouse in handcuffs. Underneath the picture was the headline:

Reporter Jailed For Refusal to Name Sources in Mayoral Scandal

Within a second black frame, this one larger, was a front page from *The Post*, March 12, 1963. The banner headline read:

Mayor Jennings Guilty on Three Counts

The third and smallest frame held a certificate elegantly embossed in black ink and gold leaf. It conferred on Lawlor the Pulitzer Prize for Investigative Reporting. The greatest honor in journalism. Every other time McCarthy had looked at the award the hair on the back of his neck had prickled erect. Now its presence turned his stomach to vinegar.

He looked away to find Lawlor's famous blackthorn cane, the finish worn and dull, standing in its familiar position in the corner. During his months in jail inmates had assaulted the editor. The leg never healed correctly.

Lawlor continued to type. Below the rolled-up sleeves, his muscular forearms popped and rolled. Even at age fifty-nine, with steel gray hair and a face etched as deeply as a printing plate, the editor exuded power. And why not? He'd won it all, hadn't he? He had the credentials for power. And on a breaking story or an investigative project he was the best advisor McCarthy had ever had.

A knock came at the door. A short, rotund, florid-faced man in his late fifties sporting a black French beret entered. Ed Tower, the Editor for Newsroom Operations, *The Post*'s number two man. McCarthy moaned.

Tower said brightly, "Got Winnie Winkle! Stole her right from under their petty noses."

Lawlor didn't respond. Tower babbled on, "I say we'll take three thousand readers from *The Beacon* on Winnie alone. Not to mention the residual effect of getting Mike Nomad and Steve Roper last month. Market research is clear: Nothing pulls readers like comics."

Without looking up from his keyboard, Lawlor said,

"Good job, Ed, but we've got something more pressing to consider."

It was then McCarthy noticed the manila folder in Tower's hand. Tower took the other red chair. He crossed his crisply creased white linen pants, adjusted his black polka-dotted bow tie, and flipped open the folder. He cast McCarthy a glance that said he would be cruel and that he would enjoy being cruel.

Tower didn't like McCarthy. The feeling was mutual. McCarthy didn't know if Lawlor actually liked Tower. But Lawlor valued loyalty and Tower had been more loyal than a Saint Bernard. As Lawlor had climbed his way to editor and then owner/publisher of *The Post*, he'd pulled Tower up behind him. The office scuttlebutt held that Lawlor probably needed Tower's social connections because, like most independent publishers, he was always looking for new infusions of cash to keep his newspaper alive.

Two years ago the paper had been in very big financial trouble and appeared on the verge of closing. Money from a silent backer had suddenly appeared. Everyone assumed Tower and his connections had been behind the investment. Beyond all that, Tower ably performed the newsroom function that Lawlor loathed. The Editor for Newsroom Operations loved to swing the hatchet.

Lawlor stopped typing. He swiveled his chair to face the window. He pointed across Broadway to the Palmer skyscraper. Editors and reporters scurried over there in *The Beacon*'s newsroom.

Lawlor said, "This time next year, one of these papers won't be publishing."

The muscles in McCarthy's jaw slackened. "I didn't know we were that close."

"*The Post* is hemorrhaging," Lawlor went on. "We're frozen. Can't hire any more reporters. *The Beacon* can't either. It's just a matter of time before a major artery bursts. Then one of us will stroke out and go dark like *The Dallas Times-*

Herald, The Houston Post, the *Los Angeles Herald-Examiner,* or any of the other papers that have given up the ghost this past decade."

Lawlor paused to point again. "Harry Plake sits right there in that office in the corner. We aren't so different, Plake and I. We get up every morning to study each other's work, to look for any little bit of blood that says we wounded the other. Know why?"

"No," McCarthy said.

Lawlor's voice became strained. "Because for all our faults, Harry Plake and me, we love our newspapers. Is this the best paper that ever was? Christ sakes, no. *The Post's* got its weaknesses like every newspaper. But when *The Post* is on, it has the faint glow of greatness. Side by side, laid out on the table every day for a month, we make *The Beacon* look like a perfect piece of shit. Am I right, Ed?"

"A perfect piece of shit," Tower said.

Lawlor turned to McCarthy. "Of all the staff members I could have predicted to lay blood for Harry Plake to see, it wouldn't have been you."

McCarthy swallowed: "I . . . don't understand."

As if on cue, Tower flipped the folder open and read from two pieces of paper that McCarthy couldn't make out: *" 'The families of the Vietnam survivors carry the scars of battle as well. They are the invisible wounded.'*

"And now this one *'The brothers and sisters, mothers and fathers carry the scars of Vietnam just like the veterans. But their wounds aren't visible.' "*

Tower skipped ahead several paragraphs in McCarthy's article to read the doctored quotes and then the actual ones from the veterans' journal. The Editor for Newsroom Operations went on this way until he'd gone over every stolen word.

"Sound familiar?" Tower asked when he'd finished.

Dots danced before McCarthy's eyes. "Covers the same points," he croaked.

Lawlor slammed his palm on the desk so hard several books slid off and fell to the floor. "Don't bullshit me, Gid! I've got a built-in detector and you're reading pure stink."

Tower said, "We got a call this morning from Professor Clapper. Said he noticed the similarities between Kraul's quotes in that journal and the ones you ascribed to her. I just got off the phone with the lady. She says she never spoke to you."

The blood that beat at McCarthy's temples threatened to turn his vision black. Lawlor, the man he respected more than anyone else in this business, was looking at him like he was worse than a street drunk.

"There are lot of crimes you can commit in journalism," Lawlor said. "You can tape someone without telling them. You could let the opposition beat you on a story you knew about first, but failed to write. You could name a source you promised would remain anonymous, and you know how I feel about that.

"But the worst crime you can commit in this business is to take someone else's work and call it your own. Plagiarism. Intellectual equivalent of armed robbery. And by allowing us to print it, on page one no less, you made everyone who edited that story an accessory after the fact."

McCarthy wanted to puke.

"By all rights, I should fire your ass, right here, right now," Lawlor continued.

"I think you should," Tower said.

Lawlor said, "But you were a fine reporter. Why did you do it?"

McCarthy's throat closed. He fought for air.

"Why?" the editor roared. McCarthy knew that half the newsroom now watched through the glass. Vultures sniffing fresh carrion.

His face contorted. "Tina's children," he mumbled.

"Oh, please," Tower began.

Lawlor held up his hand. "Give him his say, Ed."

Halting, McCarthy laid it all out: how he was bucking deadline, how Professor Clapper wouldn't speak, how he was exhausted from covering Gentry, how Charley Owens's effort to stop the adoption proceedings had made him panic. "I knew when I was doing it I was wrong. But I didn't see another way. I . . . I feel like I lost my best friend."

Lawlor pursed his lips. "You did. You lost your integrity."

"Sold your integrity," Tower said, "to make deadline."

The editor-in-chief turned away and closed his eyes. Tower busied himself scribbling on the folder. For McCarthy it was like reliving the sensation of the accident all over again. He felt apart from his body, apart from the pain, floating over the scene, a spectator to disaster.

Finally Lawlor opened his eyes. "I should fire you for this crime."

Tower allowed himself the faintest of smiles.

"But Tina Rodriguez was a great talent and her death was a tragedy," Lawlor went on. "I know you love her kids. They deserve someone to love them."

Tower made as if to protest, but Lawlor cut him off. "Hear me out on this, Ed."

Lawlor turned back to McCarthy. "Don't get the idea I'm cutting you slack because of that romantic notion. The fact is the stakes are too high right now to let you go. With the war on the brink, I can't afford to lose another reporter, even if he is a *hack*."

McCarthy shrank from the blow. The editor cleared his throat. He looked at Tower over pressed palms. "Ed, what's the shittiest beat at this paper?"

Tower appeared disappointed not to see McCarthy destroyed. Then he saw where Lawlor was going. "We start 'em all on night cops," he gloated.

"First job Gideon had here . . . what was it . . . fifteen years ago?" Lawlor asked.

"That . . . that's right," McCarthy stammered.

"Well, that's where you're going again. No more sexy investigations. Back to that dank little room in the police station. You'll file crime briefs. Your byline will rarely appear. You won't lose your paycheck because those kids have been through too much already, because *The Post* needs every warm body it can get in the trenches. But professionally? I'm sending you to back to hell."

McCarthy felt hollow, naked, alone. "It's fair," he muttered.

"It's more than you deserve," Tower said.

"I'm not done yet," Lawlor said. "You are now going out into that newsroom to confess your crime to your peers. Ed will write an account of your actions as well as your apology to appear in tomorrow's paper with your picture prominent. Any questions?"

McCarthy's fingers and toes went numb. He was a different person now, though in ways he did not yet understand. "No questions," he said.

That was three months ago. The morning papers slapped on the front stoop. McCarthy's dog jumped up in his lap and yapped twice. The reporter woke up, stiff from sleeping in the chair. He looked at his wristwatch: 4:45 A.M.

McCarthy dragged himself to the front door. He picked up *The Post* first. He looked for his story, his first step up the ladder out of the abyss.

He didn't find his story on page one. That was dominated by national news and a local article announcing that the city's mayor, Ricardo Portillo, had named Police Chief T. Lawrence Leslie as his campaign director in the race for governor of California.

McCarthy dropped the A section, the sports, and the features pages. He found his story bannered across the top of the metropolitan news section:

Seventh Body Found Slain in Desert

He allowed himself a smile. Three months without a by-line, three months of whispers behind his back, three months of shame. This was how redemption began.

He scanned the piece to make sure the copy editors had not screwed up the facts, then dropped the paper and stripped the rubber band off *The Beacon* to see what Karen Rivers had written. It was an instinctive act. In a newspaper war, comparing coverage was the way you counted bodies. McCarthy took one look at the front page and almost fell over. The headline in large bold type read:

Anti-Cop Hooker Found Dead in Desert

Only the Lonely . . .

"**B**urkhardt washes his hands a lot," LaFontaine said.

"There's a reason to go after someone," McCarthy said.

They were riding the elevator up to the newsroom just before lunch.

News said, "I'm telling you, Gid, something about him stinks."

"You sure you just weren't warm for him and he rebuffed you?"

"If I wanted someone with a ponytail, Gid, I'd date an R.G."

"R.G.?"

"A real girl," he sniffed. "And even I draw the line somewhere."

"If you feel that strong about him, head for every document room in the city. Check what sort of trail he's left on himself and Cote D'Azure."

News sniffed. "Sifting through papers stirs the old asthma, but I suppose you're right."

The elevator door opened. They walked into the newsroom, where the tempo of the day was already mounting. Stepford Editors frantically moved copy through their computer queues. Reporters cradled phones in their necks, barking questions and rapping keyboards. Clerks raced through the maze of desks, dropping books and press releases and the latest from Federal Express.

"McCarthy!" Claudette X bellowed from behind her desk amid the bedlam. "Where the hell have you been?"

LaFontaine cowered. "Sorry, Gid. I had a brutal encounter with Madame *furioso* yesterday afternoon. My delicate constitution cannot bear the thought of another." He glided off toward his desk.

McCarthy marched toward the Amazonian editor with his hands held high. "Be calm. Fisk confirmed the story. Rivers got the kid who found the body to talk. He'd looked at her driver's license. But I got some other stuff, so we're back in the game."

"The Glassholes are cracking themselves over this one," she grumbled.

At the desk behind her, Stanley Geld, the city editor, fingered the gold stud in his left ear. "Tower wants your head. Lawlor says you've got two strikes now."

McCarthy's stomach rolled over. "It won't happen again, Stan, I promise. I want this story more than *The Beacon* does."

"You're only as good as your last story, my friend," Geld said.

"Or your next one," McCarthy countered. "Quote Fisk: 'I would be remiss in my duties if I did not explore the possibility that police officers were involved in her death.' "

Claudette X whistled. "Fisk said that?"

"On the record. Said the gravel in her mouth could be taken as a warning to other informants not to talk."

"That's your lead," Geld said, excited now. "Probably told Rivers the same thing. So we're even. What else?"

"I got two sources on the grand jury to spill about her testimony," McCarthy said. "Click Patrick, one of the cops she named, forced her to have oral sex. Patrick's supervisor, Diego Blanca, coerced her into an intimate camping trip. Besides that, Gentry's a street hooker, right? But when I ran her through county records this morning, I find she owns a condo. Bought the place less than three months ago. She put down $30,000."

Claudette X screwed up her face. "Where's a street whore get that kind of cash?"

"That's my point," McCarthy said.

"Maybe she inherited it," Geld offered. "What's her background?"

"Sketchy. Came out from Tennessee three years ago. Worked in a couple of bars on the strip. Three or four pick-ups for hooking. I found the family, the brother anyway. Still lives in the little town she came from about sixty miles north of Knoxville. He's a long-haul trucker, won't be back until Monday. I'll call then."

A clerk came up and handed Geld some photographs. One was of Gentry standing outside the grand jury room, a pack of journalists around her. Geld said, "She was tall, right? I mean she looks tall here."

"Almost model tall. She might have been beautiful if she could have managed it. Her features were hard. I guess you'd call her coldly attractive."

Claudette X and Geld exchanged glances. Geld nodded. "Okay, not bad. This should keep Tower away from his ax for a while. Write it."

"What's next?" Claudette X asked. "Go after Blanca and Patrick?"

"I don't figure it that way," McCarthy said. "That's where Rivers will go because it's obvious. I'm going to start with Gentry's condo."

Geld let his attention wander to Lobotomy Lane. "You know I can't cut you free. You want this story, you got to fit it in around your night cops schedule."

"Oh, c'mon, Stan!"

"Beyond our control, Gid," Claudette X said. "As far as the powers that be are concerned, you're still the fallen angel."

McCarthy puffed and blew. "This stinks."

"Life is the pits," Geld agreed. "Get writing."

LaFontaine was busy at his terminal. He always typed up detailed notes on interviews. He always filed them with a date and time in the computer. And he always made hard copies he put in his bulging files. He hit the print key and glanced at McCarthy.

"I gather your powwow went well?"

"My ship hasn't sunk yet," McCarthy said. "But the Glassholes are looking hard for rats abandoning."

"Hang in there," LaFontaine said. "I've come to believe that surviving is about as good as it gets in this business."

McCarthy nodded, then slumped in his chair for the tiresome process of entering his notes into the computer. When he'd finished, he played with the notes, moving them around in blocks until he saw a sensible order. He thought about Fisk's admission that cops may have been involved in Gentry's death, then fashioned a lead to reflect that angle.

As McCarthy immersed himself in the writing, Isabel Perez, a trim woman in her early thirties wearing a blue designer pantsuit, dodged through the desks toward LaFontaine, who had just finished ranking the cubbyholes around him for their protective qualities; he'd decided that if the Zombie ever snapped at the obituary desk, he'd belly-crawl behind the copying machine and put a metal trash can over his head.

"Can you believe it?" Perez cried. She pointed to chief

political reporter Kent Jackson's story about Police Chief T. Lawrence Leslie being named Mayor Ricardo Portillo's campaign manager. Her head whipped with each word. Her spiked bleached blond hair sliced the air like sword tips.

"Everyone wins on some days, loses on others," LaFontaine said. "Just ask McCarthy."

"You're all heart, News," McCarthy said, without looking up.

Perez pouted. "I had a juicy little story about the fact that Tito Hernandez—the leader of that border rights organization?—thinks that Ricardo has sold out on immigrants in favor of big business."

"Didn't see it," News said. "Today's paper?"

"Tower spiked it," Perez snapped. "Said Tito didn't offer any evidence and he wasn't going to publish an unsubstantiated attack."

That piqued LaFontaine's interest. "Ed was probably just doing Ricardo a favor. They're social buddies, you know."

"Don't I ever," Perez said. "Everything I write about the guy has to go through Ed's Glasshole. Only stories like Jackson's seem to get in the paper without a fight and I didn't even get to write that."

News whispered so McCarthy wouldn't hear, "I thought your Hispanic heritage would have made you the prime contender for the Leslie scoop, Ms. Peretzki."

"For Christ's sake, News!" she hissed. "Somebody might hear."

Perez quickly looked at McCarthy and the Zombie to see if they'd noticed. McCarthy was engrossed at his terminal. The living dead reporter banged away at his keyboard, oblivious to the conversation and the wilting daffodil petals at his feet. Perez pouted again. It was unfair having someone as petty as LaFontaine knowing one of your deep secrets.

One night when Perez had too much white wine at an office party, LaFontaine, fluent in three of the four Romance languages, had spoken to her in Spanish. She had turned pale and excused herself.

Which started News digging. It took a few months, but he determined Perez had about as much Latin blood as he did. Which was to say *da nada*. She was not remotely Hispanic, and he was probably the only one outside her immediate family who knew it.

Shortly after the turn of the century a Hungarian stonemason named Igmar Peretzki got off the boat in New York. A hard-of-hearing immigration official took one look at the mason's swarthy complexion and wrote down the name Igmar Perez. The mistake would hamper the social and economic life of each subsequent generation of Peretzkis until Isabel. She learned well the lessons taught by unscrupulous reporters in the 1960s, who foresaw the coming backlash against the Euro males who'd long dominated the print and broadcast media through an old boys network that rarely hired women or minorities. Cunning careerists all, the Euro males had dyed their hair black. They Latinized their Anglo surnames. They rose quickly as newspapers and television news operations struggled to diversify their staffs in the wake of the Civil Rights movement.

In the course of her career, Perez parlayed her surname into a steady stream of jobs and promotions. Several years back she became frightened that her inability to speak Spanish would catch up with her. She took a month off and traveled to Cuernavaca in a desperate bid to learn the language. She had a dyslexic tongue. After three weeks she gave up and decided the best way to avoid being caught was to become a political reporter.

News had never told anyone of Perez's East European lineage, but he'd let her know he knew, enjoying the way she squirmed at the threat of revelation. Perez, however, was nobody's fool. She understood the commodity in which LaFontaine traded. She became one of his strongest intelligence moles, ferreting him out information on various happenings inside *The Post* with the fervor of a Mossad operative.

"I know, Isabel!" LaFontaine said. "Why don't you complain to Arlene Troy about the leak."

"News, you're merciless!" she bitched.

"A great reporter has no friends," he drawled.

Arlene Troy, a lesbian, was Mayor Portillo's press secretary and personal liaison with the gay community. In the last year and a half, Perez's spectacular career trajectory had stalled at the level of backup to chief political reporter Kent Jackson. Perez had dropped hints lately that she was a lesbian, a bisexual at the very least. The strange logic being that if she and others in the business had gotten this far on bogus Hispanic names, she'd go them one better; she'd paint herself in sapphic mystery. In a business so fixated with making the world *juste,* what could be more politically correct than a Latina lesbian political reporter? Perez figured it was only a matter of time before she supplanted Jackson as top political dog. Or maybe more.

This LaFontaine knew. Yet even he, a man who reveled in chronicling the lengths reporters will go to in the name of personal glory, had been unable to contain himself when he first heard the rumor of Perez kicking the closet door open.

"I'm sorry," he'd gagged. "If Isabel's a dyke, I read *Playboy* for the pictures!"

Perez didn't speak to News for a week after that comment, which had seeped through the newspaper and over her reputation like spilled ink.

News could see that she was at least as angry now. He was in for another week of cold silence from one of his best gossip sources. Better cool the sarcasm.

The elevator opened. A stooped older man with thick black hair, black sideburns, black eyeglasses, black leather pants, black silk shirt, and black cowboy boots stepped out. The man clutched a Styrofoam cup of steaming coffee.

LaFontaine plucked a dollar from his pocket before Perez could storm away.

"This symbol of our first president says Roy Orbison will mess his desk with yonder cup of java within four minutes of reaching his place of toil," he said.

Perez stopped short. She couldn't resist the daily spilt-coffee pool. Ralph Baker, otherwise known as "Roy Orbison," shuffled into the newsroom. Perez noted the quiver in his gait and gave value to his hand tremors. She handed News a dollar.

"Three minutes, tops," she said. "I don't think Roy even put up a fight. He was absolutely pinned by the time Ted Koppel shook his wig on 'Nightline.' "

"Tut, tut, dear Isabel," LaFontaine said. "You underestimate the range of someone who might sing 'Pretty Woman' in three octaves. I say that marvelous iron gut fought the vodka to a draw. Four minutes thirty seconds."

"You're on."

"Anybody else?" LaFontaine cried, waving the two dollars in the air. "Zombie?"

The Zombie's callused fingers beat out a wicked rhythm on his keyboard, but his eyes didn't glow hotter in response.

"Out for today as well as every other I see," LaFontaine said. "Abby, how about it? A bet on Mr. Orbison?"

Abby Blitzer, a petite woman with stringy red hair and beautiful green eyes, glanced up from her desk where she'd been rifling through *The Beacon*. She glanced at Baker. "Ralph couldn't even hold a guitar still. I give him two minutes thirty, tops. Put me and Croon down for that."

Though she had only been on *The Post*'s staff a year, Abby Blitzer had already forged a reputation as one of the city's best street reporters. And it was well-known that before coming to *The Post* she'd dried out at the Betty Ford Clinic. If anyone could handicap a journalist as far gone as Ralph Baker, it was Abby Blitzer.

"Okay, Abby, here's my buck," said Augustus Croon, a

muscular photographer perched on the corner of Blitzer's desk. "We see splashes of Chock Full O' Nuts two and a half minutes after Roy reaches his desk."

Blitzer patted his leg appreciatively. "Thank you for your support, Croon."

"Anything for you, Abby," he said. He grinned bashfully and fiddled with the cameras that hung around his neck.

"Don't moon, Croon," Blitzer said. "It's unbecoming."

"Just sort of happens," Croon protested. "You being so cute and all."

Blitzer's face hardened. "No mooning."

Croon took the deep, concentrating breath he'd been taught in Navy SEAL School, but tended to forget in her presence. He let it out slow, forcing the energy into his small intestines. "The moon has set. I promise!"

LaFontaine's lip curled in contempt. "If Croon's hetero longing has ebbed, I think we have bets to close. Velvet voice approaches."

The leather-clad wonder clutching the hot coffee had now made his way to the far window. He stared across at *The Beacon* newsroom. He raised his middle finger.

"The daily bird has been given," LaFontaine said. "Fifteen seconds to close bets."

Kent Jackson, the lead political reporter, rushed to LaFontaine, his red power tie streaming over one shoulder. He held out a dollar. "One minute thirty."

"Wouldn't be a real game of chance without you, Kent," said LaFontaine, who still found it amazing that a born-again reporter loved to gamble. News held up an imaginary gavel: "Going once, going twice . . ."

"Two minutes forty-five," McCarthy said. He had just finished the first draft of his story. "Not a second more."

"Now we've got a contest!" LaFontaine crowed.

Baker stumbled to his desk. He nodded to them, then shakily set the coffee down.

News whispered: "Time." It was 2:07:30 P.M.

"Anything breaking?" the old reporter asked.

LaFontaine replied, "The city knows better than to let anything happen until you get here for the late shift, especially with . . . uh . . . how long until you retire?"

"Three weeks, two days, eight hours, ten minutes . . ." Baker tugged a gold pocket watch from his black leather vest. "Fourteen seconds."

"Accuracy, that's the ticket," News said.

With unsteady hands Baker drew a ballpoint pen from his top drawer and placed it on the desk. He unfolded *The Beacon,* spread it out before him, and perused page A-1. With a tremor about 4.5 on the Richter scale, he reached for his coffee. He brought it in a shake and a tremble to his lips. He seared his tongue, almost dropping the cup. Gasps from every quarter. Twenty-seven seconds: a potential world record for the Daily Roy Orbison!

But the old reporter summoned control from deep in his core and managed to set the cup down without mishap. The reporters heaved a sigh of relief.

Ralph Baker was once a shooting star in local journalism, a holy terror of a reporter whose scoops were legendary. He'd begun his career with the now-defunct *Chronicle,* where he'd jousted with Mafia lawyers and covered the same corruption scandals in Mayor Jennings's administration that had won Connor Lawlor the Pulitzer. Later he did a stint in Saigon. When *The Chronicle* died, *The Post* hired him to cover Sacramento.

But that was long ago. These days, after nearly four decades on deadline, Baker's muscles constantly twitched, not with anticipation but with weariness. He was a rewrite man now, an anachronism in daily newspapers. Street reporters used to call in notes to rewriters who produced the tight, punchy copy. Advances in technology all but doomed the position at modern newspapers. But Baker was too burned out to be good for anything else and the denizens of Lobotomy Lane couldn't bring themselves to fire him.

Baker was a contemporary of Ed Tower and Connor Lawlor. He was the ghost of old news.

So he worked the rewrite shift, 2:00 to 10:00 P.M. Most days he sat quietly at his desk, suffering from hangover, drinking coffee, reading newspapers, and waiting for that rare moment when copy had to be written fast and tight on deadline.

No one could explain the outfit. He began sporting the rock star look shortly after moving to rewrite five years ago. One day he abandoned his brown polyester trousers in favor of black leather pants. The next day he added the black silk shirt. The day after that the hand-stitched cowboy boots. He grew his hair out. He had his bangs cut straight, an inch above his eyebrows. Then he died his gray hair lacquer black and changed his glasses from tortoiseshell to thick inky polymer. LaFontaine had christened him "Roy Orbison" for he was "only the lonely." The name stuck.

Forty-five seconds into the contest, more than one reporter in the betting pool shivered. They worried that unless they let their eyes glaze over and became editors soon, or decided the truth was for sale and became public relations flacks, they might wake up one day thinking it was a swell idea to come to work clad as Michael Jackson or Minnie Pearl or Judy Garland, or, in LaFontaine's case, Norma Jean.

Fifty-six seconds. Augustus Croon warded off thoughts of dressing as Jethro Bodine in the old "Beverly Hillbilly" reruns by talking to Blitzer. "Hoping for tragedy, Abby?"

Blitzer's face took on the sort of dreamy expression she used to reserve for Jack Daniel's straight up. "Don't we always, Croon? It's been so long since we really had something meaty to report on."

"There was that pileup on the interstate last week," Croon offered.

"Boo-hoo journalism," Blitzer sniffed. "Over before we

got there. Talk to the relatives, get the crying moms and dads. But nothing on the scene, you know?"

"Maybe today," Croon said. "Tragedy can come at any hour."

Blitzer got dewy-eyed. "That's the beauty of it, isn't it?"

Baker turned the page of his newspaper. He reached for his coffee.

"Dear Abby, Abby," Croon whispered.

"Ahh, sonofabitch!" Blitzer said. Dear Abby always upset Baker.

The leather-clad reporter read the disturbing marital travails of a housewife from Omaha. The other reporters tensed. Kent Jackson played with his cuff link and smiled; a minute thirty and the coffee was as good as spilled.

A miracle! A sip and no stain.

"I couldn't win a bet laid down by Moses these days," Jackson said, disgusted. He whirled in his tracks and raced off toward the sports section to lay down ten dollars on this afternoon's Dodgers' game.

One minute forty-five. Two minutes. Two minutes fifteen seconds.

"Damn it, Abby, we're going to lose," Croon groaned.

Baker turned the page to Ann Landers.

"I'm feeling good, real good," Perez said.

"He's mine," News proclaimed, knowing Ann Landers's predilection to stagger her letters so the most pathetic came later in the column.

But Ann Landers broke habit. Her first letter concerned a sixteen-year-old whose mother had committed suicide in front of her. The poor girl's plight—bed-wetting, drugs, and poor school performance—triggered a snuffle. That irritated Baker's cigarette-and vodka-charred throat, which set off the coughing jag. He hacked. He chortled. His eyes bulged. At two minutes twenty-nine seconds he reached for the coffee cup.

"Sonofa, sonofa, sonofa," Blitzer sighed.

"Life is fundamentally unfair to minorities," Perez fretted.

"One can only pray for divine intervention," LaFontaine said. "Ghost of Buddy Holly help us now."

Baker choked on the liquid. He made a nasty gurgling noise, then spewed a mouthful out onto the desk. He pitched forward, upsetting the cup. Hot coffee splashed on his hand, spurring a three-octave bellow that would have done his namesake proud. Chock Full O' Nuts ran like the Big Muddy across his desk. For a moment McCarthy stopped feeling sorry for himself. He'd won the Daily Roy Orbison.

After Baker had mopped his desk and gone in search of a dry copy of Ann Landers, LaFontaine handed over the cash from the pool. "Your analytical skills never cease to amaze me, Gid."

Blitzer nodded. "A gift."

A woman dressed in a red, embroidered Guatemalan smock, standing on the other side of the room, said, "I think it's obscene you bet on that poor man's tremors every day. Behind that black leather hide is an inner child suffering."

"Give me a break, Oracle," Blitzer said, not bothering to look in Margaret Savage's direction. "Anything behind the leather is the bastard of Stolychnaya."

"And your language! Don't you know how demeaning the term *bastard* is to children out of wedlock?"

"Why don't you go look at newsprint rolls in the printing plant and weep for the Ponderosa pine," Perez said.

When the rest of the reporters started laughing, Savage trained as much hate at them as her Zen-trained mind would allow. Fifteen months ago, Savage had never worked for a newspaper. Now she was *The Post*'s city columnist and favorite friend to Bobbie Anne Pace, the Assistant Managing Editor for News and Information. Bobbie Anne Pace oversaw the city desk. Bobbie Anne Pace, as much as anyone on Lobotomy Lane, ruled the destiny of every reporter in the room.

Savage said, "It's Neanderthals like you that are the problem with the media. Mark my words: Ralph Baker will surprise us all someday."

They all laughed again. Like most daily journalists, their vision of what could be was consistently clouded by what was. That is to say, they wore conventional wisdom like smoked welding goggles. The party line held that Baker was gone, maybe not a walking dead like the Zombie, but certainly a word musician whose internal Fender Telecaster had lost more than a few strings. Savage sneered at them all and left.

LaFontaine watched to see which Glasshole she'd head for. Perez wondered whether Birkenstocks and peasant dresses might help her dethrone Kent Jackson. Abby and Croon chatted idly about the news value of a tragedy involving a deer hunter and a vegetarian.

McCarthy tucked the Roy Orbison winnings in his pocket, filed his story, then grabbed his briefcase. "Got to go," he said. "I've got a long night ahead of me."

The reporters displayed expressions of pity as he departed. Inside they all thought: *Better McCarthy than me.*

Doing the Neil and Bobbie . . .

very day at 11:30 A.M. all editors up to the level of assistant managing editor gathered for the first of four news meetings that set *The Post*'s hierarchy of story play. The conference room was a cramped affair with a fourteen-foot rectangular table and twelve blue over-stuffed chairs. Sections of today's editions were thumb-tacked to the walls. The disparity between *The Beacon*'s shouting headline on A-1 about the hooker found dead and McCarthy's lame story on B-1 was palpable and depressing. But ten minutes into the meeting, style, not substance, dominated the discussion.

Stanley Geld grabbed the gold stud in his left ear, twisted it, and groaned, "It's fashion, Bobbie Anne, and unless there's a murdered designer to give the stories intrigue or the stories substantiate the presence of carcinogenic dyes in the fall cardigan line, it's not hard news, it's puff."

Bobbie Anne Pace, a borderline anorexic woman in her early forties, khaki-clad and imperious of attitude, replied: "I spent a decade writing that *puff* as you call it. And I'm here to tell you, you're behind the times, Stanley. There's as much value in putting fashion trends on the front page as the latest crime spree. Where would culture be without Ralph Lauren? Tell me that!"

From the exact opposite end of the table came a reluctant if extremely sexy voice: "Bobbie's right. Our most recent market surveys among women twenty to fifty-five indicate fashion coverage is an important consideration in buying a daily newspaper."

The entire pod of Stepford Editors turned as one to Neil Harpster, *The Post*'s sweet-eyed wunderkind, the Assistant Managing Editor for Form and Content. They hated him for what they loved about him: smart, thirty-nine, ridiculously handsome, married to a wealthy heiress. The fates were behind him. He could hold their careers in his hands. He could become editor-in-chief!

Harpster detested himself for taking Pace's side. She was his biggest rival for the next rung up the ladder. Still, there was no disputing the statistics. He reached to adjust his tie, in the process causing an almost-imperceptible snap in his heavily starched shirt. He paused to let the effect linger, then declared: "The numbers are clear then: Ralph Lauren has strong readership."

"See, Stanley!" Pace said, turning triumphantly to the city editor.

Geld shivered. Was he going into shock? Technically Pace and Harpster held positions of equal influence over Geld's operation. But here at the morning news meeting they constantly vied for position. Today's display of solidarity was unprecedented.

Geld glanced across the table at Claudette X, his executive assistant city editor, and twisted his lips to one side as if he were tasting something unappealing. Claudette X knew what he was doing and did her utmost to keep from laughing. In private, Geld called this meeting the "Daily Blow Job"; for every morning he came to the conference room to "Do the Neil and Bobbie."

Until quite recently Geld had been a rock-solid editorial force in *The Post* newsroom. Determined, crafty, and experienced, he was the paper's field commander. For years he'd run the hard news operation with a steady and, at times, aggressive hand. More importantly, he hadn't made any major mistakes during his tenure and seemed a likely bet for future promotion to assistant managing editor, a position he'd long coveted.

All that had changed after Pace dashed through a series of career coups d'état that culminated in her seizing the Glasshole of Geld's dreams.

Pace stole Geld's future by playing high priest to a temple built by Margaret Savage. Indeed, until Pace's chance encounter with Savage, no journalism career had a flatter trajectory. For more than a decade Pace toiled in obscurity as the fashion editor of *The Post,* a newspaper that gave little more than agate type for stories about clothes.

Then one day, dressed as usual in basic black silk, she had decided to cover a "Fight The Fur" fashion show being jointly sponsored by the Sierra Club and an offshoot group called Advocates of Pelt-Bearing Mammals.

Savage, then director of a committed public relations organization, handled spin control for the event. She wore blue shorts and a white cotton T-shirt that simultaneously managed to protest the destruction of the rain forest, the loss of spotted owl habitat in Oregon, as well as the heresy of mountain lion hunting in California. An epiphany! Pace had never before considered fashion as a political statement. Savage, in contrast, considered every word, thought, action, desire, and object, animate or inanimate, a political statement. They became instant allies.

Overnight Bobbie Anne shed her ebony spiked heels in favor of corkbed sandals. She shifted from silk to one hundred percent cotton, stopped perming her hair, gave up shaving her legs, and took up Aikido for exercise.

Pace even took Savage's advice on story selection. Within months the perception of Pace as a lightweight garb scribe was gone, replaced by that of socially conscious fashion pundit. Several post-ops on Lobotomy Lane took her out to lunch, a fact which Prentice LaFontaine had noted with wonder and spread as quickly as he could.

Pace won four major awards at the yearly journalism contest. She was promoted to features editor for her innovativeness. Her first managerial decision proved her best career move ever: she hired Savage to fill her old spot.

Savage opened up a salvo on the Southern California fashion scene, decrying fur, of course, but also leather, plastic, rhinestones, and even bikinis and volleyball wear. Young girls who sported thong swimsuits—known to Southern Californians as "butt floss"—were "victims of a denigrating, narcissistic society that demands the flaunting of flesh for acceptance." Volleyball wear failed to measure up because she got it into her mind that the game led to beach erosion.

Nothing sells a paper better than a writer readers love to

loathe. And readers adored hating Margaret Savage. A fur retailer protested that Savage was the "fashion equivalent of Ghengis Khan." An incensed volleyball player who was betting his financial future on Day-Glo shorts was arrested for spiking balls onto the hood of her convertible Volkswagen. It made the evening news. *The Post*'s circulation went up by 1,573.

The Glassholes decided that Savage needed more exposure. Pace promoted her to "New Age Culture Writer," a position which she used to rail against the "intellectual cancer of the meat culture," and surfing as an intrusion on the ecosystem of seals, blowfish, and mollusks. Many subscribers bought an extra copy on the days her stories appeared so their puppies could piss on her photograph. Circulation jumped another 648.

For its "groundbreaking coverage," *The Post*'s feature section received national recognition. The *Columbia Journalism Review* hailed it as a "harbinger of news, twenty-first century style." Pace and Savage were mini-profiled in *Vanity Fair*, invited to speak at journalism conventions, and lampooned on the editorial pages of *The Wall Street Journal*.

After six months of Savage, circulation was up thirty-four hundred, leaving the paper only twenty thousand subscribers short of *The Beacon*. To Geld's horror, Pace was named Assistant Managing Editor for News and Information.

The day after being officially lobotomized, Pace rewarded Savage with her own column on the metropolitan page. She named the column "Savage Views." Prentice LaFontaine called it "The P.C. Oracle."

In shock, Geld bought a Corvette he couldn't afford. He pierced his ear. He permed his hair. He performed drunken avant garde dances at the Slotman's Bar and Grill. As Pace's career trajectory steepened, Geld's depression deepened. His wife, Judy, threatened divorce. And he had taken lately to driving the 'Vette to the Slotman's for a lunch of three double Jim Beams on the rocks and two baskets of pretzels.

Before this morning's meeting, Claudette X had asked Geld if he thought the diet was a good idea. "Claudette," he had said, "I see it as the lesser of two evils. It's either sedation or I decide it's real smart to buy a leotard and take modern dance lessons at night."

Right now, Claudette X thought, *Stan looks like he wants to slide his pudgy legs into a pink tutu.*

Geld turned to his staff. "The numbers are on their side. But I need your opinions—fashion on the front page?"

Claudette X held her tongue. She wanted to see if her fellow assistant city editors would support their boss. As expected, they sat stone-still, a mute Greek chorus that would sing in the direction of the favorable wind. After all, this was a daily newspaper in the 1990s, not a company in the electronics or biotechnology field. Every month came the word of another daily paper laying off staff or closing its doors. To survive, to flourish, H. L. Mencken! just to pay the mortgage, you had to keep your index finger wet and high.

"Tell you what, Bobbie Anne," Claudette X said, after enduring the silence for several moments. "You have different ideas about what constitutes news. We respect that. And the statistics, too, Neil. How about we look at the series when it's done? That way we have a better idea of how it stands up against other stories we have on backlog."

Pace hesitated, then nodded in satisfaction. Harpster said, "Fine."

Geld mouthed "You're a savior" in recognition of the brilliant maneuver. Though Pace would not leave the meeting assured of page one treatment for the fashion series, she could tell herself she mattered. That meant she'd probably stay in her office, out of the way, until the paper was put to bed.

Okay, thought Claudette X, *we've done the Bobbie.* The only thing left was to get Neil to climax and the daily blow job was over.

She caught movement at Harpster's end of the table and bit her tongue in frustration. He was removing the mother-of-pearl links from his French cuffs and rolling up the sleeves Connor Lawlor style. He loosened his tie, then ran his fingers back through his expensive haircut. All proven indicators that Harpster was about to act the part of hard-driving newsman to score points after Pace's victory.

God help us! The man knew numbers, not news. He'd only worked three months as a reporter. His formative experience: six years on *The Post*'s copy desk, checking for commas. But then, as the news industry came to rely more and more on market research, he rose quickly on the basis of his undergraduate degree in applied statistics and journalism from Northwestern.

No career trajectory had been steeper. Harpster wanted to keep it that way. Like Pace, he was constantly on the lookout for ways to demonstrate his capacity for higher office. His most recent effort had been to change the titles of the senior editors.

Harpster often wondered why the paper had never achieved the status of similar-sized papers such as the *San Jose Mercury News*, the *Dallas Morning News*, or the *St. Paul Pioneer Press*.

After attending a management conference at Big Sur, during which he'd had a brief affair with a randy Brazilian-born editress from the *Miami Herald*, he came to believe that *The Post*'s underlying problem was rigidity. The editress, who adored samba, had physically demonstrated that flexibility leads to profound creativity.

In the convoluted logic of a trained copy editor, Harpster determined that rigid titles meant rigid thinking at *The Post*. He returned to announce to his fellow editors that the paper would achieve heavyweight status if it adopted more limber job descriptions. After much wailing and gnashing of teeth—and a nod to the fact that Harpster was only thirty-nine and rising quickly—the titles were adopted.

As malleable as Harpster's new title may have been, exactly what the Assistant Managing Editor for Form and Content did remained a mystery. It was well-known that Harpster ran marketing focus groups, read memos, studied the newspaper trade press, dictated to his luscious research assistant Connie Mills, and attended meetings such as this one. Everything else about the man was pure suspicion.

Sleeves rolled and ready, Harpster announced, "I've got a couple of ideas of my own I want looked into. First off, cactus rustling."

Geld's lips puckered. "Excuse me?"

"I talked to some of my neighbors. With the water shortage in its fifth year, they're turning to drought-resistant plants. Only there aren't enough around. Mature cacti are being stolen from people's backyards and probably being sold in L.A."

The Stepford Editors stared at the table, their eyes glazing as they analyzed: Was this a good idea or a bad one?

"I don't know, Neil," Claudette X said. "I mean, how often does it happen?"

"Happened to me and Lydia last week!" Harpster retorted. "Came downstairs and a beautiful barrel cactus she'd just bought as a centerpiece to our no-water garden was vamooso. Plants are her children. She took to her bed the entire day."

Claudette X glanced at Geld. He shrugged. If it was true, it was an okay story, Old West comes to horticulture, that sort of thing.

"Consider it assigned, Neil," Geld said.

"Dandy," Harpster said. He glanced inside a manila folder on his desk. "Number two. You seen these sneakers around that the kids wear skateboarding? The ones with the strange colors—neon red, green, and purple?"

The corneas of several assistant city editors cleared. A few nodded hesitantly.

"I think this is a nice trend for us to write about," Harpster announced. "They're making them right here in the city. El cheapo. Research shows people are sick of paying a hundred dollars for a damned pair of tennis shoes for their kids. I think this firm's going to take off."

He paused, thought of the Brazilian editress, then added: "I think the story has good form."

More corneas around the table became translucent. More heads bobbed appreciatively. The wind direction of this decision was easy to mark. What possible harm could a story about tennis shoes do to a career? It would make Harpster happy. That was important. A nice story, too, with color photographs of kids with vibrant sneakers playing with skateboards in the sunshine. Maybe there'd be dogs in the pictures. Nothing better than photos of kids and dogs and sneakers and sunshine in the newspaper. These kinds of pictures told readers that despite the misery, the hatred, the greed, the change, the turbulence, and the uncertainty that dominated newspaper coverage, it remained possible to carry on a life where kids could play with little pooches on a hot summer day. That, as much as the comic strips and the details of the latest yard sales, still sold newspapers.

Geld and Claudette X exchanged nervous glances. They suspected Harpster had an ulterior motive to offsetting the background terror of the common newspaper reader. Both guessed the Assistant Managing Editor for Form and Content had bought stock in the sneaker company. They got these kinds of requests during the Neiling phase of the daily blow job at least once a month. The problem, however, was that such an ethical breach was almost impossible to prove without a direct challenge to the editor. If they were wrong, their own careers could be left in tatters.

"Isn't this a story better suited for finance, Neil?" Claudette X growled, hoping she might intimidate Harpster.

"My reporters are pressed as it is without having to write about purple sneakers."

Harpster frowned. "I want the story where people can see it."

Pace chirped in from the other end of the table. "I agree with Neil. Here again, fashion is news. A story worthy of page one."

Two instances of editorial solidarity in one day. The wind blew strong and sure on wet fingers. Stepford heads snapped to and fro with the vigor of cork on rough seas. Pretty sneakers and dogs on page one: a winner for sure!

Geld looked across the table at Claudette X and mouthed the words "Please end it."

Claudette X flinched at the sight of her boss in such distress. The urge for straight Jim Beam was obviously too much for Geld to fight today. She didn't feel up to it either. She had a mortgage payment due tomorrow, which really pissed her off because it reminded her that her ex-husband hadn't sent his alimony check in two months.

"Sneakers it is," she said.

"It's an orgasm!" Geld cried.

He made as if to rise, then shrank back chagrined when the door opened and Connor Lawlor limped in, leaning on his blackthorn cane. Ed Tower followed. A rare occasion. The two top editors almost never appeared at the 11:30 A.M. meeting. They normally waited until the 3:00 P.M. conference, when stories had played out to weigh in on issues of placement, length, and future coverage.

"Sorry to intrude," Lawlor said.

"Not intruding at all." Harpster jumped up to give the editor-in-chief his chair.

"Thank you, Neil," Lawlor drawled. "Couple of things I wanted to discuss with you all. First off. I wanted to make sure we're preparing adequately for coverage of the governor's race."

"We have Jackson and Perez assigned permanently,"

Geld said, praying the editor hadn't heard him scream in ecstasy.

"And they're doing a fine job of it, far as I can see, Stan," Lawlor said, pointing up at Jackson's story on page one.

"I just want to make sure we do more than fine. Ed thinks, and I agree, that Ricardo's probably the best mayor this city's ever had and will probably be the first Hispanic governor of the state. I want to make sure we cover it right. This is *The Post*'s story, not the *L.A. Times* or the *San Francisco Examiner*'s."

"I agree," Harpster said.

"Absolutely," Pace said.

"Fine," Lawlor said. "Then I'd like to have some kind of plan for the coverage—you know, schedule stories that detail his positions, how Jim Barnes, Portillo's opponent, is responding, and a weekender each Sunday, something more featurey."

Claudette X wrote all that down on a yellow pad. "Anything else?"

"I'd also like you to draw up a detailed course of action for the last weeks of the campaign. Give me some kind of grid that coordinates it all. I know we're four months away, but it'll creep up on us. Ed will be your liaison."

Inside Claudette X cringed. The Editor for News Operations, or whatever Harpster had named him, gave her the willies. "Consider it done," she said, forcing a smile. "I'm looking forward to it, Ed."

Tower's nod was icy. "As I am. And while we're talking coverage, I'm concerned that we stay on top of this Gentry fiasco. As usual, McCarthy's work is found lacking."

Claudette X bristled. "McCarthy's already got a scoop for tomorrow, Ed. It was a fluke Rivers got that story."

"Beaten by a rookie." Tower sniffed contemptuously. "I don't know why we keep him on board."

"That's enough," Lawlor said, then he turned to Geld. "I

cut McCarthy a huge break three months ago. This is strike two."

"Given the status of our circulation, we can't get behind another step on this kind of story," Tower declared. "Readers love this sort of thing, right Neil?"

Harpster snapped his fingers. "The focus groups we conducted last month gave us a clear message: Uncover more scandals. They see it as our role to muckrake."

Lawlor thumped his cane on the floor. "I never doubted it. Enough already. Let's get back to it, people. We've got a paper to publish."

Geld whimpered slightly as the top editors left the room.

"Yes, Stan," Claudette X said. "It's officially an orgasm."

According to Sources . . .

At ten-thirty the next morning Gideon McCarthy walked in the shade of the eucalyptus trees within the condominium complex where the dead prostitute Carol Alice Gentry had lived. He had four hours to work before the hearing with the judge over Charley Owens's request to see the kids. He glanced at the sun. A California sun. A beautiful light that threatened the shadows with cruel intent.

He found her place, number sixty-one, on the third floor of a building on the far side of the man-made pond. Yellow tape stretched from doorjamb to doorjamb. The medical examiner had pasted his seal near the handle.

"You cops just can't get enough of her, can you?" came a slurred voice.

He turned. An emaciated woman in her early sixties shook a highball glass at him from the door across the way. She wore a magenta tennis outfit. The burst veins on her nose ran deep, but her eyes remained lucid. The ice cubes clinked. "Well?"

"I'm a reporter with *The Post*."

"The clowns arrive," she said. "Elephants next."

"What's your name?"

"What's yours?"

"Gideon McCarthy."

"Regina Fetterbaum. Merry widow. Next-door neighbor."

"Just who I wanted to see."

"I imagine." She sipped her drink.

McCarthy smiled. "Did you know Carol Alice?"

"We had coffee a couple of times. Women who live alone tend to look out for each other."

"You know she was a hooker?"

"She never mentioned it, but it didn't take a Louis Rukeyser to figure. Young girl like that. Lots of money. Pretty, but not pretty enough. Then she started testifying."

"She have many friends?"

Fetterbaum shrugged. "She kept to herself, but there were a couple of guys. One a big, lean kid. Wore a cowboy hat. Oh, and that little fat cop."

"Which one?"

"Don't know his name. He was balding with a thin black mustache. They had a shouting match one time. Better than something on my soap. Figured he was one of the ones she was yakking about."

"Click Patrick," McCarthy said.

"Whatever," she said, waving the highball glass. "I called him Officer Hot Pants."

"What'd she like to talk about when you had coffee? Cops?"

"Nah, her horse mostly. An Arabian. Kept it up the road at that stable. Kemper's, I think it's called. I figure that's where the cowboy came from."

McCarthy wrote down the name. "Arabian. That's a lot of money."

"Hardworking young lady." Fetterbaum shifted her stance, reached into her pocket, and pulled out a cigarette box. She lit one. She took a drag.

"She said nothing about cops?"

She thought about it. "Maybe once or twice, just that they were giving her a hard time. Maybe that they were behind the break-in."

He tried to act nonchalant. People had a way of clamming up when you showed true interest. "Break-in?"

"Oh c'mon, she must have testified about that."

"Grand jury testimony's supposed to be secret."

"Right." Fetterbaum's laugh sounded like a gargle. She took another sip of her drink. "Anyway, yeah. Two, maybe three months ago, she knocks on my door, six in the morning, just got home, all scared. Carol was one of those gals didn't seem scared of much. They forced a back window. Tore the place apart. But didn't steal anything she could find. Some money maybe. She wasn't sure."

"She report it?"

"What do you think?"

McCarthy cursed to himself. No call, no documented proof he could use in a story.

"Did she say what they might be looking for?"

Fetterbaum hesitated. "No . . . not exactly."

"But she hinted, didn't she? C'mon, this could help a lot."

Smoke billowed from her lips. She took another sip. "You have an ID or something, Mr. . . . ?"

"McCarthy. Gideon McCarthy." He fished out his press pass.

She put her drink down on a table inside the hallway to her condo, took the card between two fingers, and studied it. "You've aged."

"A family trait: gray at thirty-five, drooling at fifty."

She laughed her hoarse laugh. "Okay, McCarthy, I'll tell you. It was a mess inside. I was picking up some of the things that were knocked over in the kitchen. She rummaged around in that huge entertainment center she had, looking at tapes, counting out loud."

"Taking inventory?"

"I think so."

"Videotapes or cassette tapes?"

"Both."

"They get what they came for?"

Fetterbaum blew smoke into the air and raised her eyebrows. "She was angry and frightened that someone had been in her place. But that seemed to go out of her once she'd finished with the tapes."

McCarthy wrote that down, too. "You tell the cops this?"

"What do you think?"

The reporter smiled. "I think I like you, Regina Fetterbaum."

She raised her glass to him. "My late husband, Stan, loved to play the stock markets. I learned a lot about the value of insider information."

"And I suppose you'd be less than helpful to other reporters who come by?"

"Early bird gets the worm, I always say."

Across town, Prentice LaFontaine took deep breaths from an atomizer to ward off the asthma attack lurking at the edges of his lungs. On stifling days like this the air conditioners in the court clerk's office lifted the dust that coated the labyrinth of files, swirling it into the air to taunt him. He wheezed, then coughed at the chemical expansion in his lungs. He hated this room.

But where else could he scarf up as much dirt in so little time? Divorce records? Run a name through the A computer and ask at Window Three. Probate? B computer and

Sally in Window One. Civil proceedings? Peruse by plaintiff or defendant, then call the number over the public announcement system. Criminal cases? All there on the wall.

Sometimes, when the air-conditioning wasn't on and they'd dusted, News enjoyed closing his eyes and smelling the place. If scandal produced an odor, it was this odd mélange of scents: the onion breath of the clerks, the stale cologne of the attorneys, the mold on the old papers, the tang of the cleaning fluid they used to wash the floors, the sweat of fear, the sweat of greed. If it wasn't for the dust, he might call this room home.

He reviewed what he'd discovered already. Two cases in the civil files named Burkhardt as defendant. Routine stuff: disputes over the grading practices on environmentally sensitive hillsides that Burkhardt had developed a few years back.

In three cases Burkhardt had initiated legal action. Again they were the kind of proceedings News expected a successful developer to be involved in: breach of contract with a cement company, a suit disputing an ironworker's claim of on-the-job injury and another over a subcontractor's use of inferior materials.

LaFontaine had read the probate files, too. Nothing of great interest. Sloan was an only son. The old man's will was uncontested: he got the company and the millions. He was about to call it quits, when for the hell of it he looked in the criminal records.

Bingo! S. Burkhardt. A 1986 case. Sealed the following year? He scribbled down the only two numerical codes left on the microfilm. He got in line to talk with Carol Randolph. She was the criminal clerk he'd taken to lunch a half dozen times over the years so she'd share her expertise when he needed it.

"Carol, as always you're looking marvelous," LaFontaine declared when his turn came. "What's your secret? Oil of Olay?"

Randolph guffawed. "Just clean living, News. What can I do for you?"

"Why would this be sealed?" he asked. "Case was opened and closed in eighty-six. Sealed the next year."

"Only criminal offense?"

"As far as I know."

"Can't tell from these numbers, that's the idea of sealing, you know. But my best guess is a drunk driving case. Judge sees there hasn't been a prior, he seals it. Happens all the time, though this is kind of quick."

"Nothing else here to go on? You know, a way to figure out exactly what he did?"

Randolph looked at the code numbers LaFontaine had scribbled down. She shook her head. "That number is the judge, or whoever the judge was who had that number a few years ago. The second one is the client's attorney number. And he won't tell you squat."

"Unless he's a rat."

"Officially we have no rat attorneys in this courthouse," she laughed. "Better luck next time. Say, when's the next time you take an old broad to lunch?"

"You know I space those lunches out. Can't be around you too often, Carol."

"Why's that?" she demanded.

"Hang with a woman like you too often, I might start questioning my sexuality."

Randolph slapped the counter and howled.

The recorder's office was at the east end of the county building. Here every property record and lien was photographed and placed on reels of microfilm. News used a computer index to find the documents he wanted, then plucked the reels he needed from giant revolving stacks. He slid the first reel into an empty machine and punched in a number. It whined, spun for a minute, then jerked to a stop.

A notarized letter of intent to finance the Cote D'Azure project for $124 million from Carlton Bank. Signed Robert S. Carlton III and Thomas P. Whitney, senior vice president. Notarized by Janice Tate.

LaFontaine looked over the details of the financing statement. He was no money wizard, but the terms didn't seem out of the ordinary—heavy interest payments the first ten years, then a balloon payment of $40 million in year eleven of the thirty-year arrangement. Given the projected value of a waterfront project like Cote D'Azure, not unreasonable.

It was dated March 12. LaFontaine looked at his notes. Ten days before Carlton died at The Ranch Tennis Club. He'd pulled the clips before coming down this morning. A security guard had found Carlton around ten o'clock the night of the twenty-second on the practice court. The bank president was a member of the club, and was often seen there late at night perfecting his serve. It was his way of relieving stress, one friend said. Several sources named in the story had speculated that the strain of the federal audit had been too much for Carlton. Too many serves late at night. Pop goes the weasel.

News made a note to himself to check the autopsy report on Carlton, then rewound the microfilm and plugged in another reel. Supporting documents to the letter of intent, legal briefs and other boilerplate language that described the details of the project. Nothing new. The next four reels contained similar background documents.

He popped in the sixth and last band of microfilm. It spun and stopped. Illuminated on the screen was a legal document finalizing the terms of the loan contingent on Burkhardt's getting the city's approval of the deal. Signed again by Carlton, Bradley Whitney, and Burkhardt as president of "Blue Coast Partners."

Must be the shell entity Burkhardt organized to do the deal, News thought. It was notarized by Janice Tate on March 25. He made a note to check the secretary of state's office for information on "Blue Coast Partners," then stopped to stare at the screen.

March 25? His heart raced. Bobby Carlton was dead three days when this was signed!

He told himself to slow down, to think. Somehow a man had signed a document three days after his death. He went back over his notes, looking for a new angle of attack.

"Thomas P. Whitney," LaFontaine said. "Thomas P. Whitney."

Amateur Pornography . . .

Corporations, LaFontaine decided, were like penises, not happy unless engorged, erect, showing off.

What more proof did you need than the Carlton Bank Building? Thirty-two stories, tan granite, tinted glass, rising to a strange mushroomlike top. LaFontaine gazed up at the building and grinned. A phallic symbol in the grand tradition of the eighties, when California real estate developers and financial institutions carried on like gluttons at a Roman Bacchanalia. Downtown office space was overbuilt now. Carlton Bank had fifty percent vacancy. Another reason many people questioned the configuration of Burkhardt's development, forty percent of which was office.

News played with these facts as he rode a glass elevator up the west side of the building. The bay sparkled below him. The sails on hundreds of boats puffed and ran in the steady breeze. On a grassy knoll before the water palm fans rustled.

Suddenly he grabbed the wall to steady himself. Pain rippled along the inside of his bruised ribs. He belched and gritted his teeth. He should have known better. Thai chicken did it to him every time. Peanut sauce with cayenne red pepper and cilantro for lunch. And two cups of black coffee. He belched again.

The elevator stopped at the eighteenth floor. The doors opened into a pale gray reception area with light birch wainscoting. He staggered out, hand on stomach.

"Mr. Whitney, please," he said to the receptionist, an intense little Asian woman in her early forties. She wore a pink suit with a white carnation in the lapel.

"Do you have appointment?"

"No. I'm a reporter with *The Post*. A couple of questions I need answered."

"You have questions about federal inquiry, you speak to Ms. Gretchen Vietze, tenth floor," she said in a practiced cadence. "She's the officer of public relations."

"How very military!"

The receptionist's eyes narrowed. "Ms. Vietze. Tenth floor."

"Look, deary, I don't give a damn about the federal inquiry. Tell Mr. Whitney I'd like to ask him about a couple of backdated signatures I found on a loan agreement."

"What is this backdated mean?"

"He'll understand."

The peanut sauce reared its ugly head. LaFontaine doubled over. "Please," he gasped. "I'm not feeling well."

The reporter's greening flesh threw the receptionist. "I call Mr. Whitney!"

"Bless you." LaFontaine burped. He pressed his fingers into his abdomen, trying to calm the storm that raged within. He pulled out a roll of antacid tablets and popped four.

After three minutes of escalating gut weep, a door opened at the far end of the room and a severe-looking woman entered. She wore a black suit with an off-white shirt. Her haircut was tight above the ears, blond, masculine. She was thick with the odor of Chanel No. 5, which almost triggered another round of nausea.

"Gretchen Vietze," the woman said.

"Ah, yes. The P.R. commando," said LaFontaine, who struggled to his feet. She shook his limp hand firmly. "Sorry, a little too much to eat at lunch. It will pass."

"What's this all about, Mr. LaFontaine?"

News heard the creak of the receptionist's chair. "Is there anyplace more private?"

Vietze glanced at her watch. "We have to make this quick. I have an appointment in fifteen minutes."

He followed her through the door and into a hall decorated in deep red shades. She turned into the third office on the left.

"The receptionist said your office was on the tenth floor," LaFontaine said once she'd gotten into place behind her desk. The power position. He remained standing to offset the home turf advantage.

Vietze smiled. "Yes, well. Song does her job. What is it you want?"

He fumbled in his briefcase and came out with reproductions of the letter of intent and the final accord on the loan agreement. "Notice the signatures," he said.

"So?"

"Look at the dates."

She studied them for a moment, then lifted her head shaking it. "I still don't . . ."

"My, my how soon the passing of the powerful is forgotten."

She glanced back down at the date, then flipped back through her desk calendar. Over the years LaFontaine had honed his ability to read upside down. It's a knack most good reporters develop after time. When she got to the date of the final agreement, he scanned her list of appointments and said: "Looks like you attended old Bobby's wake the day he was supposed to have signed that."

Vietze eased the calendar shut. She fussed with several papers, then smiled brightly. "I'm sure there's an explanation."

"And I'd like to hear it from Mr. Whitney, the other signatory."

"He's busy in meetings this afternoon."

"It would look awful strange if the only quote I had to go with this story was your 'I'm sure this can be explained,' as you fidget nervously."

Her nostrils flared. The scent of Chanel No. 5 swept like a wave through the office. Despite the gurgle in his stomach, LaFontaine had the urge to giggle. The bank's information Sandinista was sweating profusely. These were the moments he lived for.

"I'll be back as soon as I can."

"Might I trouble you for some seltzer water? I have a bit of indigestion."

Vietze took a long breath. "I'll have Song bring it."

"The gulag guard turns water gal. How nice!"

News spent fifteen minutes flipping through back copies of *American Banker*, deciding in the process that there were worse jobs for a journalist than being a general assignment hack for *The Post*. Could you imagine spending your life writing about credit cards and discount rates? Better to be trussed and force-fed rancid Thai chicken by the evil Song.

"Mr. LaFontaine?"

He set down his seltzer water, lurched to his feet, and came nose to chest with Thomas P. Whitney, who stood nearly six feet seven inches in his Johnston Murphy wing tips. Whitney's hand swallowed the reporter's. Whitney was in his early forties. He was in shape, probably a runner, maybe a swimmer.

"I hear you think you're onto a hot story," Whitney said.

He lounged on the desk's corner with his arms crossed. A power position LaFontaine could not neutralize.

"Dead man's signature on a document dated three days post mortem. Pretty stinky."

"*Notarized* three days after his death," Whitney said. "Our notary had the flu. She couldn't do the job when we needed it."

"So it isn't unusual for a bank president to sign a document like that when the other signatories aren't present?"

"This bank has assets of nearly three billion dollars, Mr. LaFontaine."

"The Federal Deposit Insurance Corporation doesn't seem to think so."

The banker flushed. "That's beside the point. Mr. Carlton was a busy man. He signed dozens of documents a day. It wasn't always possible to get everyone together at once to finalize agreements. The letter of intent was the important document."

"Still, if Mr. Carlton's signature hadn't appeared there, the loan wouldn't have gone forward?" News was fishing now.

Whitney hesitated. "Officially the bank agreed to the deal with the letter of intent."

"Officially," LaFontaine said. "But it could have been undone."

This time the pause was longer. "Technically, I suppose."

"Who could have made that decision?"

"The executive loan committee."

"Chaired by Mr. Carlton. And now chaired by?"

"Me."

LaFontaine tapped his lips with his pen. "Downtown office space is glutted. Your own building is less than half-full. Cote D'Azure is a huge development. Given the . . . er, difficulties your bank now faces, do you think this loan was prudent?"

Whitney's smile was thin. "Prudent is a loaded word, Mr. LaFontaine. I think a better way to phrase the question would be was it worth the risk? The city thinks Cote D'Azure is best suited to occupy the shipyard land. Carlton Bank has long been a supporter of the city's redevelopment efforts. Mr. Carlton felt a personal commitment to that end."

"And you?"

The bank president coughed. "I share Mr. Carlton's vision."

"What does a dead man see?"

"Mr. LaFontaine, you're trying my patience."

"It happens. Listen, I get the sense the deal was so far gone when he died that you couldn't have done anything about it even if you wanted to."

"I repeat, I share Mr. Carlton's vision of the city." He reached out to shake News's hand. "I hope I've cleared up any confusion you might have had. Now I must go."

As Whitney turned, News asked: "What do you think of Sloan Burkhardt?"

Whitney missed a step, but showed no expression. "I think Mr. Burkhardt carries on in the tradition of his father."

At the same time, McCarthy was parking his Toyota in the shade of trees near the outbuildings of the Kemper Stables. Out here, where the well-trimmed lawns of the city's suburbs gave way to scrub brush, the temperature hovered near the hundred-degree mark. Morning glories withered on their vines about the faded wooden posts of the corrals. The two dozen horses vied for the tree shade. Three burros ate hay.

McCarthy thought about Regina Fetterbaum and why she'd opened up to him. He'd been developing a theory of talk for years now. It came down to this: strangers will tell you the unspeakable if there is sufficient motivation.

There were four kinds of motivation. First, extreme personal pain: grief-stricken sources who hold a grudge against the object of investigation. Perhaps the most fertile ground and the most suspect information; you have to read between the lines to get the real story. Even then it is often clouded.

Second, the ego display. Here the interviewee revels in the information and wants to share it with the world. These are often the most tiresome, yet helpful interviews.

Next came the leveraged spill. In such situations, the person being interviewed is frightened of other information about them or their loved ones coming out, so they pour out part of what they know to protect the real skeletons.

The last, and the one the merry widow fit most neatly into, was what McCarthy called the henhouse motivation. Most people will speak openly about people in classes lower than themselves as well as those of much higher economic and social standing, yet they will rarely speak freely about their peers. To do so would compromise the lies they tell themselves. At the heart of it, then, Fetterbaum talked because she believed being an alcoholic retiree was more acceptable than being a dead street whore.

"Probably right," McCarthy said to himself. He got out of the car and made sure to see that his new cardboard sign was still stuck to the rear window. It said, "No Radio, No Ashtray, No Nothing."

"Can I help you, sir?" called a gaunt man in jeans, boots, denim work shirt, and battered straw cowboy hat. He carried a saddle. For a moment McCarthy thought he might be the young cowboy Fetterbaum had seen at Gentry's. At second glance this man was older, wizened by years in the sun.

"I hope so. My name's Gideon McCarthy. I work for *The Post.* I'm trying to get some information on a woman who boarded a horse here, Mr. . . . ?"

The man closed one eye halfway. "Kemper. Clint

Kemper. And I don't give information out about my boarders. Figure people got a right to privacy."

"She's dead," McCarthy said solemnly. "I don't think she'd mind."

Kemper shot him a wicked glare. "Now that I know who you're talking about, *I* mind."

He hoisted the saddle back onto his shoulder. He headed toward a red-and-white barn. McCarthy took off after him. "I'm just here to find out about the horse."

Kemper spit. He jerked his head toward the far corral. "The mare over there, the white Arabian. Good conformation, not a bad disposition for a thoroughbred. What else you need to know? Her feed mix? Exercise schedule?"

McCarthy glanced over at the horse. A sleek animal with wide nostrils and black pepper marks about its neck and ears. "Anybody been in to claim her?"

"Nope and no one's going to," Kemper said. He continued into the barn, entered a tack room, and hung the saddle on a peg.

"Why's that?"

"What are you really after?"

"Okay, I'll come clean. I'm trying to figure out who killed her."

"I thought that was the police did that."

"They been out here?"

"No."

"Okay, then. Why won't someone come for the horse?"

"Didn't say they wouldn't come for it," the cowboy snapped. "Said no one's going to get it. I figure it's ours now for what she did."

Kemper took several halters from a box on the workbench and began oiling them. This wasn't a leveraged interview after all. Pain was involved.

"She hurt your son, didn't she?"

Kemper opened his mouth, then slammed it shut. He

pushed the halters away. "Know about it all, don't you? Just here to torture us. You reporters are all dark angels."

"I'm not here to hurt your family," McCarthy said. "I'm just here to listen."

Kemper took off his hat to reveal a shock of salt and slate hair, mostly salt. He stuck his thumbs in the pockets of his jeans and said evenly, "I don't want this in the papers. You screw me on this, I'll make sure you never walk again. Deal?"

Better to understand than not to understand, even if he couldn't print it yet. "Deal," McCarthy said.

Kemper got out another toothpick from the pocket of his shirt, played with it a moment, then said, "That bitch, Carol Alice, she shows up here about a year ago, looking for a place to board this mare she's going to buy off a breeder out in the East County. Only she don't want just to board, she wants to learn to ride, too."

"She's buying an Arabian and she doesn't know how to ride?"

"Tried to convince her we could sell her one of our quarter horses for a fifth the price. She says if I don't want to help her out with the Arabian, she'll go somewhere's else.

"I says, young lady, it's your money. So I send my son, Billy, out with the trailer to get the horse 'bout a week later. They get back, Billy's taken a shine to her. She had that smell about her. Boys nineteen can't think around that smell."

"So what happened?"

"She'd come couple times a week, always in the morning. Billy's teaching her to ride," Kemper said. "One thing led to another. Billy starts disappearing after classes."

"He's going to her place."

"Whatever. Billy, he wouldn't talk to me or his mom about it. And to tell the truth, it was none of our business. I like to think I'm a Christian, but hell, I remember what it was like to get some for the first time."

Kemper wrenched a leather thong violently about his fingers. " 'Cept one day, I go through some old boxes out back looking for a bit."

He stopped and hung his head.

McCarthy always hated this part, forcing, cajoling, doing whatever it took to get what he needed. But he had to put aside his sympathies. He needed a break on this story.

"What did you find, Mr. Kemper?"

"I find this tape, a videotape, wrapped in one of Billy's T-shirts. I take it in the house and pop it in. There's my Billy with that bitch and . . . a . . . a black gal. They're on the video. All of them . . . together like."

McCarthy's mind sprinted back to Regina Fetterbaum's description of Gentry's frantic rummage through her entertainment center. Why would she be so concerned about a tape of her, Billy Kemper, and a black woman?

"Mr. Kemper, did the video seem . . . professional?"

Kemper raised his head. "How the Christ do I know? Never seen that crap before. Can you imagine what seeing that would have done to my wife?"

"She doesn't know?"

"Intend to keep it that way, too."

"I'm sorry I have to dwell on this," McCarthy pressed. "Did it seem like the camera was still or was it shot from different angles?"

The leather thong dug into Kemper's flesh. "You're asking, was there a cameraman? No, it was still."

"Where's the video now?"

Kemper's eyes became the bores of a shotgun. "Burned it."

"Billy?"

"Gone. Five months now. I confronted them both with it next time she came in. She looks at me like I was a prude or something. Says it was a memento. I about backhanded her. Billy starts defending her, says it was his idea, not hers. And what right did I have going through his things? I told him to get the Christ out of here. Go screw his whore for the cameras."

Kemper scuffed the wooden floor of the barn with his boot.

"When did all this happen, Mr. Kemper?"

"Mid-March. Billy's living in town with some friends. Word I got is she dumped him 'bout a month after the blowout. She called in June, told my wife she was sending someone to get the horse. But no one ever came. I figure to sell it for damages."

"You know the address where I can find your son?"

Kemper didn't say anything for a moment, then mumbled, "You keep him out of it, okay? He's my only child."

"As best I can, sir."

Kemper gave him an address and a telephone number.

"I appreciate it, Mr. Kemper."

Kemper rubbed at his chin. "Do me a favor, huh?"

"If I can."

"You see Billy, you tell him his mother's been asking after him."

McCarthy nodded and left the barn. Leveraged pain. Always the most uncomfortable interview to conduct, always one of the most productive.

He got in the car, letting the excitement break through the sympathy he'd felt for Kemper. Even though the camera hadn't moved, there was still the possibility the video was professionally shot. If so, and if the video mattered, the scope of people who could be involved in her death suddenly expanded. If it was an amateur film, shot as a memento, then she was just kinkier than he thought. But what about the break-in and her other tapes?

He looked at his watch. He had to be in the judge's chambers in an hour, and then on to the night cops office.

No time to track down Billy Kemper today. But it had to be done soon. Even though he couldn't quote Kemper, he could write the story of the break-in and Regina Fetterbaum's feeling they were after a tape. The second that hit the paper, Karen Rivers would be right behind him. Despite her assurances otherwise, the merry widow might talk.

Going solo on this story was his best chance to help clear his name. But as he started the car, he conceded that even Lazarus had needed help in resurrection.

Lies and Other Allegations of Fact . . .

"Think of family court as a miniature Beirut," Jeanette Fry said. "And yourself a Hezbollah fanatic. We want to go in, wreak havoc, get the kids, and get out."

"Who are you, Carlos the Jackal?" McCarthy asked.

"Feminist version, no veil," she called over her shoulder as she hurried up the courthouse steps. An amateur bodybuilder, Fry took fluid, linear strides.

McCarthy huffed, trying to keep up with her. "We got a judge? Like I said, I don't have many friends in this place."

"As a single male you couldn't have anticipated being here," Fry said. "But those articles you wrote about family court a couple of years ago don't help much. We got Evelyn Crawford."

McCarthy stifled a groan. "She threw a bunch of files at me and chased me down the hall after the stories appeared."

"I've found that throwing marbles behind you often trips up your pursuer, gives you time to get away," Fry said. She held the door for him.

"Mr. McCarthy, what an unpleasant surprise to see you

here," Crawford said. "And forget about petitioning for a recusal, Ms. Fry. I'm probably the person with the least bias toward him in this courthouse."

Crawford, a bony woman in her early sixties, tapped a gold pen against her palm. Charley Owens and his attorney, Matthew Brady, smirked.

Dust still covered McCarthy's black, rubber-soled walking shoes. Hay flecked his sleeves. Owens sported polished Nicomo boots, an expensive two-piece blue suit, white shirt, a turquoise-and-silver bolo tie. He was so tanned that with his dark hair he could have passed for Native American. McCarthy's neck tightened. A headache coming on.

"I've read the briefs," Crawford said.

"We object categorically to Mr. McCarthy's allegations," Brady announced. His mustache was waxed. He spoke out of the right side of his mouth. "They are unsubstantiated, totally without merit, and would frankly constitute character assassination should they be allowed to enter the public files."

Crawford looked over the top of a pair of reading glasses. "Never mistreated your son, Mr. Owens?"

"If anything, I tried to prevent my wife from mistreating him," he replied earnestly.

McCarthy couldn't believe it. "That's a lie!"

Brady's response was slick and pointed. "Mr. McCarthy, if anyone here has a history of bending the truth to suit his purposes, it's you. I read all about it in the newspaper."

McCarthy glared at him. "You oily . . ."

Crawford interrupted, "Ms. Fry, please restrain your client."

Fry's powerful right hand tugged McCarthy back into his seat. She whispered, "You go crazy, you'll get more than files thrown at you. You'll lose those kids."

"Go on, Mr. Owens," Crawford ordered.

"It was a tense time in our lives," Owens said. "I am a dealer in Southwestern and Central American textiles. I did make an unconsidered move in the Navajo rug market which put at considerable risk a business in which I held an interest."

"In fact, you indebted the partnership a million dollars," interrupted Fry.

Owens tensed. "Slightly less than that, Counselor. But the allegation that in some drug-crazed frenzy brought on by the losses I abused my son, well, it's just ludicrous. Just the sort of thing Tina would invent."

"It's no invention," McCarthy snapped.

"McCarthy, if you can't let him finish, I'll have to ask you to wait outside," Crawford said. "Proceed, Mr. Owens."

Owens opened his hands. "Look, I admit I used cocaine a few times back then. Everyone did. But there was only one person in the family who had a problem. Tina. She came from an underprivileged background. I had money. And when it looked like we might lose it, she flipped.

"I'd find her up at all hours snorting the stuff," Owens continued. "There were times I'd come home and Carlos was locked in his bedroom with a bag of popcorn. He was three years old. Miriam was crying in her crib, wet."

Fry broke in, "Judge, in fact, just the opposite occurred. When Tina Rodriguez became pregnant with Miriam she entered a drug rehab center. She was clean from then on. Mr. Owens, however, continued to use cocaine on a regular basis.

"Carlos suffered from ear infections as a toddler," Fry went on. "The boy cried at all hours of the night. At the same time, Mr. Owens's business partners tried to force him out because he wasn't making good on a financial loss. His drug abuse deepened. Mr. Owens lost control one night. The boy's arm was broken in two places."

"Absolutely false," Brady cried. "Carlos took a fall from his crib. Mr. Owens considered suing the crib company because the safety bar was faulty."

"Mr. Owens," the judge began, "how do you explain the

boy's three trips to different hospitals with severe bruises and injuries in the course of six months?"

"I explain it by a having a wife who was an unfit mother," Owens bristled. "While I was out trying to recoup my losses, Tina was doping it up, ignoring Carlos. The injuries were the result of neglect."

Crawford sorted through the file on her desk. "No subsequent reports on any possible abuse from other agencies. Social services? Police?"

"Unfortunately no, Your Honor," Fry admitted.

"Because it never happened," Brady added.

Crawford said, "There is a notation here that Tina Rodriguez entered a treatment center again briefly after her separation from Mr. Owens."

"For one week and of her own volition," Fry emphasized. "She was so shaken by her last months with Mr. Owens that she needed a psychological boost to avoid slipping back into addiction. Once outside, she took the children to live with her aunt. She finished her degree in journalism and went to work for *The Post*."

Crawford drew off her glasses and chewed on one of the stems.

McCarthy closed his eyes and thought of Tina. Lawlor hired her soon after her graduation. She was smart and wrote beautifully. That first year at *The Post* she produced a series of stories about Pete Montgomery, a Grateful Dead head turned guru who changed his legal name to Sahandi. Sahandi claimed he channeled the spirit of a fifteenth century wisewoman named Sophia.

Sophia's message to the faithful was direct, wholesome, and traditional: the family was the healer of all troubles. Society crumbled as the nuclear family disintegrated. Nothing new, really, but Sahandi delivered it all in a tour de force stage show complete with lighting effects and bootleg Grateful Dead recordings. The seminars, books, and videotapes had made the counterculturist channeling the conservative spirit a multimillionaire.

All of it began to fall apart when Tina got a tip that Sahandi had fathered several illegitimate children around the country during his frequent trips to Grateful Dead concerts and was refusing to support them.

McCarthy was assigned to help Tina dig the story out. During the travel and the long nights going door to door to track down the guru's far-flung progeny, he found himself drawn by her intelligence, beauty, and strength. It was purely professional until he rescued her from a Sahandi zealot attack during a Dead concert in Colorado.

She trembled in his arms and haltingly told him about the abuse she and her children had suffered at the hands of Charley Owens. Over the next few weeks they drifted into the warm breathlessness of infatuation. For McCarthy, Tina's love and the love of Carlos and Miriam was a coming home to a place he'd forgotten.

Crawford said to Owens, "You didn't contest the custody of the children during the divorce?"

"I was scared, in danger of losing a business I'd spent years building," Owens said. "And frankly I was tired of Tina and everything about her. I felt I could only fight for one thing. I chose the business."

"Losing the boy and the baby girl didn't concern you?"

Owens swallowed. "There hasn't been an hour when I don't think of my kids. I got bad legal advice, Judge. Once Tina went into rehab and came out clean, my attorney in New Mexico told me I didn't have a chance. Paternal rights in New Mexico remain thin at best. It took me five years to pay back my ex-partners. I'm making a go of it on my own. I want them with me."

McCarthy couldn't take it anymore. "You didn't call about them when Tina died."

Owens looked straight at him. "I knew they were with Estelle. I even checked up on you, Gideon. I knew they were safe. My appearance at that time, given the level of acrimony between me and Tina, would have been hypocritical, perhaps destructive."

The measured, sincere response temporarily unbalanced McCarthy. Could Tina have been lying all that time? Then he saw her contorted face in the wreck as she made him promise to be a good father. That kind of anguish flourishes only in truth.

"I don't know what your angle is," McCarthy said. "But I know you're lying."

"They're my children," Owens replied. "They deserve to have a father."

"I'm their father," McCarthy said.

"No, you're not."

The judge signaled both men to be silent. She fiddled with the chain hanging from her spectacles, then cleared her throat. "The allegations about Mr. Owens's conduct are troubling. The problem is we get them secondhand. From a reporter who manages to dig up remarkably accurate information, but still, secondhand and with no substantiation."

Fry made as if to interrupt.

"Please, Ms. Fry," Crawford said. "I haven't begun to consider the issue of custody. However, I feel that it is within Mr. Owens's rights to have visitation privileges."

"He's not stepping foot in my house," McCarthy declared.

"Mr. McCarthy, he *will* come to your house on any weekend day, with advance notice, of course. He may take the children for six hours," the judge said firmly.

Brady said, "Six hours, Judge? My client was hoping to take them to New Mexico for a couple of days at least. Traveling all this way for a few hours is a hardship."

"Don't push your luck, Mr. Brady," Crawford said. "The

fact remains that your client disclaimed responsibility for those children for almost five years. Let's see how he does with six hours. Custody hearing in seven weeks."

In the hall outside the courtroom, Owens said, "I have business in Santa Fe and won't be able to make it back until the end of the month. I'd like to take them to a baseball or football game."

McCarthy glanced at Fry, who nodded. He swallowed at the bile that crept up the back of his throat. "They'll be ready," McCarthy said. "But Charley, I know what you're capable of."

The smooth demeanor Owens had displayed inside the judge's chambers evaporated. "Is that right?"

"You bet," McCarthy said. "The thing is, I'm capable of much, much more."

"Is that a threat, McCarthy?" Brady demanded.

"Oh, you better believe it."

They stared at each other. Brady blinked first. "Let's go, Charley."

As Brady and Owens walked away, Fry said, "It's about the best we could have hoped for."

"We got crucified," McCarthy said. "Next time I'll be a better terrorist."

She's Got a
Tragedy Jones . . .

T hree hours later the disheveled pickup truck wheezing south on the freeway in front of Augustus Croon and Abby Blitzer spewed forth a dense cloud of diesel smoke. The stench poured in through the vents, hanging about the interior of the white Ford Escort. Blitzer choked, "Jesus, Croon, get around this Okie or I'll suffocate."

Croon, who was used to sucking down noxious fumes from his days doing pushups in the SEAL tear gas chamber, startled. "Sorry, Abby."

He floored the gas pedal and shot by the truck, which was being driven by an obese woman with no teeth. "Been almost sixty years since Dorothea Lange shot those great pictures and they're still coming here," he said.

Blitzer drummed on the dashboard. "It's what makes California great: Li'l Abner can tool the freeway right next to Daddy Warbucks."

She seemed to like that idea, which warmed Croon's heart. His partner had been in a foul mood lately. It had been weeks since they'd gotten into a good tragedy. He stifled the urge to moon, contenting himself with quick peeks. He was still amazed to be head over heels with a woman half his size.

Before Blitzer joined *The Post,* action held Croon's heart. Although he'd been a straight A student and salutatorian of his high school class with full scholarship offers from the

University of Chicago and Duke, Croon had enlisted in the navy, preferring physical challenge to academia.

He qualified for SEAL training, made the West Coast team, and spent ten years swimming all night in freezing oceans, storming beaches, reading voraciously, and shooting too many bullets to remember. After a decade of corporal punishment, Croon woke up to realize he no longer enjoyed being told what to do. When his tour ended he decided to pursue a career as a photographer, one of his childhood passions.

Soon he was out prowling the streets of Honolulu with a scanner, making a name for himself as a shooter willing to go to any extreme for a good picture. After SEAL training, dodging police lines and irate relatives to snap the latest misfortune proved effortless.

The Post offered Croon a job after he won a first place prize for spot news photography in Hawaii. Lawlor assigned him to the front line: hard news. The ex–underwater demolition expert made it clear when he took the job that he worked alone, no silly reporters to interfere with his all-consuming need to capture events as they happened. After several months on the job the issue was moot; the newsroom had decided that Croon was a post-traumatic stress case who drove the streets salivating at the thought of mayhem.

All that changed the day the Stanford Hotel burned to the ground. Constructed in the early 1930s as an upscale establishment, the Stanford had steadily descended from swank to second-rate to seedy. Two years before the fire, a Los Angeles developer named Clinton Hand obtained low-income housing funds and converted the Stanford to a single-room occupancy hotel for the elderly. Hand bribed city inspectors to overlook the illegal fire escapes and the shoddy construction materials.

The fire started at 10:00 P.M. Sixty-seven-year-old Ethel Grace fell asleep while smoking in her fourth floor room. The blaze spread quickly through the thin walls. Within minutes the structure was engulfed in smoke and flames. Without adequate fire escapes, the little old ladies who lived in the Stanford Hotel had nowhere to go but out the windows.

It was Blitzer's second week at the paper. She was working nightside general assignment when word reached the newsroom. Croon was staking out the docks for an essay he was doing on violence generated by an ongoing longshoreman's strike.

Both of them arrived on the scene simultaneously, both of them instantly absorbed in the grim splendor of terrified old ladies in gauzy white nightgowns falling like snowflakes. Croon leapt the fire barricade to shoot. Blitzer talked to survivors. Two of the women told her the same story—that there'd been complaints about faulty electrical wiring, about the lack of adequate smoke detectors, about the shaky fire escapes.

"It's not just that, honey," a first floor resident named Carey Wilson said. "I worked in my brother's contracting office for years. I know when a building's up to code. Fires don't spread this quick if the walls are put up right."

Meanwhile the fire chief had ordered Croon removed from the scene. Blitzer elbowed her way past two cops. She poked her finger into the fire chief's navel, screaming, "This place is going up too fast for it to be an accident! And the only way the public's going to get the story is if you let Croon and I do our jobs."

The fire chief glanced at the fire, then at Croon and Blitzer. "Just stay out of my way, okay?"

At that moment, backlit by the flames and nightgowns dropping through the winter night sky, Croon knew he'd met a reporter as tough as himself. Fifteen minutes later he realized he'd met a reporter tougher than half the SEALs he knew.

It so happened that Clinton Hand, the developer of the Stanford, was in town to oversee the illegal conversion of another flophouse when the fire broke out seven blocks from his digs in a tony $150-a-night hotel. He arrived on the scene in a black Mercedes. A pretty young thing in gold lamé stood at his side.

Carey Wilson limped up and shook her aluminum walker at him.

"You bastard!" Wilson said evenly. "We asked you to fix those fire escapes for weeks. Now Winny and Kate and Nancy are all dead over there."

"I don't know what you're talking about, dear," Hand said soothingly. He turned to Blitzer. "She must be upset at the loss. Those escapes were built exactly to code. It's all in the city documents."

"Liar!" Wilson cried. She slapped Hand across the mouth, an event which Croon recorded with his Nikon F4.

Hand retreated toward his Mercedes. A call to his attorney on the cellular phone seemed appropriate. The pretty young thing in gold lamé, sensing her sugar daddy's impending status implosion, filtered off into the crowd. Blitzer raced after the developer. She stuck her foot in the car doorjamb and grabbed on to the frame of the open window.

"Is it true you didn't build to code, Mr. Hand?" she shouted. "What's the matter, couldn't make a profit the legal way?"

Other reporters on the scene heard Blitzer's interrogation above the roar of the fire. They rushed in behind Croon, who was capturing Hand's meltdown for the morning editions.

The developer shrunk from the media swarm's hornet whine, put the Mercedes in gear, and hit the gas pedal. Blitzer held on to the doorframe, yelling questions at him. She held on when he crabbed the car sideways over the fire hoses. She held on as he accelerated to shake the bantamweight avenging spirit with hair like flames and eyes like stormy oceans.

The Mercedes was doing thirty-five when Blitzer finally

let go; the impact broke two ribs, snapped her wrist, and gashed her forehead. Lying in the street with the pack descending on her—she'd become as integral to the story as the old birds jumping from the ledges—Blitzer felt better than she had in years. Straight Jack Daniel's had nothing on a chilled adrenaline highball served in the saloon of face-to-face confrontation!

Croon's heart swelled with joy. He knelt by her crumpled form. "Abby Blitzer, I think I love you."

"That's nice, Mr. Croon," she'd replied blearily. "But I don't think love's the right drug for me at this moment."

Croon cradled her head in his massive hands. "I'll wait, Abby Blitzer. I'll wait."

Now, as they drove toward the mid-city address where Billy Kemper lived, Croon realized it had been more than a year since he'd declared his adoration and become a fellow witness to calamitous events, an unrequited lover amid the shock of mutilation, a surreptitious mooner at graveside ceremonies.

"Abby, you don't talk much about how it was back at the paper in Philadelphia."

Blitzer flinched. She'd always been able to keep him off the subject of her past. "Not much to tell. The last couple of years I was a drunk. End of story."

"It's easier sometimes if you talk about it. Did you lose somebody back there?"

Blitzer shrugged. "Myself."

"Other than that?"

He wasn't going to let up. She decided to give Croon a little more, something that would stop him cold. "A man I was going to marry," she said. "A good man."

Croon flushed. "A reporter, too?"

"No, an engineer."

"What happened?"

Blitzer pointed at the exit. "Get off here."

Croon flipped the blinker, then glanced at her expectantly.

"Goddamned McCarthy," she said. "This isn't my kind of story, Croon. I'm your basic there's the ten-car pileup, there's the drowned child. Find the center of pathos, write it down."

Croon, who'd hung around reporters long enough to know a dodge, slipped it and came back in her face. "I've been your partner for a more than a year. I deserve to know."

"I fell apart," she said in a stony voice. "We saw each other in a different way and that was the end of it."

A pit yawned in his stomach. "You still in love with him, the engineer?"

Blitzer was quiet for a moment. "No. Not with him. Maybe with the idea of him, if that makes any sense. That's it, 2100. Pull over."

She jumped out before he could ask another question and jogged toward 2100 Pinewood, a small white house with an even smaller lawn. A red cement walkway led to a green front door. The drought-parched lawn reeked of cat. The sun hung low in the west. The blinds were drawn to block the day's last strong light. Loud country music played inside. They knocked and knocked again. The volume fell.

A woman called out: "Who's there?"

"My name's Abby Blitzer. I'm here with Augustus Croon. We work for *The Post.*"

"Don't read the papers. Waste of time, sorry."

"No, ma'am. We're not here to sell you a subscription. We're reporters."

There was silence. "What do you want?"

"Billy Kemper. Does he live here?"

"What do you want with him?"

"It's about Carol Alice Gentry," Croon said.

Silence again. "He's sick. Don't want to see no one."

"It's important, please," Blitzer pleaded.

The blinds parted and a woman in her early twenties peeked through. Thick gobs of mascara hung from her eyelids. Her face was pasty with makeup, like oatmeal with powdered sugar on it.

She disappeared. They heard mumbled conversation. Then the door opened. She stood at the screen, a woman of many curves and angles, all of them magnified by black Lycra exercise shorts a size and a half too small for her and a kelly green stretch top so tight it pinched the nipples of her big breasts into gumdrops.

"Fifteen minutes," she said. "Billy's sick."

"Nice to meet you . . . ?" Blitzer said.

"Mary."

"Got a last name, Mary?"

"Just Mary. I ain't saying nothin'. He's in there on the couch."

Blitzer came around the front of the ratty couch. Day-old containers of Chinese food sat in a heap on the cheap coffee table. She winced at the sight of Billy Kemper.

The beating had been a bad one. The left side of his face had taken the brunt, swollen, blackened, and purpled. Stitches webbed his left eyebrow. His right arm hung in a sling. Thick tape swathed his rib cage. She winced again, but forced herself to look. Taut muscles etched his body. His brush-cut hair reminded her of hand-rubbed mahogany. And behind the puffiness, perfect hazel eyes. No wonder Gentry had taken him as her boy toy.

"We're helping another reporter, Gideon McCarthy, who's looking into the murder of Carol Alice Gentry," Blitzer said. "We heard you knew her."

Kemper made a noise that wanted to be a laugh. "Could say that."

"Got any ideas who'd want to kill her?"

" 'Bout everybody."

"How about you?" Croon asked.

Kemper gave Croon the look of estimation strong men give each other when first meeting. "Maybe once. I got over it."

"What happened?" the photographer asked, pointing to the wounds.

"Got jumped three days ago. Came home from work about eleven. Mary and Tim—I rent a room from them— they was out. Soon as I come through the door I knew it was wrong. That light by Mary's sewing machine was on. She don't leave stuff like that on when she goes out. Anyways, I got low, ready. The light went off. There was two, maybe three of them."

Mary leaned against a wall by the kitchen. She said, "We found him by the door. Whole place was wrecked."

"They take anything? Stereos, television?"

"Nothin' we can figure," Mary said. "Then again, not like there's much to take."

"Carol Alice's place was broken into before she was killed," Blitzer said.

Kemper nodded. "It shook her up real bad. I was staying in another place then and she crashed there for a couple of days."

"She say what they were after?"

"Maybe." He moved and grunted in pain. "Mary, can I get a brew?"

"Doc said that's no good with them painkillers."

"Fuck the doc, Mary. I need a brew here."

Mary scowled, then disappeared into the kitchen.

Blitzer said, "Billy, we know there was a porno video with you and Gentry and another woman."

"It wasn't like that!" Kemper protested. "Who told you it was porn?"

"Your dad," Croon said.

"My dad worships at the temple of John Wayne."

Mary handed Kemper a beer. He took a long swig, staring at Blitzer over the top of the bottle. Blitzer averted her eyes. Men like Billy Kemper could look into your soul and read your dark secrets. She made a show of smoothing the pleats in her skirt. She held her notebook to one side, shook back her tangle of red hair, and said, "So tell us how it was with this movie with you and Carol Alice and the other woman that wasn't porn."

Kemper glanced at Mary in a way that made Blitzer aware that Mary's husband better stay at home at night more often.

Mary waved her beer bottle at him. "I ain't your mother here listenin'. Tell 'em."

Kemper stripped the wet beer bottle label with his thumbnail. "Carol Alice liked hoots. That's what she called them. Hoots. You know, drive her car fast the wrong way down one-way streets. Go to fancy restaurants and act like she was someone famous, then leave without paying the check. Hoots were her way of pushing out the edge."

"So the videotape of you and her having sex was a hoot?"

"Because I'd never done it before. Because she got to watch me watch myself afterward. The taping, that was routine. Videotapes, little cassette tapes. She recorded everything. She carried a recorder with her wherever she went. Said it helped her keep track of who she was and who everyone else was. She had a strange head."

"Who was on the tapes?" Blitzer said.

"I only saw a few videos. She put one on when we made love one afternoon. It was just her and the camera, you know, like by herself?"

"Jesus," Mary said.

If it was possible under all those bruises, Kemper reddened. "Yeah, and there was another time, she had a tape of a phone call. On it, this guy wants to come over to see her and she's putting him off. Teasing him, you know? She thought that tape was great. She'd get doubled over laughing when she listened to it. Couple times she'd make me . . . while she listened . . . well, you know."

"Jesus," Mary said again.

"Who was the guy?" Croon asked.

"I didn't know then, but later, when the stories started coming out, I figured it was one of those cops because of the stuff he was saying about his nightstick loving her."

At that Kemper fell quiet.

"That bothered you," Blitzer said.

"I liked her."

"You knew she was a hooker."

"Not at first. She kept everything in her life separate. But I could never see her at night and stuff. I followed her one night to the Boulevard. She saw me, saw that I knew, and it was like I'd become someone different, someone she didn't want around."

"You said everybody would want to kill her," Blitzer said.

"She taped everything. And then testifying and all. I figure it that way."

"Any friends she had that we should talk to?"

"I never really met any of them if she had them, except for Delta Ann Porter," he said, glancing at Mary again. "That's the one in the tape with me and Carol Alice. We found her working the Boulevard near Sixty-sixth Street, the McDonald's there."

Blitzer wrote Porter's name down. "You think the guys who beat you had something to do with Carol Alice?"

"Maybe she taped the wrong person. Maybe they thought I might have the tape. Now I even regret knowing the bitch."

"John Wayne's kid gets religion," Croon said.

Kemper tried his best to act indignant. He didn't succeed.

The Slotman's Blues . . .

Eight o'clock at the Slotman's Bar and Grill. The proprietor, the famed Slotman himself, patted his ample middle and analyzed the tension level. *Not bad,* he thought. Paranoia can be generated midweek.

It helped, of course, that Ralph Baker, a.k.a. Roy Orbison, slumped at the bar. Having one of the city's journalism burnouts drowning himself front and central always heightened anxiety. Which created a mad liquor lust among the other editors and reporters present. Which fattened the Slotman's retirement portfolio.

The Slotman closed his eyes to carefully gauge his latest stress enhancer. A decrepit jukebox. Its metal-walled speakers turned any song, reggae, rock, country, or classic, into an irritable music mayonnaise with the steel-drummed timbre of second-rate calypso. By the time the music traveled twenty feet it melded into an undulating dissonance that forced standing patrons to turn toward the bar for another round. Just last week Prentice LaFontaine had dubbed this neurotic Muzak "the Slotman's Blues."

The Slotman grinned. Perhaps News would come tonight. He frayed nerves better than any jukebox. LaFontaine was bad for morale and good for business.

"I'll have a beer, Slotman," Augustus Croon said.

The barkeep broke into a greasy smile. A photographer who hung with a woman hooked on tragedy. It was only a matter of time before he was slung low over the bar railing to talk old times with that leather-clad wonder, Ralph Baker.

"Sure enough, Croon," he said. "Coming right up. How about you, Abby?"

"Seltzer water with a twist of lime," Blitzer said.

The Slotman cringed. If only Blitzer would encounter a calamity so ghastly that she'd fall off the wagon. The thought of the mutual funds he could buy with her nightly business warmed his attitude considerably.

The Slotman's real name was Corey Tuft. For twenty-five years he'd been a journeyman copy editor. Worked for every paper in the city at one time or another, rising to the position of slotman at the old *Chronicle*. Though the position had ceased to exist at almost every modern paper, in its day being slotman meant power. From the central position on the rim of the copy desk he had acted as final arbiter on questions of grammar, word choice, style, and coherence. The slotman also held sway on issues of story placement and headline size, these last two most important because they could make or break an article's impact.

The Slotman loved the news business. But he never let romanticism cloud his vision. Five years before *The Chronicle* folded, he stunned everyone at the paper by taking a buy-out. He knew computers would eventually render his position impotent. Sure, some papers would continue to use the term to signify the reigning copy chief, but the slotman's power to navigate the publication of the paper like a riverboat captain would dwindle and finally end. He foresaw the personal repercussions: a slow panic as the emasculation loomed, anger, denial, high blood pressure, sleepless nights, more coffee at the beginning of the day, more booze at the end.

That awareness led to his current career. The Slotman figured if slotmen were doomed to extinction, newspapers themselves were candidates for the endangered species list. Lots of anxiety. Lots of paranoia. Lots of self-medicating. He leased this bar downtown. He had steaks flown in from Omaha. He plastered the walls with framed copies of extra editions from the various papers and installed a big-screen television that was always tuned to CNN.

As stomach acid geysered forth during the final year of *The Chronicle,* the Slotman made more money than he had in the previous decade. Though business fell off after *The Chronicle* published its last edition, word of the terminal diagnosis of other newspapers in other cities was enough to keep the anxiety of most hard news workers at subterror level. That meant a hopping bar. That meant a happy Slotman.

Things were looking up these days. Everyone knew *The Post* or *The Beacon* would rest in the coffin soon. The Slotman had a year-to-year lease on the dump. He planned to make a minor fortune on the agony of the war's final battles, then retire to Tucson to bake his skin to the consistency of iguana hide.

The Slotman drew Croon's beer, poured Blitzer's water, and brought the drinks to the table.

"We'll have New York strips with baked potato and salad," Blitzer said. "McCarthy's buying."

The Slotman did a little jig! McCarthy, the personification of news angst, was coming in! He scribbled down their order and bopped away.

To pass time until McCarthy arrived, Blitzer and Croon decided to draft a list of the top ten tragedies in the United States this century. She argued that the *Hindenburg* disaster took precedence over the San Ysidro massacre. Croon disagreed, pointing out that the mass killings at the McDonald's restaurant near the Mexican border were the work of a lunatic while the dirigible explosion resulted from unforeseen natural conditions.

"This is how I see it, Abby," Croon said, turning philosophical. "I think the delusions of man result in more profound pain than the acts of God."

Blitzer shook her tiny head. "The *Hindenburg* wasn't solely an act of God."

"Sure it was. The wind blew, created sparks, and the whole thing exploded. *'Oh the horror!'* Remember?"

"I remember. But it was man and God at odds. The *Hin-*

denburg designers knew they were taunting the natural order flying a balloon filled with flammable gas."

"A tragedy. No doubt about it."

"Man against God. Best kind of tragedy, Croon. Even the Greeks knew that."

She swirled the ice cubes against the side of her glass. "Man and God at odds. Woman and God at odds."

She burst into tears.

The ex-SEAL stood, alarmed. He'd never seen Blitzer so much as choke up, let alone sob. This was like witnessing Arnold Schwartzenegger turn all blubbery. "Abby, Jeez. . . . Uh, jeez. Are you all right?"

She sat up straight and drew in a sharp breath. "It's nothing, Croon. Just a little tired. Probably hormones, too. I need . . . I need to go to the bathroom."

She eased herself up from the table and moved methodically to the back hall, leaving Croon totally befuddled. Life had always been so cut-and-dry before Abby Blitzer. Lieutenant says swim the three miles through rough surf, you swim. Editor says get the picture, you get the picture. But who gave the orders when it came to that little redhead? He considered the foam in his beer. Perhaps a rereading of Sophocles would help him to understand. Perhaps it would help him fill the expanding hollow in his chest.

McCarthy tapped Croon on the shoulder. "How'd you guys do tonight?"

"Hey, Gid," Croon said. "We did real well. Abby will be back in a minute. Just off to powder her nose."

As McCarthy slid into the booth, Prentice LaFontaine came through the door followed by Isabel Perez. The Slotman did a quick two-step and a spin behind the bar.

"Mind if we join the brain trust?" LaFontaine asked.

"Sure, News," McCarthy said. He made room for them. "Find anything in the county records about Burkhardt?"

LaFontaine related his discovery of the sealed criminal record and the backdated loan documents. Blitzer returned while News recounted his interview with Thomas P. Whitney. Aside from the minor bags about her eyes, Blitzer radiated composure. Croon mooned at her as if nothing had happened.

When LaFontaine had finished, McCarthy asked, "Officially the loan was worth the risk, what about unofficially?"

"I was hardly in a position to inquire of his private thoughts," News said. "He had his P.R. gargoyle hovering over his shoulder. I didn't even bring up the sealed file."

"So find him off-hours and ask," Perez suggested. "He's a part owner of that new Irish place on Fourteenth Street. Place is booming. Jackson goes there from time to time."

"How is dear Kent?" LaFontaine asked.

"Insufferable as ever," Perez said. "We had a big run-in this morning. The mayor had his daily press briefing. Chief Leslie was there, too, acting all blustery with his newfound position. They were talking strategy, how they're going to deal with Barnes."

"And how's that?" Blitzer said.

"They figure with Barnes's ties to the Silicon Valley he's got the Bay Area wrapped up," Perez said. "They'll focus their efforts on the rest of the state."

"So what was the run-in?" McCarthy asked.

"I'm sitting there, being the perfect number two, saying nothing while Kent asked all these insider questions about polling and stuff. Yawn, yawn. I get to thinking about what that homicide detective said in your story about possible police involvement in the Gentry killing. I ask old T. Lawrence if it troubled him that some of his employees may be under investigation in connection with killing a woman who claimed corruption went higher in the department than street level?"

"You coldhearted Latina," LaFontaine said. "His answer?"

"Oh, you know T. Lawrence, he could convince you Charlie Manson would make a fine media consultant. He smiled and said 'Of course it's troubling. But the fact is we're investigating and got one of the best detectives on the force supervising.' "

McCarthy snorted. "Fisko is more interested in task forces than investigations."

"Anyway," Perez said, "T. Lawrence goes on about what you and Rivers have already written. That Gentry was an unreliable informant. That she was a hooker who led a life that probably placed her in a psycho's zone of opportunity. Blah, Blah Blah."

"So what's the beef with Jackson?" Blitzer asked.

"I'm getting to that. After it breaks up he asks me if I'm trying to quote 'Tilt the odds out of our favor with the campaign.' End quote. Then he starts lecturing me on the *rules of political reporting.*"

"Jackson's a right-wing butt-head," LaFontaine said. "There are no rules in political reporting. Just swallow the pablum, go back to the newsroom, and vomit it on the page."

"Not according to Kent. He says, Rule number one: If you're going to create a political scandal, make sure you've got the inside dope. It's like going to the racetrack, he says: You want a longshot to come in, you better spend time in the stable, talking to the grooms. He claimed all I'd done was jeopardize our relationship with the campaign."

"He has a point," McCarthy said.

"He's just so cocky about it," Perez said glumly. "Then he says if I want to do something 'constructive,' I should review the campaign finances. He doesn't have time."

"Did you?" Croon asked.

Perez drummed her fingers on the table. "I felt like his lackey. But it seemed better than nothing. I went to the election board and asked for all the contribution documents to the mayor so far this year. The clerk comes back with a stack five feet tall. I almost cried."

"So I guess that's out," LaFontaine snipped. "It's not like you to break a sweat."

Perez shot him a withering look. "It's sitting beside my desk as we speak. I plan to spend all next weekend putting it into my computer. A database. I figure it's murder to put it in, but once it's there I'll be able to look for the needle in the haystack. Trends, biggest givers, stuff like that."

The Slotman arrived with steaks for Blitzer and Croon. Seeing the steaming slabs of beef made them all forget the hundreds of stories *The Post* had run about the evils of red meat. They ordered the same.

"Wouldn't this just drive Margaret Savage insane?" Perez said.

"A vegetarian's nightmare," News agreed.

Everyone laughed except McCarthy, who doodled absently on a napkin.

"What's the matter, Gid?" Blitzer asked.

He told them about the court hearing that afternoon. "The kids, probably even Carlos, were too young to remember all that went on, but I don't know how I'll keep my face straight, you know, telling them it's a good thing Owens is coming to visit."

The table fell silent. McCarthy took a sip of beer, then looked at Blitzer. "Enough depressing thoughts. Tell me about Billy Kemper."

She laid the facts out tersely in the classic news structure of descending importance: how Billy Kemper had been jumped inside the house, how Gentry liked to tape people then listen to it, how it had been with Gentry and Delta Ann Porter.

"This story's getting legs," McCarthy said, happy at the new information. "One break-in I can buy. But two and a beating included, she was into something rugged."

"Blackmail?" LaFontaine suggested.

"It would figure, wouldn't it?"

"So Mr. Kemper's attacker may have been a cop?" LaFontaine asked.

"That's the best bet," McCarthy said. "If I can prove it."

The Slotman arrived with the rest of the steaks and a second round of beers. They waited until he'd gone before resuming the conversation. The Slotman was a notorious blabbermouth; he'd squeal to *The Beacon* to create bile-producing competition.

McCarthy took a bite of his steak, then tapped the edge of his plate with a fork. "Do we know what was said on the phone tape that Billy heard?"

Croon said, "He described it as harmless sex stuff. There was something about the caller asking Gentry if she'd wear 'that little red doohickie for him.' "

"Doohickie?" LaFontaine sniffed. "What is it about heterosexual men and red? I must say I find the hue a total turnoff."

"It's not like you've had a chance to be turned on lately," Perez said, sensing an opening in News's ordinarily impregnable defensive wall.

"My pseudo-sapphic goddess, I am merely waiting for the right Adonis to come along."

"Becoming discretionary in your old age, News? Been over a year, am I right?"

"And what of dear Isabel? Found a little Gertrude Stein to keep you warm at night?"

Perez choked on a chunk of steak and had to spit it out into her napkin.

"Enough, you two," McCarthy cut in before the argument got out of control. "A little red doohickie is not the sort of leverage that gets Gentry's place broken into."

"Depends on who's wearing the red doohickie," Croon said. "I mean, if it was a prominent guy?"

"Don't malign cross-dressing now," LaFontaine interrupted. "Look at how far it got J. Edgar."

"Let's be serious," McCarthy insisted. "Gentry, not the

caller, wore the doohickie, so, sorry News, it's a *red* herring."

They all groaned. Blitzer said, "What you're saying is they were after a tape. The question is which one and what was on it?"

"Who's on it is probably as important," McCarthy said. "But if those were cops who beat Billy, then you have to take it to the next logical step. Someone higher up than street level cops."

LaFontaine let a thin whistle escape his lips. "You don't suppose T. Larry himself?"

"A nice fantasy, but where's the connection? Gentry's a street hooker. I figure our bad boy is some rogue captain. And what are there, thirty-five, forty captains on the force now?"

"A lot of territory to cover," Blitzer said.

"Too much," McCarthy said. "I filed a piece tonight about the break-in at her condo and that she taped people. But I'm going to stay quiet about Billy Kemper until I've had a chance to dig deeper. I owe his father."

"Then what's next?" LaFontaine asked.

"Figure out who was on the tape that everyone seems so interested in."

Perez laughed. "Good luck. About the only person who's going to know that was getting blackmailed."

McCarthy shook his head. "At least two sources knew—Gentry and the person being blackmailed. Two raindrops make a lot of ripples."

"You gonna find Delta Ann Porter?" Croon asked.

"Got to," McCarthy said.

Blitzer said, "I know I bitched about doing your work for you, but there's a tragedy drought right now, and all this has got my interest. I'd be glad to pitch in."

"Thanks," McCarthy said. "But I'll see if I can find Porter myself. If I need you, I'll call."

"Anytime, Gid," Blitzer said. "It's getting late. I've got to go. The scanner squawks bright and early."

The sight of the group rising sent the Slotman into a tizzy. They hadn't disturbed anybody! Sometimes life just wasn't fair. McCarthy brought up the rear as they elbowed their way through the crowd. He felt a hand on his shoulder.

"Nice follow story, McCarthy," Karen Rivers said. She was standing with a knot of *Beacon* reporters he recognized by their collective resemblance to stiff-collared models in a Lands' End catalogue. Rivers wasn't wearing her glasses tonight. If it wasn't for the smarmy expression on her lips, McCarthy would have been tempted to call her attractive.

"I don't follow often, Karen, but when I do, I do it well," McCarthy said. "Breaking any news?"

"I'm working on it," she said. "You?"

"Read it and weep tomorrow."

Rivers coughed nervously. Then she pushed out her chin. "I think you'll be the one weeping."

"I don't cry," he said. He turned away, doing his best not to react when he heard Rivers say: "Classic has-been." The stiff shirts all laughed.

Bugs under the Rock . . .

Neil Harpster, *The Post*'s Assistant Managing Editor for Form and Content, lay in a sleazy motel on the other side of town enjoying the liquid buzz of hypercarnal pleasure.

Harpster had told his wife, Lydia, that he'd had to work late. In fact, he'd left the office shortly after six, shortly after picking up the phone in his office and punching in the extension of Connie Mills, his buxom, hard-rumped twenty-something research assistant.

"Connie Mills," the husky voice had answered.

"I know a motel on State Street," he'd said.

"Is that a fact?"

"It is. And I know that there will be a leather satchel on the bed in room 11 B."

"Hmmmm. And what might be in that satchel?"

"Blindfolds and earplugs," he'd whispered.

There was a pause, then Mills's voice fluttered. "There are many dark corners in room 11 B in the motel on State Street."

"Is that a fact?"

"It is," she replied. "And if two people were to start in two different corners, blindfolded, their ears filled with wax, they might be reduced to the tactile sense, groping for a . . . a generous, helping hand in the darkness."

"It might take a long time to find that helping hand," Harpster croaked.

"It might," Mills purred. "Then again, good things come to those who wait."

At that Harpster hung up the phone. He hurried from his office clutching the satchel, unaware that he was closely observed by two sets of trained eyes.

Now in the damp darkness of room 11 B, Harpster rejoiced at the heightened sensations that had resulted from this excursion into deaf and blind sex. "I don't know what I'd do without you, Connie," he announced.

Being unable to hear a thing, his research assistant said nothing; she just continued the gentle lingual ministrations on the insides of his upper thighs she'd begun after their first climactic Braille and sign language session.

Harpster groaned at the insistent pleasure Mills wrought, not allowing himself to pause more than a moment on the plain fact that Lydia would not have joined him in this psychosensual interlude in a million years.

Lydia liked flora, not fauna. A trained horticulturist and heiress to her family's PVC pipe fortune, she lived her life in the garden metaphor. She saw sex as a necessary function of procreation. She was a pistil, he nothing more than a bee carrying pollen. Trouble was, Lydia had no interest in children and therefore little interest in his stinger. It was a marriage of convenience. Harpster had financial security and a base from which to plot his ascent to newspaper power. Lydia had someone to dig holes for her on weekends.

Mills shifted. With her tongue she wrote a novel of manners on his penis. Harpster bellowed in ecstasy, then clamped his right hand over his mouth in the realization that someone outside the motel room might get the wrong idea and bust down the door. He bit into the flesh between his index finger and thumb as the hungry research assistant writhed over him, utterly delighted when it dawned on him that he was now an adventurer in the sexual world of the deaf, *dumb,* and blind.

An hour later, as they were dressing, Mills said, "Do you think Ed Tower will ever leave the paper?"

"You angling for my job when I'm promoted?"

"You know I am."

Harpster grinned. His research assistant was as crazy about status and weird sex as he was. "You'll be my number one recommendation."

She had her thong panties on now and she crossed to him, marvelous tits bouncing, and ran her fingers through his chest hair. "How is Lydia these days?"

Harpster shivered with delight. "Don't start anything you can't stop."

"I can stop it anytime I want," Mills said in dead seriousness. "How's Lydia?"

"Rooting around in the dirt as usual," Harpster said.

"She doesn't pay attention to her man," Mills remarked. "A stupid woman."

"A stupid woman with a large bank account and a prenuptial agreement."

Mills stopped the rubbing motions. "As you so often remind me."

"It's just how it is, Connie," Harpster said. "But someday when I'm editor and you're running research, she won't matter."

She came up tight against him. "You promise?"

He gazed down at the way her jutting nipple penetrated his chest hair. She reached down inside his boxer shorts. "You promise?" she demanded.

"I promise," he squeaked and they tumbled back onto the bed, groping for the earplugs and blindfolds.

Across town, Bobbie Anne Pace, the Assistant Managing Editor for News and Information, shut her drapes and turned to Margaret Savage who was busy uncorking a bottle of organically grown California zinfandel while a pot of brown rice and a stir-fry of fresh broccoli, wheat gluten, and ginger simmered.

"You appear tired," Savage said.

Pace sighed, "Dealing with the constipation of the white male editorial mind will do that to you."

The P.C. Oracle nodded without emotion. "You must imagine yourself a warrior, Bobbie Anne. Women have been underrepresented in the media power structure for too long. You're one of the few to have achieved this level. You have the obligation to push on and bring the rest of us up behind you."

"I know," Pace said, but there was no conviction in her words.

Savage said, "Think of what *Vanity Fair* wrote about us. We're offering groundbreaking journalism."

"Yes, yes, it's just that sometimes I wish there was something beyond my career," she said, then hesitated. "It's all happened so fast. Fashion writer, then features editor, now top management. I used to have so many friends, a social life before . . ."

"Before you met me?" Savage said, popping the cork from the bottle.

"No!" Pace cried. She dropped her chin. "Well, yes."

Savage set the cork down, opened the pot of brown rice, and ran a wooden spoon through it. "You have become someone different than who you were. Such transitions are painful. But this pain will make you a better leader, a better woman in the long run. The moment I met you, Bobbie Anne Pace, I knew you were born to run with wolves. You were born—and I mean this in the most positive sense—to be an Alpha bitch."

Pace listened, wide-eyed, her hands trembling at the words of a woman who seemed to know her better than herself.

Savage went on, "So if you hate me for what I've done to help you in that transition, I accept it because I know that in the long run you will realize I was right."

"Oh, Margaret," Pace said, her voice cracking. "I don't hate you. And of course I know you're right! It's just that, well . . . does being an Alpha bitch rule out having an Alpha male to snuggle with at night?"

"Beta male," said Savage, who allowed herself a rare smile. "But don't hold your breath. As the success of day-time talk shows indicate, most men are mangy dogs."

"You don't say that with any anger."

"I'm not a man hater. I'm not a man lover, either. Nor woman lover for that matter."

"Then what?" Pace stammered.

"Asexual," Savage responded matter-of-factly.

"You mean, you have both or no . . . ?"

"Please, Bobbie Anne, I'm no freak of nature. I'm a woman anatomically. It's just that I've never had feelings one way or another."

"Never?"

"Never."

"My, that's tough."

"I used to think it strange," Savage replied. "But I realize now it's a blessing in disguise. I can concentrate my energies on making the world a better place without the hormonal distractions others experience."

Pace turned the conversation over in her mind several times. She admitted to herself that she wouldn't even be an assistant managing editor without Margaret Savage. And it dawned on Pace that maybe what the sharp tongues in the newsroom said was true without even knowing it; maybe Margaret Savage was some kind of divine oracle who foresaw the future. Her future.

"Margaret," she said at last, "I'm prepared to do whatever it takes to become an Alpha bitch."

Deadline in five minutes. She typed furiously, trying to finish. Two minutes to go now. The keyboard froze. She smacked it with her hand, stared at the screen. The computer became a mouth. The pouting, rouged lips opened to reveal teeth composed of eighteen-point headline type. The teeth opened and inside the gaping cavity fire seethed from the throat. Now she was inside it, feeling the flames lick her ankles, twist past her knees. From the flames came a snake thick from years of undisturbed rest. It coiled and raised its head. Dead diamond eyes. A purpled, forked tongue flicked, then grew and came at her with malicious . . .

Claudette X woke with a start, sweating. It was pitch-black and she jerked about, trying to figure out where she was. Her living room. On the couch. "Oh, my god . . . Oh, thank god!"

She held her hands to her temples. Fifth nightmare in two weeks. She was beginning to fear sleep. She glanced blearily at the digital clock on the video machine. Only 10:00 P.M.

Last thing she remembered, she and her five-year-old daughter, Stacey, were watching a movie. Now the television was dark. A cotton blanket was drawn over her. The executive assistant city editor got to her feet, stretched, and made her way upstairs. She could see the girl's dim form in bed.

If only all parts of my life were as simple to understand, Claudette X thought. She shook her head wearily. She'd expected the news business to be tough. That hadn't scared her. Her whole life had been tough. She just never expected newspapers to become so arbitrary and bizarre.

Claudette X eased Stacey's door shut and crossed into her own room. She tried to shake off the nightmare by doing sit-ups and push-ups. When she'd finished fifty of each she walked to the window to consider her neighborhood under the streetlights.

The houses were all freshly painted or stuccoed. Solid tile roofs. Clean windows, tended lawns and gardens. Two cars in most of the driveways. A boat or two. Three or four recreational vehicles. A safe place for Stacey to grow up in. No shootings in the night. No helicopters overhead. No junkies on the corner.

Claudette X had busted into this world the way she'd busted into everything in her life. That was the way it was growing up in Watts. If you didn't fight, the pack turned on you, ate you up, spit you out, made you a criminal or an addict or a hooker. Or all three.

Claudette X's mother, Sarah Forbes, wouldn't have it that way. Her own sister had ended up a junkie. Her husband a convict. She'd be damned if her sons and daughter would end up that way. Her children would be something. They would take her anger and make it their own.

Claudette X's older brother, Marcus, was a doctor. Philip was a television producer. Carl taught history at Wisconsin. She chose journalism because she believed she had an obligation to explain the world in a different way. Her way.

She knew that *The Post* considered her an agenda hire; a black woman on staff helped the paper maintain the facade that the news business demographically represented the society it covered. The editors quickly learned, however, that

Claudette X was no agenda hire. She was the real thing: a fire-breathing reporter who relished the difficult, dangerous story. Better yet, she could write.

Still, Claudette X never forgot she was the only black woman at *The Post*. Being a good reporter would never alter that situation. She became an editor to change the system.

That was two years after she married and became pregnant by Todd Winter, a linebacker for the city's football team. He was the only man who had ever made Claudette feel small. She liked it. She knew Prentice LaFontaine had cruelly joked that they'd married for genetic purposes, but she had genuinely loved the man.

The team paid Winter very well for his abilities and, for the first time in her life, Claudette X had security. There was this house in a nice neighborhood. An Acura to drive. And soon a little girl to care for, to teach to fight. But two years ago she came home early from work to find her husband in bed with one of the team's cheerleaders.

She picked up a Louisville Slugger and chased the half-naked bimbo and one of the meanest linebackers in the NFL down the middle of this quiet, suburban street. Most of her neighbors were still scared shitless of her.

Claudette X turned off the light and got into bed. She allowed herself a nanosecond of self-pity. Though she had never seriously entertained the thought of a reconciliation, she had always figured her ex-husband would do the right thing by Stacey. He was still behind on his alimony payments. His selfish attitude ate at her. Almost as much as the newsroom these days. Too much backbiting, too many egos to stroke, too little spine in her fellow assistant city editors. And now, these horrible nightmares. Maybe she should see a shrink?

Claudette X pulled the blanket up around her chin. *I'll let it go another week,* she told herself. She tucked her anger away under her pillow and rolled over, hoping against hope the serpent wouldn't rear its head again and invade her dreams.

* * *

It was well past eleven when Prentice LaFontaine opened the door to his ground-level condominium, entered, and called out to the darkness. "Dear one, I'm home!"

There was no response. News sighed and said, "Out again with the boys I take it."

He flipped on a light in the living room and crossed to a bar. He made himself a margarita, drank it down, made another, then plopped into a black studio chair, enjoying the way the drunkenness made the room shift and roll.

The decor of the condo was deliberately kitchy—everything played off a 1950s Hollywood theme: the Dumbo, Mickey Mouse, and Pinocchio Hummels, the James Dean photographs in the loo, a painting of Ava Gardner in a cowgirl's uniform, a still of Clark Gable on the set of *Mogambo*, a replica of the handlebar of the Indian motorcycle Marlon Brando rode in *The Wild Ones*. And his pride and joy: the small working movie marquee bought at auction and mounted over his bed. Every week he changed the movie title on the marquee to fit his mood. The latest offering at Cinema LaFontaine was **The Blob.**

Underneath the sarcastic, flinty surface that he presented to the rest of the world, that's how he saw himself these days—as an amorphous, smothering, troubled sack of goo in the night.

LaFontaine went to a photo on his desk. A younger LaFontaine lolled in the arms of a dashing man in a gray beard on a beach in Jamaica. When was it taken? Six, seven years ago? Seven. It had been six since Gene left. The only decent man LaFontaine had had in his life. And he'd blown their seven-year affair, smothering the man until he'd fled off to West Palm and a new life with a Cuban-born architect. Since then it had been the bar scene and one destructive fling after another. And not even that in more than a year.

Tears welled in his eyes. "You bastard, Gene!" he shouted, and flung the picture across the room. It shattered against the wall.

LaFontaine stumbled into his bedroom and fell down on the bed whimpering to himself. "You bastard, Gene. You bastard, how could you leave me alone like this?"

At that same moment, Augustus Croon and Abby Blitzer stood at the security gate to her apartment complex. "Do you think we go to a better place, I mean after?" he asked.

Blitzer blinked several times. "I try not to think about things like that, Croon. In recovery you learn to take one day at a time."

"I was thinking of the little old ladies jumping the first night we met."

"Pathetic visions like that are often haunting," Blitzer said.

"You like haunting, pathetic things, don't you Abby?"

Her fists balled loosely. "I don't think like is the right word. But seeing them helps."

The big photographer put his hand on Blitzer's shoulder. "Helps what, Abby?"

She shrugged. "Just helps."

"I saw you cry tonight," Croon said. "I've been on beaches in Grenada and Panama with bullets whizzing. I swam in and walked the streets of Kuwait City the dawn before the attack. Nothing has scared me as much as seeing you cry."

"I told you, hormones," Blitzer said.

Croon looked down at her without speaking. She squirmed out from underneath his hand. "There's some things so pathetic they aren't haunting, okay? I got to go now."

"What's eating you, Abby?"

"Croon," she said wearily, "maybe racing off to witness

the harsh twists of reality isn't much to base a relationship on, but it's something. Can't we just share what we have for now?"

He saw he might lose her. He said: "Sure, Abby. We'll just do that."

"Thank you, Augustus," Blitzer said. It was the first time she'd called him by his given name. She stood on her tiptoes, pulled down his massive head, and pecked him on the cheek. "Good night."

A first kiss! Well, sort of. "Good night, Abby!"

Blitzer opened the gate and ran up the stairs to her apartment. She shut the door behind her. She hesitated, then crossed to a chest of drawers and pulled out some old yellowed newspaper clippings. She read the words as she had a thousand times, wishing with all her might for a drama that would make this story's pathos fade.

Tears rolled down her face as she carefully returned the clippings to the chest. She peeked through the curtains, knowing what she'd see and somehow that gave her solace. Down at the gate stood the giant photographer, his face wedged between the iron rods, mooning up at her window with all his might.

When McCarthy got home he was surprised to find a light streaming out from under Carlos's door. The boy, engrossed in a Hardy Boys mystery novel, didn't hear him come in. A large boy for nine. Big hands, big bones, big feet. All softened by his mother's brown eyes. Carlos had inherited more of his mother's American Indian blood than his sister, whose features were a smoother, muted interpretation of Tina.

"What are you doing up so late?"

Carlos yawned and shrugged. "Couldn't sleep."

"Big game tonight?"

"We won," Carlos said. "Wish you could have been there."

"Me, too, but I had to work. You pitch?"

"Four innings. They got five hits off me."

McCarthy sat on the bed. "There'll be another day."

Carlos bit at his lip, then said: "You know why I like to pitch? Not tonight, but most of the time?"

"You tell me."

"Because my part in the game comes first. Everything else comes next. So what I do kind of begins it all, you know? The swing and the catches and the throws. I like that. That and the way everyone watches you."

"I think I understand."

Carlos looked past McCarthy at the ceiling. "You think she watches?"

"She never misses a game," he said.

Carlos reached out and took McCarthy's hand. "He was in the stands, I think."

McCarthy swallowed at the bulge in his throat. "Who was?"

"My father. Tia Estelle told us what happened and Miriam asked to see his picture."

"Did he try to talk to you?"

"No," Carlos said. "He just watched."

They were quiet for a few moments. Then McCarthy said, "He wants to take you and Miriam to a baseball game in a couple of weeks. It will be all right, you know?"

Carlos nodded, but didn't reply.

"It's late. You should get some sleep."

Carlos nodded again and shut the book. McCarthy patted him on the head, then flipped off the light. The boy grabbed him around the shoulders and hugged him tightly.

"I know," McCarthy said, hugging him back. "I know."

He rocked the boy in his arms, glad that the lights were off because he knew the anguish on his face would scare the boy even more. McCarthy had always been a man who faced crises in a detached fashion, standing slightly apart as the chaos whirled, able to chronicle it for his readers. But he could not get off the line of this pain. It sucked at the bottom of his lungs and knuckled into his gut and carved out a dismal chasm at his center.

He couldn't imagine life without Carlos or Miriam or their eccentric great aunt. He rarely saw his mother anymore. She was bigoted and wanted nothing to do with the children. And he couldn't bear to return to those days when the newsroom crowd was his family. The only thing that would ever fill the emptiness was in his arms.

And yet he knew his odds of keeping Carlos and Miriam were slim. Especially now that his job hung in the balance. Owens's attorney had already mentioned the plagiarism incident once. Wouldn't he love it if McCarthy were fired?

This story he was working on, this murdered whore who taped everyone she knew, was crucial. Figuring out who killed Carol Alice Gentry was the one thing that might keep his family intact. McCarthy clenched his jaw as he lowered the sleeping boy onto the pillow. He stood up, promising the shadows he'd solve this murder or die trying.

Of Pierced Nipples and Murder . . .

McCarthy's story on the break-in at Gentry's condo made the front page, lower left-hand corner. Rivers had a metro story about Gentry's background. But she missed the break-in angle entirely. He was back on top. For today at least.

After breakfast with Carlos and Miriam, he drove to the

courthouse to examine the criminal indexes. Within an hour he'd determined that Delta Porter, the hooker who'd appeared in the sex video with Gentry and Billy Kemper, fit the journalistic cliché; she was a hard case.

During the last seven years Delta Porter had been arrested for soliciting nine times, three the last year. Street whores like Porter knew the system was too overloaded to track down small-timers like herself. As long as she created false trails she could ply her trade with minimum interference.

For instance, on each arrest report she gave her name a different way. Delta A. Porter. Del Porter. Delice Portman. Delta Portman. Sometimes the addresses matched. Sometimes the phone numbers. And the social security number was the same every time. McCarthy wrote it all down and hit the streets.

McCarthy started with the most recent address. Empty. A street kid told him Porter had moved out four months before. McCarthy relied on an old trick to keep the trail fresh. He went to the closest post office, paid a dollar, and got a copy of the change of address form she'd filed. The Sunset Court, 5350 Waverly Ave., Unit 22.

In Southern California dump apartment complexes sport perky names like the Sunset Court. This was a classic example of the species: two stories, faded pink doors, rusty iron railings, dingy curtains drawn against the sun, an empty swimming pool with four rusty beer cans floating in the green scum, not to mention the graffiti-defiled palm trees.

McCarthy missed Porter by two days. A next-door neighbor told him she and her boyfriend, Eugene Friendly, had split in the middle of the night after two plainclothes police officers had paid them a visit. Friendly was a violent ex-convict who used the name "Tabor" because it gave him a nastier image.

After much cajoling the neighbor told McCarthy that Tabor was owed a lot of money. He and Porter were wait-

ing for the cash at a motel out in Red Valley, a community
that abutted the desert.

Which made McCarthy shiver the entire drive out.
Knocking on the hideaway of a man like Tabor was like pet-
ting a sleeping rottweiler. He might roll over, slaver, and
show his belly. He might lunge for the throat. McCarthy
tried to keep his mind off the latter possibility by studying
how the city changed on the fifteen-mile drive along the
Boulevard.

Near Sixty-sixth Street the shops ran to honky-tonk
wares: rattan furniture, adult paraphernalia, cheap booze,
rolled tacos (three for a dollar), comic books, fast Chinese,
New Age books, model airplanes, the odd plumbing or au-
tomobile supply store. Brassy in the sunshine, but benign.

After dark, he knew, it took on a decidedly garish tone as
women like Carol Alice Gentry strutted in the neon glow
offering hoots to the bored, the frustrated, and the lonely.

Farther out, near Ninety-first, the street shed its tawdry
attire. Now ivy and ice plant bordered the sidewalks. Jog-
gers ran by well-trimmed palms and eucalyptus. Upscale
shops, too: specialty goods, fodder for the upper–middle-
class neighborhoods that spread out through the canyons
north and south of the street.

Gentry had lived out there about a mile in a condo she
shouldn't have been able to afford. Karen Rivers's story this
morning said Gentry had grown up dirt-poor. Her mother
left home when she was six. Her father died when she was
twelve. She lived with her aunt and uncle until running
away to live with friends at sixteen. Still no answer to where
she'd gotten the $30,000 down payment for a condo and the
cash for a purebred Arabian.

Where the Boulevard became Route 93, the condo complexes and the upscale strip malls gave way to scrub brush,
the odd twenty-four-hour store and battered trailer homes

set back from the road. Here and there swayback horses stood unmoving in makeshift paddocks.

He almost missed the Lantern Motel. The gray building with faded green trim melted into the screen of live oak that grew up on all four sides. He skidded to a stop on the shoulder, backed up, and pulled into the lot.

A Korean man about twenty lounged behind the office counter thumbing a dog-eared edition of *Penthouse*. It was the pet of the year issue and the clerk was studying her plumbing with such intensity that he didn't even look up at McCarthy's request. Mr. Friendly, the clerk said, had rented unit fifteen.

McCarthy thought about Tabor's violent streak. The razor teeth and the soft flesh at the throat. He found a pay phone on the far side of the building near the ice machine. He called the Lantern. It took the clerk fifteen rings to break away from the pet of the year, answer, and connect him to Mr. Friendly's room.

"Yeah?" It was a woman.

"Delta Porter?"

Dead silence, then a whinny. "You got the wrong number, man."

"Don't hang up. My name's Gideon McCarthy. I'm a reporter with *The Post*. I'm outside your room at the pay phone. I want to talk about Carol Alice Gentry."

"Shit. Shit. Shit." He heard the phone crash to the floor. The curtain in the window of unit fifteen fluttered. McCarthy waved.

A man came on the phone. "Who the fuck is this?"

McCarthy repeated himself.

"She don't want to talk, man."

"Look, Tabor. It's Tabor right?"

"Maybe, maybe not."

"Tabor, I'm not a cop. I'm working on a story about how Gentry got killed."

"We know how she got killed, man. You think we're sitting in this shithole for our health?"

McCarthy's heart skipped a beat. They knew who killed Gentry! He thought fast and spoke slowly. "If you know how she got killed, then we need to talk, don't we? I heard some police officers came to see you, right?"

Tabor didn't answer.

"Think of talking to me as insurance," McCarthy said. "Something happens, I tell the world."

Tabor didn't respond for so long McCarthy thought the line had been cut. Then, "Door's open. Come in slow."

Delta Porter sat cross-legged on the unmade bed, a too-thin, coal-black woman in yellow terry cloth shorts and a matching tank top. She smoked a cigarette. She watched him with a chill, hard expression. A radio playing rap music competed with the chug and wheeze of an air conditioner losing its battle with the midday heat. McCarthy stepped inside. The barrel of the gun set cold against the bone in back of his left ear. The door snapped shut behind him. The only light came from a small table lamp. The reporter swallowed hard. No one from the paper knew he was here.

"The wallet?" Tabor said.

"Front right pocket."

A thick hand rummaged for the wallet. The gun pressed hard against the back of his head. The wallet tumbled end over end through the air onto Porter's lap. She fumbled through the billfold, found his press ID, looked at it, his driver's license, and his credit cards. She took a twenty-dollar bill from the billfold and slid it into her bra. She tossed the wallet onto the table. "He's who he says he is."

The hammer of the gun made a greasy clicking noise. Then the barrel wasn't there anymore. "Sit down," Tabor ordered.

McCarthy took unsteady steps toward one of the two lime green chairs set around the beat-up table. "Nice way to greet your guests."

"We don't get many," Tabor said, coming out of the shadows to sit next to Porter.

Tabor was as white as Porter was black. Just shy of six feet, his head was closely shaved. He had bad teeth. Three gold hoops pierced his left ear. A fourth pierced his right nipple. A jagged scar ran from that nipple five inches down toward his sternum. He wore black gym shorts. He had a huge upper body and scrawny legs. He rested the pistol on his thigh. The muzzle aimed at McCarthy's stomach.

"What do you know?" Tabor asked.

He told them about Gentry testifying before the grand jury, about the break-in at her condo, about the videotape with Billy Kemper, about the second break-in and the beating the young cowboy had received. They listened impassively.

When he finished, McCarthy asked, "What do you know?"

Tabor elbowed Porter in the ribs. "Go ahead. You heard it."

She threw Tabor a dirty look. She had a husky, singsong lilt to her voice, as if once she'd lived in the islands. "First off, I didn't know Carol Alice too much. She wasn't what you call a regular, you know? I seen her on the Boulevard sometimes, but I wasn't her friend or nothing.

"Anyhow," Porter continued, "one night she pulls up to my corner in a white Camaro with that cowboy. Asks me do I wants to party? I look at her and say, who's paying this trick. She says she is. Said it was a present for the little cattle rustler. Whole night, $300. It was $200 until I saw the camera."

McCarthy wrote that down. "Go on."

"So after that I don't see her for a long time. Nothin' until she starts spouting off in the papers. I figured that woman's crazy saying all that stuff. So a couple of uniform cops want a little head every now and then. It's a cost of business."

Tabor got up from the bed. He crossed the room,

reached into a bag, and pulled out a bottle of vodka. He leaned against the wall and sipped from it. "Get to it."

"Who's telling the story here?" she complained. She turned back to McCarthy. "So she turns up dead out there in the desert where the other working girls were found, right?"

"Right," McCarthy said.

"I figures she tricked the weirdo, that's it. Until"—she clicked her fingernails together nervously—"until I sees Dusk on the Boulevard a few nights ago, in front of that Hop 'n Go Burger place near Sixty-ninth Street. Dusk's a long-timer like me. She starts crying when she sees me, saying she just read the paper and she knows who offed Carol."

"Who?"

"Like the papers said, maybe cops. Only it was."

McCarthy's palms went clammy. "Did she say who did it?"

"All she said was that during a sweep she heard cops talking about Carol getting killed."

"That's all she told you?"

"Isn't that enough? I'm ready to pee my pants at any noise outside."

"What about the circumstances? Where did she hear it? Who said it?"

Porter lit another cigarette. "I didn't want to know, you know?"

"Where's Dusk now?" McCarthy asked.

"Probably in a rathole somewhere like us. Told me she was going deep."

McCarthy looked at his notes. "Who were the cops who came to your place?"

"Homicide," Porter said. "They was looking for Dusk."

"How would they know to talk to you about her?"

Tabor burped. "Because she's got the biggest yap in town."

"Hey screw you, Eugene."

Tabor raised his fist. "I told you don't call me Eugene."

Porter jeered: "Hates his name, so he changes it. Tabor. Like he was a rock star or something."

"I told you not to dick with me about that!" Tabor yelled.

"Then don't call me no fucking big mouth, Friendly boy," she shouted back. "I was trying to do the sisters a favor. When Dusk split, I figured I better tell some of the girls so'd they be cool around the cops. I mean one of them's a killer, you know?"

"Only half the working girls are snitches," Tabor added, cooling down. "And they all start pointing at Delta."

"Did you know the detectives who came to the house?"

"Never seen 'em before," she said. "Us working girls know the vice boys."

"What'd they say?"

"Told her to keep her big mouth shut until they checked all this out," Tabor said. "Said spreading rumors like that could get someone hurt. And they wanted to know where to find Dusk. But it's like we said, she's in a rathole somewhere."

It took another fifteen minutes, but he got some information about Dusk's unprofessional life. Dusk's real name was Christine Evers. She was in her early thirties. White. Long brown hair. Hung with a guy named the Milkman. A biker.

"A thin, wiry guy with a missing upper right tooth," Porter said. "I know she takes care of his mama sometime. His mama's brains is scrambled and Milkman don't like her being in one of them nursing homes."

"Any idea where they lived?"

Porter and Tabor shook their heads. "Moved around, like us."

McCarthy tasted disgust in his mouth. This world, with the nicknames and the aliases and the ratholes and the pierced nipples, was confusing and degrading. Which was how he'd come to view Carol Alice Gentry. "Any idea what the Milkman's real name is?"

Porter brayed, "Milk. His last name's Milk. Get it? I don't know the first name."

"Thanks," McCarthy said. "You've been a real help."

"You ain't going to print what we said, are you?" Porter asked.

What was it about people? They know you're a reporter. You talk with them for more than an hour and then they ask you if you're going to write it.

"If I find Dusk and she confirms what you said, you bet I'm going to write it."

Porter looked at Tabor. "Eugene, honey, maybe we don't wants to wait until your money comes to head for Dallas."

"The name's Tabor!"

Swingo . . .

Three hours later, *The Post*'s chief political reporter was winding up to kick his desk chair. On impact, Kent Jackson's big toe snapped. He didn't notice. He wound up and kicked again. The right brace of his paisley suspenders popped. His oval, horn-rimmed glasses leapt off his nose. They broke on the floor.

"That harlot!" Kent Jackson screamed. "That harlot!"

Jackson's face contorted scarlet like a toddler uncorking a tantrum. He tore at his copy of the metro section of *The Beacon* until it lay in shreds at his feet. He stomped on the pile, then stalked from the room, throwing punches at file cabinets as he went.

Isabel Perez, dressed in black slacks and a white cotton sweater, sprinted toward Prentice LaFontaine clutching her own copy of *The Beacon*'s B section. "There is a God!"

She spread the paper out on LaFontaine's desk. The

stand-alone picture in the middle of the page showed a pretty young woman drinking wine with a handsome man.

"So?" News said, blanching at the sight of the wine. He still suffered the effects of last night's debauch.

"So!" crowed Perez. "She's Patti Jackson."

"Kent's wife?"

"None other!"

"And the guy?"

"This is where it's delicious. He's their minister!"

LaFontaine swooned. "Has anyone a hand fan? I believe I might faint!"

Perez made a show of fanning him with an imaginary ostrich plume.

News jerked upright to study the picture again. "Did he know?"

"Given the meltdown that just occurred, I'll bet he didn't have a clue," Perez gloated. "He made some remark a few weeks back about them having a few marriage problems. But nothing like this. I mean, the minister?"

LaFontaine jiggled his knee, trying to see the gossip angles. This was the best vein of dirt to surface inside *The Post* in months. His mind raced: marital discord? Violence perhaps? No, no, Jackson was too much of a Christian. Therapy? Now there was a possibility. He'd call Gertie in personnel and put her on watch for a possible request for psychological counseling.

"News!"

"Huh?" he startled.

"I was asking you a question."

"I'm sorry. Hit me again."

"Do you think this helps me, I mean on the beat?"

This was what he loved about Perez. She played the angles as often as he did. "Can't hurt, can it? Thinking constantly about his wife shacked with the holy man, Jackson loses his focus, maybe he misses a big story or two. And suddenly . . ."

"No more second fiddle."

"There's something wonderfully *The Prince* about you, Isabel," LaFontaine declared. "The trick here, of course, is to let events take their own pace. Intercede and you could turn the tide against you."

"Slow and careful," she said thoughtfully. "My chat with Lawlor this morning doesn't hurt either."

"Chat? What chat?" News hated not being the first to know.

"I came in early this morning to start entering those campaign contributions into my computer and who should wander by my desk with his morning coffee?"

"The God of local information himself."

"Fate is turning my way," Perez agreed. "He saw the stack and asked me what I was up to. I told him about the database and he said it was a great idea. Emphasis on *great*. Wanted to be kept abreast *personally* of what I find."

"She stands anointed."

Perez smiled briefly, then knitted her brows. "Of course with my luck, it will all backfire. Jackson will take strength from Patti's infidelities. My data bank will yield nothing. In a year I will be coming to work dressed like Mae West to edit the food pages."

"Such faith," News said sarcastically.

"I've been in this business long enough to be a realist."

Claudette X came stomping toward them. "Isabel?"

"Claudette, how are things today?"

"Rotten, getting worse," the massive executive assistant city editor growled. "You got to take over for Kent today. He's been . . ."

"Visited by the Holy Ghost?" News interrupted.

Claudette X crossed her arms. "So caring of others in distress, News."

"He'd do the same for me, Ms. Muslim."

Claudette X realized she would get nowhere with LaFontaine and went on. "Jackson had a late-afternoon interview with Arlene Troy. You take it, Isabel. Give me twenty inches for tomorrow."

"You've got it. Twenty to the inch." Perez hurried away.

"A star is born," News said. He turned to rearrange his desk and call Gertie.

Claudette X folded her bulging forearms. "You look not busy, News."

"Nonchalance often accompanies those in total control, dear X," LaFontaine replied. "In a matter of moments, in fact, I'm off to ambush a WASP bank president who owns part of an Irish pub. Could present interesting information on Cote D'Azure."

"Keep me posted," Claudette X said.

LaFontaine made a face behind her back as she barreled back to her desk. He gathered his briefcase and notebooks, and turned to leave. But the sight of the Zombie stopped him cold. Beads of sweat pelted the brow of the living dead obituary writer. The Zombie's lips were the color of lilies. His irises burned like molten pig iron. The Zombie glared with pure and unequivocal hatred at the Glasshole of Neil Harpster.

LaFontaine held up two fingers in the form of a crucifix before himself as he edged around the elegy scribe. Clear of the apparition, he hurried from the newsroom as fast as his thick legs would carry him.

At the same time, Ed Tower knocked on the corner Glasshole. Connor Lawlor waved him in. Tower grimly held out a computer printout of the latest circulation reports.

"Despite Savage Views' high readership, *The Beacon* bounced back last month with five hundred new subscribers," he said. "We're flat on home delivery, though slightly up on street sales because of this Gentry scandal."

The fatigue etched on Lawlor's face bordered on bewilderment. He took the printout, then handed the Editor for News Operations a memo. "Newsprint's going up another ten percent the end of the month. We'll have to cut to bare bones."

"That will hit *The Beacon*, too."

"Doesn't help much," Lawlor said. "*The Beacon* boys were smart, putting all their resources up in the north two years ago. It's growing faster than any other part of the county. They're getting subscribers. We're treading water."

"We'll survive, Connor. We always have."

Lawlor looked at a photograph of two women in their early twenties on his desk. "I've sacrificed everything that's ever meant anything to me for *The Post*. I feel like events beyond my control are conspiring to flush my life's work."

"It's not over," Tower said firmly. "You've worked too hard. We've worked too hard."

Lawlor rubbed his face with both hands. He took in the circulation figures again. He glanced at his Pulitzer Prize, at the front page of this morning's *Post*, and then back up to the stone visage of his second-in-command.

"Okay, we won't let the fat lady sing this week," he said. "Ideas?"

Tower took off his beret and said, "Swingo."

"No! No Swingo! I draw the line somewhere."

"I know your feelings about using games of chance to promote papers, but I don't think we have a choice," Tower said. "I had Harpster research it. Swingo attracts readers as much as Dear Abby, the horoscopes, or Calvin and Hobbes."

"It's tawdry."

"It works," Tower insisted.

Lawlor kneaded his temples. "What happened to the days when you could run a paper on the basis of hard news?"

"They're gone," Tower stated flatly. "They've been gone a long time. We have to be pragmatists."

Lawlor reviewed the summary of the circulation report a third time. "How much will it cost to get the game up and running?"

Tower grinned. "I'll have the projections on your desk tomorrow morning. We can be producing Swingo cards in a week."

"Have it here first thing. We'll talk at lunch."

Tower got up and made for the door, calling over his shoulder, "It's the only thing we could have done."

Lawlor nodded, letting his attention travel beyond Tower into the boil of the newsroom. He wished he could tell them what it meant to run *The Post*. Hell what it meant to be *The Post*. The newspaper was undoubtedly cast in his image, for right or for wrong.

He sighed. There had been penances to be paid for this achievement. A life of endless deadlines, grinding seven-day work weeks and agonizing decisions that kept him awake most nights. His wife, Kathleen, had left him five years ago after a marriage of twenty-six years. His daughters, all grown now, rarely spoke to him. He had no social life to speak of other than the charity events his position demanded he attend. He rarely took vacations. He lived alone in a ranch house near the ocean. The highs and lows of his existence had all taken place here at *The Post*.

Lawlor rubbed at the throb below his knee. The pain had been worse these past few weeks. It turned sharp whenever he allowed himself to think about the difficult decisions he'd had to make to keep the paper alive. For years he'd been able to keep those memories buried. Lately they'd surfaced to shoot red-hot agony through his leg.

He wished again he could tell someone what daily journalism had done to him and what he'd done to daily journalism. But such self-revelation could be dangerous in the superheated flux of gossip and backstabbing that permeated the business he'd come to dominate.

Lawlor kept these thoughts even from Tower, the closest

he'd ever had to a confidant. He glanced again at the Pulitzer Prize. He knew that Tower had done almost as much to get the prize as he had. From the moment of his arrest, through the long months of imprisonment for refusing to name his sources, Tower had been behind him. Tower wrote dozens of stories on his incarceration. Tower kept Lawlor's stand for journalistic principles alive in the public's mind.

Despite this thirty-year-old debt, there were things Lawlor could never tell Tower. Outside the newspaper Tower reveled in the social life of the city's power elite. And like that annoying reporter, Prentice LaFontaine, Tower loved sharing the latest gossip about the triumphs and tragedies of the upper crust. If Lawlor disclosed his innermost concerns with his number two man, he could never be sure Tower wouldn't use them as barter on the informational black market.

The editor-in-chief rubbed at his knee again. His personal problems were irrelevant. The important thing was keeping *The Post* alive and its reputation intact. He closed his eyes. He found a few moments of peace imagining puffy clouds in a blue sky. Then a dark vapor roiled on his horizon.

"Swingo," he muttered.

A Hatchet Job . . .

Prentice LaFontaine was perched on a barstool inside O'Branaghan's Irish Pub waiting for Carlton Bank's president, Thomas P. Whitney, to show up. The Zombie's terrible countenance haunted him. He wondered if the obituary writer saw his reflection in mirrors. He thought about buying a string of garlic to hang on his statue of Arthur Miller. He ordered a Campari on the rocks.

He looked about the bar giving it the News appraisal. O'-Branaghan's was a 1990s interpretation of an Irish pub: brass rails, bleached pine board floors, numerous photographs of the Kennedys on the wall, dreadful ditties about the old sod played in the background. The place attracted florid-faced, tweedy types in their mid-twenties accompanied by their peaches-and-cream debutantes. Ghastly!

Nonetheless, this was where Perez claimed he was most likely to find Whitney after hours. Which LaFontaine found amusing. A WASP like Whitney owned a third share in a yuppie Gaelic restaurant. Middle age does strange things to the average male.

I should talk, he thought. He allowed himself a brief pang of remorse for breaking his last photograph of Gene. Then, as was his habit, he forced himself to dwell on the future. He had an invitation to a party tomorrow night at the Pink Stag, the city's hottest gay club. Perhaps he'd meet someone! That's what LaFontaine loved about life; you created hope not by examining the real, but by projecting the possible.

At seven-thirty the bank president entered, dressed casually in pleated green slacks and a white polo shirt emblazoned with the kelly green O'Branaghan's logo. The bartender called out to him and Whitney asked him how business was going. *I'll tell you,* News thought: *The florid-faced and the peach-faced are on their way to shit-faced.*

Whitney made the rounds, then took the booth in the back right corner and ordered dinner. LaFontaine waited until Whitney was three bites into his meal before sliding into the booth.

"Mr. Whitney, what a surprise finding you here!"

The bank president reacted as if he'd eaten a rotted potato. "We concluded business yesterday."

"A reporter always has another question to ask."

"But a banker doesn't have to answer. I've explained all there is to explain. Good day, Mr. LaFontaine."

". . . it was what you said at the end of our chat yesterday . . . something about Sloan Burkhardt carrying on in the tradition of his father. I thought you might elaborate."

Whitney slammed his fork down. He gestured to one of the bouncers at the door. "I didn't want to do this, LaFontaine. But I have a right to my privacy in my own saloon."

The bouncer, a beefier version of the bar's customers, lumbered over.

"Pete, would you escort this gentleman to the door?"

"My pleasure, Mr. Whitney."

The bouncer dropped a heavy paw onto the reporter's shoulder.

"Let go of me, you steroidal Irish goon, or I'll cause a scene!" LaFontaine snarled.

The bouncer drew his hand back uncertainly. "Mr. Whitney?"

"Get him out of here," Whitney ordered.

Before the bouncer could get hold of him, News had squirmed into the back of the booth and assumed the fetal position. He squealed at the bank president, "I have friends in the Department of Health. One word from me and they'll be all over this place."

Whitney smiled. "Two inspectors were in last week. Triple-A rating. Pete?"

The bouncer leaned into the booth with a grin that turned to shock when the reporter kicked him in the chest. "Why you fucking little fairy," the bouncer said. "I ordinarily don't get rough with someone your age. But tonight I'll make an exception."

Pete grabbed him by the ankle before LaFontaine could flail again. News grabbed the edge of the table and held on for dear life. "I just want to talk about Sloan," he pleaded with Whitney. "I found this case, this sealed criminal case and I . . ."

A flicker of interest and then, curiously, of pain passed across the bank president's face. LaFontaine caught it. "No one knows what he did. Do you? That's why I want . . ."

At that moment the reporter's grip on the table's edge slipped. He flew out of the booth and thumped onto the floor. To the delight of the happy hour crowd, the bouncer got hold of his other ankle and began dragging him dead deer–style across the barroom.

News arched to look backward. Whitney was leaning out of the booth. "My spine!" LaFontaine cried. "I'm going to sue!"

The bank president stood up, napkin still hanging from his belt. "Pete! Let him go."

The bouncer turned. "Mr. Whitney?"

"I said, let him go."

"But . . ."

"Now, Pete!"

The bouncer glared down at LaFontaine, gave the reporter's foot a quick, vicious twist, then dropped him.

"Aaargh!" News yelled, and he sat up fast to rub at the ankle. "You potato-eating fascist. I hope the IRA takes you for a Protestant."

Pete made as if to grab the reporter again, but Whitney stepped in to put a hand on his chest. "Just go back to the door, Pete. It's all right."

The bouncer's nostrils flared once. "Whatever you say, Mr. Whitney."

The bank president turned to News, who still sat cross-legged on the floor alternately rubbing his ankle and the back of his neck. "Why don't we talk?"

"I still might sue," LaFontaine declared. He waved his finger around him. "I have at least a dozen witnesses."

Whitney looked at the silent crowd, then back at the reporter. "Do you wish to talk or not?"

"If you insist." He got to his feet and hobbled after the bank president.

Back in the booth, Whitney said, "What's this about a sealed case?"

"If you hadn't been so thuggish, we might . . ."

"Mr. LaFontaine, I'm tired of you. Cut to it or leave."

The reporter brushed carpet lint off his forearm and said haughtily, "I told you, there's a sealed 1986 criminal case against Burkhardt. And I want to know if you know what's in it."

The bank president studied LaFontaine. "I don't. But that such a case exists does not surprise me. However, my position puts me in a delicate situation as far as talking."

"Believe it or not, Mr. Whitney, reporters can be masters of discretion."

"Tell that to the people who watched you scream and kick a minute ago."

"Yes, well, even masters falter," LaFontaine said.

Whitney took a sip of beer. He took another sip of beer, making his decision. Finally, he asked, "How much do you know about Harold Jennings?"

"Former mayor," LaFontaine said. "Long time ago my editor pithed him like a froggie. He got my editor sent to jail. Eventually he ended up in jail himself. Did ten years, I think. What does this have to do with Burkhardt?"

"Everything, I should think. To understand a man, begin by understanding his enemies. Even his father's enemies."

Whitney broke into a long monologue about the Jennings family, which had been around since the city's founding days. The grandfather had run brothels and gin joints in an area known as "Little Shanghai" at the turn of the century. The father used the profits of sin and swill to set up a company called Jennings Concrete & Construction. The company built most of the city's early commercial projects. The son, Harold, took over the business before World War II. Harold was bright, flamboyant, shrewd, and vindictive.

"Patterned himself on classic big-city operators," Whitney said. "Harold Jennings thought nothing of making payoffs or making threats. Whatever it took to get the next job on-line."

Over the years, young Jennings forged ties with other real estate types, money men, navy admirals, politicians. One of the connections was to a hot young developer named Coughlin Burkhardt. He worked closely with Jennings on the dozens of military construction projects undertaken when war broke out.

"They were good friends, Jennings and Burkhardt," Whitney said. "Made millions together. After the war Burkhardt was the brains behind Jennings's succesful run for mayor."

In the early fifties, however, the two men had a falling-out. Burkhardt formed his own construction-development company. He focused on the growing business of building shopping malls. Jennings consolidated his political power and used it to ensure that Concrete & Construction received a steady succession of public works projects.

"No one could prove it until your editor there, Lawlor, started poking around, but it became clear that if you wanted to get a big public project through city hall, Concrete & Construction had better have a chunk of it," Whitney said.

LaFontaine thought back to the photograph in Sloan Burkhardt's office. "And then came Alta Bay," he said.

"And then came Alta Bay," said Whitney, who described how in 1956 Burkhardt proposed to dredge and fill a coastal marsh, to turn it into a tourist Mecca with hotels, beaches, sailing bays, and marinas. It was an audacious idea, one that could potentially transform the city. Mayor Jennings opposed the plan.

"Why?" News asked.

"He and Burkhardt hated each other's guts by then. But mostly because there was no room for Concrete & Construction in the Alta Bay plan. Burkhardt wanted the whole deal to himself. He had spent years paying for feasibility studies, laying the groundwork."

"Burkhardt ended up building Alta Bay," LaFontaine said.

"But not until Jennings stood behind bars and the Feds had all but dismantled Concrete & Construction. That took eight years."

"And you're saying Burkhardt had a little to do with Jennings's downfall?"

"It all happened so long ago, who's to say? I just know a little of how the old man worked."

"And how was that?"

Whitney picked up the napkin off the table and twisted it into a ball. The flicker of pain crossed his face again. "I attended UCLA in the late sixties. Economics degree. Took a couple years off, then went to business school. My first year in the MBA program, there was a scandal."

"I adore scandals," News purred. "Keep going."

"An undergraduate male brutally raped an undergraduate coed during a fraternity party. The woman never returned to campus. The boy's father made a rather staggering donation to the business school through one of its trustees, the late Robert S. Carlton III."

"The late president of your bank and, if I'm correct, the man who would eventually become the boy's chief financial source."

Whitney nodded.

"Nothing about the rape was ever made public?" News prodded.

"Money has a bleaching effect," Whitney replied. "And once people learn they can whitewash their laundry, it becomes habit."

"So you think there's something similar inside that sealed case?"

"I wouldn't be surprised."

LaFontaine could taste something in the air, something

unsaid. He looked hard at Whitney, who glanced away, the pain now steady on his face. "Who was the woman, Mr. Whitney?"

He put his hand to his mouth and would not look at LaFontaine. "My cousin, Lucy," he said. "Sloan Burkhardt beat her senseless. They let him get away with it."

News felt shitty and elated. For the first time since he'd started looking at Sloan Burkhardt he knew there was something real behind that queasy sensation he'd gotten talking to the developer. But seeing Whitney's obvious torment he knew the cousin still suffered from the effects of the rape. This was a sour victory.

Whitney composed himself. "What else do you want to know?"

"You'd like to break this deal, wouldn't you?"

Whitney shrugged. "Of course I'd like to break the deal. I'd like to see Sloan rot in hell. But it's not within my power. The bank made a commitment and we'll stand behind that commitment unless . . ."

"Unless?"

"Unless someone such as yourself manages to bring things to light that might . . . shall we say . . . upset the process?"

"Are you saying that there are things to bring to light?"

"Nothing specific, but I have no doubt you're working fertile terrain."

"Nothing else? No place to start?"

Whitney wiped a spoon on the tablecloth. "I've always believed that to understand a problem, you begin with the people involved with the people believed to be involved. If I remember correctly, Sloan was married once. That would have been six or seven years ago, about the time that case was sealed."

"I do believe I underestimated you, Mr. Whitney."

"It happens," Whitney said evenly. "By the way, we didn't have this conversation."

"Of course," LaFontaine said. He got up from the booth without offering to shake the man's hand. His stood still for a moment, balancing on his stiff ankle, then limped toward the door.

Pete smiled smugly as he opened the door for the reporter. "I hope it's a torn tendon," the bouncer said. "Better yet: a hairline fracture."

News waited until he was almost by the bruiser, then swung full force with the good leg, toe pointed out, catching Pete square on the kneecap. The bouncer buckled and fell to the floor, howling in agony.

"Take that as a lesson," LaFontaine snarled. "Never mess with someone who's paid to do hatchet jobs."

Night of the Zombie . . .

Blood streaked the back of the Zombie's hands. His knuckles were split. His feet ached. So did his back, his forearms, and his thighs. The bruise above his right eye carried hints of purple. His swollen tongue pressed thickly against his loosened teeth.

The Zombie took a deep breath to help him shove his suffering away in a remote corner of his mind. He trudged out of the brightly lit storefront past the crowd waiting to see the latest action movie toward his old white Ford pickup.

Every night of the week except Sunday the Zombie came to this Shotokan Karate Dojo and trained with men half his age. Every night except Sunday the Zombie vented his rage so he had the composure to write of the dead. Every night except Sunday the Zombie spent three hours breaking boards and sparring in full contact bouts. In his mind every length of pine and every young opponent who entered the ring lived on Lobotomy Lane.

Tonight he had delivered a devastating flying round-house kick to a surrogate of Neil Harpster, which had knocked the editorial stand-in clear off his feet. Ordinarily that blow alone would have gotten the Zombie through the weekend and to his desk on Monday morning. Of late, however, his loathing had intensified to the point where even body blows wouldn't calm the hatred.

As he had each evening for the last two weeks, the Zombie left the karate dojo, climbed in his truck, and drove north to The Ranch. He parked down the street from Harpster's new home. He sat there for several hours, staring at the whitewashed walls around the expensive house, staring at the rosebushes and the orange tile roof, staring for what seemed an eternity as the sores on his knuckles scabbed over and the blood on his hands stuck to the steering wheel.

The Zombie, whose real name was Harley Stein, had come to *The Post* in 1966 after winning several journalism prizes for exposing fraud and collusion at a horse racing track in New Mexico. He was a provocative interviewer and a tireless worker. Stein also possessed an elegant writing style that set him apart from the run-of-the mill reporters. As the copy editors put it, Stein knew how to use semicolons.

But Stein was haunted by childhood. When he was ten, his family was leaving a circus in Cincinnati. An armed man emerged from the darkness. His father struggled with the man. The pistol barked. Stein's older brother screamed vengeance and jumped at the mugger. The gun barked again. Stein held his brother while he died. He watched his father die in his mother's arms. The killer avoided the electric chair because the defense convinced the jury that the murderer's father had been bad to him when he was a child.

Though the terrible loss made him aware of the fragility of life, it forged in Stein a passionate love of truth. The primary truth: the guilty deserve to be punished. Stein joined the news business as an avenging angel.

The longer he'd remained in newspapers, however, the more Stein had to face the inescapable fact that the truth was illusory, fleeting. That imbalance nagged at him, made him susceptible to the lure of barbiturates at night to calm the chatter. Which in turn demanded a pick-me-up pill in the morning to start the internal dialogue again.

In the early 1980s, at the height of his journalistic powers and at the depths of his pill addiction, Stein was assigned to cover a debate between two fringe congressional candidates. As Prentice LaFontaine would retell the story again and again, Stein fought the assignment, screaming at then executive assistant city editor Neil Harpster that it was ridiculous to give these lunatics legitimacy.

Lawlor had backed Harpster's research-based conviction to cover the debate even if the participants were of dubious quality. Steaming with anger, Stein headed out at noon.

By four o'clock he had not called in. The desk began to worry. At 6:00 P.M., on deadline, Stein finally called the city desk. He told Harpster in a Quaalude-induced slur to come to the window and look at the fourteenth floor of the Mariott Hotel.

Fearing that Stein was about to commit suicide, Harpster sprinted to the window with half the newsroom in tow. There, fifth window from the left on the fourteenth floor of the Mariott, stood Stein completely naked, semierect, with his arm around an equally buff young lady. Stein saluted and bellowed into the telephone, "Harpster, you told me to get out there and get the fuck to it. Well, I'm getting the fuck to it, aren't I?"

Stein could have survived that debacle had he emerged from drug rehab repentant. But two weeks after his return, Stein entered the men's room to find LaFontaine standing alone at the urinal. News asked, "Any regrets?"

"Regrets, bullshit," Stein responded. "Thing that sent

Harpster off wasn't that I was chucking the story or that I was stoned off my ass. He just resented seeing my assets. It's common knowledge that while Harpster avidly chases poon, he has no balls."

The stall behind Stein swung open to reveal Harpster, red-faced, his pants around his ankles. "My sack's full you asshole. And these balls got something to tell you: it can be hell to let people hear what you really think."

Harpster had Stein demoted to copyediting the food pages. When that did not bother him enough, Harpster made him obituary writer. And everyone at *The Post* knew that Stein, because of his childhood, lived in dread fear of funeral homes and death.

A man in ordinary circumstances would have quit the newspaper. But Esther, Stein's daughter from a short-lived marriage, had contracted lupus at an early age. Stein knew that if he left the paper, Esther would lose the health insurance she so desperately needed to keep the wolf at bay.

So Stein stopped living to write about the unliving. The hatred he felt toward Harpster and the rest of Lobotomy Lane festered. By the end of his first year writing obituaries Stein decided to follow Harpster's advice—he would never again let anyone in his professional life hear what he thought. By the end of the second year he became a voluntary mute and began to train his body and his mind for future revenge.

Esther graduated from high school and went on to Stanford. Stein got his black belt, then his second degree, and ultimately his third. Esther got her bachelor's degree in May. She had her own job and insurance.

Now, as he sat in his pickup outside Harpster's house, the rage of Stein's silent decade bubbled like pressured lava under the hardened cone of a dormant volcano.

At 9:00 P.M., Harpster pulled his white Audi into the driveway, got out, and put a brown satchel in the trunk. He brushed back his hair with his fingers, burst a shot of breath spray into his mouth, and went in. An hour later the lights upstairs blinked off.

The Zombie waited another two hours until he was sure all was quiet. He pulled a black balaclava out and tugged it down over his head. He slid from the truck with the stealth of a Shaolin monk. He swept across the street dressed entirely in black. He noted with satisfaction the gaping hole where the barrel cactus had once stood. Harpster thought it was the work of landscape rustlers. The Zombie allowed himself a sick grin, then eased himself over the redwood fence into Lydia's gardens.

The Zombie stood in the shadows until he was sure he hadn't alerted the occupants. He dipped deep into the well of his loathing. He took two steps toward a blooming camellia bush and dealt the base a killing blow with the blade of his hand. The Zombie spun. He crouched low, a ninja intent on psychological assassination. He looked at the house. Still dark. He clipped an azalea to the root stems with two savage swipes. He bit the pistils and stamens from a dozen tulips. He high-kicked the trunk of a magnolia sapling. The tree cracked and the crown swung over and down.

The way the sapling dangled in the starlight made him stop for a moment before cat-crawling back over the garden wall. The Zombie believed he'd never seen anything so beautiful as that dying little tree.

Across town that strange Friday night, Stanley Geld, the Zombie's city editor, was performing sloppy pirouettes in the red silk boxer shorts and white ballet shoes he had purchased after work. "The Dance of the Sugarplum Fairies" lilted from the speakers of his living room stereo system. Geld, who was very drunk, held red and blue darts in his hand. His wife, Judy, cowered in the bedroom.

In time with the music, Geld raised his elbows parallel to the floor and pressed his hands together, knuckles to knuckles. He spun on the carpet. As he came around, he lost his balance. He tripped forward, launched the dart, and crashed.

His target: the photograph of Bobbie Anne Pace *Vanity Fair* had used for its glowing profile last year. Two darts were stuck an inch above the top of her head. One was embedded to the left of her chin. A fourth just to the right of her ear. The fifth had missed the photograph completely and hung limply from the wall. Five misses. One dart left.

Geld reached for the nearly empty fifth of gin, took a belt, lifted his elbows, and spun. Wildly off-balance his feet tangled. The city editor reeled to his right. Miraculously he released the last dart before colliding with the corner of the coffee table. It knocked the wind out of him. He landed facedown on the hardwood floor.

Geld gasped for air. He rolled over and looked up at the photograph. The dart had pierced Pace's left nostril. Geld grinned and laughed, the laugh becoming a depraved snigger. "I'm gonna get you, Bobbie Anne!"

He pounded his fist on the floor. "I'm gonna get you!"

He stopped yelling. The pounding became weak slaps on the carpet. "I just don't know how yet."

The bedroom door slammed. Judy held a small suitcase in her hands. Her lower lip trembled. "Stan, I can't take this anymore," she announced. "I'm going to my sister's."

"Can't see how those fucking Russians do that full spin without falling," Geld said.

"Stanley, I'm leaving you," Judy said.

Geld raised a leg to show her the ballet shoes wrapped around his feet. "You think I bought the wrong size?"

"Oh, Stanley!" Judy cried out. She rushed down the hallway. A door opened and slammed shut.

Unsteadily Geld got to his knees and then to his feet. If he couldn't figure out a way to displace the Assistant Managing Editor for News and Information tonight, he was determined to unravel the mystery of the pirouette.

Geld closed his eyes. He thought about the videos he'd rented of Baryshnikov. He applied it to his own history as a soccer forward and let it gel.

Raise the elbows, hands in tight, a slight drop in the center over the front knees, hips lead the arc, then snap! He spun, tripped, and collapsed again. He got up, tried another, and sprawled even harder. Gin-flavored sweat boiled out from under his permed curls. He threw his arm out and pointed at the picture of Pace. "It's all your fault!"

He looked at his arm quizzically. He threw it out again. He threw out the other one. Then both at the same time. *Balance!* he thought. He'd have to regain his balance at the end of the pirouette or crash.

Geld jumped up. This time he spun hard and, as his hips passed through his original stance, he flung his arms out at right angles to his torso. He came to a screeching halt exactly where he'd begun the pirouette. He did it again and again and again. And each time he twirled, a thought grew at the back of his sour-mashed brain until by the sixth spin it stood on point, a clear, audacious plan with all the elegance and line of a treacherous leap by Nureyev.

If Bobbie Anne Pace would trip, he must upset her equilibrium. Make that the entire balance on Lobotomy Lane! If someone must sprawl on the floor with her, so be it.

Geld pirouetted to his word processor. He opened a file and began composing.

Meanwhile, Connie Mills fumbled with the lock at the door to her condo. She got it open finally and picked up the bag of takeout Japanese food she'd bought on the way home. A fitting dinner, she supposed.

Her early evening cavort with Neil Harpster had featured kimonos and a Kurosawa film on the video machine in the motel on State Street. Neil had raced about making guttural noises and acting like a samurai. She had posed as the demure geisha.

Mills crossed the tiny kitchen. She got out a seltzer water from the fridge and opened the sushi and udon noodles. As she ate she looked around at the bare walls and the cheap couch and the television-VCR-stereo center she'd bought on layaway. She thought of her meager clothes collection. She thought of her dwindling savings account and the eight-year-old Chevy sedan she drove.

"So much for the overachiever," she muttered.

Before accepting her job at *The Post,* Mills had led a relatively uneventful life. Her mother and father were academics, he a math professor at a state university in northern California, she a research librarian. They'd lived an austere life in a farming community thirty miles from the university. She was a quiet girl, with few friends. Not much to look at until she turned seventeen and an odd mix of genetics, clean air, and hours picking tomatoes combined to produce the luscious form she now inhabited. At Stanford she lost her virginity to an insecure psychology student in a Ph.D. program who often wept after their lovemaking because he "didn't deserve to worship at a temple that belonged in *Playboy.*"

At first she rejoiced at the power her body exuded. But the crying got to be too much. She wanted someone who had a mind and physique to match her own. Then this job at *The Post* came along. At an office party she had one drink too many. Harpster whispered in her ear that putting on black sunglasses and wigs and having Rastafarian sex could be loads of fun.

Harpster had lots of muscles and a wonderful leer. She squeezed him on the butt and told him to meet her outside. They did it under a banana tree.

That was two years ago. And since then, other than the brief biweekly trysts at the motel, she hadn't had a real date. Men always asked her out. But she wanted to be free for

Harpster. She enjoyed their work together. And he'd promised to recommend her for his job when he moved up the ladder. And she enjoyed, no adored, the sex.

Often, of late, she'd been trying to determine what exactly about Harpster turned her on so much. He was drop-dead handsome, no doubt. But so were a lot of men. She'd decided it was his voice. In anticipation of carnal pleasure the timbre of his voice deepened and the tone became raw like an old blues guitar growling of the unspeakable pleasure to come. The music they created together was overwhelming.

Mills sighed as she finished the last piece of sushi. She just wished Harpster offered companionship and financial security on top of his libidinous charms.

Fashion Bulimia and Other Neuroses . . .

Twenty-four hours later *The Post*'s chief political reporter, Kent Jackson, knelt in supplication before his telephone answering machine and prayed to his Savior for redemption.

"Dear Jesus, you forgave those Roman soldiers who rolled dice for your robes," he whispered, tears rolling down his cheeks. "I'm asking you to lift this burden from the shoulders of this sinner, or I shall be smote down like Goliath before David."

Jackson knew he was mixing citations from the New and Old testaments, but figured such ecclesiastical confusion couldn't hurt. It might even create some Biblical synergy of brimstone and redemptive forces that would gather to part his personal Red Sea.

He clasped his hands to his breast. He prayed with a fervor he hadn't enjoyed in years. He didn't know what he expected in return: a masculine voice consoling him, a tongue of fire descending above his head, an archangel atop the answering machine?

When nothing happened, he collapsed in a sweaty mess on the floor wondering how in Jehovah's name he was going to come up with $56,248 he now owed his bookie? Who could have predicted that last night a journeyman palooka would knock out Iron-Fist Bean? Jackson looked skyward. How had the odds gotten so out of whack?

Ten years ago he graduated from Oral Roberts University with a degree in journalism and a vow to right the liberal wrong in media, to cover politics in the name of Jesus Christ, to counter the virulent humanistic catechism of victimology that rotted the minds of so many reporters.

He and Patti had been together since high school. She had lank blond hair, perfect blue eyes, a tiny waist, and a way of holding his hand in public that used to make him feel wanted. They'd married when he'd graduated and immediately tried to get pregnant. No such luck.

Infertility clinics were taboo. Tests and high-tech fertilization methods crossed the boundary of their fundamentalist moral code. Patti would wait as had Mary's kinswoman, Elizabeth, for the Holy Spirit to end her barrenness.

In the intervening years, Patti functioned as Kent's rudder while he navigated his way through a series of jobs covering city halls in small Southwestern towns. Then Lawlor offered him a job at *The Post*.

Jackson diligently covered local and California politics. He wrote scathing attacks on the pinkos in Sacramento in a weekly political column syndicated throughout the state. Patti became deeply involved in church life and, it would seem, their minister, the Reverend Tim Waites.

Lying on the floor in his apartment, Jackson scrounged in his pocket and came up with a virgin Lotto ticket. He rubbed off the three pots of gold and came up with zilch. He whimpered, remembering how the gambling had started.

Like most good Midwestern boys, Jackson's youthful weekends were a mix of church and football. Prayer meetings followed by high school football on Friday nights. College games on Saturday afternoon. The pros after the Sabbath service. In his mind football and religion were one; the passion play on the gridiron and the adulation of the crowd melted into evangelical ministers exhorting the faithful from their seats in praise of Jesus and back again into the overwhelming fervor of anxiety and love that surrounded a tie game with third down and goal to go and twenty-one seconds on the clock.

Two years after joining *The Post,* Tony Pritoni, the paper's premier sports columnist, wandered by with a betting pool sheet on the pro games. At first Jackson thought it unethical that a sports writer would run a betting pool. But Pritoni assured Jackson that gambling went on in the sports sections of every newspaper and magazine in America, including the weekly gospel of competition itself: *Sports Illustrated.*

Jackson knew football. He won the first seven pools and went thirteen for fourteen during the regular season. He won the March Madness college basketball tournament pool. He made money on the Kentucky Derby and Wimbledon.

He found in those moments when his picks were true a personal relationship with his Savior; he felt prescient, ubiquitous and, as blasphemous as it was, when he predicted the Buffalo Bills would lose four Super Bowls in a row, prophetic.

Those who ascribe to themselves the status of divine seer, however, are often dealt harsh punishment. He went cold and the losses started eight months ago. He couldn't even win the daily Roy Orbison spilt-coffee pool. His debts grew until they gnawed at him as a dog would the drawn intestines of a dark age martyr.

In his self-created agony, Jackson had pushed away Patti, who eventually collapsed into the warm, waiting arms of the Reverend Tim Waites.

Lying there on the floor, trying to figure out a way to pay off the $56,248, Jackson admitted that as painful as the revelation of Patti's tryst was, it paled in comparison to the news that he'd lost a bigger bet than the one he'd placed on last night's fight.

During the years of failed attempts at having a baby, Jackson had put fifty to one odds that it was Patti's plumbing at fault; but the terrible truth had come in a message on the answering machine just before the news of Iron-Fist's loss: Patti was with child by the Reverend Tim Waites.

While Jackson prayed for divine intervention, Isabel Perez sat in her condo, naked and alone. The usual for a Saturday night.

She had turned up the heat upon arriving. She closed the tan drapes. Next to the full-length mirror in her bedroom she hung today's purchases on the brass clothes rack, an exact replica of the ones they kept in the designer section at Nordstrom's department store.

Perez carefully removed her slacks and sweater, took off her stockings, her bra, and, finally, her panties. She studied herself in the mirror. Four hours of aerobics a week kept her in reasonably good shape.

She turned to an open bag of sinsemilla, rolled a thick joint, lit it, and took a deep electric toke off it. She thought of Kent Jackson and the status he had as chief political reporter. She thought what she might have to do to take that status from him and her stomach felt giddy and slightly sick. She took another deep toke to quell the nausea, then went to the clothes rack.

Slowly, as if in a caress, Perez slid the cover off one ensemble, a Donna Karan in slate blue. She held it up before her nakedness, cupping the tags in one hand so she could plainly see the $550 price. She unbuttoned the outfit and fitted it over the plastic body of one of the three size six mannequins she'd bought from a junk dealer.

The next outfit was a purple dress with black piping, a Nordstrom's original. This she held to her side so she caught the image of herself in it in profile. The purple dress went on the middle mannequin, tags out.

A mauve cashmere sweater with cream stirrup pants completed this evening's collection. With it: faux pearl earrings and necklace and off-white satin pumps. She put the shoes on, then laughed to herself when the cold pearls rolled against her breasts. She rubbed the cashmere on her skin for a moment or two, reveling in the newness of the material.

Perez put those clothes on the third mannequin, arranging the shoes and pearls just as she'd wear them if she didn't know she'd be returning all the outfits Monday morning before work.

She had her own private name for her habit. Fashion Bulimia. Whenever she felt anxious or depressed, she'd head to department stores like Nordstrom's, stores which had no-questions-asked return policies, and buy until her credit card smoked. Then she'd return home and play dress-up like a little girl. Mostly she just liked to look at the tags on the clothes. They made her feel new inside. The marijuana didn't hurt, either.

Perez brought the mannequins out from the wall. She arranged them around her as if they were special friends at an intimate cocktail party.

She thought about the fortuitous picture of Patti Jackson and her minister lover. She thought about her meeting with Arlene Troy, the mayor's press secretary, a short, muscular woman with tightly cropped hair and a raspy voice.

"A great day," she announced. "A horrible day."

She'd talked with Arlene before, of course. But the meeting last night at Troy's office was different. Both reporter and flack knew Jackson's position was in jeopardy. A new relationship might have to be established.

It had gone well, smashingly well in fact, with much information traded. When it was time to go, Troy had smiled, then said: "I'm so glad we had this chance to talk. I've heard so much about you lately. So many things I didn't know."

Goddamn Prentice LaFontaine!

Perez coughed and attempted to return Troy's smile. "Yes, well . . . you know how difficult it is to finally admit who you are."

"There are more of us admitting it every day, in every walk of life," Troy said. She put her hand on Perez's shoulder. Pink fingernails. "I hope you don't think I'm forward. But . . . well, are you seeing anyone?"

"Uh, no," Perez scrambled. "Not right now."

"Perhaps we could have a drink sometime?"

All she really wanted was to be home behind closed curtains with her off-the-rack friends. "I'm pretty busy, what with the campaign and all," she croaked. "Of course, you're busy too, Arlene. So, sure, if we can fit it into our schedules. I guess."

"Why not next week sometime? My treat."

Perez had swallowed hard. "Fine, Arlene. Fine."

Now, sitting cross-legged amid the mannequins, Perez shuddered at the things one must do to become a heavyweight journalist these days. She shuddered again and told herself these uncomfortable memories would fade. Better to focus on the unchanging symbols of her destiny.

She opened her jewelry box and brought out her most prized possession.

Perez knew the rule: as a political writer you were nothing until you worked for one of the agenda-setting newspapers—*The New York Times, The Washington Post, The Wall Street Journal,* the *Los Angeles Times*. Last year she'd suffered the humiliation of treading the national campaign trail with a plastic badge around her neck that said *The Post*.

She'd weathered the ignominy of having political handler after political handler glance at her badge, sniff, then walk away as if they'd whiffed a dead animal. A moment later these same spin doctors would encounter a badge printed with those magic words: *The New York Times*. They'd snort, then snuffle, then fawn and salivate with the raw joy of an alley stray that's found a pedigreed poodle in estrus. Oh, it was true: more than anything on this earth, Isabel Perez coveted a press badge that the badge-sniffers wanted to sniff.

So she'd stolen this one from a sleeping reporter from *The Washington Post*. Simple really. The poor woman had been suffering from exhaustion, the flu, too many Bill Clinton speeches, and three gin and tonics. In the middle of a late-night flight, Perez slipped the chain from the unsuspecting woman's purse, then slid it deep in her luggage.

It was now the nightly ritual. Perez hung the sniffable badge around her neck, a fashion accessory she'd never return. She assumed the full lotus position with the ashtray in front of her on the carpet. She watched herself in the mirror.

She smoked the rest of the joint during this meditation on self, reaching out from time to time to stroke the different fabrics around her, always returning, as a baby will to its security blanket, to the green-and-white laminated press pass.

For Prentice LaFontaine, the night was just beginning. He drove fast toward the Pink Stag, ignoring the gawks he received from fellow drivers at red lights.

Carl Tracy, the Pink Stag's owner and master of ceremonies, was throwing an AIDS fund-raiser. A man possessing a wonderful sense of black humor, Tracy expected everyone to come dressed for the event as their favorite dead military hero they believed was secretly gay. Earlier in the week, News had located a World War I doughboy outfit at an antique shop complete with dishpan helmet. He had bought an old nonworking carbine with a bayonet to complete his ensemble.

He pulled into the parking lot of the Pink Stag, telling himself that tonight he was not going to think anymore about what Thomas P. Whitney had told him. Tonight he was going to have fun even if his ankle was still killing him.

"Take fear, Huns, I'm in the trenches!" LaFontaine cried as he hobbled through the door into the Pink Stag. "Lay down your rifles or I'll shoot you like turkeys."

"Don't tell me, don't tell me!" Carl Tracy screeched. "You're Sergeant York!"

LaFontaine let fly a snappy salute. "You know I've always had a thing for Gary Cooper, Carl. And look at you, Mr. Five-Star General. Ike would just roll over and die if he could see you now."

"Wouldn't he, though?" Tracy laughed. He shook so hard his green cap slipped off his head. "Oh, go on in, Prentice, the place is just mad!"

LaFontaine scooted by Tracy into the Pink Stag's main room. John Philip Sousa marches were playing. The horseshoe bar was draped in mufti. Bunting hung from the horns of the elk head that had been dyed salmon and mounted high above the bar. Bond posters from World War I, World War II, and Korea hung from the walls. As did huge blowup photographs of Betty Grable, Rita Hayworth, and Jayne Mansfield entertaining the troops. Enlarged battle maps of the Inchon Reservoir, Gettysburg, and Waterloo were suspended over the dance floor.

LaFontaine ordered a Campari on the rocks. *First thing Monday morning I'm finding Burkhardt's ex,* he thought. *She's got to know what was in that sealed case.* He finished the Campari and ordered another. He amused himself comparing the various costumes to his own.

There was a fashion photographer at the far end of the bar dressed as Audie Murphy—a grenade in one hand and a guitar in the other. A bookstore owner clad as Charles De-Gaulle waved the colors of Free France while hugging Admiral Yamamoto. Several of the hot young male models in town had donned basic G.I. outfits and as a group kept jumping up on the stage to reenact the raising of the flag on Mount Suribachi.

Of course, there were the retro dressers. Here came a bearded gastroenterologist in Confederate gray as Gen. Robert E. Lee and his companion as Ulysses S. Grant. They carried a placard that read "Appomattox or Bust." LaFontaine sniffed at the overstatement.

As the "Boogie Woogie Bugle Boy of Company B" played, Joan of Arc took to the dance floor with George Washington. So did Napoleon, who did the lindy hop with Marc Antony. George Armstrong Custer cut in.

Behind them stood LaFontaine's vote for best costume: an abstract painter dressed as Achilles, complete with Greek warrior skirt, iron breastplate, helmet, sword in scabbard, and sandals that laced up his muscular calves. The topper was an arrow that stuck straight out from his heel!

LaFontaine was on his way through the crowd to congratulate Achilles when he noticed a young four-star general in leather riding boots, leather crop, and combat helmet staring at him. LaFontaine held his breath; the boy looked vaguely dangerous and he had so many muscles his uniform threatened to rip. My God! He's not staring; he's leching!

No guts, no glory. News slung his rifle over his shoulder, then marched crisply across the floor. He came to attention before the young man and drawled: "Scouting the battlefield, General Patton?"

"Rommel, the Desert Fox, believed in forward observation. So do I," the soldier replied in a gravelly voice.

"Plotting your attack on the grid map already?"

"Feels like I might have to move in the heavy artillery."

"Not one for guerrilla war, I see."

General Patton shook his head. "Classic attacks are my specialty. I like to whip the flanks."

Though a voice inside him told him to walk away, LaFontaine couldn't. He shivered with delight. He took a step closer and gazed deep into the general's eyes. "A warrior with a sense of history. I like that. What campaign are you thinking of now—the deserts of North Africa, perhaps?"

"Too dusty, Sergeant York, too many scorpions," Patton said as he slowly moved his riding crop up between News's legs. "I was thinking of a skirmish characterized by heavy armor and hand-to-hand combat. The Battle of the Bulge perhaps?"

"Oh, my!" whimpered LaFontaine. "Oh, my yes!"

The Milkman Cometh . . .

Mid Monday morning at a coffee shop out on the Boulevard. Even after two calming days at home, two days spent fishing and hiking around the reservoir with the kids, Gideon McCarthy still felt Carlos's terrified fingers digging into his back. Small, powerful goads that kept him on the hunt. He couldn't give Charley Owens the slightest opening.

The sun burned off the ocean fog as he reread his scrawled account of his talk with Tabor and Delta Ann Porter. Reading their words made him want to shower again. He'd been doing this kind of reporting for years and rule

number one was you had to invade the world you were investigating, learn it better than the inhabitants did. Gentry
had cavorted in the sewer. This greasy feeling went with the
territory. What had Prentice LaFontaine told him once? "If
you want to be society's proctologist, you'd better be prepared to look up some foul holes."

He'd called Claudette X at home over the weekend, telling her that he was after a story of a murder contract being
put out on Carol Alice Gentry, possibly by police officers.

"You get that story, Gid, and all is forgiven," she said.
"Connor and Ed will lose their minds."

"I know," McCarthy replied. "The trouble is finding this
hooker, Dusk."

"I have faith," Claudette X said.

"Then give me the next two nights to get her."

He heard her hesitate and knew before she spoke what
the answer was. "I got no one to cover for you, Gid. All you
got to do is grab this snake and I'll free you up."

McCarthy looked out the window of the coffee shop at
the busy sidewalk crowd, wondering if this story of a contract was real or just a snake's tail in the shadows that would
disappear down a hole when he tried to grab it.

He had to assume that what Tabor and Delta Ann had
told him wasn't just a tale, that it was real and that it was the
story. He opened a notebook. He didn't understand Gentry,
probably never would totally. But there were things he was
certain of. She had been fascinated by weaknesses, base
weaknesses, especially sex. She used it over people. It was
also true she liked the spotlight. He remembered her outside
the grand jury room, a big woman comfortable with her
body, posing for the cameras, joking with the reporters. She
liked to get leverage on people, perhaps blackmail them.
When had that started? He snapped his fingers, remembering that her brother had not called back. He put that down
on a list of priorities.

The primary focus of the day, however, was to get to

Christine Evers, a.k.a., Dusk. She was the story. She was the anchor to this ladder he was building out of hell.

Ordinarily McCarthy would have gone down to superior court and pulled files as he had on Delta Porter. But he figured he'd try a shortcut. There were still some cops in headquarters he hadn't offended in nearly fifteen years of investigative reporting. One was Sgt. Roger "Tinker" Thompson, who was second-in-command of the gang's detail.

McCarthy knew communications lines between the various police departments were convoluted. He figured it was unlikely his request for information would raise flags in Fisk's Homicide Division. With a little cajoling he got Thompson to pull the file on Larry Milk.

The road to Dusk didn't begin with her criminal record, McCarthy reasoned, but with the Milkman's. Milk had a long rap sheet, mostly minor stuff. He'd served three terms. Twice for burglary. Once for possession of crystal methamphetamine. He belonged to a bike gang called the Ospreys. McCarthy wrote down the Milkman's last three addresses, thanked Thompson, and headed for his car.

The first two addresses were busts. In each case the Milkman had moved out in the middle of the night, leaving no forwarding address. There were no changes of addresses filed at the local post offices, either.

At noon, McCarthy turned the corner onto Farnsworth Street, looking for 612A. The street was an odd collection of older, single-family dwellings. Behind many of them the owners had erected small apartment buildings. He knew from past experience that 612A was probably one of these dumps. He slowed as he passed 598, peering ahead through the web of cars along the curb and in the driveways. A short man in a blue suit came around the corner of a house half a block ahead.

"Shit!" McCarthy hissed. "He's on to it!"

Lt. Geribome Fisk paused in the middle of the lawn in

front of 612 Farnsworth, hands on his hips, talking to two other detectives. McCarthy reached over in his seat to get a baseball cap, tugged it low over his forehead, then, as inconspicuously as he could, pulled into a driveway and turned around. In his rearview mirror he saw Fisk and the cops get into a tan sedan and open cups of coffee.

McCarthy stopped in the parking lot of a strip mall three blocks away and slammed his hand on the steering wheel. Fisk was sitting on the Milkman. Had his request with Thompson at the gang's detail tipped Fisk? No matter. If Fisk got to Dusk first, the story of the hit would come out at a big news conference. No exclusive. No reincarnation for this blackballed reporter.

He rested his head on the steering wheel and looked for a way out. The Milkman had been in the joint three times. Unless he was a total idiot, he knew when he was being hunted. It was unlikely he'd return soon to Farnsworth Street unless he was absolutely desperate. Even then Fisk was assuming that Dusk would be with him.

There had to be another way! He went back over everything that Porter and Tabor had told him. It took him almost ten minutes, but suddenly there it was, a new angle. A longshot, but the only one he had.

McCarthy drove as fast as he could down to the courthouse and pulled the last case on Larry Milk, the one involving crystal meth. He jiggled his knee racing through the various court documents and filings until he found what he was looking for: a yellow envelope stapled to the inside back of the folder. A probation report. "Not For Public Review" was stamped on the cover in red ink. He paused a second to glance around at the various attorneys and legal searchers thumbing through their own cases. The clerks were too busy behind the counter to notice.

He slid a thumbnail under the staple and worked the envelope free. He opened the flap and slid out the yellow report. On the very last page of the seven-year-old report, fifth section down under the heading "Known Relatives," the Milkman had listed his mother's name and address. Laura Milk, 3345 Caminito La Bruja.

"Thank you, thank you, thank you," McCarthy whispered as he hurried back to his car.

Her Plastic, Fantastic Proportions . . .

As McCarthy performed verbal sacrifices to the spirits of the information highway, Prentice LaFontaine was rounding a corner in a swank canyon street on the west side of Los Angeles. He prayed Thomas P. Whitney was right and that Patricia Sutcliff, the former Mrs. Sloan Burkhardt, had more dirt on the developer.

Sutcliff's home was a multilevel glass and redwood affair perched on the steep side of the canyon. A bridge led to the front door. He crossed it under a blazing sun that had cooked the L.A. ozone depleters into a lung-singeing mist. He plucked out an asthma inhaler, gave himself two puffs, and then knocked.

A Mexican maid answered and when he told her he was looking for Sutcliff, she arched her brow and slammed the door shut.

"Was it my breath?" News asked the bronze statue of Buddha on the porch.

He was about to knock again when the door swung open to reveal a classic post–thirty-five, remade California woman. "What do you want Patty for?" she demanded in a thick, humid voice.

Her skin had been drawn hyper taut at the neckline, her nose bobbed so the nostrils flared ever so slightly, her breasts newly meloned to cantaloupe proportions, her ass and thighs jackhammered free of cellulite, her teeth pearled whiter than vanilla; and her hair had been dyed the hue of dried dune grass, every strand perfectly arranged to effect a sense of disarray.

She sported denim shorts and red cowboy boots and an embroidered denim tank top. She wore owly red eyeglasses. LaFontaine supposed that the hetero swells at *The Post* would find her alluring. He thought it might be more profitable to stuff her into a neon orange bikini and a set of in-line roller skates, dip her in polyurethane, and sell her to Madame Tussaud's to be used in a tableau entitled "Brentwood Plastic Surgeons Amok."

"I just want to ask her some questions about her ex-husband," News said, handing the woman his card.

She looked at it contemptuously. "Never heard of you. Why are you interested in Sloan? Has he done anything wrong? Is he in some kind of trouble?"

"Not now, not that I know of," LaFontaine replied. He was on the defensive here, a position he hated.

"Do you have the guts to go after him? Would you smear him if you got the goods?"

That threw him off. "Who the hell are you?"

"Answer the question!"

"If there's dirt and it's pertinent, I'll report it."

The woman's expression softened. She leaned against the doorway, clicking together ruby red fingernails the size of horse tranquilizers. "You know, I ordinarily don't allow strange men into my house, but since you're looking to do a hatchet job on my ex, come in."

"Patricia Sutcliff, I presume?"

"In the flesh." The woman smiled.

Or the plastic, LaFontaine thought.

"Sorry for the bitch act," she said, standing back to let

him enter. "It's just that Sloan sends up private detectives every once in a while to harass me. I've learned to deal with them."

Sutcliff shut the door, crossed the foyer, and climbed the polished maple staircase rhythmically, so her hardened ass pistoned before LaFontaine's eyes. *Must women of a certain age always thrust?* he asked himself. Scientifically he guessed it hormonal, though experience told him it was more likely a feminine gag reflex brought on by prolonged mirror bouts. He closed his eyes and imagined for a moment that this derriere was that of his wonderful new military friend, Brad Perkins. News drew in air quick and hard at the thought. Brad was such a boy!

Sutcliff took a right at the top of the landing. She led him through a door into a bedroom decorated in Laura Ashley and Patricia Sutcliff. There were photographs and collages of her on every wall. Here over the vanity was one of a miniature Ms. Sutcliff cradled in the coils of a painted python. There on the far wall her face and protuberances were partially hidden by pressed orchids. Above the bed a soft lense photo of her, back to the lens, nude in the mist on a beach.

"My, my, aren't we modest?" LaFontaine drawled.

She flopped on the bed, looked up at her naked self, and said: "I'm an artist, Prentice. I believe all artists project themselves into their art. I'm just blatant about it."

She motioned him to a rocking chair hard by the bed. He sat stiffly, sniffing the air tainted with the pungent odor of rock concert.

"This is where I do my best thinking, my best art, usually high," she said. "Though it sounds trite in the nineties, the herb lets my mind wander down interesting alleys."

"I bet."

She rolled away from him across a black-and-yellow bedspread, reached into a drawer, and drew out a manila folder. "Before we talk, you've got to agree that if you ever quote me you've got to include the fact that I'm the U.S. representative of the Tamil insurgency in Sri Lanka."

"The Tamils? Oh, no, I wouldn't dream of leaving that out." He sneezed and flipped open the folder. Inside lay a series of glassy photographs of her artwork, another soft focus shot of her, this time not nude, and copies of clippings and a résumé. This last item listed her experience as "collage artist, film producer, and international peace negotiator."

The clippings hailed from obscure art and film newsletters. In each she was quoted about her activities on behalf of the peoples of Southeast India and Sri Lanka. There was no mention of any forthcoming film or show in an art gallery. At the back of the folder a photograph showed Patricia Sutcliff hugging a sullen Tamil man in a bamboo grove. She leaned forward, showing News her cantaloupes. "They deserve to be free of New Delhi!" she whispered. "They are the niggers of India."

"Hmmn. I thought those were the untouchables?"

She tapped a finger on her lips. "Well, okay. They're the Chicanos of India. They're getting a raw deal, anyway. They deserve to be free."

"Sure, anything, free," LaFontaine replied, looking for a way to get the conversation back on course. "Free, just like you deserved to be free of Sloan Burkhardt?"

She rolled around and lay on her back. She rocked her head off the edge of the bed so she peered at him upside down. Her dark roots were beginning to show. She cooed, "Tell me, Prentice, are you one way or do you sashay on both sides of the street?"

Tabloid Witchery . . .

McCarthy cruised the length of Caminito La Bruja four times before parking. He studied each car for evidence the place was under surveillance. He was suspicious of a white panel van two blocks away, but on his third pass a workman drove it off.

He parked, got out, and took inventory. Paint curlicues hung from the eaves of the homes where pigeons roosted and crapped and decried the lack of good grass seed. The homes were all unsightly, but 3345 won ugliest house on the street hands down. Putrid green shingles. The roof cowered under the whipping of gravity and neglect. Rotting plywood hung in several of the window frames. Sparse fiddle-headed grass stalks guffawed at what used to be a lawn. A thunderhead of flies buzzed around an open can of garbage near the one-car garage.

Society's proctologist. Let's slap on the rubber gloves.

He loosened his tie and lumbered up the driveway, freezing when he heard it. A cackle. Not a good thing to attend to when approaching a house in which the mother of a rogue biker named Milkman lives. A cackle again, then a ragged whistle, and a "Hee! Hee! Hee!"

Behind all this echoed the loose babble of morning television. He couldn't tell from here—what with the odd fly peeling away from the thunderhead to attack him— whether that was Bob Barker demanding contestants guess the price of cruelty-free makeup, or Phil Donohue filleting a recalcitrant husband to the delight of the studio coliseum.

Another fly attacked. He ran to the door and rapped hard. She answered on the fourth series, cracking the door to peer out at him. "Leper Rape Spawns Monster Child," she whispered to him. "Thirteen-Year-Old Performs Self-Caesarean with Can Opener, Names Baby Campbell's Chicken Soup!"

The fetid odor of human waste wafted through the cracked door. McCarthy twisted from it, watching her side-long, sucking in fresh air from the corner of his mouth. She chanted: "DOLLY PARTON SHOCKER! BOTCHED BREAST JOB TURNS BOOBS TO KNOTHOLES!"

Laura Milk was built like a puppy, shar-pei puppy to be exact, the folds in her face cast in shades of stale ginger root and cinnamon. Her bizarre grin doubled the disconcerting effect of a pair of viciously inane eyes spinning below the flotsam of hair dyed violet. She clutched too low a once-pink bathrobe, now stained with liquids McCarthy did not care to identify. He fought off the gag reflex by focusing on the door.

"Mrs. Milk?"

"ALIENS OFFER TO REVIVE JFK, LENIN, AND DISNEY FROM DEEP FREEZE," she announced.

"Mrs. Milk, I'm looking for Christine Evers," McCarthy said.

She thought about that a moment. "TINKERS TO EVERS TO CHANCE! TEXAS CULT WORSHIPS GREAT DOUBLEPLAY COMBO."

"Mrs. Milk, I'm a reporter. I'm looking for Dusk. I'm told she comes and helps you."

Her expression turned rational. "Reporter? Do you know Jeanne Dixon?"

"No, ma'am."

She floated again. "JEANNE DIXON PREDICTS ZANY SEX HIGH JINKS AT THE WHITE HOUSE: HILLARY CLINTON IN LOVE TRYST WITH RUSH LIMBAUGH."

He tried another tack. "Do you ever see your son, Larry?"

She puffed her lips and her eyes came unscrewed. "NO GOOD SON DEFRAUDS HELPLESS MOMMY!"

"Could you repeat that?"

A thin line of spittle drooled from the corner of her mouth. "NO GOOD SON DEFRAUDS HELPLESS MOMMY," she repeated. She made a sound like a sledge-hammer hitting a tin roof, then howled: "TONIGHT ON *'A CURRENT AFFAIR!'* "

"What about his friend, the one who helps you?"

"SEX SLAVE KEPT ALIVE IN BASEMENT. HER STORY WILL SHOCK YOU!"

"She's in the basement?"

She raised a finger skyward. "Work for the *Enquirer,* sonny?"

"No ma'am, *The Post."*

"Too bad, I know all about Jacky Hoffa and Elvis."

He decided to humor her. "Tell me, Mrs. Milk."

She looked both ways, batted her eyes twice, then picked up the hem of her bathrobe and whined in a little girl's voice: "MUUURDEERRR!! MUUUURDERRRR!!!!"

She jigged in place, her gray breasts slapping her chest. "MUUUURDERRRR!"

A fly rebounded inside the reporter's slack mouth. He spit it out, coughing: "Yes, ma'am. I believe it, too."

"Got your story then, sonny boy!" she snapped, suddenly angry. "Bye-bye. Eleven o'clock. Time for 'Hard Copy.' "

The door slammed. Over the yip and keen of the television it came again, the cackle and the "Hee, Hee, Hee!" and then a screeching: "MUMMIFICATION! ANCIENT EGYPT OFFERS LAURA MILK HOPE OF AFTER-LIFE!"

McCarthy's stomach roiled again at the stench that boiled behind her. The flies tore about his head, looking for the source of the vile odor. He backed away from the house, got his breath, and almost left. When his head cleared he decided to go around to find an entrance to the basement.

Several pigeons flushed when he opened the gate. A mangy orange cat leapt from the empty pool, charged across the patio, and vaulted the back fence. Old blankets and what appeared to be black trash bags hung on the inside of the windows. No basement bulkhead. He knelt down, ripping away at a tangle of vines. A crawl space. No basement at all. Just a back door under a portico of sorts. He felt vulnerable here, wondering what the Milkman might say if he caught him slinking around his demented mother's backyard.

He was turning to leave when he noticed it, a footprint in the dirt beyond the portico. A narrow footprint of a woman's shoe with a small heel. A woman had come through this door lately, probably in high heels. Laura Milk was in no condition to manage high heels. He smiled to himself. "I've got you, Dusk."

He looked at his watch. Two-thirty. He had to be at the cop shop in half an hour. He glanced at the footprint again. He thought of Charley Owens. He thought of Carlos and Miriam. He thought of Claudette X and Ed Tower and Connor Lawlor, then made his decision. He wasn't going to work night cops tonight. He wanted out of this limbo. Get the story or lose the job. One way or another it would be over after tonight.

He crossed back to his car and got it turned around so he could see 3345 Caminito La Bruja. He prayed to the spirits of the information highway that sometime in the next twenty-four hours Christine Evers, a.k.a. Dusk, would play whore with a heart of gold and come to change the diapers of a senile crone obsessed with yellow journalism.

Keeping the Weirdness at Bay . . .

P rentice LaFontaine stared in abject horror at the woman writhing obscenely on the bed in front of him.

"Well?" demanded Patricia Sutcliff. "Do you, or don't you?"

"Perish the thought, Ms. Sutcliff," Prentice LaFontaine replied. "To even sit here in the, er, rampant femininity of your boudoir gives me the heebies."

"Too bad," she sighed, and stilled her squirming hips. "Aside from good herb, I've found afternoon sex promotes profound creativity."

"To think it! I chat with a female Georges Simenon."

She grinned. "My theory is that engorgement draws blood down from the brain. Orgasm is a moment of anoxia, complete deprivation of oxygen. When the air comes back the brain's fire is hot. Art results."

"That why so many snooze afterward?"

"They've just got to get up, right after!" She performed a leaping sit-up that startled him. She landed on her feet on the far side of the bed, pivoted, and flopped, protuberances down, her head resting on her forearms, her expression all business. "Okay, enough philosophy. What do you want to know?"

"Why did you get a divorce? Your records about it all are sealed."

"Figures," she laughed. "Sloan's got more secrets than the CIA, real and imagined."

"Tell me, tell me."

"He washes his hands constantly."

"This I know."

"Know why?"

"It's been nagging at me. Ignorant fear of AIDS?"

"You could understand that, couldn't you? No, Father—as Sloan referred to old Coughy—told him that to accomplish anything one has to soil the hands. A gentleman washes them as soon as possible."

"Sloan took it to heart."

"The man's a compulsive."

"You divorce him because of the hands?"

"Not at all. I can tolerate retentive tendencies."

"If the relationship is profitable?"

"You're fast, Prentice."

"Just experienced, Patricia."

"Sure you don't play both sides of the fence?"

"The thought of a nonphallic frolic nauseates."

"Too bad," she said again. "No, I divorced him because he had quick hands."

"Figure that would be a benefit to someone who fancied the afternoon roll about."

"Not that kind of quick," she admonished. "The sort that's quick to swing. Never understood why some people accept violence in their lives. I never would."

Inside LaFontaine stiffened at the thought of the riding crop in Brad's fist last night. He knew he might be getting into another dysfunctional relationship, but damn it, he was lonely. Brad was different. News was sure of it.

He displayed none of these conflicting thoughts to Sutcliff. He projected the aura of concerned therapist. "Sloan hit you?"

"Three times on separate occasions. Three and you're out as far as I'm concerned."

"When did the hitting start?"

"Year six of our marriage," she said. "I was in my house,

he was in his. You didn't know? Oh yes, separate dwellings. He preferred it that way, as if he was Prince Charles and me Lady Di keeping different shacks on the same estate."

She sat up. "It was a nice arrangement at first. We got together in the afternoon every so often. It worked."

"The modern marriage."

"I thought so. Anyway, I knew Sloan was a bit strange when I married him, but—"

"All that cash," News interrupted.

"An artist has two choices, starve and pray future generations remember you fondly, or . . ." she said.

"Live well and pray future generations remember you fondly."

"So you understand!"

"Did you know that he beat and raped a woman during his college years at UCLA?"

The knowing smirk that had accompanied her easy bantering fell away, replaced by shock. "No . . . I didn't."

LaFontaine told Sutcliff everything the bank president had described.

She was quiet for a long time. "That poor woman."

He nodded. "He has a sealed criminal case from 1986. Know anything about it?"

"No! From when? Eighty-six?" Her mouth hung open for a moment, then shut. She got up and walked around, snapping her fingers. "That figures, doesn't it?"

"What does?" News demanded.

"It must have been July of eighty-six when the police came," she said, talking more to herself than him.

"What happened?"

She tapped a finger on her lips. "You should probably know something else before I tell you. Sloan enjoys scenes. Every day must have at least one scene, one moment of high drama. 'Apollo battling Dionysus' as he put it."

News made as if to interrupt again, but she uncoiled her fingers to stop him. "Hear me out now, I've had a lot of time to think about this aspect of his personality. Sloan operates in a money world. Where there's money there's tension. Everyone's trying to figure out what makes the other person tick. Everyone's got a hidden agenda. So much at stake in these mega projects. It's perfect for him."

"But some days are boring, right?"

"I used to have a saying, a drama a day keeps the weirdness at bay."

"Catchy."

"Words, paint, just different mediums, Prentice," she said. "I hate to admit it, but the scenes were what got us together, Sloan and me. I was an assistant manager of a gallery over on Melrose. He came in looking to buy some art for his office. One thing led to another. He played Pablo Picasso."

"You were Françoise Gilot?"

She rolled her eyes. "Dora Maar, please!"

"Sloan found your rendition of the artist-muse scene pleasing?"

"Married me, didn't he?"

"Indeed. What about the event?"

"It's coming. So anyway, when he'd have a bad day, no scene, he'd invent one. And we'd play it out."

"Always as some cubist?"

"No, no, no," she laughed. "Sloan has a ranging, if troubled, mind. Let me see, over the years there was Keith Moon and Janice Joplin, Liz Taylor and Richard Burton, Fred and Ethel Mertz."

LaFontaine screwed up his eyebrows.

"I swear!" she cried. "That day Sloan even bought a cassette tape with Ricky Ricardo playing 'Babaloo' and put it on the stereo in the room just above us. Who else? One time there was Julie Nixon Eisenhower and Abbie Hoffman. Then Dorothy Parker and Harpo Marx. I got to be cuttingly erudite; Sloan blew a lot of whistles."

"But what about the cops?"

"Okay, okay. I was in Dallas July 1986. I came back at night. I saw a police car leaving the estate. I asked Sloan what they wanted. He decides to play Jimmy Cagney. Knocks me around, shoves a grapefruit in my face, screws me against my will."

"Never told you what they wanted?"

"No."

"Drunk driving, maybe?"

"Not a chance. Sloan controls his booze, like everything else in his life," she said.

"But after that visit from the police he started acting violent?"

She nodded. "He was building a mall in Arizona at the time. Pressure scenes four times a day at work. He was on the boards of several charity organizations, more scenes. He was doing some fund-raisers for Portillo, the one running for governor? More scenes."

"He came home and . . . ?"

"Created grim scenes." She tugged off her red glasses. The taut skin was now puffy. "They got darker. He seemed to be spiraling downward. No drama, just a foreboding of violent climax. I left, got a good lawyer."

Sutcliff slid the glasses back on her face. "Help any?"

"Well, it makes me more determined than ever to find out what's in that sealed case," he said. "You know Robert S. Carlton III?"

"Bobby the banker? Died playing tennis. One of Father's old cronies. Father knew everyone. Everyone owed him something. That was another thing the old man taught Sloan: there's no greater friend than one who owes you."

"What did Bobby the banker owe Father?"

She cocked her head. "I don't know, why?"

"Because Carlton was Sloan's banker on the project I'm interested in."

"That doesn't surprise me. Bobby was like Sloan's uncle, you know? Sloan even made him one of the Lollipop Kids."

"The what?"

"You haven't heard about them? Another thing Sloan got from Father. Coughlin set up this little eating club called the Wizards of Oz that grew into a philanthropic, good deed group. Very select bunch of old boys down there. It sort of petered out when Father died. Couple of years later Sloan formed its successor—the Lollipop Kids. Most of them are middle-aged professionals, attorneys, developers, bankers."

"You ever attend a meeting?"

She laughed. "Guys only. They'd have this big bash at his house every few months. I'd head to Palm Desert or San Francisco to shop."

"You're sure Bobby was a Lollipop Kid?"

"The oldest one. Sloan made him join after his wife, Helen, died."

"Maybe being a friend was what Bobby owed Sloan."

"Doubtful."

"Sloan just won the right to develop twenty acres of the downtown waterfront. I think there's something peculiar about the deal."

"Guaranteed," she said. "It wouldn't be a scene if it wasn't."

News puffed out his cheeks and blew. "But, as far as the newspaper goes, I've got nothing I can print yet. Nothing hard and fast."

"You just have to look close at everyone in on the deal," Sutcliff said. "Figure out who's got something to gain. Who's got something to lose. You can bet Sloan will have all that figured out. That's how Sloan gets all of his deals."

LaFontaine looked at her thoughtfully. "If I come across something of interest that I don't understand, may I ask your opinion?"

"For what it's worth." She grinned.

"Thanks for the help," he said, reaching out to shake her hand. He headed for the door, turning before opening it.

"One more question. If Sloan's obsessed with sex, at those Lollipop Kids gatherings, were there scenes?"

She tapped her pouty lips with a single red fingernail. "I don't know. But if there were that many guys, I know who Sloan would cast himself as."

"Who?"

"Caligula."

Behold a Pale Horse . . .

hree hours later, as McCarthy continued his vigil for Dusk, LaFontaine sat in traffic twenty-two miles north of the city, sweltering in the afternoon heat. He wondered whether today's solar radiation—exhaust mix was bad enough to set the crazed Southern California commuters to wobbling and their fingers to quivering in search of the .357 Magnums and Glock 9 millimeters they kept stashed under their front seats.

Especially troubling was the pasty-faced guy with the snow-white hair ranting and pounding his fists on the steering wheel of the white Mustang in the breakdown lane next to him. Scrawled in fresh blue paint below the driver's window were the words "Pale Horse." A moment ago, the guy had leaned out his window and shrieked something about the end of the world. And what the hell was that moving in the backseat? A dog? No. A pony! One of those true miniatures you see at the circus! Oh, dear God, look at the twit's license plate: "ARMAGDDN."

News moaned. The world was coming to an end.

Or at least becoming so confusing he didn't understand any of it anymore. He'd spent the better part of two weeks tracking Sloan Burkhardt and what did he really have to print? Nothing. He knew the developer had a violent, kinky past and a strong history of collecting dirt on people. *The same could be said of me,* News thought morosely. He supposed that if Burkhardt were a public figure running for office, the information Whitney and Sutcliff had provided would be enough to go to print with. But Burkhardt wasn't a public figure and there weren't any records on the rape at UCLA.

He drummed his fingers on the steering wheel. There had to be another way to get at that sealed case. And what about the Lollipop Kids? What frustrated him was that he had no clear reason to believe any of it fit in with the Cote D'Azure development. He was overlooking something. He should sit for several hours and reread all his notes. It was something McCarthy did all the time, but it was just so much work!

The blare of a horn jerked him from his thoughts. The albino in the Mustang leaned out the window, eyes wide and pink, phlegm spraying from his lips as he pointed to a gap in the pavement that had opened up in front of LaFontaine's red convertible Miata.

"Get your ass moving brother or a pale rider will haunt you!" the man screamed. The little pony whinnied and shied at the rear window.

The nut had a gun! LaFontaine popped the clutch. He jammed down hard on the gas, leaving forty feet of smoking rubber.

The traffic flow opened nicely after his chance encounter with the prophet of doom, enabling News to arrive at *The Post* newsroom at exactly 4:20 P.M. He would later describe the events to follow as "messianic," for that afternoon he would witness a resurrection.

He trotted into the newsroom, noting with satisfaction that everything was as it should be. Ralph Baker in his best black leather and a new hair dye job had already spilled the afternoon coffee. Isabel Perez was happily writing in the vacuum created by Kent Jackson's absence. Abby Blitzer and Augustus Croon were huddled by the police scanner, praying for a downturn in human relations. The Zombie's dead fingers slapped the keyboard at a frenetic pace. Claudette X and Stanley Geld had emerged from the afternoon meeting and busied themselves assigning copy flow to the Stepford Editors. Barring any unforeseen circumstances, tomorrow's paper was set.

LaFontaine dropped his briefcase on his desk, then, as was his routine, opened a file in his computer and typed in his notes [*and opinion, in brackets*] concerning his meetings with Thomas Whitney and Patricia Sutcliff. It took him thirty-five minutes to complete the task. He was tagging the file with a date and time as the system demanded when the phone rang.

"Mr. News?" said the elderly woman.

"Gertie, dear, what have you got for me?"

Gertie was his mole in the human relations department, a deep source he'd cultivated with years of chocolate confections, her singular vice.

She whispered, "You wanted me to keep a watch out on Mr. Jackson's file."

"I did indeed."

"Just as you thought, he's requested counseling, only it's not marital, it's psychological. He's seeing Dr. Hoffman, two visits so far. The notation also mentions a gambling problem. And Dr. Hoffman's prescribed a sleeping pill."

"Poor man," News said sympathetically. He told himself he'd get great information from Perez in return for this dirt. "What kind of truffles would you like, dear?"

"White chocolate with strawberries would be nice."

"Consider them delivered. Thank you, Gertie," News said.

He hung up the phone. He opened GOSDI, his daily journal of *The Post*'s underworld, and entered the information about Jackson. Done, he refiled the Whitney and Sutcliff interviews, hit print, and was rising to go get the hard copy when a divine finger reached inside *The Post* newsroom.

The scanner crackled and crackled again. The closely cropped hair on Croon's head stood on end. Blitzer bent to the machine, then jumped in the air and cried "HALLELUJAH! IT'S A TRAGEDY! WE GOT OURSELVES A TRAGEDY AT THE POST OFFICE!"

She elbowed by Croon, stood on her tiptoes, and screamed at Claudette X: "A shooter right on the loading docks! Two down, six held hostage."

Claudette X tugged at her ear. "Another postal worker? This is getting cliché. Let's let McCarthy handle it as an item."

The tiny reporter's entire body was jerking now with the random fury of an epileptic in petit mal. "Gunman's an albino! Got four weapons: two semiautomatic rifles and two pistols. And here's the best part: he's got a pony with him and he's threatened to shoot it next!"

A gunman holding a pony hostage! "You're gone," Claudette X shouted.

Croon already lumbered toward the door, three cameras, two lens bags, and a light meter bouncing about his neck. Blitzer sprinted right behind him, mainlining on the promise of real-life drama. Margaret Savage stood from her desk and bellowed "I'm going, too!" She took off after them, a whirl of beaded hair and brilliant peasant cloth.

News called out, "Abby, did you say albino?"

Blitzer twisted in mid sprint. "A real pink-eye!"

LaFontaine raced toward Geld and Claudette X. "I saw him, the shooter! Not a half hour ago on the freeway. He waved a gun at me."

Geld dismissed him. "So what. A gun in the hand is the California turn signal."

News gave Geld a look of utter contempt. "An Albino

with a miniature pony in the backseat? License plate 'A-R-M-A-G-D-D-N?' "

Claudette X dropped her huge frame into her desk chair. "Tie me up and sit me down. A Biblical tragedy! News, run the license plate through DMV. Find out who he is!"

Blitzer's expression was blissful, almost serene, as she, Croon, and the P.C. Oracle raced down Broadway toward Fifteenth Street, the site of the city's main post office. Out of the corner of her eye as she crossed Eighth, she saw a similar detachment of *Beacon* reporters barreling out of their skyscraper.

"They're after it, too!" she screamed at Croon, already a half block ahead, charging the crowded city sidewalk as if it were a Middle East beachhead. He pivoted in full stride, saw the *Beacon* team, tore back, and grabbed Blitzer as though she was a football and dashed toward Fifteenth Street, where the sirens already wailed.

"Jeeeesus, Croooon," Blitzer cried, her voice oscillating with every thud of the giant photographer's feet. "Yoooou're knock, knock, knocking the wiiiind out ooof meeee!"

"Sorry, Abby," Croon said, mooning just a little bit at the little bit of a woman whom he held in his arms at last. "But we got to get there first or you'll be pissed for days."

No arguing with that. Blitzer took a big breath and held tight to the ex-SEAL's belt as the photographer dodged through the crowd bellowing "Get out of my way! News media! Breaking story!"

Seventeen police cruisers, an animal control truck, and two ambulances from a veterinary hospital had already surrounded the main post office, a neo-Federalist building three blocks from city hall. The front of the structure faced Fifteenth Street and was lined with marble columns. The SWAT team was set up in the rear, about 250 feet from a series of loading docks. Somewhere beyond the steel roll-up doors of the docks an albino was holed up with two down and four held hostage. And a miniature pony.

A SWAT lieutenant named Tim Conrad, who respected Croon because he used to be a SEAL and Blitzer because she'd once held on to a speeding car just like cops did in the movies, let them cross the line.

Savage puffed up behind them, her sweat triggering the heavy cent of patchouli in the air. "She okay?" Conrad asked.

Croon and Blitzer glanced at each other. "I don't know, Tim. She hates Chuck Norris," Blitzer said.

"Sorry," Conrad said. "Chuck haters watch from here."

"You can't do this to me!" The P.C. Oracle protested. "I'm a columnist. I have a right to be here. The First Amendment guarantees . . ."

Automatic gunfire ripped the air.

"The Pony Express failed to deliver on time!" roared a voice from inside the third dock from the left. "The legend's a lie!"

Two more bursts of gunfire followed, snapping the gravel and blowing out the windows of two of the cruisers. Silence. And then the whining of a terrified animal.

Tears welled in Blitzer's eyes. The *Beacon* team was trapped a half block back and she was within earshot of an albino shooter with a hatred of the Pony Express! It just didn't get better than this. Except maybe when there was a sex angle. Then something happened that negated her longing for a thread of prurience to weave itself into the story. Behind her, Savage sang to herself in a trembling soprano: "All we are saying, is give peace a chance . . ."

The gunman inside yelled: "I have demands! I have demands to be met."

Conrad sighed and took out a notebook. Ordinarily he would wait for the hostage negotiator to arrive, but the expert was stuck in traffic. The SWAT lieutenant spoke through a bullhorn: "This is Lt. Tom Conrad. What's your name, son?"

"Behold a pale horse and I the pale rider," the gunman shouted. "Know my name? Know my name? Hell follows with me."

"Oh, for Christ sakes," Conrad mumbled to himself. "I got a Bible whacko who hates the Pony Express and loves guns."

Blitzer's and Croon's watery eyes met and locked. What joyful anguish they were sharing! This story would run page one for days.

"What are your demands, Pale Rider?" Conrad asked.

There was silence for a moment, then the shooter bellowed: "I want the Postal Service to tell the world that Express Mail is just as much as a lie as the Pony Express was at getting the letters there on time. I want you to put their confession on TV."

Croon rolled to his left, then belly-crawled in back of a sniper, who had his rifle trained on the third truck bay from the left. A shadow of a man was visible inside the door, nothing more. Then at the end of six feet of rope a tiny blond pony shied out walleyed from the shadows. The photographer pulled out his weapon, a Nikon with a four-hundred-millimeter telephoto lens to the top of which he'd mounted a laser gunsight. He put the red laser dot on the pony. He squeezed off fourteen frames. A dramatic inside-the-A-section photo for the next day!

Lieutenant Conrad dug his fingers into his temple. "We can't do a taped confession on such short notice."

Inside the shooter shrieked: "You don't, old Pale Rider's going to blow little pony's head right here to kingdom come."

Lying in the gravel, desperately scribbling the words of a madman, Blitzer believed she'd died and gone to heaven.

* * *

Back in the newsroom Claudette X frantically edited the copy already in before the Albino shooter stories started flowing across her desk. Geld watched the live television coverage of the tragedy. Croon and Blitzer were visible in the foreground of the picture. Beyond them the parked Mustang and the apocalyptic license plate.

LaFontaine was arguing with a lazy bureaucrat in Sacramento who didn't want to pull the registration on the shooter's car. "We have an account with you, lady," he informed her. "We pay for it. I don't care if it is half an hour until quitting time, there's a crazy man on the loose down here."

"Sir," answered the nasal voice wearily, "there are two Los Angeles crazies holding hostages, not to mention the one who's taken over the Oakland schoolroom. We're not pulling names for the media in those cities either. It's just too late in the day."

"Our crazy's different. He's an albino."

"They all have their little twists, sir."

"He's killed four people."

"The whacko in L.A. has already shot five."

"He believes this is the end of the world."

"And you don't?"

News was desperate. "He says he's going to execute a pony next."

"A pony? You mean a defenseless little horsie?"

"That's right, miss. A cute miniature pony."

"Mr. LaFontaine, I don't care if it is half an hour until closing time. I'm going to get that nut's name for you."

"Bless you," News said.

Up on the television set, Paul Fairbanks, a particularly annoying television reporter, was describing the scene. The station promoted the twerp as an enterprising sleuth. The truth was he stole most of his ideas from the newspapers. Worse, he wore a thin gold chain on his left ankle.

"C'mon," News whispered into the phone; Fairbanks

was an ass, but he had connections inside the police department.

"Lester Hale," the nasal voice said. "H-A-L-E. Born . . ."

News didn't wait for the DOB or the address. He yelled the name across the room just as a hand gave Fairbanks the same information and more. "Lester Hale," the television reporter intoned. "A postal worker on the graveyard shift recently fired for showing up for work late and trying to convert fellow workers to a religious sect in East County."

Now the volume of gastrointestinal fluids being produced in *The Post* newsroom increased tenfold. Albinos and postal workers and Biblical sects! Not to mention the Pony Express and the demand for a television confession to the inefficiency of overnight Express Mail! Hale had killed two people, but goddamn it! this guy was threatening to blow an innocent pony to kingdom come!

No sex, but it was by far the strangest story in months.

Several of the Stepford Editors cringed and snuck away from their desks. A story this volatile was dangerous. One missed fact, one false assumption, and a career could be left in tatters. Geld almost leapt into action, but was rendered catatonic by the sight of his arch nemesis, Bobbie Anne Pace, racing out of her office. From the opposite side of the room came Pace's arch nemesis, Neil Harpster. Both assistant managing editors were shouting instructions as to how the story should be written and played from the perspective of form and content, not to mention news and information.

"I want a backgrounder on miniature ponies," Harpster demanded. "The research on animal love among newspaper readers is clear!"

Pace cut in, "I want a sidebar that tells parents how to explain the mistreatment of animals to their children."

"Claudette," Geld whispered. "Save me."

Claudette X saw the panic in Geld's face and knew he was as useless as if he'd had two liquid lunches and a tango lesson from Twyla Tharp.

She jumped in front of her boss. "We've got it under control," she said in the deepest voice she could muster. "We'll talk at a meeting we've called to plot coverage. We've asked you to be there as well as Connor and Ed. You will be consulted on approaches and space. Just let us get our people in the field."

Harpster and Pace glared up at Claudette X. How dare this . . . this sub-editor presume to keep them out of the action! Then again this sub-editor was massive, mean, and a minority; and they'd already proven to themselves once today that they mattered; and an opportunity now presented itself to prove it again soon, in front of Connor Lawlor and Ed Tower, who really did matter.

"I'll be in my office monitoring the situation," Harpster blustered. "By the way, I still want an update on the cactusnapping story. Things are out of control at The Ranch."

Geld looked like a basset hound with an earring. "Okay, Neil."

Claudette X turned to fire orders: two reporters to Hale's neighborhood to get the personal angle; another reporter to chase down the story of how he was fired; two more to profile the religious sect. And where did he get that pony?

She speed-dialed the cop shop and let it ring ten times. Five-thirty. Where the hell was McCarthy? She slammed the phone down.

"News!" she shouted to LaFontaine. "Call every horse farm in the county. Find that animal's owner."

Juggling the assignments and controlling the approach to the coverage of the shooter so consumed Claudette X that she couldn't muster her normal hostile veneer when someone tapped her on the shoulder and said: "Don't you think it would be a good idea for someone to phone the post office, see if there's anyone inside who'll talk?"

She turned to see the ghost of Roy Orbison weaving back and forth on unsteady legs. Claudette X shivered involuntarily at the thought this specter might be a part of a future nightmare, then spoke to him as if he were a little boy. "You sure you don't need more coffee before you start work, Ralph?"

"No, I'm all right. Just a little fuzzy."

"You call, then. Tell me if you get anything."

The leather-clad reporter shuffled off to his desk and called up a blank screen on his computer. He opened the white pages of the telephone book. He found the listings for the post office, including the central receiving room, and dialed the number.

A strained voice answered, "What is it? You got that commercial done yet?"

"Commercial?" said Baker, confused. "No, no commercial. I'm Ralph Baker, a reporter with *The Post*. To whom am I speaking, please?"

"Newspaper? Well, I was hoping for television, but better than nothing. Ralph, have you ever looked into the lies behind the Pony Express legend?"

"Can't say as I have," said Baker, very confused now. He wished he'd taken Claudette X up on that second cup of coffee. "But can you tell me what's going on? I understand there's been some shooting inside."

"No real people, you know? Just supervisors who live the lie that Express Mail can be delivered overnight and on time by a government-controlled corporation."

Baker thought about that for a second, then said: "What did you say your name was, sir?"

"Lester Hale, but you can call me Pale Rider, Ralph."

As News would describe it later, Baker achieved the benefits of the twenty-eight-day Betty Ford program in about six seconds. His hands stopped shaking. The dregs of last night's vodka evaporated. The florid veins that webbed his nose ebbed to fine white lines. He scribbled the words "I'M TALKING TO THE SHOOTER!" on a notebook, then tossed it onto LaFontaine's desk.

News looked up from the tack shop listings in the Yellow

Pages, glanced at the message, then up into the perfectly sober eyes behind the black polymer glasses. He made the sign of the cross. "Godspeed Roy Orbison."

Baker gave News the thumbs up. "You still there, Pale Rider?"

"Here but not so happy to be so, Ralph," Hale said.

"Why's that?"

"Had a kind of rough time of it lately. No sleet or snow, but lots of dark of night. And the mail's not getting through. Can you understand?"

"I can," Baker said, trying to type down the shooter's words as quietly as he could. He asked himself how Dear Abby would proceed, then said: "Seems sometimes, Pale Rider, that nothing gets through anymore."

"That's a fact, Ralph. That's a fact."

"How many people are dead in there?"

"Two."

"And how many others are with you?"

"Five, including Peterson. And Teddy, of course."

"The postmaster Peterson?"

"Biggest liar of the bunch!" Hale screamed. "Liar! Liar! Pants on fire!"

Baker heard the sound of metal striking flesh and several moans. A woman sobbed.

"Calm down. Calm down now, Pale Rider," soothed the reporter. "If you think about Peterson, you won't be able to tell me everything you want to see in the paper tomorrow. Now who's Teddy?"

"Pony. Symbol of everything that's wrong with the Postal Service today."

"You want to hurt the pony, Lester?"

"Teddy's my neighbor's girl's pet," Hale said. "Why would I want to hurt him? But no one pays attention to people getting hurt no more."

Hale's breath became labored. "Just you make sure you write down that Peterson was a liar, lived a lie, okay? Told the world that he had an above ninety percent rate of getting Express Mail there on time. Liar! See, I was here, Ralph. Fourteen years. I know how poorly treated the mail was . . ."

Baker struggled to keep up with Hale's rantings. "I'm taking it down, Lester . . ."

"Pale Rider!"

"Sorry, Pale Rider. Let's just keep talking. Okay?"

Hale wheezed. "I'd like that . . . But first, Ralph, I'm going to ask you a very important question. Have you accepted Jesus Christ as your savior?"

Baker paused, unsure of what to say; he didn't want to lie and yet he didn't want to lose Hale. "No, I haven't, Pale Rider. I'm a reporter. It's my job not to get involved."

"Even with your Savior?"

"It's a strange business."

"Sounds as nuts as the Postal Service."

By now LaFontaine had spread the word. Lawlor had emerged from his office as had Tower, Harpster, Pace, and the rest of Lobotomy Lane. They all stood behind Claudette X, who had hacked into the computer system so she could watch Baker work in real time. Several of the Stepford Editors commiserated on the periphery of the crowd, assuring each other that they knew all along that even with a week to go before retirement, Ralph Baker remained a reporter to contend with.

"How's he doing?" Lawlor asked.

"He's out of his mind," Claudette X said. "Ralph's got this guy thinking he's his buddy."

"McCarthy getting us stuff from the inside?"

She hesitated, then lied for her friend. "And Blitzer and Croon are on the scene."

"Okay. We sched Ralph with a leading story for A-1. Slug it: A talk with the shooter."

"Absolutely," Geld said.

Harpster said, "But if the nut shoots the horse, we'll play the news story higher than the conversation."

Lawlor ran his tongue along the inside of his cheek. "Done." He walked back toward his office, shaking his head. "Ralph Baker!"

Tower stared at the leather-clad reporter for another minute. He clenched his fist and stalked back to his office.

For the next hour and a half Baker played personal advice columnist to Lester Hale. It was, in News's words, "a case of the dyed leading the bleached." Three times the police tried to get Hale to talk to their negotiator, who had finally made it through the traffic jam. But the shooter seemed to find in Baker a kindred spirit and he refused to speak with anyone else. The negotiator came to the newsroom to observe and advise.

In fits and starts, between rants about liars, above the echoing of the police bullhorns, Hale told Orbison how he'd come to be in the central receiving room of the main post office with two dead and five held hostage. And a 9mm Glock held to the head of Teddy the pony.

Hale was thirty-seven. During his first five years as a letter carrier the Southern California sun burned his skin so bad that several times he put in for disability. All his requests were denied. At the same time he married a woman named Cary Burns, who believed they were living in end time, the era in which the Bible prophesies that Jesus will return to Earth to judge the living and the dead.

Ten years into his career Hale took to preaching to customers of special delivery about end time. There were complaints. He was transferred to the central sorting room. Soon after, Cary Burns Hale decided that perhaps Jesus was not returning to judge the living and the dead quite so soon and that perhaps she might be better off as a croupier at a Las Vegas casino. Hale never forgave "the Jezebel," as he called her. He asked to be transferred to the graveyard shift.

"Didn't like the sun. Hurts my eyes, Ralph. Besides, at

night you think more, see clearer. That's when I came upon the big lie. All these blue overnight packages, *the express ones*, that wouldn't get there on time. And the public being charged double the going rate, for a LIE!

"That's when I decided to go into the past, check out the Pony Express. A lie, too! Sure the mail got there, but almost always late. Killed horses to do it, too. That operation only lasted eighteen months. You should check it out, Ralph."

"I appreciate the tip," Baker said, sadly.

"Something wrong there, Ralph?" Hale asked.

Baker looked around the newsroom, at all the people watching him, at all the machinery and the quirks of character and process that went into making *The Post*.

"I was just thinking how strange life gets, Pale Rider. How it turns and twists and buries itself on you."

"For you, too, huh?" Hale said. "They made fun of me here a lot. It's like when you don't conform, they shun you, you know?"

"Pale Rider, is that what made you angry? Is that what made you want to kill?"

There was silence on the other end of the line for a long time, then Hale said: "No, Ralph. I just heard a voice the other week, after they fired me for being late so much. Kept saying I had to ride the white horse to the end of time. So here I am."

"You sound tired, Pale Rider."

"Not so much. God has always looked kindly on those who toil. How they doing on that commercial, Ralph?"

"I'll check." He put down the phone and looked at the police negotiator. "What should I tell him?"

"The SWAT team is set," said the negotiator, a short black man in a cream sport coat. "Ask him to give himself up."

Baker picked up the phone. "It's going to be on the news, Pale Rider, everything you said and did and why you did it.

Don't you think it's time to go out and let those people and little Teddy go?"

"Told you I'm going to ride this little white horse in," Hale scolded. "After my chores are done. Got to clean up here, Ralph, starting with liar Peterson."

Baker looked at the photo of Abigail Van Buren above today's column. He ran his finger across the newsprint, smudging the picture. "They've got you surrounded."

There was silence on the receiver, then: "I've been surrounded for a long time, Ralph. I'm used to it. I've got chores now. No more questions. Time to die. Time to die."

The police negotiator said "Go" into his radio. Over the phone Baker heard the crackle of gunfire, people screaming, and behind it all, shrill neighing.

"Pale Rider? Pale Rider, are you there?"

When the SWAT team opened up, Croon was ready. He caught the movement of the three officers belaying from the roof on a rope. He fired his camera as they pitched through the open door of the loading dock. Then he was running behind the sniper, squeezing off frame after frame of the tragedy as it unfolded.

Blitzer dodged two patrol officers assigned to keep her at bay and tore at the real-life drama. Hale made the sign of the cross, then head-shot Peterson the postmaster. One of the female supervisors on the floor kicked Hale in the testicles as he crouched over her dead boss. A SWAT team member completed the pacification by shooting Hale through the right thigh. The bullet continued on and blew a hole the size of a chestnut in Teddy the Pony's gut. Hale hugged the horse as it died, crying, "Oh, Teddy! Teddy. These are they which came out of great tribulation, and have washed their robes, and made them white in the blood of the little horse!"

Croon and Blitzer bulled their way into the climax scene

and knelt before the madman. She scribbled down his fumings. He photographed the gone prophet's agony and Teddy's final moments.

When the medics carried Hale out on a stretcher into a white ambulance, Croon and Blitzer silently thanked the skies for bringing this harsh reality into their lives. It was by far the best misfortune of the year. And it had wound up an hour and a half before final deadline: A perfect package! Then they pointed and giggled: the P.C. Oracle had peeked in to view the carnage. One look at the dead pony and she had keeled sideways and was now on all fours, retching in the bushes.

Ralph Baker watched it all on television.

"In a tragic conclusion to today's hostage situation, a SWAT officer shot a miniature pony to death," Fairbanks began. "Three others lost their lives in the storming of the city's post office, including Carl Peterson, the city's postmaster."

The voice of the evening anchorwoman broke in. "You say that the SWAT team shot the pony, Paul. Will there be repercussions?"

"Undoubtedly, Sharon," Fairbanks replied, pressing his earphone tightly into his canal. "Already in the crowd behind us, animal activists are gathering to protest the killing. Some are questioning whether the police acted in haste, not taking the pony's safety into account before storming the loading dock."

The camera shifted to show a group of people yelling obscenities at the police. Margaret Savage stood before them, writing down every word.

Claudette X hoisted Baker out of his chair and hugged him. "Roy Orbison, you were unbelievable. Absolutely unbelievable."

All around him the members of the newsroom cheered and clapped.

He murmured, "It's nothing to be happy about, Claudette. That was a real tragedy."

"Nonsense," Lawlor said. "You did us proud. Ed?"

Tower seemed as if he didn't want to be there. He coughed. "You kept your objectivity in a tough go of it. Congratulations. Only a week left?"

"Yes," Baker said.

Tower looked at Lawlor. "Hard to believe the three of us started out together more than thirty years ago. And look at us all now."

Baker gave Tower a strange, knowing look that seemed to unnerve the Editor for Newsroom Operations.

Tower hemmed and hawed, then said, "Well . . . Ralph . . . a good job. I, I look forward to reading it."

Tower hurried back toward his office.

Lawlor stared after him, then returned his attention to Baker. "Why don't you take the week off, on us. Start your retirement early. You earned it."

He clapped Baker on the shoulder and went off. Baker plopped down at his desk, exhausted. "I didn't prevent him from killing Peterson. Ann Landers would have."

Claudette X said: "No, she wouldn't have. Ann Landers and Dear Abby sit in offices reading letters and composing responses. You did your best at something you weren't prepared to do—negotiating with a lunatic. Now I want you to be your best at something you are prepared to do: writing a good news story."

Baker tugged at his impossibly black hair, then nodded: "Claudette, I'm going to need some coffee if I'm going to write this up."

Claudette X beamed. "Now you're talking! I'll get it myself, Ralph. Cream?"

"And sugar." He paused. "And maybe just a splash of vodka . . . to still the clanging, you know?"

Claudette X fished in the pockets of her jumpsuit and pulled out a five-dollar bill. "Split of vodka, cream, and sugar it is."

Twenty feet away, LaFontaine smiled at the tangy taste he got in his mouth watching the meanest woman he knew hugging the second most burned-out reporter he knew. He opened GOSDI on his computer and took notes for future oral renditions of the day when Roy Orbison rose from the deathbed of his career to sing strange harmony with an end time crackpot and a pony named Ted.

Dusk Falls . . .

McCarthy heard much of the action on an all-news radio station. His forehead pounded cold as if he'd been force-fed a gallon of ice cream. Part of the story belonged to him and he hadn't showed. He slouched in the front seat, asking himself what he'd do if he lost the job. Few alternatives suggested themselves: teaching, he supposed, advertising, or public relations. He shuddered at the latter course, then quelled these thoughts by following radio developments in the Hale shooting until eight o'clock, when a reporter cornered eight-year-old Tess Knight as she left a ballet class. She was the pony's owner. Her parents hadn't told her that Teddy was missing. Tess's sobs made McCarthy think of Miriam and the way she slept with Malice curled at the foot of her bed. He'd told her that her father was going to visit. She just smiled and said, "That's nice. Will he bring me a present?"

Depressed, McCarthy switched the broadcast off. There used to be among news outlets an unwritten limit on how deep a reporter would intrude into ordinary people's lives caught up in extraordinary events. Only tabloid slimeballs ignored the restriction.

In the past ten years, however, the demarcation of legitimacy had been obliterated between grocery store weeklies and great gray ladies. They all ignored the line that said don't talk to a little girl who thinks her pony is safe in the barn, not assassinated by a religious lunatic. He didn't know exactly what started the rampage. Economics, competition, an expanding number of news outlets without a corresponding expansion in real news. Ego. All had played a part though the latter force seemed paramount.

The sad thing was that he knew the role well. He could see the radio reporter gleefully telling comrades over a beer about how she "broke the Tess Knight angle." Grief is as hard a currency in the news business as sex and scandal.

By nine o'clock his butt hurt. He was ravenous and thirsty. He fished in his glove compartment and came up with two stale peanut butter cups. He used Laura Milk's outdoor faucet for a drink. He fell asleep around eleven.

At two in the morning he awoke, got out and urinated, then fell asleep again. He was startled awake at three-thirty by the sound of a car door shutting. He shivered. A fog had rolled in off the ocean. Footsteps on the sidewalk now. Two people appeared out of the mist, then evaporated through the back gate at 3345. McCarthy's breath turned shallow and rapid. At times like these—when a reporter knows he's on the verge of breaking something really big—the danger lies in allowing preconceptions to obstruct the flow of possibilities. He rapidly raised his arms up and down. He jogged in place to bring blood to his tired brain. He slipped to the rear of the house, waiting just inside the gate for ten minutes, then knocked softly at the back door.

"Bill?" came a deep gravelly voice from the other side. A male's voice.

"My name's McCarthy. I write for *The Post*. I think you

and Dusk are in trouble and you need to tell someone what you've heard. I spoke with Delta Porter and Tabor."

There was a shuffling noise and then murmurs and then nothing for several minutes. McCarthy rapped again. A hurtling form in his peripheral vision shot out of the night, clouted him high in the shoulders, and blew him sideways through a trellis and into pricker bushes. Warm liquid the taste of copper trickled from his lip. Something quick and small moved in the mist to his right. He groaned, "Hey, I'm a reporter, I'm not here to . . ."

A wildly flung boot grazed McCarthy's ribs, swung back, and prepared to kick again. McCarthy rolled to his left, dodging the next blow, frantically trying to remember some of the self-defense moves he'd learned in a class several years before.

He got to his feet and crouched in a triangular stance. The man rushed straight at him. McCarthy stepped off the line of his attack and threw his forearm at what he figured was the man's head. He missed the head, but caught the neck flush. The man crumpled with a soft grunt. A knife clattered at McCarthy's feet. He grabbed it, more terrified now than during the fight. The man choked and clawed at his throat. He rolled over onto his knees. McCarthy knelt next to him and held the knife to his neck.

"I got your knife here, right where you don't want it," he said hoarsely. "I'll tell you again, I'm not here to hurt you."

"Fuck you, this is deadly," the man said, sounding like cellophane being torn.

"I told you . . ."

A woman behind McCarthy and to his left said, "There's a baseball bat in my hand. I won't miss. Put the knife down."

On instinct, the reporter said, "You may hit me, but I'll fall forward onto his neck. I don't put it down until you agree to talk."

McCarthy pressed the knife into the man's skin. He brayed hoarsely, "Chrissy, for fuck's sake hit him!"

"Carol Gentry's dead," McCarthy blurted. "People who knew her have been hurt. If you don't tell someone outside the system, you could be next. Homicide is watching the place on Farnsworth. You're just lucky I figured out Larry's mother lived here first."

The next thirty seconds were the longest of McCarthy's life. In the chill darkness he focused on the faint glint of the knife. It was as if everything he'd done in the last few months could be absolved by that glimmer.

The bat thunked on the cement pool deck. "Okay, we talk," she said.

"No," the man complained. "We don't know who he is."

"I don't care. People got to know. And I'm sick of being all hopped up like this."

A door opened. Light flooded out onto the patio. McCarthy squinted at the retreating figure of a woman in a brown bathrobe then down at the scrawny little man in dirty Levi's, a tan tank top, and a black leather motorcycle vest. The Milkman hadn't shaved or showered in several days. His brown hair clung oily to his scalp. A falcon tattoo graced his left forearm. Milk winced in the glare and said, "The blade, man."

McCarthy relaxed the pressure. Milk slowly got up, rubbing his neck. McCarthy motioned with the knife toward the door and followed the biker inside past a six-foot stack of tabloid papers into a bedroom lit by two naked light bulbs. A cage occupied the center of a three-legged card table jammed against the wall. The white rat inside wiggled its nose at McCarthy. The competing odors of rodent and Laura Milk hung in the air.

McCarthy tossed the knife out into the darkness, then shut the door. Dusk gave McCarthy a short appraisal, then disappeared behind an army blanket clothespinned to a rope slung across a doorway. Milk straddled a chair with two broken slats and considered the floor as if it were his enemy. Dusk returned with a washcloth.

"You're bleeding," she said to McCarthy. "Wipe yourself off."

Dusk dwarfed her boyfriend. She was close to six feet, with heavy bones and generous weight. Her dark hair framed an oblong face dominated by wide brown eyes, pretty by themselves. The dour set of her lips and cheeks stunted the overall effect. She sat, uneasy, on the other chair at the card table. Her fingers trembled as she drew out a cigarette and lit it. "What do you want to know?" she asked.

McCarthy lowered himself gingerly onto the burst springs of a green sofa and pulled out his notebook. "Just what you heard."

"Hold on," Milk said. "I know how this reporting stuff goes down. Right now, you know you can hear it all. But no names."

McCarthy grimaced. "Without names I can't attribute. Without attribution to what I think you know, I can't publish."

"I don't give a shit," Milk said. "You want to hear it, you play by our rules."

McCarthy asked Dusk, "That how you want it?"

"Got to cover our own, you know?"

McCarthy thought about it a second, then said, "Deal."

Dusk told him that Gentry was not a regular on the Boulevard. She had an attitude and talked about attending sex parties for big money. Gentry even offered the phone number of her outcall service to Dusk and some of the other street whores. Only one, a girl named Shirley Barfield, ever called.

"You have the phone number?"

Dusk said, "Yeah, maybe. Hold on a second."

She disappeared through a door. Somewhere down the hallway, Laura Milk stirred. She cried out "MARY MAG-

DALENE REINCARNATES AS FLORENCE NIGHT-INGALE!"

Dusk shushed her.

Milk jutted his chin toward the door. "She's the only one can keep my mama in line. Otherwise, they'd have her down to county mental health in some lockup."

"You know she can't stay here much longer."

"We'll care for her here long as we can. It's her home."

Dusk entered the room and handed McCarthy a slip of paper with a phone number and a name on it.

"Tiger?" McCarthy asked.

"Probably the brains behind the outcall," Dusk said. "I never wanted to be under anyone's thumb like that."

McCarthy folded the slip and put it in his pocket.

Dusk went on, telling McCarthy that Gentry claimed to have screwed an old rich guy to death at one of the parties. She had the money that went with that kind of scene, so Dusk believed her. When McCarthy asked why an outcall hooker making big money would work the streets, Dusk said that Gentry was a freak who liked the danger of the Boulevard, who liked to taunt the police, letting them know she wasn't afraid.

McCarthy decided to press Dusk. "This is all interesting, but Delta Porter says you heard some cops talking about killing Gentry."

Dusk twisted a length of her hair between her thumb and forefinger.

McCarthy said, "I have to hear it if I'm going to protect you."

Dusk nodded, fumbling for another cigarette. "It was probably like eight weeks ago, about a month after she first testified. A Friday night and I'm out early, six, seven o'clock, and they roll through with the wagon."

McCarthy looked at her confused.

"You know, a wagon. When they do sweeps on the Boulevard, they bring in a rolling cage to put us all in so they don't have to make twenty trips to the jail. It's standard. Anyway, I'm the first one to get popped and thrown in the cage. It's parked in an empty lot up there at Seventy-seventh."

Dusk swam in the flow of her story now. "I'm sitting in there alone wanting a smoke, and I hear these two cops start talking and pretty soon I know who they're talking about. They're saying shit about 'this bitch Gentry making trouble for them.' "

"How come they're talking in front of you?"

"Not in front of me. They're out by a patrol car. But what they're saying is echoing off the wall of the furniture store. I could hear it almost as clear as you and me right now."

"What did they look like?"

"A short fat cop with reddish hair and a tall Mex, he was in charge. After they found Carol, I went to the library to look up the stories about Gentry testifying. The little guy was the one they call Click. The other one was Blanca, the lieutenant she testified about."

McCarthy closed his eyes for a second. *I'll be a son of a bitch,* he thought. *I got it.* "You're positive?"

"You don't forget faces when they say stuff about killing someone. Click, he was pacing back and forth. He says maybe she could disappear and the whole thing would be dropped. Blanca kind of nods, but says they can't be involved. But maybe there's someone who can do it for them. And Click says he knows someone who owes him, who'd do it as a favor. Blanca just stands there stone-faced, saying he wished he'd never met her."

"Then what?"

"Then nothing."

"Nothing?"

"That's all of it, man," Milk said. "Then a bunch of other girls was brought in and they stopped talking."

McCarthy's lungs suddenly collapsed inward. Four-thirty. He hadn't slept well in weeks. He'd crossed a desert and wanted nothing more than to press his face into cool water. And then the need to sleep was washed away by the understanding of what was required before publication. He breathed deep again, reaching for his second wind. He had Dusk repeat the story.

Satisfied he had it all, he said, "Couple more questions. How come you haven't gone to the cops with this?"

Dusk pursed her lips in disgust. "Jesus, who are they going to protect, me or one of their own?"

"If I write this, Fisk, the homicide lieutenant, will want to talk. I mean, it's obvious he already does."

Milk screwed up his face. "I guess that's okay, then. Cause the fuckers can't just ignore it once it hits the papers, can they?"

"No, they can't," McCarthy said. He looked at both of them with a critical eye. They were lowlifes, but even lowlifes can tell the truth. "I believe you heard what you said you heard and I'm going to try to write it."

"No names," Milk reminded him.

"They're going to come out eventually if you're called as witnesses."

"Let that happen when it happens," Milk said. "We had a deal."

"Yes, we do."

"When's this going in?" Dusk asked.

"We're going to try for tomorrow."

Dusk crushed the cigarette package and began to shake violently. "Tomorrow? Christ, I don't know . . ."

"It's better that we move quickly," McCarthy said. "Get it out in the open. Homicide's right behind me. If it's printed, they have to act righteously."

She waved the crushed package in a gesture of helpless agreement. "Okay."

McCarthy got up to leave. As he opened the door, Laura Milk cut loose with her strange cackle. The Milkman looked at Dusk. "We got to get her fed, then get out of here before it gets light."

McCarthy shook Milk's hand, then Dusk's. He glanced at the white rat sniffing at the cage door and left.

He leaned his head on the roof of his car and chuckled. A hit, a goddamned contract let by cops! Cops with motive. His teeth and then his whole head spreading to his body pulsed with the electrical current of giddy knowledge. He jumped and did a three-sixty in the air. The best story he'd gotten in years, maybe ever! Think of the headlines! Think of the sick gut feeling Karen Rivers will get tomorrow about this time when the phone rings and some panicked early morning editor wakes her!

Think of what Connor Lawlor will say. Think of the expression on Ed Tower's face when he knows I'm back.

In the eastern sky the first pale fingers of light glowed incandescent. McCarthy gazed at the rosy, otherworldly display and smiled. The dawn was no longer a sickening event. His longest night was ending at last.

Part 2

DON'T KILL THE MESSENGER

Her Story Ain't
Doodly-Squat . . .

*T*he *Post*'s city editor slipped up to the long bank of open cubbyhole mailboxes in the back hallway of *The Post* newsroom. From his briefcase Stanley Geld took two interoffice memo envelopes. He looked around to make sure no one was watching, then popped one into Bobbie Anne Pace's box and a second into Neil Harpster's.

He smiled, then rushed off toward the city desk. It was only 9:00 A.M., but Claudette X was already there. She held up the front section of *The Beacon* to him, then whipped it down on her desk.

"McCarthy's history."

"What?" he said, still thinking about his surreptitious deed. "Oh, yeah, I saw that. I'll be putting together his discharge package this morning."

"You seem real upset."

Geld shrugged. "No one said this was a socialistic business. No one's entitled to a job. McCarthy made his choice, now he suffers. Anyway, I got other things on my mind."

Geld went off toward the elevator. Claudette X shook her head. Geld was acting weird these days, but what else was new? As for McCarthy, they had no choice now. McCarthy had disobeyed her direct order by not showing up to work night cops. Because of that *The Post*'s coverage of the Lester Hale fiasco lacked a crucial angle: the ballistics report on why Teddy the Pony died in the shoot-out.

Karen Rivers had the ballistics report story on A-1, right next to her latest scoop on the Gentry slaying. That piece included an interview with the estranged brother McCarthy was supposed to have followed up on. Gentry's brother told Rivers that as a teenager she developed an unsavory reputation in her hometown for sleeping with middle-aged businessmen, then leveraging money from them in return for not telling their wives. It had all blown up when one of the wives tried to shoot Gentry, and she'd run away.

The executive assistant city editor swiveled in her chair. Only a handful of reporters had arrived yet. Most of those who were here were still talking about the resurrection of Roy Orbison. She allowed herself to feel agreeable and sad about that at the same time.

Claudette X had remained with the old reporter long into the night as he framed and fitted his article. Four coffees and three splits of vodka later, they had gone together to the plant to watch the first edition roll off the presses.

"Great story," she had said simply.

"Best I've had in years," Baker replied. He held the paper as if it were fine china. His story began in bold print at the top of the page above one of Augustus Croon's photographs of the SWAT team subduing Lester Hale while he clung to the dead pet horse.

Abby Blitzer's roundup jumped off the right side of A-1. A shadow box alerted readers that Margaret Savage had an obtuse opinion on the entire event in the Metro section. The P.C. Oracle believed Hale drew his rage less from his treatment by the U.S. Postal Service than from the fact that society used the term "Albino" to describe him. She considered it psychologically brutal and proposed "Melanin Challenged" as an alternative. She planned a follow-up story on the symbolic import of the pony's death.

"So this is it for you," Claudette X said to Baker. "Connor says you've got next week off. You're retired as of now. How does it feel?"

"I don't want to take next week off," he protested.

Claudette X crossed her arms across her massive chest. "Not too many people drive a home run into the bleachers on their last at bat. You're only Ted Williams if you make this your last at bat."

Baker adjusted his glasses, gazed up at the huge editor, and felt the urge for a double vodka. "I guess so, it's just that . . ."

"Just nothing," Claudette X said. "You should know better than most that this business is cruel to those who stay too long."

He scuffed his black leather boots on the cement floor. "It's just . . . well . . . I don't know how to leave."

Ordinarily that would have annoyed Claudette X. This day, however, she'd witnessed a miracle. She summoned up as much empathy as she could muster and put her densely muscled hand on the old reporter's shoulder. "I don't think anyone knows how to leave something they love, even if the infatuation is memory and the love has become painful. In the end you just try to walk out with as much dignity as you can."

"A newspaper is all I know."

"You're thinking about tomorrow. That's something different," Claudette X said. "I'm talking about the leaving— with the crowd cheering."

Baker watched the gigantic presses thunder with the force of his own words on paper. Claudette X watched, too. He turned finally and put out his hand. "Thank you," he said. "Thank you for being a kind person."

Claudette X winced. "I wasn't being kind. I'm not kind! Ralph. I was . . . I was."

The rock star reporter smiled at her embarrassment. "Dear Abby would have been proud of you," he said. He picked up another copy of the paper off the stack, tucked it under his arm, and walked through the plant door into the foggy night.

Sitting at her desk the next morning, Claudette X wished every reporter who'd stayed in the business past burnout could leave like Ralph Baker. But the plain truth was that the majority would dwindle like the Zombie, embittered, wondering how the riptide of current events had eventually worn them down, left them far from shore, drowning in a filthy brine they didn't understand.

She pondered for a moment how well she was swimming these days. No nightmares last night. Probably too tired for it. But she knew they threatened every time she shut her eyes.

McCarthy stumbled into the newsroom. His salt-and-pepper hair flying in six directions, his white polo shirt stained with coffee and peanut butter and blood. Bags hung under his eyes. His mouth was swollen.

"McCarthy!" she roared. "You're fired!"

McCarthy turned bleary-eyed to her. "Do that and you'll be the sorriest editor alive tomorrow morning."

She picked up *The Beacon*. "You seen this? You're fired!"

"My tale is red-hot, her story ain't doodly-squat!"

She stopped, his words like water on her fury. "You got it, you got the hit?"

"Close enough," he said. He sat on the edge of her desk and related all that he'd learned from Dusk and Milk.

"They had her killed," she said in awe. "I don't believe it."

Geld arrived. "You're fired, McCarthy."

"Hold it, Stan," Claudette X said. "You won't believe this."

She had him repeat it all again for the city editor. Geld

took notes, thought about them, then said, "Connor won't publish without attribution. Too explosive."

"What are you talking about?" McCarthy demanded. "We know Fisk is after them for the same reason. I just got there first."

"We don't know that," Geld said. "You're assuming it."

"No offense, Stan, but you haven't been on the street in ten years," McCarthy said. "You couldn't see the connection here if it bit your thigh."

"McCarthy," Geld bristled, "I may ride a desk, but I still know news and this story will sit until you get attribution."

"I want Connor to make the call on this one," McCarthy said.

Forty-five minutes later they all trooped into Lawlor's office, Claudette X, Geld, Ed Tower, and McCarthy. As they seated themselves, Neil Harpster and then Bobbie Anne Pace, who'd gotten wind of the story, arrived from opposite ends of Lobotomy Lane.

Lawlor glanced at them and waved them off. "No need to make this more complicated than it is. I'm sure you both have business to attend to."

Harpster fiddled with his tie knot, nodded awkwardly, and left. Pace curled her hand into a fist, made as if to say something, then followed Harpster. Geld shut the door behind them, then sat, a bizarre expression plastered across his face.

Geld's facial cast unnerved Claudette X so much that it was a long time before she realized McCarthy was telling the story again, how he'd tracked Gentry, how her house had been broken into, how Billy Kemper had been beaten, how Delta Porter and Tabor were on the run, how Dusk had overheard Click Patrick and Diego Blanca talking about having Gentry killed.

Lawlor sat forward in his chair, his chin in his hands. He

squinted at McCarthy. "How many times has Dusk, or Evers, or whatever she calls herself been arrested?"

McCarthy shifted in his seat. "Dozens."

"Hardly an unimpeachable source," Tower observed.

"It takes a snake to know a snake," McCarthy replied.

"That's my problem with this whole story, it's filled with snakes," Tower sniffed. "Whores and killings, it all strikes me as a seedy world *The Post* has no business chronicling."

Everyone in the room, including Lawlor, groaned.

"You're outvoted on that one, Ed," Lawlor said. "The plain fact is that it's a hell of a story. But I'd be more likely to publish if our serpentine source would use her name. If she knows she's going to be called eventually to testify in public, why not?"

McCarthy threw up his hands. "These people are all paranoids."

Lawlor pushed back in his chair. "This would be like dropping an A-bomb on *The Beacon*. But, damn it, the story comes from a shaky source."

Tower added, "And we intend to let a reporter with a troubled past tell it."

The tips of McCarthy's ears burned, but he said nothing.

Tower went on, "One must be clear-eyed about crossing thin ice."

"You saying we can't publish?" McCarthy said. "Because if you are, I'm gonna quit and take this across the street."

Lawlor broke into a toothy smile. "That's the first time in nearly two years I've seen the old McCarthy passion. But son, I agree with Ed, we can't publish."

"There you are," Geld said.

McCarthy stood, fists clenched.

Lawlor waved a finger at him. "Even an old horse like me can see this story's a keeper. What we don't have is a vehicle with which to print it. By that I mean some source with more credibility than this Dusk or whatever she calls herself that we can pin this on without wading into serious libel problems. Basically, because of the anonymity you granted, you are asking we, *The Post*, to call these two officers killers, am I right?"

McCarthy hated to admit it, but he said, "Yes."

"Okay, then. You know we can't do that without giving some damn attorney the keys to my dwindling bank accounts. We need an authority to call those two cops killers."

The seven sat silent, thinking. After nearly five minutes, Lawlor snapped his fingers and said, "You saw this homicide lieutenant staking out their house."

"Fisk? Yes."

"So he's probably heard the story somewhere or a version of it."

McCarthy saw immediately where the editor was going. "So I tell Fisk that I've heard the story straight from the source and I know he's following it . . ."

Geld broke in, "And you get him to admit it's a prime vein of the investigation in return for the specifics."

"And we back door the story into print on Fisk's admission that he's looking into it," Claudette X finished.

Lawlor drummed his open palms on his desk. "And tomorrow *The Post* publishes a story that gives Harry Plake and the rest of *The Beacon* staff the peptic ulcer of a lifetime."

Everyone, with the exception of Tower, grinned like idiots. Lawlor spun in his chair to look over at *The Beacon* newsroom. "I haven't had this much fun in years."

Then he turned serious. "So what are you waiting for? Get that lieutenant on the horn. This will have to go through every damned lawyer I have before 9:00 P.M. tonight."

McCarthy bolted for the door.

"Gideon!" Lawlor yelled after him.

The reporter stopped and turned. "Yes?"

Lawlor said, "I still don't excuse you your recent transgressions. But I would be remiss if I did not tell you that you can be one hell of a reporter when you want to be."

McCarthy smiled at the editor-in-chief. "Thanks, Connor. It means a lot."

When Geld and Claudette X had returned to their desks, Tower remained behind.

"Ed?"

Tower shut the door. "I have a problem with this story."

"So you said." Lawlor seemed preoccupied.

"I think we put the paper in a very awkward position if we publish this."

"Out with it, Ed."

Tower cleared his throat. "This will be extremely embarrassing to Ricardo's campaign. We're saying cops under Chief Leslie ordered a contract murder. Leslie's Ricardo's campaign manager. I wonder if we do a disservice to both of them by acting on the word of a street whore."

Lawlor picked up the roll of magnets from the desk. He didn't reply for several moments, then said, "I don't give a damn what effect this has on the campaign. We are not in the business of taking sides."

Tower's skin turned magenta. "That's not what I . . ."

"That's exactly what you meant, Ed. I know you have to deal with these folks at social functions. So do I. But our job here is to get at the truth and let it play out. Ricardo's been a good mayor, the best, I think. Leslie's been a good chief, probably the best, too. One bad story won't hurt either of them."

Tower made as if to argue. Lawlor cut him off. "End of discussion. I've got some calls to make now."

Tower clenched his teeth and slowly walked out.

*   *   *

McCarthy made repeated calls to Fisk's office the rest of the morning. Only when he told his secretary that *The Post* was about to publish a story that would blow the Gentry case wide open did Fisk finally call about two in the afternoon.

"What's up, McCarthy? Need a quote so you can follow up Rivers's latest?" was the first thing the diminutive lieutenant said.

"Gee, Fisko, you get any better with your quips and you'll get your own late-night talk show," McCarthy replied.

"My agent's taking meetings in Hollywood as we speak," Fisk said. "Now what do you got? I have to be somewhere in ten minutes."

"Out in front of Larry Milk's house, perhaps?" McCarthy asked.

The silence on the other end was so profound McCarthy wanted to cheer.

"Larry Milk?" Fisk said finally. "I don't believe . . ."

"I saw you staking out the place yesterday, Lieutenant," McCarthy said. "Too bad, I got to Larry and Christine first. Heard the whole thing. Sounds like you got some bad bad boys in your department."

Fisk didn't say anything for so long that McCarthy thought he'd passed out.

"Lieutenant?"

"I'm here," Fisk said at last. "Tell me what she said."

An oblique admission of interest. Not enough to print the story. McCarthy needed a clear confirmation.

"I'll show you mine if you show me yours," McCarthy said. "You've got an idea what she overheard and this is a prime avenue of your investigation, correct?"

Fisk hesitated. "Told you before, McCarthy, I don't discuss the particulars of an ongoing investigation."

McCarthy decided to bluff. "Too bad. I guess you'll have to read about it in the papers tomorrow. Kind of look strange to the average reader to see the newspaper opening up an angle the homicide supervisor hadn't even considered, especially when it seems that two police officers might be involved in the murder."

Fisk cleared his throat, "You're prepared to publish?"

"We are," McCarthy fibbed.

"I'm going to have to get back to you. Will you be there in five minutes?"

"Awaiting your cheery voice with bated breath," McCarthy said. He hung up the phone and smiled. Lawlor was right; he hadn't had this much fun in years!

"Wipe that silly smirk off your face," said Prentice LaFontaine, who'd just arrived at his desk. "I'll have you know you missed the best gossip of the year. Last night Roy Orbison sang better than Buddy Holly."

McCarthy's smile intensified. "I heard."

"I'm surprised to even see you here this morning. Ms. X was all set to give you notice last night."

"I seem to have redeemed myself."

LaFontaine saw he was serious. "The lady of the night talked?"

McCarthy wiggled his eyebrows.

"My, my. Next thing we know, the Zombie will deliver a soliloquy from *Hamlet* right in the newsroom. Or heavens! I'll write something!"

"Still nothing concrete on Burkhardt?"

"The man's a rapist and a power-mad deviate. Problem is I can't prove it. Yet."

The phone rang on McCarthy's desk. He picked it up. "Hello, Lieutenant."

"That confident, huh McCarthy?" Fisk replied.

"When you're hot, you're hot."

"I imagine you'd be willing to share with me what Ms. Evers said."

"If the right words come from your mouth, I imagine so."

Fisk said tersely, "We have heard a rumor on the street concerning discussions by certain police officers regarding the arrangement of the killing of Carol Alice Gentry. We take the rumor seriously enough that we are actively investigating it. End of statement. You got that, McCarthy?"

McCarthy pumped his fist above his head. "Every word, Lieutenant. Every beautiful word."

Sex, Satyrs, and Howling Wolves . . .

Neil Harpster dug his fingernails into the finish on his desk top and stared at the memo he'd found in his mailbox earlier that morning. A letter responding to a query from Ed Tower. Obviously a case of someone in human resources stuffing the wrong memo in the wrong envelope. The letter gave the Editor for Newsroom Operations a full breakdown of what he could expect in income from his pension plan and 401K.

Harpster's first thought had been to reseal the memo and send it on to Tower immediately; after all it was personal and confidential. His second thought was to rejoice at his great good fortune. There was no other explanation: *The Post*'s number two man planned to retire sometime in the next year! Harpster photocopied the memo, then sent on the original, his mind whirling at the possibilities.

Harpster picked away the gobs of varnish under his fingernails. Dramatic upheaval coming soon. Harpster's moment. He'd been a good manager of the 1990s, studied the writings of William Tecumseh Sherman. He knew that those who act with decisive and ruthless intent often reap great victory. Unless Connor Lawlor did the unthinkable and looked outside *The Post* for a replacement, he only had one rival for the position: Bobbie Anne Pace. A fashion flake. No real competition.

Now was the time for Harpster to demonstrate his leadership ability. He'd had a chance yesterday when the albino took the pony hostage, but that Ubangi giantess on the city desk, the one with the perpetual attitude, had brushed him off. He was tired, too. Lydia had kept him up to all hours whining about the bastard vandal who was destroying her beloved garden. And then this morning, the final indignity—shut out of the editorial conference on the most explosive story to be broken by a *Post* reporter in years.

He followed the loops and twirls in Tower's signature, trying to plot another course of action. But as often happened to the Assistant Managing Editor for Form and Content during times of mental stress, his efforts to assure his long-term future gave way to the need to assuage his short-term physical needs. He tried to deny it, but the demand grew in his gut and spread through his loins until he could think of nothing else. He had to rid himself of the sensation or the day was lost.

He put the memo back in his desk, allowing his attention to wander to the black a-line short skirt worn by Connie Mills as she keyed in the results of his latest reader focus group into the computer. No need for her to know about the memo. It might disturb her concentration and he could feel that he needed her to be extra concentrated today. He picked up his phone and punched her extension.

"This is Connie."

"I know a motel on State Street," Harpster whispered.

"Is that a fact?"

"It is. And I know that in about a half hour there will be a brown satchel there in room 11 B."

"Hmmm, what might be in the satchel?"

Harpster gripped the phone tightly, "Fur leggings with zippers up the back, a pair of little horns, and a flute."

There was a slight, sharp intake of breath on the other

end of the line, then, "I know there's a big, big bathtub in room 11 B."

"Is that a fact?" Harpster replied.

"It is. And if you use your imagination that tub becomes a pool off in the woods. Beside it a wood nymph sits, pondering her reflection, unaware that a satyr watches."

At that, the vision of Mills' firm backside and plump tits slipping into the warm bath as he cavorted about blowing on a pan flute seized Harpster. He forgot about pension memos and garden vandals and fashion flakes and cops and tattletale hookers. As if in a trance he hung up the phone, walked out to her desk, and said loud enough for half the newsroom to hear, "I'm off to lunch, Connie. If anyone needs me, I'll be back in an hour."

Mills nodded dreamily and ran her finger lazily on the top of her desk as if she were dipping it in the waters of a cool, sylvan stream.

One hundred feet away, Bobbie Anne Pace glanced up to see Neil Harpster hurry out of the newsroom red-faced, clutching a brown satchel. She studied him for a moment as one would a dread enemy then returned to the memo on her desk describing what could only be the impending retirement of Ed Tower.

She picked up the phone, punched in an extension, and said, "Will you come to my office? I have a change in fashion to discuss."

Two minutes later, Margaret Savage closed the door behind her. Pace slid the memo across the desk without expression. The P.C. Oracle read the letter twice, crossed her legs, and said flatly: "It's come finally, what we've waited for. From the managing editor slot, you can effect needed change in the domination of this institution by Eurocentric white males. You can bring a female warrior's sensibility to

The Post. Bobbie Anne, if we act well in the coming months, you will run with wolves."

The Assistant Managing Editor for News and Information glanced at the framed photograph of herself and Savage that had appeared in *Vanity Fair.* Hovering in the air over Margaret's head she imagined the headlines that would eventually come her way:

"Swashbuckling Editress Lays Waste to Old Boys' News Network." "From Fashion Scribe to Information Trendsetter, Bobbie Anne Sets the Pace."

And dare she think it?

"Lawlor Retires. Names First Female Editor-in-Chief in Southern California."

Pace did not allow herself to smile at these imaginings. Savage would see any indication of pleasure before attaining their goal as a sign of weakness. And she needed the columnist's creative mind to chart the typhoon waters ahead.

"Neil Harpster," Pace said simply.

"You must get by him," Savage responded.

"But how?"

Savage did not blink. "I do not know him well enough yet. But flaws in character will reveal themselves to the careful observer."

Pace shifted uncomfortably. "I'm uneasy using dirt to get ahead. The Aikido classes have taught me that confrontation is not the way to achieve harmony."

"The hell with Aikido," Savage said. "That's martial art for art's sake. This is a street fight. To become the Alpha bitch, you must lay bare the necks of your rivals."

She said this last with such frigid conviction that Pace shivered. Pace thought of the alternative: having to listen to Neil Harpster tell her what to do the rest of her newspaper career. She returned her attention to Savage. Her features sharpened. She drew back her lips and bared her teeth. She growled.

At that the P.C. Oracle's expression softened perceptibly. She leaned forward in her chair, echoing Pace's growl with her own low-tone howl.

Prentice LaFontaine cocked his head: "Is there a dog in here?"

Isabel Perez peered up from behind her computer screen where she was working on a list of people to call for a story about the media tactics planned for Mayor Portillo's gubernatorial bid. "What are you talking about?"

"A dog, a pooch," News said. "I swore I just heard one . . . make that two pooches barking. Ahh, well. No matter. Tell me some good gossip."

"Nothing to tell."

"Please, Isabel," he whimpered. "After the scandalous antics of Ralph Baker yesterday, I'm coming down hard. I'm a frantic snoop junkie in need of a defamation fix."

"Sorry, News, the well is dry," she said. She looked back at the lead she'd been fashioning. "As you can see from the front page, I've been terribly busy."

An angle! He took two steps back to appraise her with arched eyebrow. "Already assuming the status and arrogance of chief political reporter, I see."

Perez reached involuntarily to her collarbone. She wore a navy turtleneck cotton sweater under which lay the badge the badge-sniffers longed to sniff. Since she'd started wearing it to bed at night, fate had gone her way. Now she regarded the press pass as a sacred talisman capable of warding off all evil in her path.

"It's not like that," she said.

"It certainly is," said someone behind LaFontaine.

News turned to find Kent Jackson with his thumbs

looped in his paisley suspenders. "Ask and ye shall receive," LaFontaine said, delighted at the prospect of a showdown.

Jackson ignored him and turned to Perez. "I've been . . . distracted. But I'm not about to let Patti's obvious bout of insanity ruin my career. I'm back, Isabel."

Perez hesitated, stunned by Jackson's reappearance. "Of course," she began. "I was just making sure we didn't get behind."

"Come, come, Isabel," Jackson said, throwing his brief-case onto his desk. "You expected me to dwindle into quivering ineffectual jelly. Just isn't going to happen. I believe in a higher power. He gives me strength."

Perez pressed her index finger against the sniffable press pass. "Give me more credit, Kent," she said. "I understand your talents."

He grinned. "As well you should. Now, I believe there are quite a few faxes and press releases to go through. I'll be taking over the media strategy piece."

Perez bit the bottom of her lip so hard she tasted blood. She opened her mouth slightly, and said, "I wouldn't have it any other way."

She stood without another word, wiped the blood from her chin, and made her way toward the wire basket where the clerks stacked political correspondence.

She froze when she saw the two-foot pile of political dross. She thought of Arlene Troy's longing. She became steely and detached. She reached for the first five inches of paper, understanding for the first time just how far she would go to become worthy of the holy fetish that hung about her neck.

LaFontaine was about to return to his desk, when he remembered that Gertie said Jackson was in therapy.

"You seem well rested for a man whose wife just left him," he said.

Jackson didn't even bother to look up. "Get out of here, you circling vulture."

"Placing yourself square within the carrion metaphor," LaFontaine taunted. "You are suffering."

"Get out!" Jackson yelled.

The chief political reporter watched the insufferable gossip trot away, wondering with dread what LaFontaine would do if he ever learned that he'd borrowed $56,248 from a loan shark to pay off his Vegas bookies. The loan was for forty-five days, no extensions.

Jackson was betting on a wild anonymous phone tip he'd gotten last night about the relationship between Mayor Ricardo Portillo and Chief of Police T. Lawrence Leslie, something that if uncovered could end the gubernatorial bid.

If Jackson could nail it down, it would serve a twofold purpose: he'd probably get that six-figure book contract to write about California politics his agent had been shopping around. And he'd be putting a death sword in the most liberal politician he knew.

Six hours later, while dusting his collection of Disney Hummels on the mantelpiece, LaFontaine recalled with glee how unnerved he'd made Jackson. He would have to do more research into this gambling problem. It could provide many more delicious moments.

When he'd finished with the porcelains, LaFontaine went through the rest of the condo looking for the slightest bit of dirt. How he hated dust in his personal life.

He paused to watch Brad Perkins do finger push-ups on the rug and glanced in at the movie marquee above the bed. **Spartacus** was playing. *Perfect*, LaFontaine thought, bringing his attention back to his new live-in.

Out of his General Patton outfit, in blue Lycra shorts, no shirt, News thought Perkins looked exactly like Kirk Douglas in his younger days. His skin was flawless. It popped and rolled and smoothed over the taut musculature of his back. Sweat gathered at the nape of his thick neck. At one hundred, Perkins flipped over and into a set of stomach crunches.

"I've already made reservations for the Bull Ring at nine," LaFontaine announced. "We have a table near the window and an order of Raphael's famous Tapas waiting."

Perkins had shifted into cross abdominal work, taking each elbow to the opposite knee. "Not me," he grunted.

"Are you mad?" News demanded as he untied his housework apron. "Do you understand how difficult it is to get a window table at Bull Ring on such short notice?"

"Too much work to do," Perkins said. "Besides, Tapas make you fat."

Perkins relaxed back onto the carpet, his ripped pectorals heaving from the exertion. He grabbed one knee and pulled it toward him in a stretch.

LaFontaine took two steps toward Perkins and tickled his butt with the feather duster. "C'mon, Old Blood 'N' Guts, for Sergeant York?"

Perkins lashed out his foot, knocking the duster away. "Jesus, Prentice, I'm trying to stretch here."

News saw something in Perkins's reaction, something bordering on the flared rage his father used to display. He felt unsure, scared, and yet pleased with the response.

Perkins returned to the stretch, blowing air long and smooth out through his mouth. In an act beyond his control, LaFontaine reached forward with the duster and tickled the bodybuilder under the nose.

Perkins jumped up. His hands curled into fists. His nostrils quivered in anger. Inside News felt nice and wanted.

Reaction . . .

By seven o'clock the next evening, Gideon McCarthy was on his second beer at the Slotman's Bar and Grill. He waited on a stool bar for Prentice LaFontaine, who'd called him from home.

"I needed a mental health day off," News had said. "But let's have a drink tonight to celebrate your Virgil-like ascent from hell. I'll bring Brad for you to meet."

McCarthy declined at first, wanting to be with Carlos and Miriam after the endless days of work, but Estelle had insisted he go for a little while. He didn't have much of a social life. The kids would wait up for him.

He sipped at the beer, knowing he should be ecstatic at breaking the biggest story of his career, but he wasn't. Several of the events of the past twenty-four hours nagged at him. He sat there trying to block out the Slotman's irritating Muzak, thinking about it all.

Carlos and Miriam woke him early, jumping on his bed with the paper. The headline over the copyrighted story said:

Cops Heard Arranging Murder of Prostitute

All hell had broken loose. Mayor Ricardo Portillo and Police Chief T. Lawrence Leslie called a press conference at 11:00 A.M. in city hall to handle the media clamor.

McCarthy sat front row center with Isabel Perez and Kent Jackson. They were all loving the way Paul Fairbanks and the other television reporters held up the front page of *The Post* to the cameras as they did their stand-up introductions.

Even better was Karen Rivers's reaction. Her normally olive-tone skin had paled considerably. Her eyes were puffy, probably the result of a 3:00 A.M. wake-up call from *The Beacon*. She bit at the quick of her fingernails. No doubt about it: she evinced all the signs of making her first trip to the hot seat of the missed big story. *Better to give than receive,* McCarthy thought.

Mayor Portillo, a handsome man, some would say an elegantly handsome man, in a navy blue suit and matching tie, strode to the podium. He was ordinarily a consummate politician, cool under pressure, articulate without appearing slick, forceful but not a tyrant. This morning he fumbled with the paper his statement was typed on. Arlene Troy, who was flitting in the background with a sheaf of papers, stepped forward. Before she could reach the podium, Chief Leslie, a tall man with a deep tan that spoke of weekends on the tennis court reached over and found the mayor the correct page. Fisk leaned against the wall well behind the chief and the mayor, obviously annoyed. Next to him stood Steve Cohen, the district attorney's right-hand man.

"I have a brief statement and then we will open the floor to your questions," Portillo said. "Two of this city's police officers were arrested this morning on charges of conspiracy and first degree murder. Officer David Patrick, a patrol officer assigned to the Boulevard precinct and Lt. Diego Blanca, a shift supervisor in the same precinct, will be arraigned later today in connection with the slaying of Carol Alice Gentry."

Perez leaned over and whispered to McCarthy, "You got 'em."

McCarthy nodded and kept writing as fast as he could. Behind them Fairbanks whispered to his cameraman to get a close-up of Leslie, who stood with his head bowed.

Portillo continued, "This is a sad day for the city and, I think Chief Leslie will concur, a very dark day for the police force."

Portillo went on. "Shortly after the arrests were made,

Chief Leslie offered to resign from his position as manager of my campaign."

Jackson broke in, "Did you accept his resignation?"

"I did not," Portillo said firmly. "I still believe that Chief Leslie is the best man to run my campaign and the best man to run the police force. That is not to say that I minimize the gravity of the arrest of these two officers. But this city employs more than four thousand full- and part-time police. In any organization, there may be bad apples."

Jackson followed up, "Frankly, Mayor, you've made crime a major issue. Your opponent, Larry Barnes, says having Chief Leslie run your campaign indicates you're wishy-washy about keeping California's streets safe."

Portillo shook his head. "Larry Barnes is a high-technology executive, with no public experience. Chief Leslie is a man of integrity and a committed public servant. I think the fact we are here now, announcing these arrests, says a lot about our dedication to rooting out criminals no matter what they do for a living."

Rivers shouted, "Excuse me, Mayor, but it was well-known that Patrick and Blanca were under investigation for extorting sex in return for protection on the Boulevard. Why weren't they placed on leave? Why were they allowed to continue to work, and, if the allegations are true, get rid of the woman who fingered them?"

Good question, McCarthy thought. She's not cowering like a whipped dog.

Chief Leslie held up his hand. "I'll answer that, Mayor. That was my decision based on an investigation carried out by Internal Affairs. The fact is that the grand jury decided not to indict Blanca or Patrick or any other member of the Boulevard precinct because of a lack of substantiation to Gentry's claims."

McCarthy snorted and whispered to Perez. "That's bullshit. I've heard at least three other hookers tell me the same stuff."

"However," Leslie went on, "our internal investigation showed otherwise. We believed that the two officers in question were involved in questionable activity, but we did not have enough concrete evidence to suspend or fire them. The removal of civil servants is covered by a stringent set of union rules. But we were actively moving toward relieving both officers when the information about the contract came to light."

Perez said, "Do you regret not suspending them now?"

Leslie scratched at his cheek. "I guess what you're asking is do I believe that by suspending them I could have saved Carol Gentry's life? I suppose I'll be asking myself that question for many years to come."

"What's your answer today?" she pressed.

"I should have suspended them," Leslie grimaced. "I'll have to live with that."

Fairbanks shouted, "Any ideas of who carried out the hit? Another police officer?"

Fisk winced. Cohen, a bearded fellow in his early forties, said, "There's nothing to indicate other police officers are involved at this time. But as the mayor said, we are continuing the investigation and will prosecute without fear or favor."

McCarthy finally spoke. "Do you believe Gentry was blackmailing these officers?"

Leslie looked at Fisk and Cohen, then down at the reporter. "We are looking into that angle."

"What was she blackmailing them about?" Rivers cried.

Arlene Troy moved in front of the dais. "I believe that's all the questions we'll take now."

The reporters groaned. Portillo and Leslie moved quickly toward the door. Jackson, Perez, Fairbanks, and Rivers raced after them. McCarthy ignored the obvious and cornered Fisk.

"You looked pained when Fairbanks asked about who carried out the contract," McCarthy said.

"Guys with abnormal hairdos and chains around their ankles bug me."

"C'mon, Fisk. You know something."

"I know you're sticking your nose in where it doesn't belong, as usual."

McCarthy waved his notebook in front of the little detective's nose. "I made you look pretty good in my piece this morning. I could have rubbed it in that *The Post* got to Dusk first, but I didn't. You owe me."

Fisk's expression didn't change. Finally he said, "We've got some leads, but nothing's panned out yet. Talk to me in a couple of days. Fair?"

"Fair."

McCarthy walked away. He waited until Jackson and Perez had finished. He said, "I've got the arraignment in half an hour."

"We've got the rest," Jackson said. "Isabel will write the lead analysis piece and the news angle that Leslie offered to resign."

Perez seemed shocked. "You're giving me the reaction story?"

Jackson nodded. "I want the insider's view on this, how the campaign attempts to recover from the blow. Teddy White stuff. Besides, you deserve it."

Perez and McCarthy looked at him suspiciously. "What are you up to?" Perez asked. "Magnanimity has never been your strong suit."

Jackson pressed his palm to his chest. "I've undergone a difficult time of late," he said. "I'm trying to change."

"Don't argue," McCarthy said as Jackson hurried away.

"I won't," Perez said. "But Kent's wily. I'll have to cover my back."

Now McCarthy saw Perez sitting in the corner of the Slotman's with Arlene Troy, having a drink. She looked pretty damn uncomfortable about something. He swiveled on his stool, stirred his drink, and mulled over a couple of facts that bothered him.

Cops, probably Blanca and Patrick, had broken into Gentry's place looking for a tape. What tape and what was on it? It was one thing to talk generically about blackmail. But it was the details that made motive clear. McCarthy liked things to be clear.

Then there was the way Patrick and Blanca had appeared at their arraignment. Patrick, a rotund balding man with an unkempt, walrus mustache, had come into the courtroom as if he didn't understand where he was. He stumbled twice. The bailiff helped him to his chair, where he stared blankly at the floor. Blanca, a muscular guy with raven black hair and a square jaw, acted defiant. After taking his seat, he turned to Sue Tripp, a public defender McCarthy knew, and said something. Tripp pointed at McCarthy.

Blanca looked at him carefully, then mouthed: "This is bullshit. We never killed anyone!"

When it happened, McCarthy tossed it off as the usual protests of innocence. Sitting in the Slotman's six hours later there was something in his memory of Blanca's face that unnerved him. He thought about it a moment. Blanca wasn't angry. He was confident.

Playing against the back wall of it all was the fact that Gentry wasn't a regular on the Boulevard. It bugged him, but he couldn't figure out why. He reached in his wallet and drew out the outcall phone number Dusk had given him.

"Drink on the house for the conquering hero?" the Slotman asked cheerfully.

McCarthy refolded the slip of paper and returned it to his wallet. "Why are you so happy?"

"Call me a marketing genius," the barkeep grinned. "A freaking marketing genius!"

The Slotman tossed his head in the direction of the

kitchen door through which Ralph Baker came in a full-length black leather apron emblazoned with the words "The Slotman's Bluesman." McCarthy put his head on the bar and moaned. He saw immediately what the Slotman was up to: having one of the city's journalistic burnouts—even one who'd pulled a Lazarus on his final day of work—pouring cheap booze for reporters and editors would heighten anxiety, which in return would create a mad lust for liquor and continue the steady rise in the value of his retirement portfolio.

"You're evil, Slotman," McCarthy said.

The Slotman cried, "I'm telling you Madison Avenue lost a great one not recruiting me! Ralphie, a beer on the house for McCarthy!"

Baker picked up a beer glass with trembling hands, then pulled the tap. He almost got it filled before it slipped and shattered. The half dozen patrons seated at the bar stared in horror. All of them ordered another round. The Slotman served them himself.

"Here's your beer, Gideon," Baker said after he'd cleaned up the mess. "Great story yesterday."

"I appreciate it, Ralph," McCarthy said. "Your piece on Hale was dynamite."

The Roy Orbison look-alike nodded appreciatively, but didn't say anything.

McCarthy said, "Never figured you to work for the Slotman."

Baker leaned toward McCarthy as if he were a first-time singer approaching the mike on amateur night. "Didn't see much else I could do. Tried to call up a couple of P.R. firms in town yesterday. But every time I heard them pick up the line, I'd get sick and hang up. Slotman offered me the job last night, said everyone I know comes in. Kind of like home. And I can work the evening shift. Gives me my days to walk and think."

"What do you think about, Ralph?" McCarthy asked, trying to get his mind off the Gentry case.

"How it all goes. How it's tough to keep up. I don't know why it should surprise me. Lester said it was the same down at the post office, just kept piling up on you."

"Lester? As in Hale?"

Behind his thick black polymer glasses, Baker's eyes grew watery. "Couldn't get him out of my mind, Gid, the image of him lying on top of that pony at the end. Went down to see him at the hospital this morning. Figured he might be lonely, you know?"

At that revelation, McCarthy needed another drink. Something stronger this time. Maybe Slotman was a marketing genius. "I need a bourbon, Ralph. Straight up."

"You got it," Baker said.

"Ralph?"

"What's that?"

"If you don't mind me asking: why did you start dressing up like . . . well, like that?"

Baker adjusted his glasses and flicked a piece of popcorn off his black silk shirt. He hesitated, then said, "Used to be all a reporter had to do to succeed was get down, get dirty, and break stories. It made sense: work and payoffs. Then something happened after I'd been in it a while that made me change my mind. Since then I've seen it all get screwed up with quotas, and politically correct stories, and all the power plays of the newsroom. Hell, you can get to the top just on image now."

"What happened?"

Baker shrugged. "I figured out that news is a commodity now, like corn or sowbellies."

"You saying the black leather was all a form of protest?"

Baker shrugged again. "I was sending a message."

That was a funny thing to say. "To whom?"

Baker twisted his apron and didn't respond.

"Ralph, you're not in the business anymore. You can't get hurt."

Baker thought about that, then said simply, "Ed Tower."

McCarthy hunched over the bar. "What about him?"

Baker described how in the early seventies he'd worked on a story involving an investment guru who was really running a Ponzi scheme. He'd written the story, but Tower sat on it for months before allowing a watered-down version to run. A couple of years later, after the guru had gone to jail, Baker figured out that Tower had been invested. He'd used the story to force the guru to pay him back before the pyramid collapsed.

McCarthy shook his head. "I knew he had marginal ethics, but I never would have figured him for this kind of thing. But who am I to talk?"

"At least your dirty secrets are out in the open," Baker said. "There are a lot more buried inside *The Post*, believe me."

"Like what?" McCarthy asked.

But before he could answer, the Slotman bellowed: "Ralphie. We got wet whistles down here. C'mon. C'mon. This isn't newspapers anymore. We're in *business* here."

Prentice LaFontaine yelled, "Wet whistles here, too, my good Mr. Orbison. A daiquiri and a tequila neat, if you please!"

McCarthy swiveled in his chair to find News standing behind him with arms held open wide. He wore a pair of sunglasses.

"Sporting the celebrity look now?"

LaFontaine's raffish grin fell. He took the glasses off to reveal a black eye. "Took a terrible fall down the stairs last night. Part of the reason I took the day off."

A ball formed in McCarthy's stomach. He felt very small. "Prentice, you don't have a very good record with this sort of thing."

"I don't know what you're talking about," News sniffed.

"I've sat next to you for the better part of thirteen years. History repeats itself."

"Brad's not like that, you'll see," LaFontaine said.

"Just tell me he hasn't moved in."

News ignored him, turning to greet a fashionable man in his early thirties. McCarthy could have picked out LaFontaine's new beau anywhere. News loved faddish guys.

"Gid, Brad," LaFontaine said. "And the vice versa."

"Charmed," Perkins said dully.

"Yeah, pleasure's all mine," McCarthy said.

"Gid broke the story of the prostitute being murdered by cops," LaFontaine said.

Perkins examined his fingernails. "Isn't there a *boite* with more class than this we can frequent tonight, Prentice?"

LaFontaine gritted his teeth. "I told Gideon I'd buy him a victory drink."

"Suit yourself," Perkins said. "Maybe you can catch up to me at Pony's or the Bull Ring."

"Don't be like that, Brad," LaFontaine complained.

This was the last scene McCarthy needed to be involved in tonight. He downed the shot of bourbon. "Actually, News, I've had my fill. I'll head home to see the kids."

"Too bad you had to leave so soon," Perkins said brightly. He reached past McCarthy to retrieve the shot of tequila and drank it.

LaFontaine hurried after McCarthy. "Sorry I was so late, Gid. Brad can be . . ."

"Difficult?"

For an instant News's shoulders sagged. Then he tossed his head back, his normal bravado intact. "Challenging is how I prefer to see it."

McCarthy smiled sadly. "You take care of yourself."

"Always," LaFontaine said. "I may be a hard news reporter, but I'm no victim!"

McCarthy patted him on the shoulder and exited through the door of the Slotman's into the night air. He almost knocked Karen Rivers over. She jumped back in embarrassment. She looked at the pavement, then adjusted the strap of her pocketbook over the shoulder of her blue denim dress.

Rivers said, "I, I guess I owe you an apology."

"Yeah, for what?" She looked better than she had this morning. He liked the way she'd braided her hair and flung it over one shoulder.

"I called you a has-been," she said, still studying the pavement. "You may be many things, but that isn't one of them. That was a great story today. I almost threw up."

"I was kind of hoping that would happen."

"I said almost." Her jaw was set when she finally looked up at him.

"You did at that. An admirable opponent."

Now she smiled. "Can the admirable opponent buy the cagey veteran a beer?"

"The cagey veteran has to go home to see his children."

She seemed surprised. "I . . . I didn't know you were married."

"I'm not," McCarthy said. "A rain check on the beer?"

"Sure," she said. She adjusted the pocketbook again, hesitated, then yanked open the door to the Slotman's.

The blare of the bar faded behind McCarthy as he walked north on Broadway. Rivers had a quality about her that annoyed him and intrigued him. She could play the charming naive one moment and the hardened reporter the next. She'd make a very good journalist someday.

The ocean breeze made the night air cool. He drew his jacket in and buttoned it. He walked quicker now, thinking how good it would be to sit with the kids, maybe read them a book or two before bed, talk about their lives, smell their hair after their evening baths, hug them before they slept. He hated not being there every night, especially with the visit from Charley Owens looming.

McCarthy turned the corner onto Ninth Avenue. There

were fewer streetlights here than out on Broadway. He always kept his battered Toyota at a lot on Ninth between L and M Streets. It was the only spot in town that charged less than ten dollars a day to park. He was entering the nearly empty lot from the far side when he saw a shadow move inside his car.

He shouted, "Can't you read, asshole?! There's no radio inside!"

Then the whine of the old starter motor echoed and died. "Oh, shit, he's going for the whole thing!" He didn't have money for another car. He began to run.

McCarthy was fifty feet away when the whine came again and then the ball of fire ballooned out orange and blue. The roar smothered him like a blanket and twenty horses kicked him in the chest all at once and then there was darkness.

A Deft Double Backstab . . .

Fifteen days after the explosion, Claudette X glowered into the reflective glare of her computer screen and begged the powers that be for sleep without nightmares. Make that anytime, day or night, without nightmares.

Gideon McCarthy had been home more than a week. He'd spent seven days before that in the hospital with a concussion, four broken ribs, and a hairline fracture of the jaw.

That was bad enough, but the bombing had been a herald of dark events, the coming of a shitstorm the likes of which *The Post* had never seen.

Day in and day out, the police scanner had squawked

with word of tragedy after tragedy upon tragedy. Just this morning, Augustus Croon and Abby Blitzer had squealed tires from a helicopter crash in the foothills to a canyon fire that engulfed the homes of two quadriplegics and an abortion-rights activist to the drowning of three divers entangled in the kelp beds offshore. A report of a copycat weirdo threatening to blow up a pony stable unless immigration laws were changed had just come in. Blitzer had radioed to the newsroom that she couldn't keep up.

There had been a series of preliminary hearings on the Gentry murder trial. Requests for bond by both Patrick and Blanca had been denied. The prosecutor had persuaded the judge that the police officers were a flight risk.

Lawlor was still on a rampage over the bombing. He had Kent Jackson hounding the offices of the mayor and Chief Lawrence every day, demanding answers on why a reporter from his paper could almost be killed by a car bomb after identifying two cops as murder suspects. Prentice LaFontaine had been drafted to write a "police force out of control" story, which was published yesterday.

All this despite protests from Lieutenant Fisk that the attempt on McCarthy's life was likely a case of mistaken identity. Lao Pot, the seventeen-year-old killed in the blast, was a fringe member of a violent Asian street gang known for drive-by shootings and pipe bombings.

"Our intelligence indicates Pot was being initiated into full membership," Fisk was quoted as saying in this morning's edition. "We believe he was carrying the bomb and trying to steal McCarthy's car when it accidentally detonated."

Claudette X didn't know what to think. The explosion had come so quick on the heels of the Gentry hit story that it reeked of retaliation.

But the worst nightmares had been newsroom generated. The morning blow jobs had rarely climaxed. Bobbie Anne Pace and Neil Harpster didn't think they mattered. Or maybe they didn't think they mattered enough. And both assistant managing editors had requested separate meetings with Claudette X and Stanley Geld this morning. The gaping mouth that haunted her dreams appeared in her mind. She trembled.

"Claudette, hurry up please. It's time," Geld said.

Claudette X shook off the hallucination, nodded morosely, and trudged after the city editor to Harpster's office. The Assistant Managing Editor for Form and Content was blowing his nose.

"Bad cold," Harpster said. He rubbed at his rheumy eyes. "But that's what you get sitting out in the ocean air all night."

"Bonfire on the beach with some friends, Neil?" Geld said.

Harpster shut the door to his office. "There are many things afoot, some of which I cannot inform you. But I'm here seeking your advice and, well, your loyalty."

Loyalty? thought Claudette X. *In a newsroom?*

"Well, we respect you if that's what you mean," she said, unsure if that was enough to get her the hell out of the Glasshole before Harpster's red nose appeared above the mouth in her dreams.

"It's a beginning, I suppose," Harpster said. He wheezed into a Kleenex. He tossed his head from side to side like a horse trying to rid itself of a persistent fly. "Oh, I've got to tell someone. I'm being harrassed. Or Lydia is actually, but that means me, too."

Geld curled his finger in the locks of his latest perm. "Who's harassing you, Neil?"

Harpster laid his forehead in the palms of his hands. "If I knew I wouldn't feel so defenseless. I could sue the bastard or have him arrested or shoot him."

He jerked his head up. "Ten thousand dollars worth of plants have been destroyed at my house in the past month. Tulips. Azaleas. Hydrangeas. A Japanese maple. Ten different types of violets. All dead. Plants are like kids to Lydia. The doctor's got her on Valium. The cops say they can't sit around protecting a garden from vandals, so I'm out there with a shotgun on sentry duty all night."

"That's good, right?" Geld asked soothingly. "I mean, you kept the plants safe."

A perceptible tremor began in the lower lip of the Assistant Managing Editor for Form and Content. "Everything seemed so perfect at dawn this morning, even the new spirea I put out as bait. Then we went in the greenhouse. Lydia has four Bog Rein orchids she'd bought from a specialty shop in New Mexico."

Claudette X thought Harpster might cry. "What happened, Neil?" she asked.

Harpster said, "It looked like someone had chewed them, bitten them in places on the stalk, maybe even eaten the flowers! Lydia had to be sedated."

Harpster hunched low at his desk and let his eyes wander beyond the city editor and his chief assistant through the glass of his hole. He whispered, "It's somebody in this newsroom. I'm sure of it."

"Oh c'mon, Neil," Claudette X said. "It's probably just kids."

Geld said nothing. He was engrossed in thought.

"Explain these, then," Harpster said. He tossed two pieces of paper across the desk. They were copies of the latest tax assessment on his home and land in The Ranch. $785,000. Scrawled across the bottom of the page in red Magic Marker ink were the words: "Not to mention extensive landscape improvements."

Harpster said, "We found one in the greenhouse. Another was in my office mailbox when I came in this morning."

Claudette X tried to appear concerned, but all she could think was $785,000! *How the hell could he afford that kind of place on an editor's salary? Lydia must be loaded.*

Geld said, "I'm sure there's no one here out to get you. Even Bobbie Anne wouldn't stoop this low."

"Bobbie Anne?" Harpster's forehead knotted. "What does she have against me?"

"I'm sure it's nothing," Geld said.

Harpster glared out the glass walls of his aquarium. "What do you know, Stanley? C'mon, we've been friends . . . well colleagues anyway . . . a long time."

Geld paused a moment. "Neil, it's probably nothing, just that she mentioned something the other day after the daily blow jo . . . I mean after the morning meeting, about Form and Content being, well . . . slightly flaccid these days."

"Flaccid!" Harpster blustered. He jumped up, grabbed today's *Post,* and waved it at them. "Flaccid! Why this paper's never been so . . . so *turgid!*"

His cheeks flared a brilliant red. Beads of sweat popped out on his forehead. "It's that crazy series she's talking about with that holier-than-thou columnist of hers. That's what it is, only she's turning it into a power play, trying to drive me nuts!"

Geld said, "Calm down, Neil. You'll give yourself a heart attack!"

Harpster took a silk handkerchief from the top pocket of his suit coat and mopped his brow. He loosened his tie. "Heart attack? I wouldn't give her the satisfaction. Who would have thought that fashion plate could climb garden walls?"

"Now, now, Neil," Claudette X said. "There's no way Bobbie Anne Pace is behind those attacks on your wife's garden. She's too . . ."

"Feminine," Geld agreed. "Now . . . Margaret you'd never know about."

Claudette glared at Geld. What the hell was he up to?

Harpster's breathing slowed. His chin stopped quivering. His posture shifted to angular. "So Bobbie Anne's not content with News and Information. Her trajectory's too steep for that. She wants Form and Content, too. And who knows what else? Well, we'll just see how flaccid Neil Harpster really is."

An awkward moment followed during which Harpster sneered at some unseen apparition.

"Neil?" Claudette X said sharply. "We've got another meeting."

"Go, go." Harpster was deep in thought, writing on a yellow legal-size pad.

Geld closed the door behind him. Claudette X waited until they were around the corner, out of Harpster's sight, and almost to Bobbie Anne Pace's office before she said, "What's going on, Stan?"

Geld merely whistled before knocking.

"Come in, come in," Pace said. Margaret Savage perched on the edge of a chair.

"Sit, please," Pace said. "We'd like to talk with you about a series of columns Margaret has begun. We think they're groundbreaking and should get marketing attention."

"That's Neil's decision," Claudette X said.

"True," Pace said cautiously. "But he's been acting, well—between us—strange, of late. I wanted to make sure I had your support for this."

"We're listening," Geld said.

Stan's beaming, thought Claudette X. *Stan doesn't do beam. Stan does mope.*

Savage said, "As a columnist I have freedoms that other reporters here don't. I can call the kettle black even if I don't have it on someone else's authority."

Claudette X counted backward from ten; the idea of someone with thirteen months in journalism lecturing her on the news business made her blood simmer.

"It's a big responsibility," Geld observed.

"One I take very seriously," Savage said. "I choose my subjects well, try to stake out the correct ground. I can't tell you how many nights I lie awake."

"Nor I," Pace said. She smiled at Savage.

"I'm sure," Geld said.

Savage went on. "I'm preparing a series of columns about the disparities of pay between men and women. I plan to name names, use my contacts to get actual salaries and compensation packages for men and women holding the exact same job."

"Then you publish them," Geld said in a way that made Claudette X think he already knew about all this. She eyed him suspiciously. Geld was still talking. "It will take a lot of support to get the go-ahead."

Pace said, "I know. I messaged the rest of the senior editors earlier this week. Several are supportive. Others are, well, lukewarm to the idea. How do you view it?"

Claudette X looked at Geld again. That's how he knew about the series. He'd been snooping in the computer system.

"I'm for it," Geld said. "Count on my support. Claudette's too; am I right?"

Savage yawned. Claudette X stared deep inside the P.C. Oracle's mouth.

"Claudette?"

Claudette X felt as if a thick fuzzy lens had been placed over her eyes. She wondered whether this was what the other assistant city editors felt like. "This is out of my league, Stan. Your call."

"Then we're for it," Geld said. Then, slyly, "Now, Neil, I don't know about."

"Why's that?" Pace demanded.

Geld made a show of appearing restless and on the spot. "I'd rather not say."

Savage said, "I'm new at newspaper politics. Your insight would be a big help."

Geld nodded conspiratorially to Savage and then to Pace. "It's something I heard."

"What?" Pace demanded.

"It's probably nothing."

"Out with it, Stanley," ordered the Assistant Managing Editor for News and Information.

"If you insist. The way it was put to me was, how could Neil possibly afford that house in The Ranch if he was being paid scale? What I mean is, everyone knows Lydia inherited a bundle, but is it enough to cover a place up there?"

Geld let the implication sink in. The only person on the totem pole who should be making a wage at a scale comparable to Harpster was Pace.

"Stanley," she began, "in strictest confidence . . . what do you think he's . . ."

The city editor drew out a ballpoint pen and scribbled a figure on a slip of paper. Savage and Pace gasped.

"It's just what you've been saying, Margaret," Pace said.

"We've got to fight this," Savage said. "You can't stand still for this kind of inequity. Bobbie Anne, newspapers can't be immune from scrutiny; if this is true, I want to publish Neil's salary in my series. We've got to fight."

Geld wanted to hug them both. Instead, he said, "Please, keep me out of this."

"Of course, Stanley. We appreciate your candor."

"Oh, one more thing," Geld said.

"Yes," Savage said, eagerly.

"There's another possible explanation, just so you don't go off half-cocked, assuming that the story is what I assume it is."

"To Assume makes an Ass out of U and Me," Pace said.

"Basic journalism," Geld agreed. "And I know I'm out of line here, but honestly it's bothered me for quite a long time."

Pace slid forward in her chair. "What is it?"

To Claudette X's utter chagrin, he laid out how he'd long feared that Harpster was using his position to tout stocks and make a profit on *The Post*'s sterling reputation.

Geld went on, "Have you ever noticed how Neil goes out

at lunch several times a week with this brown satchel? I think he carries files on his investments in there. I'd like to know where he goes and who he meets with."

Claudette X wanted to crawl into a corner and suck her thumb. She and Geld had long suspected that Harpster went off at lunch for quickies with Connie Mills at a sleazy motel down on State Street. What in the name of Malcolm Little was Geld up to?

"I'll follow up," Pace promised. "Stanley, if things turn out as I plan, you will be remembered. You just might be a Beta male."

"Huh?" Geld said.

"Never mind," Savage said quickly. "We thank you and urge the both of you to keep this to yourself."

"I wouldn't breathe a word," Geld said. He rose from his seat to shake their hands.

"No . . . word," Claudette X said. She walked out of the office, thinking she'd better have her eyes checked. Cataracts were definitely forming. Better get a good sleeping pill from the doctor while she was at it. Blow her mind blank with a strong sedative. She barely made it to her desk, where she laid her head on her keyboard.

"Stanley, please tell me what's going on?" she moaned.

He pulled his chair up close to hers. "They think Tower's retiring."

Claudette X peaked out from behind a massive arm. "Is he?"

"Not that I know of." He held up the two bogus memos he'd retrieved from interoffice mail before they could be delivered to Tower. He grinned weirdly.

She read enough of one to understand what was going on. She closed her eyes and moaned again.

"Trust me," Geld said.

"Trust you?" Claudette X snapped, her anger returning. "I don't even know who you are anymore, Stan. You used to be one of those nice depressed Jewish guys you find in every newsroom. Now you're a stranger."

Geld's expression hardened. "Listen, Claudette, every night for the last four months I've awoken in a sweat from a terrible dream."

"Join the club," Claudette X said.

He went on as if he hadn't heard her. "It's always the same: I trot out into a dance studio dressed in a black leotard that's too tight up the crack of my ass. Neil's playing piano. Bobbie Anne's this wrinkled old doyenne rapping out time with a wooden stick. My feet can't stop dancing."

Geld's weird grin returned. "But given what I just saw in those two Glassholes, I'll tell you one thing: whatever the future holds, old Stan's going to sleep tonight without danger of going *en pointe!*"

The Physics of Quid Pro Quo . . .

Just then Isabel Perez ran up. "I'm onto a big story."

Claudette X shook her head to clear the horrors of the last half hour. "Tell me."

"The company owned by none other than gubernatorial candidate Barnes has been dumping toxic wastes from the making of silicon chips."

Geld said, "I thought you were supposed to write that political items column."

"It's done, Stanley," Perez said, irritated. "Don't you listen? Look, I was back there working on my database of the campaign financial records, when, bang, I get this anonymous call about an hour ago."

"Tell me," Claudette X said again. She desperately wanted a real story to work on.

"It's a guy. Says he's a concerned citizen."

Geld said, "Probably some dirty trickster hired by the mayor's campaign."

"Probably," Perez nodded. "But you know how it is, Stan. You listen and if they don't sound loony, going off in every direction at once, you check it out."

"You did," Claudette X said.

"With the Environmental Protection Agency and the California Bureau of Water," Perez said. She flipped open her notebook. "Fourteen separate violations by his company in connection with the disposal of acetone and twelve with another solvent, a known carcinogen I can't quite pronounce. Polypebbles or something."

Geld said, "Barnes was running the company when they did the illegal dumping?"

"Chief executive officer," Perez said. "Now here's where it gets good. Barnes has made speeches calling for relaxing environmental regulations and he made a speech about it on the same day his company got slapped with the largest of the dumping violations."

"Very nice," Geld said. "What does the mayor say about it?"

"I haven't spoken with Portillo yet, but Arlene is outraged, of course."

"Of course," Claudette X said. She whirled in her chair and called up the city desk queue on her computer. "Any chance *The Beacon* is onto this?"

"Sure there's a chance," said Perez, who knew there was no chance.

"Have you got everything you need to write?" Geld asked.

"I could use a little more time to get it fleshed out."

"All right," Geld said. "Claudette, slot it for Sunday, page A-1."

Claudette X looked at Perez. "You tell Kent you're working on this story?"

Perez threw her hands on her hips. "Would he tell me?"

Claudette X scowled. "At least let him know before it runs. I want a draft ready when I get here tomorrow to edit."

Perez rushed back to her desk, thrilled at the good fortune that embraced her. This was the kind of story that gets attention. This was the kind of story that sets a political reporter apart from the pack. Did it matter that it probably came from Mayor Portillo's campaign tricksters? She knew it did. She didn't care.

Talking to Arlene the night McCarthy's car was bombed outside the Slotman's, she'd mustered every slippery move mastered in twelve years of hiding her Slavic past. Arlene's lust was obvious and unsettling. Every time it seemed Perez might be backed into a corner, she attacked or dodged or slid just out of reach of Arlene's grasp. That two cops had been arrested was a wonderful political angle for a story and an equally wonderful defensive posture. In the end they'd negotiated common ground.

"You beat us up pretty bad in there today," Troy had said after they'd ordered drinks.

"Part of the job, Arlene. Doesn't look good for Chief Leslie's boys to be putting out contracts on talkative hookers."

"They're under arrest, aren't they?" Troy said.

"They are," Perez admitted. She felt a tickle on the inside of her calf. It was Troy's toe! Perez swallowed and drew her leg out of range. "Doesn't mean, though, that this is over, the controversy, I mean."

Troy laughed. "Where would you dear reporters be without that word?"

"Writing for the food pages," Perez said. "Conflict makes the news world go round, Arlene."

"Even if you have to invent conflict."

"McCarthy didn't invent this."

"But it's being blown out of proportion," Troy said. "I know how it works: coverage is based on a vacuum. The pages have to be filled, the monster fed, so reporters get sucked toward whatever is happening. There must be some kind of physics equation to explain it, something like: The Size of a Scandal is Directly Proportionate to the News Void that Exists at the Moment. I mean look at Kent this afternoon, running around asking secretaries and clerks questions all over city hall. You'd have thought he was Carl Bernstein in *All the President's Men.*"

"Nervous?"

"Not at all," Troy said. She batted her eyelashes at Perez, who responded by rearranging her napkin. The Slotman brought them their drinks, leered for a moment at Perez's obvious discomfort. She gulped her wine.

Troy went on, "You know as well as I do, Isabel, that the media these days is amok. There are no standards of what a story is. The big newspapers and networks won't break an obviously tawdry, unsubstantiated, gossipy story, but they'll sure follow it once a paper with lower standards prints it."

"You trying to say *The Post* has low standards?"

"No, I think *The Post* is a very good paper. But there's a corollary to what I just described. If the reporter has motivation to break something, anything, you know as well as I do that a clever writer can harness circumstantial facts or buttress the claims of a dubious source."

Perez made as if to interrupt, but Troy cut in. "Hear me out. Kent, for example, obviously has that kind of motivation these days. He's been made the laughingstock of the local press after his wife appeared *in flagrante* on the front page of *The Beacon*'s Metro section. He wants to prove to the world that he still counts. Understandable. But I won't have him force a story which would end up ruining Ricardo's chance at the governorship."

Perez took a second gulp. She realized she had leverage.

"Let's say you're right, Arlene, about that basic physics equation. If so, there must be another equation."

"And what's that?" Troy said.

"The Speed and Impact of a Scandal Slows and Lessens in the Presence of Another Scandal," Perez said coolly. "Unless of course, the scandals involve the same people, in which case there is an exponential effect: the intrigue takes on a new mass and velocity."

"Are you saying we're about to be hit with another scandal?" Troy asked, suddenly worried.

"Not that I know of," Perez said. "But I've just finished entering most of the campaign finance data into our computer. Who knows what I'll find?"

Troy was all business now. "That kind of story doesn't bother me. Campaign contributions are a fact of political life. We can handle that, as long as it's factual."

"Spin is a dangerous thing, isn't it, Arlene?" Perez said. "I mean like you said, a reporter can look for the agreeable or the controversial in just about anything."

They said nothing for several moments, each woman studying the other. Finally, Troy said, "I didn't take you for a hardball player."

Perez said, "Stand in the shadows for as long as I have, you get tough."

Troy ran a finger along the skin between the thumb and index finger of her other hand. "The Speed and Impact of a Scandal . . . how did that go?"

"Slows and Lessens in the Presence of Another Scandal," Perez said.

"That was it," Troy said softly. She hesitated. "We might, uh, know some things about Barnes that we were, uh, holding in reserve."

"I'll bet you do." Perez batted her eyelashes at Troy. "Friends tell friends secrets."

"Mmmmm," Troy purred. "And what might a friend tell me?"

"How about what reporters at *The Post* are working on at any given moment. What might a friend tell me?"

Troy leaned forward and said huskily, "That she wants to be more than friends?"

Perez wet her lips deliberately. "Every thing in good time, Arlene," she said. "Why don't we begin by slowing down Kent Jackson before he hurts our dear mayor?"

Troy ran a fingernail along the outside of her wineglass, then said, "I suppose you might be at your desk some morning soon and just might be willing to receive a call from an anonymous tipster."

"I suppose I might," Perez said. "And I suppose you'll be at your desk from time to time to listen to a voice from inside the media machine?"

"I suppose I might," Troy smiled. She looked longingly into Perez's eyes. "And after the campaign is over, who knows?"

Perez mustered all her guile and stared humidly back at Troy. "Yes, who knows?"

Now in the newsroom, typing in her notes from the anonymous tipster, Perez again paused to fondle the sniffable badge. She'd kept her part of the bargain, snooping around in various reporter's files and pumping Prentice LaFontaine for all the latest dirt inside *The Post.* Just yesterday she'd told Troy that Jackson was in some kind of gambling trouble and seemed interested in finding out more about the financial relationship between Chief Leslie and Mayor Portillo. He'd evidently heard a rumor that they were involved in a mutual investment somewhere. The item hadn't phased Troy a bit.

"Ricardo gives away most of his excess income to charity," Troy said. "His investments are limited to a savings account for his kids' education fund, his home, and a piece of property over on Lake Mead in Nevada where he plans to retire."

Whatever. For a little information Perez now had the makings of a blockbuster story. A story certain to be seen across the country by agenda-setting reporters and their editors. She snatched the phone from its cradle and began punching in numbers.

Welcome to the
Jungle . . .

The next morning, Gideon McCarthy sipped from a disgusting concoction Estelle had whipped up in the blender: milk, two eggs, a carrot, and a powdered protein supplement the hospital nutritionist had recommended. The doctors had wired his mouth shut with a gap of about a quarter inch so he could talk and get the straw into his mouth. Two weeks of this crap and his stomach now turned at the first whiff.

"Is good, no?" Estelle asked.

"Dear Estelle, that's like asking the poor boy if a bed of nails has the feel of silk," Prentice LaFontaine said. News sat at the dining room table near the kiva fireplace eating a huge plate of *huevos rancheros.*

McCarthy lay on the couch in the living room in a pair of shorts and a T-shirt. Surprisingly he looked fit. With the wired jaw and the long walks he'd been taking, he'd lost fifteen pounds.

"No, really, *Tia.* It's good," McCarthy said. He glanced at the clock. Ten minutes to ten. The house, ordinarily boisterous this time on a Saturday morning with the children's playing, was quiet, subdued.

Estelle fumbled with her apron and hurried away into the

kitchen, calling over her shoulder, "Mr. News, you want some coffee?"

"Thank you, dear one, yes," LaFontaine said. He turned to McCarthy. "I must say I'd forgotten how much the gleaming steel in your mouth did for your general appearance. How long did you have them on after the car accident?"

McCarthy drew his lips back to reveal the full extent of the wiring job. "A month, so I got another two weeks to go."

"How pleasant." News jiggled his expensive black loafer. "Anyway, here's the gossip: the newsroom is still humming about the attack. The Zombie has called George Romero and demanded a legion of walking corpses to invade police headquarters. Abby and Croon have named you to the list of the top twenty living survivors of tragedy."

"Well after the Kennedy family I hope."

"I think you're number twenty exactly, displacing that little girl who fell down the sewer hole in Texas a few years back? The Kennedys' number one ranking remains intact. What else? The Slotman is pushing a special drink he named after you."

"C'mon."

"True! True!" LaFontaine chuckled. "A double bourbon with a dash of lime juice on the rocks. Up on the chalk board above the bar it says 'The McCarthy: Drink one of these and your jaw won't move for a month.' Roy Orbison said the Slotman made a fortune on them last Friday night."

"Just what I always wanted," McCarthy said. "To occupy a soft spot in the Slotman's heart."

LaFontaine grew somber. "Some people are wondering if you'll come back."

In the kitchen Estelle's bustling stopped. McCarthy glanced in her direction and saw her looking at him. He spoke to her more than News. "I'm not giving up."

The doorbell rang. Malice tore out of a back room, yelping, skidding sideways across the hardwood floor toward the front door, almost tripping Estelle, who spun neatly and wiped her cheeks with the folds of her apron. Carlos and Miriam appeared in the doorway to the back hall holding each other's hands. McCarthy forced a smile onto his face, "Baseball game time, guys. Ready?"

Carlos said nothing.

Miriam, a lovely little girl with shoulder-length dark brown hair, said, "Do we get to eat cotton candy?"

"You'll have to ask Mr. Owens," McCarthy said.

The doorbell rang again and a third time. Malice barked and leapt at the door.

Estelle said, "Well, does no one answer?"

McCarthy got up off the couch, picked up Malice, and opened the door. Charley Owens stood there in white linen pants, blue polo shirt, and tortoiseshell sunglasses, holding two California Angels baseball caps. "McCarthy."

"Owens," McCarthy said. Malice snarled and bared his teeth.

Owens took two steps backward. "Is the show of force necessary?"

"The kids love him."

"I bet. May I see my children now?"

"I'd like a word outside first."

Owens didn't seem to like the idea. "Can we lose Bowser at least?"

McCarthy tossed the dog inside and shut the door.

Owens peered at the yellowing bruises on McCarthy's face. "Judges don't look kindly on these dangerous professions in custody battles."

"We're here to talk about today, Charley. You go to the baseball game, then you come home, no side trips, no 'Gee I'm sorry we're late,' or I'll be on the phone to the judge to block any further visits. Clear?"

A vein pulsed along Owen's neck. "Clear."

"Another thing. I want you treat the boy like an egg."

"I'll treat him any way I want," Owens said. "He's my son, not yours."

McCarthy took a quick step forward, took Owens by the collar, and opened his mouth so the steel work gleamed. "Do I look like I'm in a negotiating mood here?"

Owens smiled wanly. "Not really."

The door opened behind them. McCarthy released his grip and stepped back. Miriam said softly, "Mr. Owens, can I have some cotton candy at the game?"

Owens knelt as Miriam came out through the screen door. "Sure, you can, honey. As much as you want. And you can call me daddy, you know."

"No," Miriam said. "I'll call you Mr. Owens."

She said it in such a sweet, matter-of-fact manner that McCarthy wanted to hug her. He looked up. Carlos stood in the doorway with Estelle behind him. Owens came erect and offered the boy his hand. Carlos shook it limply.

Owens said, "Hope you like the Angels. They're playing the Twins."

"I like the National League," Carlos mumbled.

"Well," Owens said. "We'll make the best of it, all right?"

"Okay," Carlos said uncertainly.

Owens looked beyond the boy. "Estelle, black becomes you as always."

Estelle said, "As always, you the same, Charley."

Owens gave her a forced smile, then slipped his sunglasses back on. "Okay, let's go kids. It's a long drive to Anaheim. Who wants to sit up front?"

"I do," Miriam said. She tugged her new baseball cap down over her ears. She marched toward Owens's rented white Lincoln, calling over her shoulder, "Bye, Gideon! Bye, *Tia!* You bring any cotton candy with you in the car, Mr. Owens?"

* * *

When they'd gone, McCarthy stared at the fabric of the sofa and the pattern in the Navajo rug Tina had brought to his home. LaFontaine chatted merrily about how Brad Perkins planned to open a personal training and nutrition counseling service for the gay community. He was calling himself the Physique Motivator.

"You haven't heard a word I said, have you?" News asked after several minutes describing the pending venture.

McCarthy said, "Brad's planning to open an eat vitamin and pump iron so you can give your significant other a bruise organization."

LaFontaine scowled at him. "I know you're feeling down, but was that necessary?"

McCarthy closed his eyes. "I guess I'm getting sick of me and my friends cast in the role of sucker."

"I tend to enjoy that role myself," LaFontaine said.

"Ha, ha," McCarthy said. "I'm serious, News. . . ."

The doorbell rang again. Estelle answered it and murmured for a few minutes. She leaned around into the living room. "Is two ladies, Gideon. They say they have to talk with you about some men named Patrick and Blanca."

McCarthy got up from the sofa. "Let them in."

A plump woman in her early thirties with lank brown hair, wearing a pink exercise suit entered. She was followed by a striking Hispanic woman in a tight-fitting, basic black jumpsuit. Her dark hair cascaded down to her shoulders in tiny ringlets. The plump woman said, "Which one of you is Gideon McCarthy?"

News extended a finger in McCarthy's direction. The woman rushed at him, raising her fists. "My husband didn't kill anyone!"

McCarthy grabbed her wrists before she could strike. The woman struggled, then broke down and bawled. Estelle came forward to lead her to a chair. McCarthy looked at the Hispanic woman and shouted over the din, "Mrs. Blanca?"

"Please, I'm Click Patrick's wife, Maria," she said in a streetwise tone. "I'm here to tell you Click doesn't have the *cojones* for murder."

McCarthy pointed to the sobbing woman. "So she's?"

"Anna Blanca. Been blubbering since your bullshit story appeared two weeks ago."

At that, Anna Blanca's histrionics settled. "I hate you for what you wrote," she said between hiccups.

"It was my job," McCarthy said, knowing that sounded ridiculous.

LaFontaine piped in: "He was only the messenger. Don't kill him, dears."

"Who are you?" Maria Patrick snapped.

"The messenger's friend, Prentice LaFontaine, esquire."

Maria frowned at McCarthy. "I would not have figured you for a *maricon.*"

"A queer's *friend,*" News said, annoyed. "Not his companion."

"Gee, so sorry," Maria said. She took a broad stance. "Okay, messenger, get your notebook. Me and Anna got a message to send to you."

McCarthy did as he was told. An interview with the wives of the accused was a good story. He brought a notebook and pen back into the room and handed them to LaFontaine, who looked at him questioningly.

"I'm on codeine, News," he said. "Do me the favor?"

LaFontaine grumbled, "Your stenographer awaits."

Maria Blanca said: "How much you know about my husband, Click?"

"Eight years on the force, hasn't made sergeant," McCarthy said. "Gentry testified he and a bunch of other patrols who worked the Boulevard extorted her for sex. Sorry to say it, but he isn't exactly a model officer."

"Yeah, yeah," Maria said, tapping the tip of a sharply pointed high heel on the rug. "Click's not the brightest guy in the world. But that's no crime. And he can be a very caring person. Click adores his children."

"Duly noted," News said.

"Right. Now this second thing, you know, about him extorting her for sex."

"We have that from several sources, including her grand jury testimony," McCarthy said, anticipating her protest.

"I don't care what you got," she insisted. "Did he lean on her for sex? Probably. We was . . . well, we was having problems earlier this year. But anyone was extorting anyone after that first time was her. She put the arm on Click."

"Diego, too," Anna Blanca whined. "She had a tape of them on the telephone."

That backed up Billy Kemper. "What did they talk about?" McCarthy asked.

Anna raised the tissue to her nose. "Diego didn't say. But I could figure, you know, based on the news stories. Sex probably."

McCarthy said, "I know Click called Gentry and talked to her about wearing a little red nightie to their next meeting. She taped that conversation. What I'm saying is that no matter who was extorting who, after her testimony, there's a lot of motive here."

"Yeah, yeah," Maria said dismissively. She hesitated. "A *red* nightie?"

"Fire engine red," LaFontaine said.

"That little prick," she said. "I'm gonna bust him in the chops next time I see him."

She fumed a moment, then continued. "But that still doesn't change things. Like I said, Click's a jerk, but he's no killer."

"Didn't have to be," News said. "The story said they hired someone to kill her."

"I can read," Maria snapped. "Look, Click's dream was to get off the streets, become an evidence tech. He talked a macho game to be accepted by the other cops. But do your job here, McCarthy. Get ahold of his record. He's a scaredy-cat."

Anna Blanca cut in. "But my husband's not. Diego's got a mean streak and that's why it doesn't make sense. If Diego wanted to kill someone, he'd do it himself. I know that doesn't sound like an alibi, but you'd have to know him to understand. Hiring someone would be like backing down."

McCarthy and News glanced at each other. Not too convincing, but it would make for a decent story.

"Look," Maria said as she pawed inside an oversize black pocketbook. She drew out a copy of McCarthy's story, already yellowing. "You say here the whore heard Click start the conversation about the contract and Diego having to be convinced."

"That's how she described it."

Anna said, "That's not how it would happen if it was true."

Maria interrupted. "If they was talking this for real, it would have been Click saying no and Diego doing the persuading."

"Absolutely," Anna said.

McCarthy thought about that a moment. "So you're not denying they said it?"

Maria rubbed her chin and took a quick look at Anna. "Like off the record? Yeah, they said it. But Click was fucking around, acting the tough guy. It was just talk."

LaFontaine said, "Gentry ended up dead three days later."

Suddenly all the bluster went out of Maria Patrick. Tears welled up in her eyes and she blurted out: "Look. We been to Internal Affairs. We been to Homicide. They all said the same thing: Our husbands are killers. I'm telling you this is wrong. Someone's got to believe us. This is wrong!"

* * *

"You think they're right, don't you," LaFontaine asked after they'd gone.

"Do you?"

"I hate to admit it, but I do. Their reasoning is convoluted, but it's the sort of understanding that only intimates can have."

McCarthy nodded and rubbed his sore jaw. He told LaFontaine that Gentry was not a regular on the Boulevard and that she boasted of working for an escort service, the number of which she'd given Dusk.

"Called it yet?"

McCarthy said, "Not yet. Maybe I'll head in to work, do just that."

"No!" Estelle cried. She'd been listening to the entire conversation. "I'm very frightened of all of this, Gideon. The children, oh, everything."

McCarthy went over and hugged her. "I can't sit around here all day thinking about them. Work will do me good."

He turned to LaFontaine. "You interested?"

"In making an appearance at *The Post* newsroom on a Saturday afternoon? I think not. It's 2:00 P.M.—daiquiri time somewhere. But you have fun."

LaFontaine dropped McCarthy at the door to *The Post* a half hour later, Estelle's angry clucks still ringing in his head. Inside, a skeleton crew of reporters and editors worked on what little breaking news there was on a Saturday. In a far corner, Isabel Perez and Claudette X hunched over a terminal editing the story about Barnes and toxic dumping.

McCarthy went to his desk and called the number Dusk had given him. The line rang once, then made a clicking noise, then a lower-toned ringing began.

A woman, her voice deep, throaty, and sensual answered, "Welcome to Tiger's Jungle. Can I help you?"

"I hope so."

"I'm having trouble understanding you. Can you speak up?"

McCarthy realized the way the doctors had wired his jaw slurred his speech. "I got a toothache," he said.

"Sorry to hear that," she said. "You should see a dentist. Any other aches and pains we can help with?"

"I was a little lonely this afternoon."

"With your toothache and all."

"That's right. I guess I'd like to play in Tiger's Jungle."

"What's your name?"

"Bob."

"Have you been on safari with us before, Bob?"

"No," McCarthy said. "I got your number from another great white hunter."

"Funny, Bob. Does the hunter have a name?"

McCarthy hesitated, "Actually, I don't know his name. He was just having a drink in a bar with me the other night and one thing led to another. He gave me the number."

"No can do, Bob," the woman said. "We work on referral by trusted clients only."

"I have lots of cash."

"I'd hope so. Adventure travel can be expensive. But a policy's a policy. No referral, no jungle tours. I sincerely hope your toothache gets better. Ciao."

The line went dead.

"Ciao," McCarthy said into the silent receiver. He considered calling the number again, then decided against it. No use getting the woman more suspicious than she seemed. He took the number downstairs to the library and found the crisscross directory, a book which allowed him to look up the phone number and find out the address it corresponded to. It took him ten minutes to find a match: 8390 Commercial Way, Suite H.

Interior Designs . . .

McCarthy checked out a staff vehicle with *The Post*'s bright logo on the side. So much for stealth. On the drive he decided coffee and M&M's were a reporter's best friends; they could give even the foggiest of scribes enough of a grip on reality to do their jobs. *Look at Roy Orbison. Hell, look at me: flying up the freeway on a funny-bone airline of painkillers, fear, caffeine, and melts-in-your-mouth.*

"Runway seven niner, we're making our approach," he yelled to himself as he exited off the freeway.

He passed a sporting goods store. A boy and his father tossed a football to each other outside. The giddy sensation deflated. The sober understanding that his children were traveling far away with someone their mother despised flooded in. He glanced in the rearview mirror, saw himself, and felt terribly inadequate. *Focus on moving forward,* he thought, *and you'll get by this.*

He got lost several times negotiating the maze of low-roofed, tan buildings surrounded by hibiscus and other flowering shrubs, but finally found Commercial Way, one of several cul-de-sacs at the rear of the Weber Industrial Park. Eighty-three-ninety sat at the back against the orange soil of a desert bluff. Smoked, reflective glass filled the doorframe of Suite H. "Flower Ltd." was painted chest high on the glass. Nothing else. He pulled at the handle. Locked.

McCarthy paused in the warm sunshine, listening to the breeze shuffle the leaves of the two poplar trees planted in front of Suite H. It was a longshot anyway. He knew a little about the escort racket. The clicking he'd heard on the telephone line suggested that 8390 Commercial Way, Suite H was probably a relay station and mail drop.

Questions remained. To what telephone number did the relay switch incoming calls? And who was the husky-voiced woman who answered on the other end? Maybe she had known Carol Alice Gentry. Then again, maybe she hadn't. For all McCarthy knew, Ms. Sultry Voice was a sales rep, and the escorts free-lance contractors.

He went to Suite I, a computer repair service. No answer. A sign said Saturday hours were 8–12. He'd missed them by forty-five minutes.

The sign in the window of Suite J said "For Lease." Suite K was also for rent. A short, lean, balding man in his late twenties holding a blowtorch answered the door of Suite L—*The Bird Bicycle Co.*

"Can I help you?" the man said.

"Gideon McCarthy. I'm a reporter with *The Post.*"

"Yeah? About time. I'm Steven Bird owner and sole proprietor, Bird Bicycles. I'm making the mountain bike of the future in here. Shock absorbers, fiber frame, twenty-one gears. Climb the Himalayas with what I'm building in here. Good story."

"Probably is," McCarthy admitted. "But not the one I'm interested in today."

Bird appeared crestfallen. McCarthy quickly added: "But if you'll give me a minute, I'll pass your card along. Somebody will probably come out."

Bird set down the torch. "Fair enough. What can I help you with?"

"I'm interested in your neighbor in Suite H. Flower Ltd."

"Don't know them," Bird said. "To be honest, I'm in my shop here most of the time testing prototypes. The only people I do see regularly are the computer guys. And there's the foxy older lady down the other end who comes in and out in her white Mercedes convertible a lot."

"Never saw a delivery van, like a floral delivery van pulling in there, to Suite H?"

"Not that I can remember," Bird said. "Why the interest?"

McCarthy shrugged. "It's a loose end of a story I'm working on."

"Anything to do with your teeth there?"

"No," McCarthy lied. "Got that trying to ride my son's skateboard."

"A bike's much safer," Bird said. "Got to get back to it now. Like I said, try the fox at the other end of the complex. She's here a lot."

"What's her name?"

"Don't know. It's Suite E or F."

Diane Tressor, Interior Decorations occupied Suites E and F. The hours listed on Tressor's door indicated she was closed on Saturday afternoons and open during the week to "The Trade Only," whatever that meant.

But the white Mercedes was parked out front, so McCarthy feigned ignorance and knocked. A platinum blond woman five feet eight inches tall wearing stone-colored stirrup pants, a black silk tank shirt, and lots of silver jewelry came to the door. She had the kind of high-culture beauty that makes lesser mortals like street reporters feel uncomfortable. She could have been in her late thirties. She could have been in her early fifties. She gave McCarthy the once-over, pausing briefly on his black high-top basketball shoes. "We're closed," she mouthed through the glass before turning away.

McCarthy rapped again, pressing his identification card against the glass. She examined it, studied him again, then twisted the lock open.

"Yes, Mr. McCarter?" she said.

"McCarthy. You're Diane Tressor?"

"I am," she said. She had a graceful, melodic voice. "And I'm fairly busy. I have a presentation to make Monday morning."

"I just have a couple of questions," he began.

The phone rang inside the office. She turned and looked back inside. It rang twice more, then stopped. "Can we make this quick?"

McCarthy nodded. "I'm interested in Flower Ltd."

Tressor hesitated for a moment. "Flower Ltd., are they an interior design group?"

"No, they're right around the corner here, Suite H."

She took a step outside to see where he was pointing. "I confess I don't pay attention to my neighbors. Why the interest?"

Before he could answer, the phone rang again. This time it kept ringing. "Excuse me a moment," she said. "My answering service doesn't seem to be on duty."

She darted back through the door. McCarthy followed. One side of the space was carpeted, open and quite large. He saw a closed loading dock at the far end. Expensive pieces of furniture, some wrapped in plastic, others bare, filled one section. Thick binders of carpet, fabric, and tile samples lay open on oak tables. And there, against the wall, stood a white plastic model of a large development.

Tressor had her back to him, speaking softly into the phone. She pecked at a computer. McCarthy crossed to the model and was surprised to see it was Sloan Burkhardt's Cote D'Azure project. A carefully calligraphied card noted that Tressor was the decorator for the hotel and office building planned.

"I know who you are now!" she cried. She was off the phone, moving toward him. "You're the reporter whose car blew up a few weeks back, the one who wrote the story about the two police officers who had that prostitute killed."

"Guilty as charged," McCarthy said. His reporter's instinct came on alert. His photograph had been on the front of both newspapers, but that was two weeks ago. The average mind processes and discards all images but celebrity.

"I thought I recognized you," she said. Tressor came very close to him. She wore expensive perfume. She had dazzling blue eyes and under the tank top her breasts were unnaturally perky. It had been a long time since McCarthy had been this close to a beautiful woman. It had been a long time since he'd been this close to any woman.

"Does it hurt? The jaw, I mean?"

"Only when I laugh."

"I promise not to be amusing," Tressor said. "Does this Flower Ltd. have anything to do with the bombing? Sorry to be so nosy, but I'm kind of a mystery buff. I read them all the time and well, my job is sort of mundane."

Mundane wasn't the word McCarthy would use to describe a business that catered to multimillion-dollar projects, but he couldn't help himself. He wasn't used to having stunningly attractive women fascinated with him. He smiled.

"So," she said. "Tell me. What have my neighbors done?"

"Nothing for sure," McCarthy said. "Their phone number came up in a conversation I had with one of the hook . . . um, prostitutes."

"The one who told you about the killing?"

The alert signal faded. McCarthy knew he probably shouldn't tell her, but she seemed innocent enough. And she smelled better than anything had in a long time. Was it the codeine-caffeine-sugar mix? Who cared?

"Yes," McCarthy said. "But I'd rather not go into what it's all about."

"Maybe I can help? I mean, I'm here all the time."

McCarthy shrugged. "I don't know. If you ever happen to see anybody going into that place, Suite H, could you give me a call, maybe write down their license plate."

Tressor frowned. "Is that legal? Writing down a license plate, I mean."

"It's a public document," McCarthy said.

She laughed and delicately touched him on the arm. "I never thought about it that way, but then again, I'm no investigative reporter."

McCarthy smiled again.

"Don't smile now, your jaw will hurt."

"I'll get over it," McCarthy said.

There was a moment of awkward silence, then Tressor said, "I really have to get back to work."

"Oh, right," McCarthy said. "The Cote D'Azure project."

Her enticing smile evaporated. "How did you know about that?"

McCarthy pointed at the model. She clapped a hand over her mouth and laughed again. "God, of course. You see, my involvement's supposed to be hush-hush. And you being a reporter and all."

"That's the sort of thing they write up in the real estate section."

She touched his arm a second time. "So I'm safe with you?"

"Absolutely, Ms. Tressor," McCarthy said.

"Please call me Diane," she said.

"Gideon, Diane. Well, I guess I should be going." He pulled out his wallet and handed her his card. "You'll call if you see anything?"

"I wouldn't miss it."

McCarthy was on his way toward the front door when from the rear of the warehouse, a woman with a thick, deep voice called: "I'm back. Sorry, I went to get a cup of coffee and some water and . . . Oh, sorry again. I didn't know you were with a client."

McCarthy turned to see a tall woman in her early twenties with an amazing shock of red hair that tumbled about her shoulders. Freckles dotted her creamy skin. She wore a black, sleeveless dress that hugged the kind of body McCarthy had seen only in photographs. She seemed embarrassed and went quickly to the desk with the computer.

"Caitlin Harris," Tressor told him. "One of my assistants."

"Your answering service?" McCarthy said.

"That, too." She gently steered McCarthy toward the door.

Just before he went out, he looked back over his shoulder and shouted, "Ciao Caitlin!"

"You're sure it was the same voice?" Prentice LaFontaine asked an hour later. They were at News's condo near the park. LaFontaine was wearing a bathing suit and jacket in a brilliant blue floral design. He was three daiquiris on his way to oblivion; the Physique Motivator was supposed to be home two hours ago and hadn't showed.

"If it's not, it's her twin's voice: sort of deep and sensual and, well, erotic," McCarthy said.

"Erotic?" News sniffed. "When was the last time you had real sex, Gid?"

"That's irrelevant."

"Frustrations play havoc with the imagination in the course of an investigation."

"Sir Arthur Conan Doyle?"

"P. LaFontaine."

"You're drunk."

"I'm severely depressed and actively pursuing the state of intoxication."

"You're throwing your life away on another of these bad boys," McCarthy said.

"Life!" LaFontaine laughed. "Life, as we who cover it know, is a savage, scandalous comedy with an equal number of satisfying and not-so-satisfying sex scenes and weepy moments that ends in tragedy: We all die. I'm just playing out my bit part in the drama until the denouement."

"You could at least try to pick your partners so you'd be happy."

"Piffle. What kind of story would that be to tell? No matter, back to your erotic voice. That forwarding telephone could be ringing anywhere. What's the possibility that it rings two suites away in the offices of a well-to-do interior designer?"

"Who designs for Sloan Burkhardt," McCarthy added.

News drew his glass away from his lips. "OOOH, you didn't say that."

"She's got a model of Cote D'Azure in her offices. She told me she recently got the contract. Supposed to be a secret."

LaFontaine got to his feet and trotted to a file cabinet on the far side of the room near the sliding glass doors that led out to his balcony. McCarthy couldn't help himself; while LaFontaine dug through the file cabinet, he peeked in at the movie marquee to see what was playing. **Beach Blanket Bingo.**

News turned from the file cabinet, saw him in the door to his bedroom, and said sadly, "I'd planned a matinee performance, beach trunks and everything. Anyway, Ms. Tressor is lying. She's had that contract from the get-go, listed here in the appendix to the filing Burkhardt had to make with the city as Decorating Consultant/LTD."

"LTD? She has a stake in the development?"

News frowned and shuffled through the stack of papers. "I don't think so. Burkhardt's the general partner of Blue Coast Ltd. And Carlton Bank's involved, of course. And Sankyo Bank of Tokyo, too."

"But she could be one of the limited partners, right?"

"I suppose it's possible."

"Which raises the question of who the others are?"

LaFontaine stared at the stack of paper. "Okay, I'm interested, but where does Gentry fit in?"

"I don't know," McCarthy said glumly. "Maybe I'm just hopped up from all the codeine I've eaten and trying to avoid thinking about Charley being with the kids."

"Or maybe there's something to it," News said. "Maybe Sloan Burkhardt is dirty, dirty enough to have been involved with a slain hooker. I say we go after it."

McCarthy thought about that a moment. "Okay, I'll go through the secretary of state's filings on Monday, try to figure out who the limiteds are. You use your contacts to find out more about Tressor."

News went to the blender, added more ice, and flipped it on. "Actually, Gid, I think we should trade assignments. You're only recently out of newspaper hell and this is a lowodds proposition. I think you should solidify your reemergence, write some follow-up stories to the arrest and your miraculous escape from the bomb."

"Even if I don't believe Blanca and Patrick did it?"

"Without a doubt. We might come up with zero on this angle. I can afford a zero. But you—even with the wallop you've laid down of late—can't."

McCarthy didn't like being out of the action, but he knew his friend was more a newsroom scholar than he was. "All right, I'll talk with Fisk, see what he thinks."

News sipped from the daiquiri. "You learn so quickly."

"How's that?"

"You're only as good as the piece you wrote yesterday. A two-week-old news story produces methane in the landfill."

Later, at the
Pink Stag . . .

66**W**hy the interest in a nouveau decorator, and
one of the wrong sex at that?" Carl Tracy
asked.

Prentice LaFontaine shrugged. "Call it men's intuition."

"C'mon, Prenty, you can do better. You know how the
gossip universe works: you titillate me, I electrify you."

News hesitated. They were in the Pink Stag's back office
behind the stage the female impersonators used for their
evening shows. Tracy, a small man in his late fifties, reached
across the table for an espresso cup. Tracy was among the
most socially and politically active people LaFontaine knew.
He was also one of the biggest blabbermouths in town. The
subtle withholding of information was crucial.

"Okay, okay. She's got the contract to decorate the Cote
D'Azure project. And I don't know who she is." All that was
true. Tracy needn't know that McCarthy also suspected she
was the second coming of Mary Magdalene.

"That's better," Tracy said smugly. He rearranged himself in his chair, then confided that Tressor had moved to
town three years before from Chicago. She was highly visible on the social scene, often at political fund-raisers with
Sloan Burkhardt. Several designers in town were furious
that Tressor, a relative neophyte in the field, got the plum
Cote D'Azure deal.

"They figure it was rigged from the get-go," Tracy said.
"I mean, honestly, News, how can you compete with a pillow talker?"

"From what I hear his pillow talk borders on the perverse." LaFontaine went on to explain to Tracy all that the ex–Mrs. Burkhardt had related about the developer's sex life. With the exception of the UCLA rape. Throw the guy a bone, not the carcass.

"Lovely!" Tracy giggled.

News grinned, too, praying silently that Tracy would reveal something that would make this morning's work make sense.

California secretary of state's records had given him the following picture: Blue Coast Partners Ltd. was composed of Sloan Burkhardt as managing and general partner and Diane Tressor as the only identifiable limited partner under the name Tressor Ltd. The rest were blind corporate entities: River Inc., Rock Inc., Tree Inc., and Perennial Inc. All, according to the snotty bureaucrat, were Nevada corporations.

The Nevada secretary of state's office was only slightly more helpful. The corporate offices of River, Rock, Tree, and Perennial were all at 1190 Pierce Way, Suite 3B, Las Vegas. An attorney, Max L. Crisp, was listed as agent and sole director for each of the companies. On a hunch he asked them to run Tressor Ltd. Same thing. He'd called up Crisp's office, and, as he expected, Crisp politely declined to discuss his clients.

News decided the only fresh angle was to find out as much as he could about Diane Tressor. Which was why he was in Tracy's office. Tracy grinned, then told him he wasn't surprised at Sloan's activities. His father, Coughlin, was the same way. A very well connected, tightly controlled bastard and political advisor to the mayor.

"But that was before he decided to build Alta Bay," News said.

"No, no, Prentice. You're thinking of Jennings. I'm talking about Portillo, the mayor now. Back in the seventies when Ricardo first ran for city council, Coughlin was behind the scenes, running the campaign, raising money. Funny, Ricardo really came out of nowhere. He was an obscure district attorney and then, bang, the most powerful man in town was on his side. I always wondered what the connection was."

"Maybe he just realized Ricardo was a bright guy."

Tracy laughed. "No one in politics does anything for altruistic reasons."

"Coughlin was making some kind of payback to Ricardo?"

"It was always my assumption."

"For what?"

"I've been trying to figure that one out for years."

LaFontaine thought about all of that for a minute, then asked. "And you figure Sloan has the same relationship with Portillo?"

"Possible, though certainly not as public as the relationship his dad had."

News smiled and got to his feet. "Appreciate it, Carl."

"Glad to help, Prentice. That little bit of slime about Sloan and the scenes is worth its weight in gold. Maybe I can get your delicious young friend with the big muscles to play opposite me in a scene featuring leather loincloths?"

LaFontaine tensed up inside. "I didn't know you knew Brad."

The nightclub owner made a dismissive gesture with his fingers. "Oh, we've met."

"Uh-huh. Any loincloth scene will be played *chez moi.*"

"So Brad's still with you?" Tracy looked up at LaFontaine half-lidded, a gossip iguana. "I'd heard he's been . . . out and about."

LaFontaine swallowed at the ball in his throat. *Don't let him see you sweat. Don't let him see your fear. Throw him some gristle, then get out the door.* "We had a little row over the weekend, but all was patched up by last night."

"So, so happy to hear it," Tracy said.

* * *

McCarthy studied News's chart of Blue Coast Partners. He'd just come in for his shift and caught LaFontaine about to leave for a dentist's appointment. "There's got to be some kind of connection here beyond the same lawyer we're not seeing."

"Maybe, maybe not," News said. "I mean, what are the odds there's any kind of link between a streetwalker like Carol Gentry and these companies?"

"Thousand to one," McCarthy admitted.

"I don't think they'd even give you those odds out at the Sea View Race Track."

"Last day of the season, isn't it?"

"Post time at four. All the fashionable ladies will wear their straw hats for the last time. And their wealthy fops in blue blazers, linens, and cream bucks."

"You usually attend."

"Not this year," LaFontaine sighed. "Brad finally returned Saturday night."

"Beach Blanket Bingo?"

LaFontaine smiled. "You know I never kiss and tell."

"You just show off your bruises."

LaFontaine turned away and pouted.

"I won't mention it again," McCarthy said.

"He told me he loved me if you must know," News declared. "We're attending a bodybuilding contest tonight. Love has its costs."

"All those oily bodies and you aren't interested?"

"I was never one for the vicarious."

"You're a reporter. Vicarious thrills are your life."

"Don't make things difficult, Gid. I have enough contradictions in my personality to justify as it is."

McCarthy checked his watch. "I have a meet with the ever-forthcoming Lieutenant Fisk. Feed the monster, protect my hide."

He grabbed a notebook and headed toward the door.

"Gideon!" LaFontaine called. "You forgot to tell me how it went with the kids and Charley Owens."

McCarthy stopped, his face clouded. "They had a good time."

"A serious complication," News said.

I'd call it the shits, McCarthy thought two hours later as he sat in his car in the parking lot outside Diane Tressor's office. When he had returned home Saturday evening the kids were playing out back. Miriam said she ate two huge puffs of cotton candy and a foot-long hot dog. Carlos said Charley had explained the system of relay throws from outfield to infield.

Outwardly McCarthy had done his best to show pleasure that the visit with their father had gone well. Was he an asshole for thinking it would be somehow better if Charley had hurt Carlos? That notion, which had been plaguing him since last night, sickened him. Then it twisted and became a panicking force that said: get your butt out of here with those kids and don't look back. He laid his head on the steering wheel. Maybe it's too much. This story. The bomb. He laughed, then began to dry heave at the absurdity of it. The explosion could have resolved the custody issue once and for all.

His cynicism deepened when he thought of the conversation he'd just had with Lieutenant Fisk. He'd gone to the homicide detective's office directly from *The Post*. Fisk continued to maintain that the bombing of his car was a coincidence. McCarthy argued the point, which annoyed Fisk. Then Fisk slipped him a story lead. The department was looking into Patrick and Blanca as possible suspects in the serial killings.

McCarthy was stunned. He told Fisk he didn't believe it because of everything Anna Blanca and Maria Patrick had described about their husbands. At that point Fisk had gone ballistic, calling him and all other reporters he knew hacks.

"The first thing you learn as a cop," Fisk said, "is that wives and mothers would tell you that Hitler was an okay guy."

Then Fisk threw him out of his office.

McCarthy lifted his head off the steering wheel. Pegging Blanca and Patrick as possible serial killers was a good tale, better than their wives' protests of innocence. He thought about what Fisk had said about being a hack only interested in a flashy copy. Not true, but it did raise the question: where did reporter end and investigator begin? Being an investigator implied following the trail until truth was discovered. Being a reporter was something altogether different; one could legitimately chronicle the different trails of information, even if they didn't lead to a final truth.

When Dusk told him the story of the hit, he believed it. Was it because the story was good for his comeback or because it held water? He shook his head, confused. But one thing was certain: McCarthy didn't believe Patrick and Blanca were serial killers.

Carol Gentry's killer? A chance of that. But the two police officers didn't fit the mold of murderers who slew women for twisted sexual gratification. While logic might play a supporting role in a single murder, contorted desire drives the protagonist through strings of slayings.

He tied together the threads of what he knew until they knotted and frayed. He slammed his hand on the steering wheel in frustration. Then he remembered something Lawlor had told him years ago when McCarthy was a cub reporter. "Don't try to prove what you think you know, try to disprove it. If it stands up, it's real; it's a story."

As good a method as any right now. He couldn't spend his time disproving Patrick and Blanca as serial killers. That could take months. He couldn't disprove what the wives said. Their analysis was too subjective. That left Diane Tressor and whether she was connected to Flower Ltd. and Tiger's Escort Service. That was disprovable. That was why he was here in the parking lot outside her office.

Steven Bird came out of his shop and rode down the street on a black matte-finished mountain bike with an odd-looking pair of handlebars. A couple of customers went into the computer store. McCarthy was about to get out to stretch when a black BMW sedan cruised into the lot and parked before Suite H. Sloan Burkhardt in a blue blazer, white pants, and white bucks got out. The developer considered himself in his side view mirror, then took the sidewalk past the flowering bougainvillea to Tressor's suite.

Two minutes later, Burkhardt held the door for Diane Tressor, who wiggled down the walkway toward the BMW, pressing a huge floppy straw hat to her head. The band about the crown was purple silk to match the color of her outfit, which included a backline that plunged almost to the rift of her ample fanny.

They climbed into the car and drove off. McCarthy followed, keeping a car between them as they traveled east through steep canyons, past vast housing tracts and strip malls, over an estuary toward the ocean where for five weeks a year the Southern California horse-racing scene gathered at the Sea View Race Track. The lot beyond the gates was mobbed. College kids in baggy white pants and Doc Martin boots stood shoulder to shoulder in the brilliant sun with grandmothers in floral print muumuus, grizzly bikers in leather skullcaps, and marine buck privates raw from boot camp. Above it all, the din of touts brayed the value of their racing tip sheets.

Like a lord among the great unwashed, Burkhardt drove his BMW crisply into the VIP lane, where he showed the attendant a red card. A gate opened. The black sedan disappeared in a cloud of dust. McCarthy swore and crawled through the general admission lane, finally passing the gate a full ten minutes later. Inside, he shouldered his way through the crowd at the betting windows. He climbed the stairs above the grandstands, looking for the entrance to the exclusive glass boxes and the turf club.

McCarthy was halfway up the staircase when Augustus Croon and Abby Blitzer appeared out of the crowd. Dark bags hung under Blitzer's eyes, which were devoid of their normal spark. "We're here to do a feature on bonnets," she said dully.

"A few of them could be called tragic," McCarthy offered.

"This is farce, not drama."

Croon put a hand on Blitzer's shoulder. "Abby's pissed."

"I'm not pissed, I'm feeling nothing," Blitzer interrupted.

Croon nodded. "Claudette pulled us off the calamity beat for a couple of days."

"Said I couldn't handle the constant agony we've been getting the past week," said Blitzer, who rocked on her feet. "Humph! No one can handle agony better than me. So my lead wasn't right on that day-care center fire yesterday, so what?"

"You didn't include a verb, Abby," Croon gently chided. "And you sort of moved the facts around to make it seem like all the kids didn't make it out safe and sound."

Blitzer twisted from underneath his hand. "Whose side are you on?" she snarled.

"Yours, Abby," Croon said. "I'm always on your side."

Her jaw twitched. She flexed her hand so hard she broke her pen. Tears formed in her eyes. "Then show it! You just show it or I'm busting up this partnership."

"I'll try to do better," Croon soothed. "Why don't you wash your hands?"

Blitzer examined her ink-stained hands. "Wash?"

Without another word, she wandered off, clutching her

notebook. Croon played with the leather tabs on his camera bag.

"Ever since that nut with the pony," he said, "she's been talking crazy, talking about how she's been reading the Bible at night after she goes home and should be sleeping, how the Old Testament's just chock full of bloody pathos and nothing seems to match it. It's like she needs more every day, Gid, like she wants to see the ripped limbs and floating bodies of old Pharaoh and his boys after Moses laid the Red Sea on them. It's scaring the shit out of me, Gid, and being an ex-SEAL, I'm not easily spooked."

"Get her to take some time off," McCarthy suggested.

"I asked her a dozen times the last two days. She hasn't had a vacation since she got out of Betty Ford. She says she wants to work. Says work is a vacation."

"Vacation from what?"

Croon looked like he'd just broken his best camera lens. "I don't know."

Then his cheeks softened. Abby was coming back through the crowd. She seemed surprised to see McCarthy. "What're you doing here, Gid?"

McCarthy let it pass. "The usual, Abby, nosing around in somebody's business. You have a pass into the turf club and the swank seats?"

Blitzer nodded. "I suppose that's where the story is. As you can see the masses don't go for five-hundred-dollar dyed straw hats."

"Mind if I tag along?"

"Suit yourself," Blitzer said. "Let's get this over with, Croon."

Croon sighed, picked his green canvas camera bag off the floor, slung it over his shoulder, and hurried after the love of his life like a sergeant after his major.

Inside the turf club, McCarthy kept to the walls, trying not to stand out. He slunk along, scanning the upper crust crowd for Burkhardt and Tressor. It was almost fifteen minutes before he caught a fleeting glimpse of the interior decorator's muscular back.

Tressor sipped from a tall glass of champagne. One bejeweled hand rested lightly on Burkhardt's arm. The developer leaned against a white pillar. His attention lazily focused on a tall man with dark hair who had his back to McCarthy. Tressor giggled at what the man said, then reached out to touch him, too. The man turned, obviously engulfed in the same energy McCarthy had felt talking with her the other day. Police Chief T. Leslie Lawrence sported the leer of a sailor heading for shore leave after six months at sea.

"This has potential," McCarthy murmured to himself. He considered tactics for a moment, then went on instinct. The direct confrontation can be a wonderful lever. When you let the quarry know he is a bull's-eye, he often makes fatal mistakes.

"Chief Leslie!" he cried gruffly. "I didn't know you were a race fan."

Leslie turned, grinning at first in his practiced political manner, the smile melting from his face when he realized who had called to him.

"McCarthy," he coughed, then reached out to shake his hand limply. "How are you?"

"Wired." McCarthy opened his mouth in a mock grin.

"Yes, err, I heard," Leslie fumbled. He gestured toward Tressor and Burkhardt. "Do you know . . . ?"

"Mr. Burkhardt? Just from the stories in the papers. But Diane and I have met. Just the other day in fact. Her receptionist, Caitlin, has a resonant, sultry voice."

Tressor glanced at Burkhardt, who held his hand just below the break of his jaw.

"I've never had the pleasure," Leslie said, coughing again.

"It's distinctive," McCarthy went on brightly. "I've only heard one other like it."

"And when was that?" asked Tressor, without expression.

"Sort of embarrassing to admit it, but when I called an escort service called Tiger's. The woman who answered had the same kind of deep, well, sexy way of talking."

Burkhardt's lips thinned. Leslie frowned as if he couldn't quite believe what McCarthy had just said. His face reddened. "McCarthy, you're on thin ice here. These people are personal friends of mine. To imply . . ."

"No, Larry, wait," Tressor said. She thrust her shoe out provocatively and balanced the weight of her leg on the spike of the heel. "I want to hear him out. It's amusing. What are you trying to say, Mr. McCarthy?"

McCarthy shook his head in mock dismay. "The other day it was Gideon. Oh, well. It's like this, Ms. Tressor. I called a phone number last week and talked to an extremely sexy woman. I traced the number to a suite two doors down from yours. Then I hear Caitlin, who has a voice so similar I lie awake at night thinking about it all."

Burkhardt pushed himself off the pillar between McCarthy and Tressor. His chin trembled. He sputtered, "I find your insinuations insulting. If you continue to make them, I'll take legal action. Diane Tressor is one of the most talented designers on the coast."

Leslie pointed a finger. "I'm a witness."

McCarthy showed his palms. "No one's accusing anyone of anything. I just notice things. Voices that sound alike. Who talks to whom at functions like this."

Leslie's eyes narrowed to slits. "You want to know how I know these fine people? Sloan and I sit together on the board of a charity—the Lollipop Kids. We help bedridden children get out to zoos and parks."

"We send them over the rainbow where skies are blue," Burkhardt said sharply. "But I suppose that kind of thing doesn't appeal to a reporter."

Tressor edged into McCarthy's space. She spoke in the

tone of a gently scolding teacher. "You intrigued me the other day with that Flower Ltd. company so I asked my landlord about it. The suite hasn't been rented in nearly a year, not since a company that cared for office plants moved out. There's nothing inside, no desks, no telephones, nothing. I'm afraid you must have traced the wrong number."

For a moment, McCarthy succumbed again to the intoxicating energy that floated around the interior decorator. Then he heard the sultry voice again.

"I didn't trace a wrong number," McCarthy said. "Make all the threats you want, but something stinks here and I'm going to find out what's rotting. I hope you all have a pleasant evening."

With that he strode off into the crowd. It was almost five and he should have been in the night cops office by now. It wasn't until he was almost to the car when something Chief Leslie said came back to him.

"The Lollipop Kids!"

Spiked! . . .

66I didn't accuse anybody of anything!" McCarthy protested. "I just pointed out the strange coincidence of the voices and the proximity of Flower Ltd. to Tressor's offices."

He was sitting in the editor-in-chief's office the next morning along with Ed Tower, Neil Harpster, Bobbie Anne Pace, Claudette X, and Stanley Geld.

Connor Lawlor gritted his teeth. "Cuteness doesn't become you, Gid. This is damn serious. I've been getting calls all morning."

Tower held up a copy of this morning's *Beacon*. "To make matters worse, *The Beacon* publishes a story saying Blanca and Patrick are serial killer suspects while we lead with an apology from their wives."

"I included the stuff about the serial killer," McCarthy said.

"But you buried it," Neil Harpster said. He looked tired and haggard from lack of sleep, but was doing his best to appear leaderly. "That was the story."

"That serial killer stuff is as full of holes today as it was yesterday. To my mind it didn't even deserve to be in the paper. But I put it in because it came from Fisk."

"You missed the lead," Bobbie Anne Pace said coldly.

"Something's going on with Fisk," McCarthy insisted. "He's not dealing straight with me, but I can't figure out why. What the wives were saying makes a lot of sense. Prentice was there when they talked to me. We both believed them. Why doesn't Fisk?"

"Now we're ceding to LaFontaine as arbiter of truth," Tower said, rolling his eyes.

"But, *as you know*, Ed, he gets remarkably accurate information," McCarthy said.

Tower sputtered and flushed red. "Yes . . . he . . . does."

McCarthy turned to Lawlor. "Connor, there's too many questions left unanswered if Blanca and Patrick did kill Gentry."

"Such as?" Lawlor said. Word was Swingo had circulation up twelve hundred, but he still seemed harried.

"What's the real motive?" McCarthy said. "Sure she humiliated them, but she gave no hard evidence to the grand jury. Her word against theirs and it doesn't seem to have accounted for much. There's been no indictment."

"Maybe she had evidence she never revealed," Claudette X said.

"But we don't know that," McCarthy replied. "There's a lot more leverage—and potential motive—in the kinds of clients she was servicing as part of Tiger's Escort. Remember Rivers's story awhile back? Gentry's brother said she had a thing for leverage."

Lawlor hesitated, then said, "Who's to say she wasn't blackmailing Patrick and Blanca?"

"I think she was. But there's also the possibility she was blackmailing other people, more powerful people."

"Like Sloan Burkhardt or Leslie?" Geld asked incredulously.

"Why not?" McCarthy bristled.

"We've maligned the police department already," Tower said, regaining his composure. "Now you want us to smear the chief, a leading developer, and the developer's girlfriend?"

"If I can prove it! Listen, there's a lot about Burkhardt and Tressor that's rancid. Prentice has found all sorts of things about them that don't make sense."

"People Don't Make Sense," Tower snickered. "I could have written that headline thirty years ago when the judge sent Connor to jail for refusing to name his sources."

Lawlor puffed out his cheeks and blew. He rubbed his thumbs against his temples. "LaFontaine's working on this, too?"

"No . . ." McCarthy began. "Well, sort of."

Geld ran his fingers through his permed hair and made a moaning noise. "Connor, honestly, I had no idea they were off on a wild-goose chase . . ."

Lawlor held up his hand. "Get News in here."

Claudette X left the room and came back with LaFontaine, who beamed upon entering the meeting. "A seat in the inner sanctum at last. *Je suis arrivé.*"

"Sit down and shut up," Lawlor ordered. "I want everything you know about Gentry and cops and developers and interior decorators."

LaFontaine cleared his throat conspiratorially, loving the center of attention. He told them how he'd been suspicious of the loan to Cote D'Azure because of Bobby Carlton's death. He talked of the cover-ups involving the rape at UCLA, of the sealed record from seven years ago, and of the oblique structure of Blue Coast Partners. He told them that Tressor had no background in interior decorating, yet she had managed to land one of the largest local contracts in recent history.

Lawlor said. "But what's Burkhardt doing now? I don't see the story."

News shrank in his chair. "It's a feeling. And it seems to go back and be somehow involved with his father. I mean, you knew Coughlin, didn't you, Connor?"

"Who didn't?" Tower said before the editor-in-chief could reply. "What's the point?"

"Lots of people who know Sloan, even his former wife, say he isn't like Coughlin. He doesn't ride the line of what's right and wrong. He routinely goes over it."

Lawlor stared off into space. They all waited a moment.

"Connor?" Tower said finally.

The editor-in-chief started and reached down to rub at his bad knee. "Sorry. I've had a rough week. Yes, well . . . Coughlin. He pointed me in the direction of a few things back during the Jennings days, but I didn't know him well. You're chasing ghosts here. Oddities, minor skeletons that don't add up to a story."

McCarthy said, "But three of these oddities, as you call them, seem to have a shape. One, Gentry may have had something to do with Tressor and so, maybe, Burkhardt, who has a history of hurting women."

News piped in: "Then there's this sealed record that I think has to do with the Lollipop Kids. And Chief Leslie belongs to the Lollipop Kids . . ."

Tower threw up his hands and roared, "What do you think the Lollipop Kids do?"

LaFontaine stammered, "Burkhardt's ex-wife said they were an all-male group, sort of a dining club. She said he had parties at his house with the Lollipop Kids and maybe during one of them was when the sealed case happened."

"What do you suspect?" Lawlor asked in a cutting tone.

"I don't know, exactly," News fumbled. "Something sexual, I suppose."

"Like what?" asked Harpster brightly. Then he frowned. "I really don't want to know. We're not the *National Enquirer.*"

Lawlor chortled. "If these two were in charge, we would be."

"Hey, just a minute," McCarthy protested.

Lawlor's face clouded. He pointed a finger at him. "No, you wait just a minute! You have again caused this paper embarrassment. And you missed the lead on a damn good story. You get so horny for a blockbuster—while on painkillers, I might add—that you peg this paper's reputation on the fact you think you've heard a voice twice."

Lawlor turned to LaFontaine. "And you! There are probably two hundred prominent people in this city who belong to the Lollipop Kids. Including Cardinal Mahoney, Mayor Portillo, half the corporate CEOs. Also Ed. Also me. Am I part of your theory?"

LaFontaine's mouth drifted open. For once he was without a comeback.

McCarthy felt very small. "Connor, we never said . . ."

"Not another goddamned word!" Lawlor growled. "This escapade is over. *The Post* will no longer support it. And if I find out either of you are spending my time—my time!—on anything this frivolous and potentially damaging to my paper again without my direct supervision, you'll be on the street. Clear?"

"Clear," McCarthy said.

"Crystalline," LaFontaine said.

Tower gave them his patented shark's smile and opened the door to show them all out.

* * *

"I want a stronger look at the serial kill angle for tomorrow, 750 words for metro," Claudette X said. She loomed over McCarthy's desk with her arms crossed.

She turned to LaFontaine. "As for you, there's a rubber chicken political thing downtown I want you to cover tonight."

Both reporters nodded morosely. Then the executive assistant city editor said: "I think after you turn in these stories, a few days off are in order."

"I just got back," McCarthy said. "I'm not tired."

"Moi, non plus," News mumbled.

Claudette X sat on the edge of LaFontaine's desk. She tossed her wrist at McCarthy. The dozen thin silver bracelets she wore jangled like high-pitched wind chimes.

"You and I have a date at the preliminary custody hearing day tomorrow afternoon, don't we?"

McCarthy nodded.

"Then take the time to prepare. And recover. Two days."

McCarthy didn't answer.

"That's an order."

When he shook his head, she whispered, "Think of it this way: what you do with your own time is your business, not Connor's or Ed's."

McCarthy glanced up at her. "You think we're right, don't you?"

"Not saying I do, not saying I don't," Claudette X replied. "All I know is that this place has been haywire lately. All sorts of pressures. General nastiness. Harpster's losing his mind over this vandal that's ravaging his garden. Pace is plotting with her flunky to control the world. Stan's gone totally nuts. I think Connor's too wrapped up in the war to see the possibilities. Ed, I can never figure him out."

News said. "I guess what Lobotomy Lane doesn't know about our own private investigation won't hurt them."

"Like the Zombie, I speak no evil . . . as long as it's out of my newsroom," Claudette X said. "Once you come back in here, you will abide by the law. Clear?"

"Crystalline!" LaFontaine cried as she walked away.

None of the three was aware that the Zombie had been listening in on their entire conversation. He had been eating a sandwich of wilted Bog Rein orchids, priceless fern, and mayonnaise on homemade cactus bread. Now he put the strange luncheon combo down. His eyes fired up the color of molten pig iron at the news he was reading between their lines. He watched Claudette X weave her way back through the desks, silently thanking her for the invaluable information.

Claudette X had her own problems to deal with. Ever since Geld had planted the seeds of power lust and paranoia along Lobotomy Lane, the bureaucracy of the paper had lurched more wildly than ever. Earlier this morning, Harpster had asked her to check Pace's hands and forearms for scratches from the rosebushes sabotaged over the weekend. And she'd hung up on Margaret Savage when the columnist called seeking advice on how to research investment portfolios and personnel files.

The executive assistant city editor slumped into her chair in front of her computer terminal, acknowledging that she'd better see a shrink soon or risk a nervous breakdown. The nightmares were so bad over the weekend, she didn't dare blink.

The overwhelming fatigue had stripped away her anger by Sunday afternoon. She and Stacey had watched a preseason football game, starring her ex-husband, who had six unassisted sacks. He was an adulterous shithead. No doubt about it. But during the game, seeing him guzzle Gatorade on the sidelines, she'd found herself missing him. It was the pits raising a daughter without a man. She was thirty-six, hadn't had a date in ten months and was unlikely to in the near future. Women six-foot-four with biceps like small mountains weren't the flame of the average male moth.

Ever since the divorce she'd managed to use work to keep these kinds of thoughts at bay. Of late, however, the balance inside *The Post* had heaved like a ship in gray waters. The constant splash on the deck had quenched the furious inferno she needed burning inside to feel right. In its place were emotions she'd rarely allowed herself before: pity, goodwill, loneliness and . . . dare she admit it? . . . fear?

Her right hand trembled. She grabbed it with her left to still it, looking around to see if any of the Stepford Editors had caught the tremor; the slightest show of weakness and that mutant cadre of Ivy Leaguers would come alive with pack fury and devour her. None of them noticed. On deadline they rapped away at their keyboards with the passion of certified public accountants in early April.

It took nearly ten minutes of concentrated effort to get the tremor to subside. Only then did she look up from the keyboard, her attention wandering over the city desk and coming to rest on Stanley Geld, whose arms snaked and sinewed through the air like a Hindu prince in an ecstatic sacrificial dance to Siva. She followed his gaze. A tsunami crashed over her gunnels. Neil Harpster was leaving the newsroom with his brown leather satchel in hand. Bobbie Anne Pace was fifty feet behind him in a black trench coat, a camera over her shoulder, a cassette recorder in her hand.

Claudette X fought back the bile that crept up her throat.

Ciao, Baby! . . .

A t the same time, Kent Jackson was sitting in the Café de La Plage near the harborfront, his favorite luncheon spot. He squirmed in his chair, excited. He felt the cataclysmic rumblings of a big bang story about to break. He didn't know what it was yet, but he knew where it was going to occur—somewhere in the dark, gassy inferno of the ongoing gubernatorial race.

He glared at the Sunday edition. Isabel Perez's article on toxic waste dumping by Jim Barnes, the Republican candidate, was bannered across A-1. He told himself to calm down, let her have it, this wasn't what he felt boiling below the surface, this wasn't what would land him his book contract and a new life free of debt. For a split second he wondered if the foreboding was a side effect of the antidepressants he'd been wolfing since learning Patti was pregnant. He looked at his lap. Could God have really dealt him a short hand in the reproductive poker game?

No way! He knew he had the juice in the same way he knew there was a big story, probably a Pulitzer, lurking out there, right now.

He'd been prowling city hall ever since McCarthy broke the murder contract. He was convinced that was only the tip of the story. He'd seen the evidence in the sudden silences and the forced greetings of Mayor Portillo's aides, in their skintight smiles, and in the way they jingled change in their pockets when they spoke to him.

Arlene Troy was avoiding him. So was Chief Lawrence. He hadn't had an interview with Mayor Portillo in nearly two weeks. They were shutting him out and he knew it. What were they hiding?

One of his prime sources, a paralegal assigned to the mayor's office, had told him that there had been a late-night strategy session among the campaign's top operatives in the wake of McCarthy's story. She'd gotten a hurried glance at notes Leslie had taken and, among other things, seen a cryptic reference in the margin to a land deal outside Las Vegas.

He'd asked Troy if Portillo owned property in Nevada. The mayor's press secretary was very, very good, controlled, jovial, cool; but she'd clenched her teeth ever so slightly before answering that, yes, he'd purchased property on Lake Mead for his retirement. Troy characterized it as a straightforward deal and he, not wanting to spook her, had let the answer stand.

Immediately afterward, however, he'd gone to the city clerk's office and requested the financial disclosure documents Mayor Portillo and Chief T. Lawrence Leslie were required to file every year. The clerk informed him that unfortunately the files were in a rear room that had suffered a burst water pipe. It was under reconstruction. The files wouldn't be available for a few days.

A woman's velvety voice broke Jackson's thoughts. "You don't mind if I take a seat, do you? It's so crowded here today."

The Post's chief political reporter raised his hand to his brow to block the noonday sun. A very tall woman in her early twenties with an amazing shock of red hair that tumbled down about her shoulders. Freckles dotted her creamy skin. She wore an emerald cotton jumpsuit that outlined a body that even a born-again Christian doped on Prozac would have trouble forgetting at night.

"Not at all. Please, sit down," he said, standing to pull out a chair for her. Was his hair combed? His tie straight? Did his wire-rimmed glasses make him appear the politically savvy reporter or policy dork?

She put a salad and a flavored seltzer water on the table and a large leather portfolio next to her chair. She smiled ever so wonderfully. He fumbled with his newspaper.

She opened the seltzer water. "That's a good paper."

"I . . . I write for it."

"Really? What's your byline?"

He pointed to his piece on the metro page about Portillo's planned media tactics.

"Kent Jackson," she said. "I read that article this morning. Taught me something. I hate it when articles don't teach me something. I'm something of a self-improvement nut, read three newspapers a day, a book a week, yoga . . . oh, listen to me go on."

"No, no," he stammered. A beautiful woman who read the newspaper. Goddamn it, a beautiful woman who read his articles and said they taught her something!

She reached her hand across the table. "Caitlin Donnelley."

He shook her hand. It was a soft hand.

"I wouldn't have figured you for a reporter," she said.

"Why's that?"

"You're dressed so nice. Calvin Klein braces, nice tie, fitted dress shirt, and worsted khaki pants. Doesn't fit the image. I tend to notice these things. I'm a model."

"No kidding. Must be a glamorous life."

She rolled her eyes. "For some, I suppose. I'm too large in the chest for *haute couture*, so I'm not on the runway much. New York once or twice a year. Certainly not Europe. Tits aren't back in Europe yet. And my skin's too fair for most bathing suit shots, so it's not like I travel to exotic islands for *Sports Illustrated.*"

"Then who do you model for?"

"Department store ads mostly," she said. "This afternoon I do lingerie. With my eyes and hair I shoot well in satin and lace. I'm your basic take your jeans off, put these on, and look hungry kind of model."

The thought pinched at his lower lung until he had to remember to breathe. Damn Patti! He'd show her!

"So you live here?" he asked.

"I just moved in. By the way, are there any good Thai restaurants in town?"

He blanked. "Thai, uh, yeah, the Golden Triangle, it's uptown near Fourteenth."

"That's great to know, thanks, Kent." She cocked her head. "I hope you don't think I'm pushy or anything."

"Not at all."

"Good," she grinned. "Then how about you and me going to the Golden Triangle. I don't know anyone in town yet really, so it would be nice for me. My treat."

The pinching got worse; now it extended to his intestines, which went liquidy. "You're asking me out? You barely know me."

"You seem sweet and it would be nice to talk to someone with a brain for a change," she said. She cocked her head again. "Unless you're married or something?"

"Separated and divorcing," he said.

"Good for me," she said, patting him on the hand. "How's tomorrow night sound, around seven?"

"Okay," Jackson said. "Okay. All right. I'll meet you there. I'll do that."

She grinned. She shook her hair back and put on a pair of wraparound sunglasses. She picked up her portfolio. "Time to get hungry! See you tomorrow. Ciao, Kent!"

"Ciao, Caitlin!" Jackson cried. "Ciao!"

Bobbie Anne Pace clicked off the tape recorder. She bit at the quick of her fingernail. She peered out through the wall of her Glasshole toward Connie Mills, who was gathering her things to leave for the day.

Pace said, "You know he's forcing her to do it against her will."

Margaret Savage stared at the tape machine. "How long did it go on?"

"My God, an hour at least," Pace said. "Her begging 'No, Neil! No, Neil! Please!' The man's an animal."

Savage twisted in her chair so she could see into Neil Harpster's office. The Assistant Managing Editor for Form and Content was busy perusing a stack of files with a contented grin on his face.

Savage said, "And Geld thought Neil was involved in an investment scam."

"Geld's a fool," Pace said. "We have to figure how to help that poor woman."

"Yes, that poor, poor woman," Savage said. She continued to stare in the direction of Harpster's office.

"Margaret? Margaret?" Pace demanded. "Are you all right?"

Savage shook her head as if coming out of a trance. "Right? Of course I'm all right. I was just considering the possibilities."

"And?" Pace asked.

"What else would you call that? Sexual harassment. Of the most vicious kind," Savage said. "We talk to Ms. Mills, find out how long he's been coercing her into that sordid little motel room, and convince her to sue."

Pace gasped. "It's brilliant, Margaret! The ensuing publicity will crush Neil's chances of getting Ed Tower's job."

"I told you it was only a matter of time before he revealed his true character."

"You did, oh, you did," Pace crooned. "Now, who should approach Connie?"

"You'll be out in front on this," Savage said without hesitation. "She's young and relatively new here, obviously in a difficult situation. You represent a power figure, someone of Harpster's stature she can rely on in case of reprisal."

"I'll have to be delicate. I don't want her to run scared."

"You'll do fine," Savage said. The columnist took the cassette tape from the machine. She dropped it into her colorful Peruvian cloth purse.

"What are you going to do with that, Margaret?" Pace asked.

"Don't worry," the P.C. Oracle soothed. "I'm going to take it home and make a copy. For *our* protection."

An hour later Neil Harpster climbed out of his Audi into the perfect Southern California twilight. He closed his eyes and stood still. He reveled in a silence broken only by the freeway din. Inside Lydia would carp about the floral killer that stalked their garden. Even though the sicko hadn't struck in two days, Lydia was sure to force Neil out into his sleeping bag against the garden wall to spend another night in the damp ocean cold clutching the twenty-gauge pump shotgun.

He yawned at the thought of another night upright in the lawn chair. He yawned again and attributed his advanced state of muscle fatigue to today's luncheon with the fair and lascivious Ms. Mills.

It had been her idea this time, the naughty girl. She'd called and suggested a new game. She called it "No Means Yes." She'd gone to the costume store on Twentieth and Market Streets and rented outfits that made them look like the characters on the cover of her favorite new historical romance novel, a bodice ripper entitled, *Love's Furious Fury*. It was, she'd told him, a tale of virginal conquest in old New Orleans.

He had felt foolish at first wearing the maroon pirate's shirt, the knickers, the bandanna, and the long blond wig. In the mirror he was an anemic version of the muscular hunk on the cover of the paperback. But seeing Connie come out of the bathroom in a crushed velvet ball gown with the bodice laced tight over her pink boobs, he threw aside all misgivings. Call me Bluebeard!

Connie had two copies of *Love's Furious Fury* and had dog-eared the sections they were to reenact. Each one began with her crying "No! No! No, Neil, No!" to which he invariably replied something along the lines of "Yes, Yes, you know you can't resist your desires. Let them go, because No means Yes."

Harpster opened his eyes and sighed. It wasn't much as literature goes, he thought; but the memory was more than enough to get him through another night in the lawn chair.

1-800 I-Boozer . . .

Fernando Lazzard Trujillo loved nothing more than news of a wealthy drunk driver stewing in the downtown holding tank. Suffering a few hours of one-sided, migraine-soiled conversations with transvestites, street hoods, and junkies down from their latest whoop was usually all it took for them to call his now infamous 1-800 I-BOOZER line and agree to his exorbitant retainer. He put up the first billboard with his smiling face and the 800 number seven years ago. Now they pocked the landscape from Pasadena to the Mexican border. The billboards had vaulted his stature from obscure ambulance chaser to crown prince of the Southern California D.U.I. Bar. Prentice LaFontaine figured it must have been a bumper crop night for the prince. He'd been sitting at this outdoor café outside Trujillo's office the better part of two hours now and no Fernando.

News had finally gotten the energy up to review his notes last night and stumbled onto an overlooked sliver of information that opened up this possible chink in Sloan Burkhardt's armor. The California Bar Association gives all attorneys a coded identification number. That code follows them everywhere they go. It is entered every time they are involved in a court proceeding, even when the details of the proceeding are sealed.

For the hell of it, News called the state bar association office and asked them to run the attorney code on Burkhardt's sealed case. If the name of any other lawyer in the city had popped up, LaFontaine would have spent the day at the beach. But lotuses of hope sometimes spring from brackish water.

The third espresso and croissant of the morning boiled in his stomach when Trujillo appeared. The attorney padded across the intersection as if he were barefoot and the asphalt thorns. He stopped every few feet to peer down at a pair of bright white socks protruding from black leather, open-toed sandals. LaFontaine threw some cash on the table and hurried after him, catching Trujillo just as he reached the foyer to his office building.

"Good morning, Fernando," LaFontaine said.

"Prentice, I thought they fumigated you years ago," Trujillo said. His thinning hair was brushed back. The jacket of his green poplin suit strained against a stomach News didn't remember. The attorney shuffled into the elevator.

"Some bugs are impervious to DDT," News said. "Can we chat a bit?"

"About?" Trujillo held an alligator hide briefcase and a white bag that reeked of fast food. He yanked at his tie until it loosened. He unbuttoned his collar.

"An old client of yours."

The doors to the old metal cage elevator opened. "That, Mr. Bug, would violate ethics."

"Never thought of you as a champion of virtue, Fernando."

Trujillo sniggered. "What I always liked about you, Prentice, you never stood toe-to-toe, always looking below the belt. You'd a been a decent gangster."

"An instinctive street fighter always looks for weakness," LaFontaine said. "I apologize."

"For what?" Trujillo grunted. "I've been in this business thirty-one years. I'm beyond taking offense. Besides, my feet are killing me. Podiatrist cut three bunions out of my poor dogs day before yesterday."

He opened the door to his office. A woman a third Trujillo's age with a teased hairdo sat at a new computer in a freshly painted waiting room.

"Any messages?"

"You got these two an hour ago, Mr. T. I think they're still in the tank. The second one there, Palmer, third offense, says he can't lose his license."

"Probably has to chauffeur Bill Clinton to the airport this afternoon, right?" Trujillo glanced at his watch. "Find out the arraignment schedule. Get Tony L. to pull the past records on the three-timer. I got to eat some breakfast and soak my feet, then I'll be down."

She was already picking up the phone.

"Uh, Fernando?" News said.

"You still here, Bug?" Trujillo asked. "Told you, client privilege."

"Give an insect a chance. I've been chasing Sloan Burkhardt so long without a break I feel like a fanatic."

"Sloan Burkhardt!" Trujillo drew back his lips to reveal a gold cap on his front right incisor. "A member of Fernando's Asshole Hall of Fame. Why didn't you say so?"

The carpet in Trujillo's office was two inches deep. The desk near the window looked freshly refinished to match the row of new oak filing cabinets.

"D.U.I.'s been very, very good to you," said News, looking around. "I seem to remember this place as a way station for various vermin."

"1-800 I-BOOZER. My one fucking stroke of genius,"

Trujillo said. He crossed into a small bathroom, ran hot water into a plastic bucket, then poured Epsom salts in and carried it to his desk. He stripped his feet of sandals, white socks, and bandages, then laid them gently in the steaming water. He closed his eyes momentarily and smiled. From the white bag he got a cup of coffee and two burritos that reeked of *chorizo*. Trujillo reached into a drawer and brought out a silver hip flask. He poured a bit into the coffee, took a drink, then asked, "What do you want to know about the Sloaner?"

"He has a sealed file. You got it sealed. I want to know what's in it."

Trujillo chomped through half of the burrito. Egg and *chorizo* squirted on his chin.

"Jesus, you butterfly boys go for the balls right away, huh?" he said. He laughed, then wiped away the grease with his napkin. "A sealed case. That's serious business, you know? What's your interest?"

"I can't tell you it's confidential?"

"Nope."

LaFontaine figured as much. He told Trujillo everything, except the suspected link between Burkhardt and Carol Gentry. When he'd finished, the attorney said, "What's in this for me I talk?"

"You said he was in your derriére hall of fame. Maybe I can make him a public asshole without even mentioning your name."

Trujillo wiggled his eyebrows. He took a last bite of his burrito. He finished chewing, then cracked his knuckles and stared at LaFontaine. "Bug, you're never going to get anyone else to confirm this. In fact, if I hear you even try, I'll sue you silly. Got it?"

"I'll take what I can get at this point," LaFontaine said.

"Just so we understand each other." Trujillo sat back and eased his bruised feet up on the mess of his desk. "Must have been seven, eight years ago, the year before Coughlin Burkhardt died as I remember. I'm sitting here having my *chorizo* and eggs, just like now. Only the office didn't look so plush. Anyway the old man himself comes through the door with Sloan. Now Sloan's maybe thirty, thirty-three, successful, and married at the time I think. But Coughlin pushes him through the door into my office the way a pissed-off father would a teenager who's fucked up. Seems Sloan had gotten himself into trouble with a lady, a pro. She's not taking it well that Sloan beat the shit out of her. She was pressing charges until she heard that there was money to be had, maybe a plane ticket to another town. Only there was the problem of the case being on the books. So, anyway, they ask me to participate as their representative in the complex and delicate negotiations with the lady and the judge over sealing the whole matter."

"Why you?"

"That's the thing," Trujillo laughed. "I think Coughlin was too embarrassed to go to one of his highbrow legal beagles to cut the deal, so he came here. I wasn't exactly a household name back then, and he wanted it all quiet. He even had me pay a couple of the low-level detectives something to keep their mouths shut."

"Did they?"

"Hey, for $10,000 apiece and no heat from the chief, you bet your ass they did."

"What do you mean the chief?"

"Leslie. Wasn't chief then, assistant I think. But he was in on the whole thing, making sure it all ran smooth. It was wired."

"Let me get this straight," LaFontaine said. "Leslie was in your office that day?"

"*Jesu* no, I haven't talked to Leslie in years. He was outside. I watched Coughlin and Sloan after they left, through that window there. They met Leslie on the sidewalk. Then all of them got into that big black Lincoln limo Coughlin used to tool around in."

Trujillo poured some more liquor into his coffee and laughed again. "Funny as hell, Coughlin coming to *me* to clean up his kid's fucking mess. I don't think they remembered me. But why should they? I was just a bit player back then."

"Back when?"

"I worked for Mayor Jennings maybe two years out of law school. I was what they called a liaison to the Mexican-American community. Jennings was cutting edge about that kind of thing. Mostly I think he saw how potentially powerful a voting block we Hispanics were. Wanted us on his side."

"So how did you know Coughlin?"

"Not really know, you know? But I was around with Jennings long enough to understand there was an enemies list. Coughlin was enemy number one. And I got involved in some stuff that wasn't . . . how should I put this? . . . too pleasant in retrospect? Anyway, I came within a short hair of being indicted myself. Testified at the grand jury same day as Coughlin. He didn't remember me when he came to my office."

"Or maybe he did and just didn't want to let you know."

"Possible."

"You ever talk to Lawlor back then?"

"Sure. Twice, I think. And, after he was in jail, to Tower. But who didn't? Those two were good. They had the whole story wired."

"What did Coughlin testify about?"

Trujillo shrugged. "I don't know for sure. Grand jury asked me about kickbacks on contracts out at the navy base. Probably asked Coughlin about the same stuff."

"The kickbacks. True?"

"Jennings was a crook, but they're all crooks, and he did some good things while he was raiding the till. Hey, what the fuck, it's history now."

LaFontaine looked back over his notes. "You're sure you saw Leslie that day?"

"Sure I'm sure. Even before he was on television all the time, I knew him."

"Thought you said you've never talked to him?"

"No, I said before I saw him outside my office I hadn't talked to him in—oh, Christ—more than twenty years. Last time was probably at Jaime Ramirez's wake. He and Ricardo Portillo showed up."

News screwed up his face. "Who's Jaime Ramirez?"

"The jumper. The one who brought it all down—Bobby Kennedy's Justice boys, FBI, everyone—on Jennings's head. Jaime worked on Jennings's personal staff. He was the one your editor linked to the Quintanas, the one who his anonymous sources said was involved in drug smuggling. Just after Lawlor went to jail for not revealing his sources on that story, Jaime took a dive off the top of city hall."

"Jesus," LaFontaine said. "I didn't know that."

"Very dramatic shit. Leslie and Portillo came to Jamie's wake scrambling after the fact to show they were on top of things. Lawlor hit everyone cold with that story."

"I don't get it. Why Leslie and Portillo?"

"You don't know shit, do you, Bug?" Trujillo said. "Leslie was a D.A.'s investigator back then. Portillo was one of the eight or nine research attorneys assigned to the Jennings probes. Portillo has always known how to be in the right place at the right time, always building the sweet résumé. We were active in the *La Raza* movement together, late fifties. So was Jaime and his brother, Pablo. Then me and Jaime went to work for Jennings. Portillo went to work to get him nailed. He's mayor now, running for governor. Jaime's dead. Me, I got these swell offices, the hooves of a Clydesdale, and all these upstanding clients to tend to."

"Jaime's brother still around?"

"Pablo? Sure. He runs a small import/export company down near the border, Aztec something or other."

Trujillo looked at his watch. "Speaking of upstanding clients, I got to visit a couple before they get too used to their nice new digs."

"Just a couple more questions," News said. "I was told Coughlin was an early backer of Portillo. True?"

"True. Probably saw him as the bright youngster. Hard not to, you know? Handsome, smart, well spoken. Goddamn choirboy."

"Someone suggested it was a payback from Coughlin for services rendered."

Trujillo shook his head. "If it was, you'll never find it. Ricardo's too shrewd. He's running for governor of California, right? All you local clowns and the East Coast media heavies been looking at him for months now and nobody's laid a hand on him yet. Barnes? Christ, your colleague there, Isabel Perez, she's just pulverizing him on the toxic dumping shit while our mayor's sailing calm water."

News knitted his brows. "If he's so clean, why'd you agree with me that Sloan probably got a sweetheart deal from Portillo's administration?"

"That's how it works," Trujillo said. "Probably not a direct payoff. Ricardo wouldn't risk his virginal image that way. Ricardo sees himself as an indebted *amigo* of the old man who helped him. He's going to pay close attention to Sloan's bid for the waterfront. It's not illegal, it's . . ."

"The system," LaFontaine said.

"You bet yours," Trujillo said. He dried his feet, laid fresh gauze on his stitched wounds, then gingerly drew his socks and sandals over his toes. He got up slowly and winced. "Have a nice day, Bug."

As they went through the door, LaFontaine said. "Why'd you say Sloan's in your asshole hall of fame?"

Trujillo made a spitting sound. "I got that seal in place in six weeks, a goddamn record. A couple of years later, I made a name and some money for myself with the billboards and all. I get invited to this political fund-raising party. The Sloaner's there, standing alone having a drink. So I walk up to shake his hand."

"Let me guess. He wouldn't."

"That fucking woman beater looked at my fingers like I just pulled 'em outta the ass of a dead dog at the Tijuana dump, just rotting in the heat. But, I'm a man. I walk away cool, figuring I got the better deal out of sealing that case."

"Tell me, tell me," News said.

"How do you think I got the cash to pay for that first billboard?" Trujillo laughed.

The Depths of Despair . . .

Gideon McCarthy cradled his father's trumpet. He watched Miriam and Carlos play on the swing set out beyond the porch. They seemed to move in slow motion. Each pump of leg and pull of arm to make the swings go higher, each smile at the swoop upward, each gasp at the arc down, took on terrible meaning. He was lost forever.

When Prentice LaFontaine came out on the porch and saw the anguish on his friend's face, he knew. He hugged McCarthy. "You haven't told them yet, have you?"

"I don't know how to." Tears welled in McCarthy's eyes. "It's not final, is it?"

"No. But the way it went we have to prepare for the worst. Everything against Owens was circumstantial. Everything against me was tangible, especially the damaging effect my job has on the kids."

"It's not like you're a cop."

"I might as well be, according to Brady. The bastard crucified me. He took what Dr. Hammond—the counselor I had the kids seeing?—was saying about our family life and twisted it. Got her to talk about how I'm never here until late at night, how the kids say they're frightened about the bombing. We thought Claudette, because of her friendship with Tina, would be my big character witness. She talked about how Tina and I knew we were made for each other from the first moment. How we spent all our free time with the kids and planned for the future. But Brady ignored all that on the cross and got her to talk about the dirty little secrets of journalism—the rate of broken families, the incidence of drug and alcohol abuse, the eighty-hour work weeks for low pay, the shrinking job market, the depression, the burnout, the despair."

"Oh, come on," LaFontaine said. "The carnage is what makes journalism fun!"

McCarthy managed a weak chortle through the steel that still held his jaw shut. "That's what makes gossip fun, you cynical queen."

"News, gossip. Same difference. What your other witnesses said didn't hold weight?"

"The best we had was Roger Dean, Charley's ex-partner, talking about the coke addiction and the money problems. But Brady got Dean to talk about Tina's coke problem. It was a wash and Charley's still the biological father."

"Crawford disallowed Dean's testimony about Owens's mother?"

McCarthy turned the trumpet over, seeing himself in the finish and almost choking again. "Hearsay. Brady objecting left and right. She had no choice."

"You think it's true."

"From what Tina said about the guy and his family, nothing would surprise me."

"It turns my jaded abdomen to think he might be after the kids just to satisfy some whim of his mother's that he have a family."

"Dean said the rumor in Santa Fe is that it's financial. If

Owens gets the kids, he gets the money he needs when she dies. She's in her late seventies."

"Subpoena his mother."

"She's out of state. The subpoena system is convoluted. And we could get her here and she could lie. And that would bolster Owens's case. Brady tells the judge we're inventing stories to damage his client. We're screwed."

News dug through his mental dirt files, retrieving a courthouse gossip item he'd heard a few months back. He was about to mention it when Carlos ran up onto the porch.

"Play some catch?" the boy asked McCarthy. He slapped the ball into the palm of the glove.

McCarthy put the trumpet down. "You bet."

Miriam got down off the swing to sit in the grass and watch the ball fly back and forth. After the fifth toss, she announced, "I don't like cars."

McCarthy missed the ball. It sailed by and struck the house with a thump. He motioned to Carlos to get it. "Why's that, honey?"

She toyed with her sneaker tread, but didn't reply.

"You're afraid of what happened to my car?"

She nodded. "Mommy's, too."

McCarthy knelt to stroke her hair. "I don't like cars either. It would be better if we still rode horses."

Carlos came back with the ball and said, "Do we get to go to the courthouse to talk to the judge?"

Looking at their expressions McCarthy understood for the first time how rotten life had treated them at an age when it should have been simple and pure. "Maybe sometime."

Miriam tugged at her lower lip, looking just like her mother. "If we go, will they ask us who we want to live with?"

"Maybe," McCarthy said. His stomach tightened.

"That will be easy," she said. She threw her arms around him. Carlos hugged him, too. McCarthy looked over his shoulder at LaFontaine. He felt as alone as the night Tina died.

Estelle called from the porch. "Okay, children, your dinner is ready. Gideon, you and Mr. News in twenty minutes, okay?"

"You go along now," McCarthy said. He barely saw them run across the lawn.

When the kids had gone inside, LaFontaine came down off the porch, trying hard to suppress his own emotions. If he witnessed too many more of these scenes, he might change his mind and decide all children were not evil pests.

"I'm afraid . . . I'll have to leave after dinner. A rendezvous with Brad."

"It's okay," McCarthy said. He wiped his face on his sleeve again. "I need some time with them to figure out how to explain it. But enough of that. What the hell was Leslie doing there that day outside Trujillo's office?"

"Riding shotgun, making sure everything went smooth," LaFontaine said, glad for the change in subject.

"You don't ride shotgun if you're an assistant police chief unless there's a serious debt you're paying back," McCarthy said. "What do we know about Leslie, his finances, his background?"

"I got that covered. I went to the city clerk and asked for his disclosure forms going back ten years. There was some kind of water pipe break in a back room a couple of days ago. The whole place is under tarps. It could be seventy-two hours before they get to it. It's on order. Funny thing. Kent Jackson has asked for it, too."

"Jackson? What's he up to?"

"I wouldn't even bother to ask. You know what a prick he is when he thinks someone's trying to invade his turf."

"Let's focus on what we've got for now. With Sloan's history of abusing women, he's got to be a possible suspect for killing Gentry."

"Round three," News nodded. "Question is: did he do it for kicks or was he provoked?"

"I say if he did it, he was provoked. She had something on him."

"Like what?"

McCarthy kicked at the stoop. "If only I knew."

Inside Miriam giggled. McCarthy's attention immediately traveled to the voices inside the house. He didn't answer when LaFontaine asked what he planned to do tomorrow. "Gid?" News said again.

McCarthy startled. "Huh? Oh, I think I'll go back and talk with Dusk, see if she remembers anything else Gentry might have said about Tiger's outcall. You?"

"I'm going to dig some more on Leslie. Maybe pay a visit to the courthouse," he said. He didn't bother to mention Trujillo's description of Portillo and Leslie during the Jennings years, nor a possible side trip to see Jaime Ramirez's brother, Pablo. The sort of historical background he enjoyed knowing. Gossipy bits to store away for a rainy day. Nothing to do with the real story.

McCarthy fitted the straw of his drink into the gap between his teeth and sucked in the cool, tart liquid. The booze fired off a synapse in the back of his head. "Trujillo said he paid off two detectives at ten grand apiece. Who were they?"

News slapped himself on the forehead. "I was so agog to learn that Leslie was in on the sealed file I never asked."

"Something to check out," McCarthy said.

"On my list of things to do," News promised.

"Another drink before dinner?"

"Did Plato love Socrates?"

Augustus Croon gently knocked on the door to Abby Blitzer's apartment. A shuffling and a dead bolt thrown. The door opened two inches.

"I brought some things I thought might cheer you up," Croon said. He held out three videos. *"The Poseidon Adventure, Earthquake* and *Othello;* it's the black-and-white version with Orson Welles as the Moor."

In the dim light Blitzer clutched the lapels of a faded blue terry cloth robe. Mascara and newsprint streaked her cheeks. "I didn't deserve to be suspended," she said weakly.

"Not suspended," Croon said. "Geld just thought you needed some time to get your batteries recharged."

"I'm ever ready. I don't need a recharge."

Croon set his jaw. "Abby, you weren't acting like the woman I've mooned over for more than a year."

"And who's that Abby?" she snapped. "Sweet tough Abby? Soft coldhearted Abby? So sensitive feel-nothing Abby?"

"The workable Abby," Croon said. "The way she used to be."

"You don't know what I used to be!"

For the first time in fourteen months Croon didn't feel lunar in her presence. He handed her the videos one by one. He stooped down and picked up a bag and handed it to her. "Mutton shank. Boiled potato. Yorkshire pudding. It's take-out British food."

She threw him a queer look. He forced a grin. "Most tragic meal I could think of."

Blitzer took the bag and, in spite of herself, smiled. She reached up, pulled his massive head down, and planted a kiss full on his lips. "Good night, Croon. And thank you for caring."

He walked away dazed. He'd never been kissed like that before. There was the promise of romance in that kiss. Which swelled his heart. But there was something else, too, something that reminded him of the chaos he'd endured in combat. The photographer made it down the stairs and through the gate to his car without once looking back.

Blitzer shut the door. She padded through the dark

apartment into the kitchen. She unloaded the meal, put it on a microwave tray, and zapped it for four minutes. The mutton chop came out steaming. She went into the living room, popped in the *Earthquake* video, and fast-forwarded it to the scenes where the walls start tumbling. She did not allow herself to look down at the pile of yellowed clippings with the picture of the sandy-haired ten-year-old boy that littered the coffee table.

On the television screen, a woman driving a car screamed as the freeway buckled. Blitzer bit into the hot mutton, scorching her tongue. She bit again and again into the searing flesh until her mouth had no sensation. She nodded to herself as she cried, affirming her conviction that unlike revenge, tragedy was a meal best served flaming.

Margaret Savage didn't know whether to cry or sing or punch the wall until her knuckles split. There it was again— the shimmer in her spine, hot and humid like a gusty wind on a July day. A raspy thick blues guitar voice surrounded her, told her to rewind the tape and play it again. For the twentieth time in the last two days, Margaret Savage turned on the cassette recorder.

When she'd first heard the tape in Pace's office, Savage had turned from the primal sounds as if hearing an animal dying. At home she'd listened again. And again. And gradually, without reason, like unfamiliar music slowly revealing its quality, the animal dying became the siren of wanting. She listened to Neil Harpster's demands and Connie Mills's cries. She knew for certain that the research assistant had gone to that motel room of her own free will. Connie's wanting echoed within Savage, too, a slim peal at the beginning, then deeper, a clang that resonated in her knees and her belly and shimmered in her lower back.

Hearing it now, for the twentieth time, she gave way to a desire that had been building the past twenty-four hours.

She longed to be in Room 11 B in the motel on State Street, longed to give way to the animal instinct she'd suppressed her entire adult life.

She sat up on the bed and drew her knees in close. She was further tortured by the fact that when she thought about what was happening to her it was always in the syntax and rhythm of the ridiculous prose in *Love's Furious Fury*.

Savage listened to Harpster's insistent voice. She looked down at her copy of the paperback on the bed. She picked the book up, hearing in the background Connie's voice say, "Page ninety-one now, Neil. Get to 91!"

Savage thumbed the pages until she found it. The scene in which Damien, the young, athletically chested master of the White Oak Plantation, seduces Laura Lee, the school-teacher from New Orleans. She read along as Neil acted Damien and Connie his Laura Lee. Again the clanging and the longing and the wanting and all the other passionate gerunds she could think of took hold. Until she could bear it no more.

She threw herself on the bed and began to sob uncontrollably.

The strict, linear thinking that had served her so well had gone circular, even spiral. No longer could Savage compartmentalize and judge the justness of every action with cold, socially correct logic. Random compulsion shook her like the mother of all hot flashes. The sobbing became a wailing. She punched at her pillow, sweating and denying it, then cursing and cursing again when it came to her clear, painful, and unavoidable.

She bit at the knuckle of her finger aware that it wasn't the sweet morning sick love she'd anticipated as a teenage girl. This was needy and hurtful, the first desperate yearning of a sexual obsession. And she couldn't do anything to stop it.

Vicious Twists of Fate . . .

C onnie Mills said, "Bobbie Anne, you're way out of line. This is between Neil and me."

Pace clasped her hands to her chest. "Dear, we all know from reading the advice columnists how difficult it is to admit being caught up in a destructive relationship, especially with someone who wields power over you."

They sat on the blue couch in the living room at Mills's apartment. Harpster's research assistant brushed the film of sweat away from the purple band about her forehead; she'd been flexing her butt muscles in time with the platinum blond in the "Righteous Rumps" exercise video she bought last week when the Assistant Managing Editor for News and Information had knocked on the door and asked to talk.

"I'd hardly call it destructive," Mills said. "It's fun. Don't you and Margaret ever have any fun?"

Pace ignored the question. She had rehearsed the scenario from every angle she could think of this afternoon. But she hadn't considered the remote possibility that Mills might be going to the motel on State Street because she wanted to. What was wrong with this woman? If Mills read the papers these days, she'd see that no woman really wants to have sex with her boss, with her husband, with anyone. Except, of course, young, confused artistic guys. Other than that, it's all rape and domination and harassment. Or at least unfulfilled desire. Didn't Mills keep up with the times? *Better take another tack,* Pace thought.

"So you and Neil have a fulfilling relationship outside Room 11 B?" she asked. "Go to movies, art galleries, candlelit dinners on the harborfront?"

"It's not like that."

318   *Mark T. Sullivan*

"No, it isn't, is it?"

"What's your point?"

"How old are you?"

"Twenty-seven."

"You think you'll still be his *research assistant* at thirty?"

"If I want to be. I may have a knockout body, but I got the job because the brain is Stanford trained. B.A. in economics with a minor in applied statistics."

Pace's laugh rattled. "So smart and yet so naive. Take it from a gal who's been there. You don't have a chance."

"I think I do. Remember, I've seen what he's like in Room 11 B."

"Right. He'll leave his rich wife for lust."

"Everyone shows love in different ways. Anyway, Lydia's hardly what you'd call a real wife. Her idea of a hot time is composting."

"Money, dear, is a strange lens. It makes people see the world differently. When that taut body of yours begins to sag, and it will, Neil will shift his gaze. Because whatever you give Neil is over when he puts his pants back on. Lydia gives him much, much more."

"Lydia will be history when Ed Tower finally leaves," Mills insisted. "He's promised me."

"So he does know about Tower," Pace said. She bit at the quick of her fingernail. "I'd suspected, but wasn't sure."

"Know what about Tower?" Mills asked.

For a brief instant, Pace took on the insightfulness of Margaret Savage. Even if Harpster didn't know for sure, this was an angle she could exploit. "Then he hasn't told you that Ed is about to retire?"

Mills didn't want to hear that. The bombshell research assistant jumped up and made her way to the refrigerator, where she fished for a jug of distilled water and a banana.

Pace followed her. "He hasn't, has he?"

Mills would not look at her. She drank the water. She

wanted to throw the glass against the wall just to hear it shatter.

"Has he?"

"No," Mills said finally. "How long has he known?"

Pace saw the lines in the young woman's face, lines that hadn't been there ten minutes ago, lines that made her seem suddenly older. "I've known for almost three weeks," Pace said. "I'd assume he found out about the same time."

Three weeks, Mills thought. Fur leggings and a pan flute. Romance novels and torn bodices. Not a word about the promise he made her. She looked out into the condo at the bare walls. She thought about the two years she'd lost in the motel on State Street. Time to look out for herself.

Mills put her water glass down and said, "He put me in a situation where I found it difficult—no, downright impossible, to deny him sex. I was forced into it."

Pace was overcome with a vision of herself with her feet up on Ed Tower's desk. A scribe from the *Columbia Journalism Review* took notes on her every word about changes at *The Post* under her watch. She took a deep breath to clear the vision, then said, "Admitting you have no control is the hardest part and the first step in recovery."

Mills went on as if she were rehearsing it all for her day in court, "He made it clear that I'd lose my job if I didn't submit to his every sick whim."

Pace played Greek chorus. "You're going to be a survivor, Connie."

"He robbed me of two years of my life, of my dignity, of my self-respect."

"You've got to fight to get your self-esteem back!"

"He degraded me."

"And made you wear strange costumes."

"I want $1.5 million for my suffering."

Pace thought of the wonderful American legal system and how it granted reporters the right to quote freely from

the stipulation of facts in law suits. No matter how slander-
ous. No matter how trumped-up. Harpster was finished!

"My dear, I think the slavery you've endured is worth at
least $3 million."

Mills leaned on the countertop, already preparing herself
for a life without Room 11 B. Too bad. Neil could be so
imaginative. But she knew she could be just as creative. She
thought of life with a muscular male research assistant/sec-
retary of her very own.

"After Neil resigns in disgrace, *The Post* will require a new
director of market research," Mills said.

"I know the perfect candidate."

Kent Jackson couldn't believe his good fortune. He'd just
had a remarkable dinner with the most beautiful woman
he'd ever met. Now she was back at his apartment for an
after-dinner drink! He poured from a bottle of Amaretto
that had been gathering dust in one of the cabinets. Caitlin
Donnelley was in his office making a phone call to her agent
about a photo shoot scheduled for the next day. If he'd put a
thousand on the odds any right-minded bookie would have
laid on this happening to a political hack like himself, he'd
be free and clear of debt right now.

He shrugged off a moment of concern over the interest
mounting daily with his loan shark to listen to Caitlin's
sweet murmur from beyond the closed door to his office.

Jackson beamed, thinking how well dinner had gone.
They'd chatted of current events over spicy Thai pork and
shrimp dishes. He'd sprung for a bottle of expensive wine
and had drunk much of it at her insistence.

He made it a rule not to talk of himself or his work with
acquaintances. But Caitlin had a way of making him seem
like the most savvy guy around. She laughed at his com-
ments on the local political scene. She clucked sympathetically at his explanation of Patti and the minister. (He left out

that nasty detail about his virility.) She put her lovely hand on his and asked him what he was working on now.

"I'm really not supposed to talk about it," he'd said.

"Oh, c'mon. It's not like I'm going to spill it to the photographers or hairdressers," Caitlin pouted. "I just think your job's so fascinating."

He'd looked into those perfect emerald eyes above that boudoir body. A safe bet. Roll the dice. He told her he thought there was a scandal brewing inside the campaign of Mayor Ricardo Portillo for governor.

She leaned on her elbows, her eyes wide. "What sort of scandal?"

"I'm sure the mayor and the chief are involved in some kind of shady land deal. Most likely in Nevada. Historically, real estate scams are the most likely ways a politician will meet his Waterloo. I'm just waiting for some documents to be freed up that describe the deal. I should have them in a couple of days."

Caitlin cocked her head to one side. The reporter couldn't help but admire the planes in her face. "But all politicians have skeletons in their closets, it's part of the game, isn't it?"

"Only if you let it be part of the game," Jackson insisted. "I won't let it be part of the game."

"You're an idealist," she said, smiling.

He smiled back. She seemed to like the idea he was after the story for noble purposes. Better than admitting the truth: that he needed the scandal to help him get money to pay off his enormous gambling debt.

Caitlin asked, "So what do your editors say about all this? I mean, I saw in that movie *All the President's Men* that you guys always talk with them."

Jackson squeezed Caitlin's hand and was thrilled when she squeezed back. "I'll let you in on a secret," he said. "The key to getting a big story into a newspaper is not to get the editors involved too early. Most of them have been away from the action for so long that they have a skewed view of the world. They'll try to impose their slant on your facts. Nothing wrong with slants; they're in every story. But their slants are uninformed, manufactured at cocktail parties with their cronies.

"The best thing for a reporter to do is get enough of the story nailed down so you can present it to them your way. Then that becomes the conventional wisdom editors can deliver at cocktail parties and is the one most likely to make it into print."

"So you haven't told them, yet?"

"And probably won't until I nail down the exact nature of the land deal."

Caitlin took a sip of wine. "I never knew so many secrets were kept inside a newspaper."

"A newspaper is as much about rumor and secret as it is about fact," he said, shamelessly borrowing a line from Prentice LaFontaine, that vulture.

"I'll remember that," she'd said.

Jackson put the brandy snifters on a tray and brought them into the living room. He daydreamed about what her body would look like nude. The door to the office opened behind him. He turned around with a big grin only to find the lingerie model frowning.

"Bad news?" he asked. "The shoot's off for tomorrow?"

"Sit down, Kent," Caitlin said.

Jackson did as he was told, moving over to make room for her on the couch. She took the studio chair across the glass coffee table. The muscles in her face tightened.

"What's the matter?" Jackson asked. This wasn't going the way he'd hoped.

She held up her hand to stop him. "Let me say for the record that this is just business. I kind of like you."

Jackson put his brandy snifter down. "What are you talking about, just business?"

Caitlin fished in her pocketbook, came up with a piece of paper and slid it across the table at the political reporter. He picked it up and felt immediately ill. It was a copy of the loan shark's note on his gambling debt.

"How did you? Who are you?" Jackson stammered.

"A friend who has friends," she said icily. "And friend, you owe these friends a great deal. They know you can't afford to pay this off, that the revelation of a gambling problem and indebtedness to a loan shark would mean the end of a promising career. So they propose a win-win situation for everyone involved."

Jackson's tongue had dried. "Who's they?"

The model shook her head. "Irrelevant."

"What do you want from me?"

"Laziness and ineptitude."

"What?"

"Be a lazy reporter. Be an inept reporter. Don't follow through on your instincts. Don't go fishing for big stories that might cause certain people trouble."

Jackson sank back into the couch. "This is bigger than I ever thought. Oh, my God."

"There is no God, Kent. Haven't you figured that out by now?" Caitlin said impassively. "People and institutions have power in other people's lives, not some being up there in the sky."

Jackson shrank from those words. "And what if I just decide to go on and dig this story out anyway, the repercussions be damned?"

"I don't think you're big enough to handle the repercussions. You make one more inquiry and a copy of this loan note will find its way to your editors. Story or no story, you'd be finished, disgraced, ruined."

Jackson was quiet for several moments. "And if I choose

to be a lazy reporter, just writing up press releases, no more questions?"

She smiled. "A thousand dollars a week comes off the note. I meet you, you sign at the bottom."

"Nice touch," Jackson said. "So if at the end of fifty-six weeks I should get the idea to start digging again . . ."

"Evidence suddenly appears that you had a hand in a cover-up."

"You've got me."

"We do."

The Cinema LaFontaine . . .

The strange blare of tabloid television was missing at the Milkman's mother's house. McCarthy knocked on the back door, telling himself that motion was good, go forward on the story, it was the only way he had to keep his mind off the children.

On his fourth rap, Larry Milk opened the door. He was shirtless. His belly hung like dead fish skin over his jeans. He held a broom and dustpan.

"Great, our savior," Milk said, disgusted. "Thanks for nothing, pal. Couple days after homicide came to talk to us, county mental health stopped by. Took my mom away. Declared her incompetent. We have to be out in two days."

"I didn't know," McCarthy said.

"Yeah, right," Milk said. He turned and walked off.

McCarthy stepped inside. Dusk was packing. Her hair was drawn and tied at the back. She wore a drab tan dress. She turned away when she saw McCarthy.

"I'm not talking to you," she said. "Fisk says you don't believe me no more."

"That's not true," McCarthy protested. "I think you heard exactly what you said you heard. But maybe there's more to Tiger's Escort than meets the eye."

Dusk chucked off her shoes and plopped down on the corner of the bare mattress. She was quiet for a few moments, then, "Shirl's sister said the same thing."

"Who's Shirl?"

"I told you 'bout Shirley Barfield," Dusk said. "Gentry gave her the number to Tiger's, too. Only her sister, Lorraine, says Shirley called it and went to one of them parties with Carol. She's scared."

"Hold up a second. How do you know that?"

"I ran into Lorraine downtown yesterday. She said Shirley 'bout freaked when she read that story you wrote 'cause it was wrong."

"Where do I find Shirley?"

Dusk said nothing.

"Did Fisk tell you not to tell me where to find her?"

She said, "Didn't tell him about it. He'd probably get mad at me. As it is, he keeps acting as if I must have heard more than I did through the window of the van. I've told them what I know. I'm not going to make nothing up."

"C'mon, Dusk," McCarthy pleaded. "Give me Shirley, or at least, Lorraine."

Dusk stubbed the cigarette out and lit another, then looked at Milk, who now leaned against the wall nursing a beer. He said, "Ahh, go ahead. We're out of here anyway."

"You don't think I was lying 'bout what I heard?" she asked McCarthy again.

"I told you I believed you," McCarthy said. "Still do."

That seemed to satisfy her. "Lorraine said Shirley got the willies after Carol turned up dead. Split for L.A. She got popped up there for carrying with intent to sell. She's in the L.A. County Jail under another name: 'Annie Carris.' She don't want to make bail. She's hiding out until this blows over."

A half hour later, McCarthy hung up the phone in a booth off the Boulevard. Visiting hours at the L.A. County Jail were over. He slammed his open palm on the side of the booth. "Damn it!"

If what Dusk said was true and Shirley Barfield had gone to a Tiger's Escort party with Carol Gentry, she might be able to link Diane Tressor to this whole mess. He phoned LaFontaine's house to tell him what he'd found. No answer. He tried News's pager and waited ten minutes for a call-back. Nothing.

He was at a standstill. Without motion to quell them, the memories of last night came back. Of how the children went limp when he told them that they might have to go live with their father. Miriam crying, "I want to stay here and no one can tell me I can't."

And McCarthy saying, "Honey, a lady at the courthouse probably believes it's better for you not to be here."

Carlos, quiet, so very quiet up to that point. "What'd we do wrong?"

And McCarthy, going to him, holding his chin up with his hand, "Nothing, son. If anybody's done anything wrong, it's me."

He'd woken up this morning to find them both in bed with him.

He checked his watch. Half past noon. He had a 1:30 P.M. appointment with the doctor to remove the wires from his jaw. Nothing more he could do on the story today. He'd take the kids up to the reservoir, rent a boat, and go fishing this evening. Try to give them good memories to take away.

Four hours later, Prentice LaFontaine did a jig in *The Post* elevator. He raised his hands high over his head, gave the

Richard Nixon victory sign, and bellowed "I am King
Snoop! Gossip personified!"

The elevator slowed, dinged. News composed himself.
The door opened. He lifted his briefcase, heavy with documents and an interview that broke it all wide open.

He took ten steps into *The Post* newsroom and froze
within the fury of a paper approaching deadline, seeing it all
as if for the first time.

Kent Jackson, stoop-shouldered, trudged to the fax machine for a press release. Isabel Perez pranced about with a
copy of her latest front-page story on the Jim Barnes toxic
dumping scandal. Augustus Croon mooned over an empty
chair, his ear glued to the police scanner. Margaret Savage
whispered furtively into a phone. The Zombie flipped
through an old copy of *House & Garden*. The Stepford Editors slapped mindlessly at their keyboards. Claudette X held
her forehead as if someone was drilling there. Stanley Geld
bobbed to some unseen dance music before his computer
terminal. Over there on Lobotomy Lane: Neil Harpster listened intently to the phone, face flushed, eyes closed. Connie Mills perused a law book. Bobbie Anne Pace read this
morning's *Beacon* with her feet up on her desk. Ed Tower
gestured wildly to Connor Lawlor. The editor-in-chief
stared unbelieving at the newest circulation report that
showed that Swingo had them up three thousand.

News paused for a moment, fighting off the urge to climb
on top of his desk and spread his arms like Moses, the original reporter just down from the mountaintop, to tell them
he believed he understood it now, the code that solved the
mystery, the words that had opened his eyes to dirt he could
not have imagined in the weirdest of closets.

Drawing on an inner peace he hadn't possessed earlier in
the day, News restrained himself. The pieces of the big picture were definitely in place. And he thought he knew how it
would appear when finished: one of those odd drawings that
seems to be one thing looked at from one perspective, then

from a slight shift in angle reveals itself to be something very different. A beautiful woman and then a hag.

Being this close to the exclusive of his life he was determined not to blow it. He had to work now. He had a ton of checking and reporting to do before the picture could be unveiled.

LaFontaine slipped quickly to his desk. He hunkered down behind his terminal so he wouldn't be drafted into action should travesty break out on deadline.

A quick chore first. LaFontaine got a white notebook from his briefcase. He paged through it until he found the details of a rumor having to do with Judge Evelyn Crawford and its proof discovered this morning in the courthouse. This he outlined in a memo to McCarthy. He filed and printed it, put it in an envelope, and stuffed it in the top drawer of McCarthy's desk.

He returned to his own terminal. The phone rang.

"Prentice?" It was Brad Perkins.

"Hello, lover," LaFontaine cooed. "We have reason to celebrate tonight."

"Yeah, got your message earlier. Can't make it. Got a meeting with someone about the personal training service."

"This is important," News bristled. "More important than any job."

"Potential business," Perkins said, equally tart. "I don't think sharing drinks while you crow about some stupid story is worth screwing up my future."

The reporter put his forehead in his hand. McCarthy was right; he was too old for these kind of relationships. End it now.

"Listen, you brainless hunk of muscle . . ."

"Watch it, Prenty," Brad cut in.

"No, you watch it. I'm onto the scandal to end all scandals here and you're being more than indifferent. You're a tiresome 1960s movie, Brad. I want you out of my house by the time I get home. Maybe your business date will . . . put you up."

Brad's voice turned menacing. "If I leave, who'll be around to slap the little puffball around? Or should I tell our friends along the bar scene exactly what the hardnose Post reporter loves to do behind closed doors? There are lots of people dying to get the lowdown dirt on you, you know."

LaFontaine went ballistic. "Get out of my house! I want you and your weights and your foolish Lycra outfits out in an hour. Or I'm calling the cops!"

News slammed the phone down and looked up to see half the newsroom—city desk, Stepford Editors, a few reporters, the Lobotomites on the Lane—watching him. He wiggled his fingers at them all, then shrank down behind his terminal. Claudette X lumbered over. "Thought I told you to get lost for a couple of days."

"I'm just getting a few things in order," LaFontaine said, doing his best to control his quavering voice.

"Love problems?"

"Nothing I can't handle with an eviction notice."

"Sorry to hear that, but I'd rather the rest of the newsroom not listen to the gory details. Know what I mean?"

"Heard and understood, Ms. Muslim. Now if you please, I'm officially not here and I'd like to conclude my unofficial business and go home to make sure my personal affairs are in order."

Claudette X made a clucking sound, then said. "By the way, unofficially, you make any headway on our little . . . um . . . project?"

"I'm in no mood to talk, right now. Can this please wait until tomorrow?"

The executive assistant city editor noted the slight tremble of LaFontaine's lower lip. "Sure, News. We'll talk tomorrow."

When the fire left his skin and the first hint of the loneliness to come reached him, News opened a new file in his

computer, dated it, and began typing in his notes. Brad had
spoiled his relishing of the delicious scuttlebutt before him.
He looked at the quotes and their implications objectively.
He typed them as fast as he could, putting in brackets his
suppositions, the links he needed to flesh the story out.

The picture of the pretty woman, he thought, before closing the file and printing it. He brought the seventeen-page
document back to his desk, then drew out the manila file
folder marked "Burkhardt" and added these pages to the
notes he'd taken over the last several months. Next he
reached into his briefcase and brought out a thick bound
report. It was yellowed with age.

On the back of the Burkhardt file News scribbled the
phrase "Other Documents:", and under it "U.S. Justice Department Report 1963." He opened the bottom drawer he
used for material too large to keep in his active file drawer
and dropped the report inside.

Last, he opened GOSDI, his computer gossip file, and
typed up a description of what he believed was the deeper,
scarier implications of the Burkhardt story. It was almost
entirely conjecture. But that was the thing about an altering
of perspective; the two stories could be based on the same
facts and yet be entirely different by a change in interpretation.

The writing took half an hour. The entry contained a
basic narrative of what he knew had occurred as well as several possible explanations for certain events and motivations
he had not yet fact-checked. Time would winnow out the
details. *Such is the lot of a newsman,* he thought, *we put down the
first flawed draft of history. The passing of years allows the historian to
cull the lies from the truth.*

He closed the file and hit "P." He raced to the printer
and grabbed the document before any other reporter or editor could see it. He put it into his hard copy gossip file
folder. He put both the Burkhardt file and the gossip file

into a drawer. He shoved a key in the desk lock, turned it, and heard it click.

With the cool demeanor of a card shark who has drawn a straight flush queen high, he snapped his briefcase shut, stood, gave brief appraisal to the battlefield on which tomorrow, the day after at most, he would launch the equivalent of thermonuclear device, then headed for the door and the elevator and home.

LaFontaine never noticed that from the moment he raised his voice to Brad, the Zombie had put aside *House & Garden* to study and listen to him with an intensity he normally reserved for the denizens of Lobotomy Lane.

The Zombie watched the elevator door shut. He stayed Zen-still for forty-five minutes, until nearly seven o'clock, when the fever of *The Post*'s deadline was at its zenith, when no one noticed a presumed brain-dead reporter sliding his chair behind the desk of a fellow journalist. He found the file drawer locked. The center drawer, too. He tugged at the bottom drawer. It groaned, clicked and gave, a fortuitous malfunction in the mechanism.

The Zombie drew out the yellowed report News had brought in. He read the title on the cover. His eyes flared like rocket exhaust. He slid his chair back to his desk, tugged his shirt out from his pants, and slid the report up against his Karate-chiseled abdomen.

By eight-thirty Neil Harpster was frantic. All day long someone had rung his office phone line and then breathed heavily into it. Never a word. Just the breathing. Who was harassing him?

He picked at the vegetarian dinner Lydia had left on the kitchen counter. He gave thought to the enemies he'd made over the years. He glanced at the insulated gardening jumpsuit he'd been sleeping in outdoors the past ten days. It hung on a hook near the back door.

The phone rang. Harpster picked it up. "Hello?"

"Damien?"

"Damien? No, I'm afraid . . ."

"Damien, it's Laura Lee. Tell me that No means Yes."

"Connie?" he whispered. "I told you never to call here like this."

Upstairs, Lydia yelled, "Who is it, Neil?"

Harpster held his hand over the mouthpiece. "No one, honey. Wrong number!"

The voice said, "It's not Connie. I'm much more than Connie could ever be." There was a clicking noise on the line. Then, "I'm your living Laura Lee, your secret admirer."

"Were you the one calling my office all day? Are you the breather?"

"I just wanted to hear your voice. Your blues guitar voice."

Harpster's tongue dried. He listened closely. He knew that voice, didn't he? Wait, what was that? Something about the breathing on the line; it echoed as if there were two people listening.

"I'm thinking about you in your tight black pants and your maroon pirate's shirt," the woman said. "I want to touch . . ."

Harpster couldn't help it. "You want to touch what?"

A creak behind him. Harpster wheeled to find Lydia in her flannel nightgown clutching a trowel. He slammed the phone down. "It was an obscene phone call!" he cried.

"I was listening!" Lydia sneered. She swung at him with the trowel. "You pervert. You loved it!"

"I didn't!" He ducked the first swing and the second and the third. She grunted with effort, but kept coming. Long days filling in the root holes of assassinated plants and the side effects of the psychotropic drugs the doctor had prescribed had combined to give her superhuman strength. Harpster backed up against the open broom closet.

"I was trying to keep her on the phone long enough for a trace," he yelled as the tip of the trowel caught him hard in the rib cage.

"Liar!" Lydia raised the trowel over her head and let it come flying down.

Harpster dodged at the last second. Lydia reeled forward. The trowel struck the rear of the closet. He slammed the door shut on her arm and leaned on it with all his weight. She screeched and snarled and spit at him.

"No, it's true," he said, lying with every inch of his being. "I saw it on one of those reality-based cop shows. You try to keep them talking so the record of the call shows up at the phone company."

The contorted rage on Lydia's face ebbed ever so slightly.

"It's true," he said again. "How could I want to be degraded like that?"

"You sounded interested," Lydia whined, doubting herself now.

Neil bit at the inside of his lip so his expression would appear pained. "Obscene phone calls are as bad for a man as they are for a woman."

Lydia's features softened. Tears welled in her eyes. "Do you love me, Neil?"

"Oh, Tulip," he cried. "There's no one in my garden but you."

All the tension went out of her shoulders. He reached out to stroke her tortured face, but kept the full force of his body against the broom closet door. Just in case the phone should ring again.

It took News just under an hour to pack Brad Perkins's gear and lug it outside onto the patio of his condo. He taped a note to the front door: "Mr. Pecs, you'll find your muscle-inflating devices out back. Don't bother to say good-bye."

That done, he changed into silk pajamas and bathrobe, which always made him feel better. He changed the name of the movie on the marquee above his bed, then put the sound track from *South Pacific* on the stereo.

He mixed himself a margarita. A troublesome choice, he knew, but easier than facing the love loss cold turkey. He guzzled the drink and poured a second from the blender.

That was better. Not good, but better. He pushed aside negatives, imagining how his life would change once the story hit. He knew well that many considered him a buffoon, a cartoonish newsroom sideshow. Perhaps that's how he'd wanted it. The angry clown is a brilliant defensive posture to mask insecurity. Now they'd see him differently.

Oh, how he'd wanted someone to share in his news tonight. That was the thing about gossip: the pleasure of knowing grows in the telling. He looked around his condo and then at the clock and understood if he did not have companionship tonight he'd become self-destructive and either drink too much or head out to a leather bar.

LaFontaine had planned to make the unveiling as much of a surprise to McCarthy as to the rest of the newsroom. They were friends, of course, but this was such a singular triumph he did not want to share in the glory.

He admitted, however, that the events of the day were too much for a lonely rumormonger to handle solo. He needed to boast. He needed a shoulder to cry on. He dialed McCarthy's home.

"I have gone where no man has gone before," News replied to McCarthy's hello.

"What are you Captain Kirk?"

"Everyone knows he had a thing for Spock."

"What's up, News? I tried to get in touch with you earlier. I've got something interesting . . ."

"McCarthy, save your triflings. I've figured it all out. I

know the answer to the mystery. It was under our nose the entire time."

"Burkhardt? Leslie?"

"One does not deliver such dramatic messages over the phone. Too impersonal. Hurry over and I'll render a story that will drop your BVDs about your ankles."

"Just as long as you aren't standing behind me."

"Your humor smacks of the playground."

"Yeah, yeah. Give me an hour to get there. I'm just getting the kids to bed."

"Destiny awaits you," News said. He hung up the phone.

He busied himself preparing a guacamole and mixing up a fresh batch of margaritas. Thirty minutes passed. The doorbell rang.

"McCarthy!" LaFontaine cried as he trotted toward the door. "You're not going to believe it!"

He flung the door open and held his hands out before him palm up, playing to his audience like a magician who has just made an elephant disappear. He stopped short. He drew his lips back into a sly smile.

"You got to me quicker than I ever thought you would," News said. "Then again, anyone who's as good at this game as you are must feel it when a big story's about to bust open."

McCarthy parked his rented Buick in the lot next to LaFontaine's Miata. He yawned, wincing at the ache in his newly unleashed jaw. Prentice's news better be good, he thought, as he climbed out of the car. He heard someone running behind him and turned to see Brad Perkins in full sprint toward the park.

"Oh, no!" McCarthy said. The last thing he wanted to be involved in was another of LaFontaine's histrionic break-ups. He almost got back in the car, then remembered the knowing tone of News's voice on the phone.

The gossipmonger's condo was the last unit in the complex and faced a canyon developers had not yet managed to rape. The torn remains of a note was taped to the door, which was ajar. The stereo blasted. A woman sang *"I'm going to wash that man right out of my hair."*

McCarthy pushed the door open. "News?" He took a step inside and almost slipped on the tile in the foyer. He stood in a pool of blood. There was something black and bloody next to it. He stooped and turned it over. A toupee.

He turned around and saw a bloody handprint on the foyer wall as if someone had staggered from a blow and reached out for support.

That same disconnection, that hovering over himself he'd gone through the night Tina died, swept him aloft. He followed the red splatters down the hall. More bloody handprints. Gushes of blood on the rug. The living room was a shambles. Drawers opened and flung on the floor. Papers from his filing cabinet strewn everywhere. The bloody handprints were on the floor now. A trail of them led to the bedroom double doors. McCarthy pushed them open.

News was sprawled at the foot of the bed. His bald head was caved in on the right side. His dead eyes were open. Blood seeped dark from his nose. At first McCarthy thought that the blows had knocked LaFontaine's teeth out. Then he saw dentures next to his friend's face. News's robe was open. A girdle was cinched tight about his waist.

He fell to his knees and stroked Prentice's shoulder. Then looked up and broke into sobs when he saw the movie marquee.

From Here to Eternity was playing at the Cinema LaFontaine.

Part 3

THE GHOST BETWEEN THE LINES

Requiem for a News Reporter . . .

66**C**onnor gave Prentice a wonderful elegy," Isabel Perez said.

"Called him a newsman's newsman," Augustus Croon said. "Unafraid of the consequences of his probing style of journalism."

"But a bit misguided at times," Abby Blitzer said.

"He was that," Stanley Geld said.

"Oh, hell, he was a bitch," Claudette X said. "But when he was on, he raised bitchiness to an art form."

"I'll miss him," Perez said. She began to cry.

"We all will, honey," said Claudette X, who threw an arm around Perez's shoulder. Were those price tags she felt under Perez's beautiful black mourning dress?

Kent Jackson shrugged off the sensation he was being watched. "I was no real friend, but I can't believe Tower didn't go to the funeral, yet shows up here."

They all looked over at the Editor for Newsroom Operations who was sipping white wine at the bar watching Paul Fairbanks interview Lawlor for the evening news.

"Ed always hated Prentice," McCarthy said simply.

The reporters and editors gathered around the long table

inside the Slotman's Bar and Grill nodded. At one time or another almost everyone had hated News.

Behind them Ralph Baker, a.k.a. Roy Orbison, was pouring another round of drinks while the Slotman hung a framed copy of the obituary the Zombie had written. It carried the headline:

Death of a Messenger

Next to it, the Slotman fashioned a banner of black crepe paper around a publicity photo of LaFontaine he'd gotten from *The Post*. The Slotman looked about himself, vaguely disappointed. Though the place was packed with mourners, all of them drinking heavily, this was hardly a record-breaking angst.

Not that he hadn't made an effort on such short notice. He'd convinced the jukebox supplier to bring him a couple of Gregorian chants and some Peter, Paul and Mary tunes ("Abraham, Martin & John" in particular) for the machine. He'd taken a color coordination tip from Roy Orbison and rushed out to buy a mortician-black two-piece suit. A business expense. The last time he'd be able to use Prentice LaFontaine to create gloom.

He rang open the cash register and took a peek at the receipts. Not a record setter at all. Probably all the working reporters here from *The Beacon* and the radio and television stations kept the place from descending into the longed-for mawkish guzzle-fest.

The Slotman brought a round of drinks to the stiffest group in the bar. Somehow in the crush following the graveside ceremony, Bobbie Anne Pace, Margaret Savage, Connie Mills, and Neil Harpster had all been squeezed into a corner. The Slotman took their money, noting more than grief in their eyes. He told himself to come back in five minutes. This crew looked ready for a protean swill.

Harpster threw back a vodka martini. He grimaced at the fact that Pace's dress featured long black sleeves. He was sure if he could raise those sleeves he'd find scratches on her forearms. And was it possible she was behind the obscene phone calls? Connie had denied knowing anything, though she did seem a bit remote.

"What do you think of gardens, Bobbie Anne?" he asked.

Pace took a belt from her Sea Breeze. "I think they grow well if they aren't force-fed fertilizers."

Mills sipped furiously on her Madras. She prayed Pace wouldn't blow her cover; the attorney they'd hired said the lawsuit was still a few days from being ready to file.

Savage said, "I find the plant world sensuous." She hiccuped. She rarely drank hard liquor. She was halfway through her fourth Kamikaze.

"Sensuous?" Pace asked.

The columnist waved her hand in space. "A turn of phrase. I like the smell and . . . touch . . . of flowers."

Harpster froze at the way Savage said "touch." He took her in sidelong, a voice inside screaming: It's her! She's the one calling me!

Savage smiled at him. She reached up slowly to readjust the sleeveless top of her black cotton dress. For some reason the need on the columnist's face frightened Harpster more than Lydia armed with pruning shears.

"I think I'll be going," he managed to say. "Do you need a ride, Connie?"

"I'll stay a while," Mills replied.

"I could use one," Savage said sweetly.

At that Harpster hyperventilated. "I, um . . . I, um . . ."

"I'll give you a ride, Margaret," interrupted Pace, now studying her chief advisor with growing concern.

"No, no," Savage said. "I'll go with Neil."

"I'm sorry, I forgot." Harpster was sweating profusely. "I'm supposed to meet Lydia in half an hour at a restaurant at the beach. So, um, sorry."

He rushed off through the crowd.

Savage started to follow, but her boss grabbed her by the wrist. "Margaret! What's the matter with you?"

Savage turned, spitting venom. "Get your hands off me!"

Pace's stunned reaction broke through the haze of desire that had enveloped Savage. The columnist shook as if a bitter wind had blown about her new silk panties. She thought fast. "Don't you see? He's such a lecher that he might have tried to force me to do something against my will!"

Pace released her grip. "And you could join the lawsuit."

"Yes," Savage said. "That's right."

Pace took her friend in her arms and hugged her. "A martyr for me."

Mills tossed aside the straw from her Madras and sucked down the rest of it. And she thought being alone in a motel room with Neil was weird! She better get at least $2 million out of this fiasco.

The two women ended their embrace. "I promise not to interfere again," Pace said. "Sometimes I just can't keep up with the way your mind works."

"It's understandable," Savage said. "I think I better go for a walk now, clear my head. Is there a bookstore nearby?"

"Bookstore?" Pace asked. Ooops, she'd promised not to interfere again. "Yes, of course, down the street at Eleventh and Broadway."

Savage shook hands with Mills and made for the door.

Pace watched her go. "I've never seen her like this."

"You mean horny?" replied Mills. She waved at the Slotman for another round.

"What are you talking about?"

"You know: excited, turned on, wet?"

"Impossible! Margaret's never had a sexual feeling in her life."

Mills stopped waving for a moment. "You're kidding?"

"That's what she told me."

"Well, she was having a whopper of a sexual feeling just then. Neil has that effect on some women. It's something about the way his throat resonates when he's tense."

Pace stared in disbelief at the door closing behind the columnist.

"Don't take it so hard, Bobbie Anne," Mills said. "It's just sex."

Pace stammered, "But I feel like I'm losing my best friend."

By then the Slotman had caught sight of Mills's waving and cut through the crowd to deliver another round. He leered when Pace took her Sea Breeze, inhaled it, and demanded another. He waddled off through the crowd, gleefully telling himself that the night could be saved; record-breaking inner turmoil was within his reach.

Geld had witnessed the confusion from across the room. He wanted to rise and pirouette, but given the solemn nature of the occasion restrained himself. *Got to keep calm,* he thought. *Got to be patient, let events play themselves out.*

He asked McCarthy, "How'd your kids handle it?"

"I try to tell myself that they're resilient, but they've seen too many funerals in their lives. They went home with Estelle after the service."

"The Zombie sure stayed at graveside a long time," Blitzer observed.

"He was there when I left," Jackson said. "Probably still there."

"Prentice would have said something reprehensible about that," Perez said.

Ralph Baker brought their drinks to the table. He stroked at his black sideburns and asked morosely, "They get Perkins yet?"

McCarthy shook his head. "Four days and not a peep. I should have gone after him when I saw him running."

Geld said, "You couldn't have known."

McCarthy put his head in his hand. "If I'd been there twenty minutes earlier, maybe I could have stopped it."

"SEAL training teaches you not to think like that," Croon said. "Death waits for no one."

They all took long belts off their drinks at that thought. The silence went on for almost a minute, until Claudette X said to no one in particular, "He wore a wig?"

They all looked up from the table and burst into gales of laughter.

"I can't believe he got away without us knowing that for years!" Perez cried.

"And a goddamned girdle, too," Geld said. "Remember how he always used to boast about his physical fitness regime?"

"Dentures," McCarthy chortled. "He liked to lecture me about how he kept a perfect smile via dental floss, hydrogen peroxide, and baking soda."

"News was all surface," Blitzer said. "Can you imagine what he would have said if we'd come apart like that?"

They laughed again and gradually quieted.

A shadow fell across the table. "Laughing, drinking, and crying over the dead," said Lawlor. "You'd have thought he was Irish."

"Everyone's Irish at a wake," McCarthy said.

"True enough." Lawlor put his hand on the reporter's shoulder. "We'll all miss that tough, sneaky, whining, belligerent, secretive, beautiful gossipy bastard."

He raised a glass and his blackthorn cane. "To News!"

"TO NEWS!" they roared.

And behind them the entire crowd packed into the Slotman's heard them and joined in. **"TO NEWS!"**

When the cheering and the hubbub had died down, Lawlor wiped tears from his eyes. "Can I have a word with you a moment, Gid?"

McCarthy got up and followed the editor-in-chief as he limped to the back hall.

"Quieter here without the Slotman's depressing music grinding at us," Lawlor began. "How are you holding up?"

"I've been better."

"It's a great loss when you think what Prentice might have been had he applied himself."

"The last couple of months he was applying himself," McCarthy said. "He was coming into his own."

"But he always seemed to chase tangents like that Lollipop Kids angle."

McCarthy didn't feel like arguing, so he let it slide. "He had an eccentric's mind."

"You do, too," Lawlor said. "Which is what I wanted to talk to you about. I'm considering starting a special investigations unit that would report directly to me. I'd like to know if you'd be interested in leading the team as its assistant managing editor?"

McCarthy put his hand to his forehead in disbelief. "You mean . . . ?"

Lawlor laughed again. "Whatever News used to think of we who reside in the Glassholes, you don't have to undergo a lobotomy to get one."

McCarthy jerked his hand down. "That's not what I was doing. I . . . uh, actually it was . . . I, uh . . . honestly don't know what to say."

"Don't say anything right now," Lawlor said. "Claudette told me about the situation with your kids. I want you to take a week off, get over News's death. It's a big move with a lot of responsibility, not to mention a healthy pay raise. If you come back and accept, I'll want you to commit one hundred percent. If not, I'll understand."

"Okay," McCarthy smiled. "I'll think about it."

"Good," Lawlor shook the reporter's hand. "Oh, and one more thing. I've been giving interviews all afternoon about News. Karen Rivers of *The Beacon* wanted to talk to someone who knew him well. I suggested you, if that's all right."

"Sure, I'll talk to her," McCarthy said.

Lawlor pointed across the crowded bar room toward the

jukebox. "She was over there somewhere last time I saw her."

McCarthy shouldered his way through the increasingly plastered crowd, thanking those who offered their condolences, turning down several of those who offered to buy him a drink. Halfway across the room, he eased by a rotund Stepford Editor and came face-to-face with Ed Tower.

Tower opened his mouth, then closed it, then opened it again. "Anything kind I might say to you would appear hypocritical."

"I know," McCarthy said.

The editor's face reddened. He sputtered, "Any word on his boyfriend?"

"Not yet," McCarthy said.

"Connor has informed me of his offer," Tower said. "I would hope whatever differences we have could be put aside."

"Anything's possible, I suppose," McCarthy said. "If you'll excuse me, Ed, I'm supposed to talk to someone from *The Beacon*."

Tower put out his hand. "One thing. I read in your story that LaFontaine's place was torn apart. What do you think Perkins was looking for?"

McCarthy paused. "I hadn't even thought about it."

"Something we might want to ask the police."

"Sure, next chance I get," McCarthy promised.

He spotted Karen Rivers perched on a stool at the far end of the bar hard by the jukebox. He tapped her on the shoulder and yelled over the blare of a Gregorian chant, "What do you want to know?"

With her white reporter's notebook, Rivers pointed over to an empty table. When they'd gotten seated, she batted her eyelashes, and said, "He was a dear friend of yours."

McCarthy screwed up his face. "Spare me the Barbara Walters/Connie Chung routine, okay? I'm not going to boo-hoo for you."

"I was trying to be nice."

"You were and you weren't. By being nice on the surface you hoped to crack me open for the sake of your story."

Rivers took a deep breath and let it out. "No, I was actually trying to be nice. I've heard a lot more about you since that night when they found Gentry. I know you've suffered a lot. I feel bad about the way I've acted. I feel bad that your friend died."

McCarthy saw that she was telling the truth; there was nothing of the hyena about her. He hesitated, then said, "I guess I feel bad about the way I've thought of you, too."

It started slowly with him telling her what she needed to know, that LaFontaine was from Louisiana, that his mother was dead, that his father considered him dead years ago, that he'd been a first-rate reporter at a small weekly outside New Orleans and an erratic reporter, but colorful character at *The Post*, that he loved old movies, that his own personality confused him, that he cared deeply about many people even though he tried to hide it.

"And he had dark side as everyone does," McCarthy said.

"That arrest years ago?"

"It's public knowledge," McCarthy said. "I'd appreciate it, however, if you didn't play that up. It was the sensational part of him, but it's not what I choose to think about when I think about News."

"You cared for him," Rivers said.

"I sat next to him and listened to his dreams and his disappointments for more than ten years."

"He was gay."

"Obviously."

"I mean it's unusual for a heterosexual male to be so close to a gay man."

"I guess I never thought of it that way. We didn't let our sexual orientations interfere with our friendship."

Rivers chewed on her pen thoughtfully. "You're an unusual man."

"Not really. After all I've been through, I just believe in getting by."

"Getting by what?"

"Getting by life . . . with the people who are important to me safe and warm. A pipe dream I have."

She closed her notebook. "I've got to call in these notes for the final. Do you have any plans, afterward, I mean?"

McCarthy shook his head.

"Could I ask you to dinner?"

"You could."

The bright sun shining in through the open window roused McCarthy. He opened his eyes. He saw hardwood floors and a hooked throw rug and a framed jazz poster on the far wall. He smelled her then, the thick woman smell he'd lost himself in last night. He felt her heat behind him and the sure rhythmic movements of her breathing.

He closed his eyes and thought of it, how they'd left the Slotman's and gone to eat at a Greek place she knew. She'd lost her father, a steelworker in Pittsburgh, the same year he'd lost his father. He told her about Tina and the children. She talked about being so far from home and wondered whether this was the right business to be in.

Outside in the first light rain of the year, a fluke rain coming this early, she'd turned her face to him and he realized how terribly lonely he'd been the past two years and how much worse it might become in the future. He'd kissed her and they'd come here and he'd fallen into that wonderful mushy smell and the sure powerful movements of her body.

McCarthy opened his eyes. He inhaled through his nose and felt himself aroused. He rolled over and found her looking at him from underneath tousled hair.

"How long have you been awake?" he asked.

"About an hour," she said. "You looked so relaxed I didn't wake you."

Rivers slid up tight against him, her scent everywhere and he felt himself drifting away. From somewhere in the room came a high-pitched peeping noise, followed by another. They broke, both up out of the bed to claw through the pile of clothes they'd left on the floor in the rush of the night before.

McCarthy pressed his beeper. "City desk."

"Me, too," Rivers said. "I go first, my apartment."

"I thought we had something," he said, feigning hurt.

She grabbed him hard by the buttocks and kissed him. "We do. But this is business."

She crossed to a nightstand and reconnected the phone and dialed.

"This is Karen. . . . Sorry, I've had some problem with the phone." She listened intently for a few moments, then said, "I'm on my way."

"What's going . . ." McCarthy was saying, but she was already by him and on her way to the shower.

McCarthy ran to the phone and dialed *The Post* newsroom. Claudette X answered, "Where have you been? They got Brad Perkins. Arraignment in an hour."

"I'm on it," McCarthy said. He dropped the phone, sprinted into the bathroom, and jumped into the shower.

"Really," Rivers said. "A lady likes to be alone at times."

"You're not a lady," McCarthy said. "You're a journalist. And journalists have to suffer sometimes for a story."

He took a bar of soap and began to wash her. She shivered in the hot water and murmured. "But the arraignment's in an hour."

McCarthy grinned and said, "That's okay. I'm used to working on deadline."

Playing It Venomous . . .

P aul Fairbanks hopped from one Gucci loafer to another while his field producer did a sound check on the microphone. He loved the strike and clang of heavy gold chain at his ankle on every re-bound. It made him think of the thick ankle bracelets slaves wore in movies about ancient Rome and Greece.

Wearing the ankle bracelet was a reminder to Fairbanks of what he was, an admitted pagan. His golden calf: the snout lens of the television camera. Six days a week he gazed into it and offered up human sacrifice. The idol gave him the power to alter reality, to cut and trim events to meet his sound bite vision of the world. It granted him eternal life. His image and his producer's words emblazoned on video for all time.

"Paul Fairbanks, Channel 10 Eyewitness News," he intoned. "How's that sound?"

His producer, a short Jewish woman named Rose, saw what he wanted, and, being a lackey to the talent, she gave it to him. "You're in wonderful tone this morning, Paul."

Fairbanks beamed. "How should I play this?"

"Venomous," Rose said. "One of your own has been murdered. His killer's been brought to justice."

Fairbanks hesitated. "Um, what's venomous mean?"

Rose sighed, knowing her mother had been right; she should have gone to law school. "Angry, with a touch of evil."

"Oh!" Fairbanks said. "I can do that."

"On the first take, I hope," Rose said. "Ready? Three, two, one and you're on."

Fairbanks snapped his six-foot frame erect. He curled the

right side of his upper lip just like Clint Eastwood always did before he blew away the whackos. "A homosexual reporter's lover and suspected killer brought to justice, we'll have the details live at six!"

"Beautiful!" Rose said. "We'll run that promo the two hours running up to the show. Now the stand-up."

Fairbanks resumed the Dirty Harry pose. Rose signaled the cameraman to run tape just as the sheriff's van pulled into the garage of the courthouse.

McCarthy and Rivers stopped watching Fairbanks's broadcast antics. Perkins was led out the back door. His hair was disheveled. A couple of days' growth of beard shadowed his face. They already had him dressed in an orange jailhouse jumpsuit.

Perkins hunched over and covered his head when the klieg lights burst on. Fairbanks broke in perfect transition from his introductory monologue to wheel to let the camera catch him in near-perfect profile and shouted: "Brad! Brad! Did you kill him? Was it a lovers' quarrel?"

Rivers was yelling out the same kinds of questions. McCarthy couldn't bring himself to say a word. He wanted to jump the barrier and strangle them. McCarthy led the pack up the back stairs to the third floor, where the superior court arraignments were held. It all went quick and perfunctory. A plea of not guilty was entered on Perkins's behalf. Bail was denied because he was a flight risk. The pack surrounded the deputy district attorney and Millie Dubrovsky, Perkins's public defender whom McCarthy had known for years.

McCarthy hung back, waiting until the other reporters had their fill. He caught Dubrovsky's eye finally and she motioned to him. Rivers tried to follow, but Dubrovsky said, "Sorry, this is private."

McCarthy walked backward, hands out to Rivers. "I'll call you."

Rivers pouted and nodded.

They walked to a window overlooking Broadway. Du-brovsky said: "Over my objections my client wants to talk to you."

"Nothing to talk about," McCarthy said. "He killed my best friend. I saw him leaving the scene."

"There's more to it than that."

"Prentice had a thing for guys who liked it rough. Brad's a classic example. He killed him, sure as I'm standing here."

"Gid, I always thought you reporters liked to hear the other side."

McCarthy thought about it for a moment, then said, "Make sure we're talking through glass. I don't know what I'll do if I know I can get my hands on him."

Two hours later, a guard led Perkins to a chair in a glass booth inside the downtown jail. He had the sleeves of his jumpsuit rolled up to expose his beefy forearms. Without expression he picked up the black phone that hung from a cradle inside the booth.

McCarthy didn't pick up his phone for almost a minute. All he could see was News's head bashed in and the bloody handprints on the rug and the way his friend's body had contorted in death.

"Please," Perkins mouthed.

McCarthy finally put the phone to his ear.

Perkins talked fast: "I know you saw me running from the condo. But I swear I didn't kill him. He was dying when I got there, lying on the rug in the bedroom, making these awful noises."

"You hit him enough times."

"No! I didn't hit him. I never hit him."

"Bullshit. It's what you did together. It got out of control because he told you to leave and you started swinging."

"No! No! What we did alone was different. That was

role-playing. That's what he seemed to like, so I fed into it. But whoever killed him was there before me."

Perkins shivered now. McCarthy wanted to smack him upside the head.

"Look," Perkins said, "the last time I talked to him he said he was onto the biggest story of his life. He said something about 'the scandal to end all scandals.' How do you know he wasn't killed because of that?"

McCarthy had been so caught up in the grief and the funeral arrangements that he hadn't had time to think clearly about the phone call he'd had with News that night.

Before he could reply, Perkins continued, "The story in the papers said his place was ransacked. If it was a lovers' quarrel, why would I tear the place apart?"

"I figure you were looking for money."

"I had money. The reason Prentice got mad at me that afternoon was I had to meet with an investor who was interested in backing me in a personal training service. He agreed and gave me five thousand dollars to get me on my feet and start buying equipment."

"You have this investor's name?"

"Carl Tracy," Perkins said.

"The guy who owns the Pink Stag?"

Perkins nodded. "Carl has a thing for me and Prentice suspected it. We were trying to keep the deal under wraps until I was up and going. Ask Carl; he'll tell you it's true."

McCarthy hated himself for thinking it, but it was possible that Perkins was telling the truth. News's memory surrounded him, telling him he'd better check it out.

"Did Prentice say how he broke the scandal?"

"To be honest, I didn't ask him. I was sort of taunting him. And I feel so bad about it, because when I tried to tell him I was sorry, when I was holding him there in his bedroom, he died. And I got scared when I knew he wasn't breathing anymore, and I ran."

Perkins's shivers became violent shaking. McCarthy hung up the phone and left.

Ed Tower came up to McCarthy's desk while he wrote the story of the arraignment. "I heard you got an exclusive with Perkins."

"He talked for a while. Said he's innocent. Said News was alive when he got there, died in his arms."

"Doesn't hold water?"

"I saw the guy running from the scene," McCarthy said. "They found his bloody prints all over the place. But I'll quote him to be fair."

Tower hesitated, then said. "He mention anything about the place being torn apart?"

"He said that's why I should know he didn't do it. That he had no reason to go through his papers."

Tower looked off toward the distance.

"Why the interest, Ed?" McCarthy asked.

Tower's lips twitched. "I take it personally when one of my people is bludgeoned to death and that part of it bothers me. Keep me posted on what happens."

"Sure," McCarthy said. The Editor for Newsroom Operations stalked back through the newsroom, shut his Glass-hole door, and immediately got on his phone. McCarthy shrugged it off and worked on the story another fifteen minutes when his phone rang.

"Post. McCarthy."

"Gideon, this is Jeanette Fry."

"I was hoping I wouldn't hear from you."

Silence, then, "You should know I received a call this morning from Judge Crawford's clerk. She's scheduled a disposition hearing a week from Friday."

"Ten days? Can't we stall or make some kind of motion to hold it until I can get more information on Owens?"

"Brady called me this morning, too. In so many words,

he implied that if we try to block the hearing on frivolous grounds, Owens would file a lawsuit against you."

Since finding LaFontaine's body, McCarthy had not allowed himself to do anything but move forward. Now, time seemed to stand still.

"What are my odds?"

"I'd say seven to three against."

"Any chance I'll get visitation rights?"

There was a long pause. "It would be unusual, but this is an unusual situation. It depends on whether Crawford looks at this from precedent or her own sense of justice."

McCarthy didn't hear Fry say good-bye. He didn't hear anything until Claudette X growled directly in his other ear, "How much longer until that story's ready?"

He hung the phone up. He looked at the screen. "Ten minutes . . . I'm going to lose the kids."

"Oh, no!" she moaned. "It's final?"

"Not until next Friday. But the odds are against me unless some miracle happens."

"Gid, I'm very sorry. Why don't you finish the story and go on home, okay?"

He nodded. He typed in the last three paragraphs of the story on autopilot, filed it, printed it, and then sent it to the city desk. When the computer beeped to indicate it had been received, he opened his desk drawer to file his hard copy. A manila envelope addressed to him in Prentice LaFontaine's handwriting lay on top of his hanging files.

He slit open the envelope and drew out a single piece of paper.

PL 10/1;Gid:1

Gid—Today I've come to understand we live in a time of subjective reality, where the flood of information is so great that it is impossible to trust any one analysis of events. In the end, each person must interpret facts to find his own truth, a truth he can live with.

Here are some facts I thought you should know:

Item: The disclosure forms of Judge Evelyn Crawford indicate her husband has taken heavy financial losses each of the past two years.

Item: Crawford is sixty-four, due to retire next year. Her husband is sixty-two. She might work, then again she might not. Her pension will hardly cover the cost of their home and condo in Scarsdale.

Interpretation: ??????

McCarthy read it through three times, then folded the paper in half and slid the memo into his coat pocket. On his way out, he thought about what Perkins had said about the condo being ransacked. It hit him. He ran back to his computer and quit out of his personal work area.

It took him nearly twenty minutes, but he finally struck the two-word combination—Yankee/Clipper—needed to open up Prentice LaFontaine's work area. An enormous directory of files appeared on the screen. He typed in a series of commands that culled through the files by date, specifically the date News was murdered.

He hit enter and immediately the words NO SUCH FILES FOUND sprang up on the screen. Impossible. Must have made a mistake. He typed in the code and the date again. He hit enter. NO SUCH FILES FOUND

He pulled out LaFontaine's memo and typed in the exact file code that appeared at the top of the page. NO SUCH FILE FOUND.

McCarthy slouched back in his chair. It was possible that News had deleted the file, but unlikely; LaFontaine had been an information pack rat. No speck of dirt, no snippet of intrigue, no thread of gossip went . . . Gossip!

If McCarthy had learned one thing sitting next to LaFontaine all those years, it was that he kept a running log of the intricacies and outrages inside *The Post*. News used it to create the top twenty gossip items of the year, an underground list he published every Christmas. McCarthy typed in GOSDI with the 10/1 suffix.

NO SUCH FILE FOUND

McCarthy chewed on the inside of his cheek. Prentice had been at his desk for more than an hour the afternoon before he was killed. That's where he was when he'd had the argument with Perkins everyone had overheard. Emotional turmoil, bureaucratic or personal, always sent News to his keyboard.

He slid his chair over to LaFontaine's desk and tugged at the drawers. They opened, chock full of neatly arranged files. He bent low over the bottom drawer and thumbed his way through them. *BURKHARDT, SLOAN*.

He took the file from the drawer and opened it. LaFontaine would have made a wonderful clerk. All his notes were dated at the top and filed in reverse chronological order. The most recent printout vaguely described his interview with Fernando Trujillo. It mentioned T. Lawrence Leslie, Sloan, and Coughlin Burkhardt, but didn't give the detailed account News had related to McCarthy. That was strange. LaFontaine always prided himself on keeping specific notes. He glanced at the computer tag. Truj;9/30; 4/5/ The last page was missing.

He thumbed his way forward through the file, trying to find page five. It wasn't there. But on the inside back of the folder he found a yellow Post-it note, scrawled with News' handwriting. "For 10/2—GET T.L.L DOCS; FIND P.R."

GET T.L.L. DOCS. That had to be Leslie's disclosure documents, the ones LaFontaine had ordered at the clerk's office. But what or who was P.R.?

McCarthy shut the folder and tossed it over onto his desk. He dug deeper into the drawer until he came across the hard copy version of GOSDI, three folders, each of them more than four inches thick. He shuddered to think what he might find here. He flipped open the first one and was dumbfounded to discover that, again, the most recent entry was September 30, the day before News died. Nothing about his fight with Brad Perkins.

He read quickly through the September 30 entry, grinning at News's scathing description of Trujillo's eating and drinking habits, including a reminder to himself to ask *The Post*'s medical reporter if bunions were related to gout.

The next section made him wince: News speculating on the psychological effects of McCarthy losing the kids. He glanced up at the model LaFontaine predicted he'd emulate. The Zombie stared back at him with dead eyes. The fire was out.

"Just looking for some things we were working on together," McCarthy said.

The Zombie nodded, but didn't reply. McCarthy looked away, shut News's drawer, and rolled his chair back to his desk. He opened an empty drawer of his own and dropped the gossip files inside. He reached for the Burkhardt file and saw the note scrawled on the back: "Other Documents:", and under it "U.S. Justice Dept. Report 1963."

LaFontaine always kept cumbersome reports in his deep bottom drawer. McCarthy opened it, looking for the Justice Department document. Not there.

It was almost as if LaFontaine's files had been sanitized. But by whom? McCarthy jerked his head up to look toward Ed Tower's glasshole. The editor had swiveled his chair so his back was turned to the newsroom. He was still on the telephone.

McCarthy gathered up as many of News's files as he could and dumped them into his own drawers, locked them, then hurried home.

In the Shadow of the Snake . . .

The late-day sun shone hard and hot on the pale rock outcropping at the top of the hill. McCarthy held his hand to his brow to block the light, looking for the white terrier that wiggled and snuffled in the undergrowth of the canyon below him. Every once in a while he heard a faint yip as the dog flushed an animal or a lizard, then several bays as it gave chase and finally whimpers and frantic scratching when he lost it down a hole.

"Malice's over there," Miriam said. She pointed to a rustling bush about eighty yards away, back toward the house.

"He'll be all right," Carlos said. "We come out here all the time."

McCarthy smiled. "I used to play out here when I was a kid, too."

"*Tia* said your daddy played the trumpet on the rock," Carlos said. He pointed to the instrument in McCarthy's lap. "You going to play today?"

"No," McCarthy said.

"Why bring it, then?" Miriam asked.

"You like to sleep with your elephant, don't you?"

"Babar's my friend."

He turned the horn over in his hand. "This is kind of like my Babar."

"Oh," Miriam said, accepting it naturally. Despite the pain she'd gone through she still trusted. She balled up the hem of her blue dress. "Does Mr. News have a Babar?"

"He's dead, honey."

"I know," she said. "But you said being dead is like going to sleep for a long time."

"I did, didn't I?" McCarthy said. He didn't know what else to say. Carlos wandered off toward one of the dozen avocado trees, all that remained of his father's orchard. Carlos picked up a fallen avocado and threw it down the hill near Malice. There was a flash of white in the underbrush as the dog raced to the sound.

Miriam got up to join the game. McCarthy didn't allow himself to watch her go. He wondered if he'd have the same strength when she left with Owens.

He thought about LaFontaine's memo. His attention traveled down the length of the little canyon to where the Oklahoma gas man lived in a red-roofed hacienda. He stroked the surface of his father's rock and tried to tell himself he could do it.

Malice began barking then, crazy, loud, hoarse, jaw-stretching brays cut with high-pitched yips and snarls. And then above it screams, Miriam's screams. "Gideon! Gideon!"

McCarthy sprinted along the canyon rim before she could scream again. He ducked under the thick branches of an avocado tree. He skidded to a halt. Fifty feet below him on a broad flattopped boulder among a tumble of bone white rocks Carlos trembled like an off-balance washing machine. To Carlos's left the terrier leapt side to side, its muzzle drawn back to reveal angry, sharp teeth.

The triangular head arched over thick scaly coils. Disturbed from sleep on the warm rocks, the snake hissed, fangs revealed. The stiff bony rattle argued with the air. Black pearl eyes darted from the boy to the dog and again to the boy.

"Don't move, Carlos," McCarthy said.

"It's going to bite him," Miriam cried. She was in the rubble above them. "It's going to bite him."

"No, it's not," McCarthy said calmly. He edged toward

them, soft, quiet, all focus on the snake and the boy and the dog, which raced back and forth, just out of range, snarling, nostrils flared.

He reached Miriam. She moved to hug him, but he gently pushed her away and murmured "It's going to be all right."

The snake was no more than twenty feet below him now.

"Look at me, son," McCarthy said.

"I can't," Carlos said. Tears welled in his eyes.

"Yes, you can," McCarthy said. "I want you to look at me as if the snake wasn't there. It's just you and me."

The tears came heavier now, but the boy didn't lift his head from the snake.

"Carlos, tell me what you do when you're two and two on a fastball hitter."

"I can't."

"Two and two on a fastball hitter."

As if it were a heavy weight winched from mud, the boy's chin oozed up and through the blur he looked for McCarthy. "Change-up."

"Right. You show him something he doesn't expect."

"I'm . . . I'm scared."

"That's okay. Because we're going to throw this snake a change-up, okay?"

"I . . . I guess so."

From the rubble McCarthy picked up a fist-sized stone. "I'm going to count to three and then I'm going to throw the rock to the snake's right. He's going to forget you and Malice and think about that rock, just like a change-up. You're going to jump backward."

"I can't see what's behind me."

"I can. You'll fall a couple of feet and land in a big bush."

Malice darted toward the boy, yapping. The snake rolled and made a mock strike at the dog, but didn't stretch its body in full attack.

"Wait, Carlos," McCarthy commanded. He held the

rock behind his ear, focusing on a deep pile of avocado leaves six feet from the snake. "One, two, three."

The stone flew straight. The dry duff exploded into a cloud of leaves and twigs. The snake struck sideways into the cloud even as Carlos leapt backward and fell. Malice sprang after the stretched rattler to sink his teeth into the flesh at the base of its neck. The terrier's turtle jaw held tight. He snapped his head to and fro while the snake's body writhed in the bright evening air, looping around the dog's body, rattle lashing at his eyes. The dog summoned all of his strength to buck like a horse shedding an unwanted rider. His head thrashed in one savage crack of a whip. The snake went limp. Blood turned the dog's muzzle bright pink.

By then McCarthy rocked Carlos in his arms. "It's okay, nothing's going to hurt you." He looked down the canyon at the home of the Oklahoma gas man. "Nothing's going to hurt you ever again."

McCarthy made the necessary phone call much later after the terror of the day had ebbed and the children were asleep in their beds. Hanging up the phone he felt the fetters of old rules of conduct slip from his wrists.

LaFontaine was right. There was no such thing as an objective observer. People couldn't be clear lenses, recording without a flinch life's appalling comedy. Everyone had to marshal the facts to fashion an interpretation that they could live with. The key was to control the interpretation, to spin it, to give it direction, your direction. To do that you had to have all the facts. Information was raw power.

He was up until two that morning, reviewing every note he had, reviewing every note he'd taken from News's file cabinet. He made a long list of the strings they hadn't tied tight. Somewhere in that list of unanswered questions was the reason why Carol Alice Gentry and Prentice LaFontaine died. And he intended to find it. No matter what the cost.

McCarthy arrived at the city clerk's office two minutes before 8:00 A.M. A low-ceilinged, bureaucratic maze with walls the color of stale oatmeal. The only relief from the institutional effect were poster-sized photographs of the zoo and the park and Alta Bay.

A young clerk with spiked black hair and razor-thin lips waited on him. She came back with the documents LaFontaine had ordered the week before. "You want the stuff, the other guy, Jackson, wanted? The stuff on the mayor? He never came to pick them up."

"Why not." Screw Jackson.

She returned with another stack. "That'll be $16.50 for the both of them."

McCarthy paid and went to a desk in the corner. He went through Chief Leslie's disclosures first. As chief of police Leslie made $119,000 a year. He had a stock portfolio worth more than $10,000 and less than $100,000. He owned bonds with a similar assessment. His three-bedroom condo on Alta Bay was valued in the low six figures. Three years ago he'd bought raw acreage worth less than $100,000 on Lake Mead, Nevada. He had an equal amount sunk into a Texas limited partnership called Countryside.

Net worth? Probably half a million. Not out of line for an unmarried man in his late forties with that kind of annual income. But nothing here that might lead News to believe he was onto the biggest story of his life.

McCarthy put the Leslie disclosure forms aside and started in on Mayor Portillo's. Portillo grossed $106,000 a year. A politically astute move to keep his salary substantially less than that of the police chief, the city manager, and the city attorney. It made him look like a humble servant of the people. His mutual funds had a net value of between $5,000 and $50,000. His five-bedroom house abutting the south barrio—another politically astute move: stay close to your roots—was worth less than Leslie's condo.

McCarthy turned the page to "Other real estate investments" and gaped. Three years ago the mayor had bought raw acreage worth less than $100,000 on Lake Mead in Nevada. He had an equal amount of money sunk into a Texas partnership called Cityscape Ltd.

He forced himself to analyze. Leslie and Portillo were close friends and had been for years. Maybe one of them found out about the land, and, knowing they'd have to retire sooner or later, brought the other in on the deal as a place to spend their waning years. But that didn't explain the Texas investments.

It was 9:00 A.M. He needed more facts. He would not draw conclusions, nor shade them with interpretations until he had exhausted the facts.

He got himself to a pay phone and called a title search company in Lake Mead, Nevada. For $100 on his credit card he was assured he'd have the relevant documents faxed to him in the newsroom by midday tomorrow. He made a second call to Austin, Texas. For another $150 he employed a paralegal there to dig out the articles of incorporation on Countryside and Cityscape. They, too, would be faxed tomorrow.

It was now ten-forty-five. Fifteen minutes until the appointment he'd arranged by phone last night. He exited city hall. He walked north seven blocks, then took a right on Twelfth. He went into a combination coffee shop and bookstore halfway down the block.

Peter Crawford, the husband of Judge Evelyn Crawford, had already taken a booth in the back corner. A fit man in his early sixties. Silver hair and beard. Nattily dressed in a blue blazer with matching red tie and handkerchief. No hand was offered.

"I'm not at all comfortable meeting you like this," Crawford began.

McCarthy said, "Did you tell your wife you were coming here?"

"No."

"Good. I'm not going to beat about the bush. Here's the situation. My fiancée died and left me her children. They're the most important things in the world to me. Her ex-husband is a bastard and he wants them now for reasons I believe are less than altruistic."

Crawford held up his hand. "I know about your case, McCarthy. Tragic."

"Then you probably know that I'm probably going to lose them."

"My wife hasn't made that decision yet. Just get her the facts and I'm sure you'll be the winner."

McCarthy stared at Crawford. "The facts are that your wife's sixty-four and tired. You're sixty-two, on the verge of bankruptcy, and more tired than she is."

Crawford got up. "I think I'd better leave."

McCarthy reached out and grabbed the developer's wrist.

"As judges go, your wife is pretty good. I know that. You know that. She knows that. I also know that she deserves better than bankruptcy and a state pension after retirement. I'm prepared to make that possible."

Crawford swallowed and sat back down. "I'm listening."

"I own prime acreage abutting The Ranch. A very wealthy man has been after the land for the last several years. He's offered a considerable sum, far beyond its assessed value. The land has significant emotional value to me. I have been reluctant to sell."

"Go on."

"The marketplace is a strange and wonderful thing. It doesn't question why a man might choose one buyer over another. It doesn't question what a man might sell his property for as long as it seems reasonable."

Crawford hesitated. "And what might reasonable mean?"

"A thousand dollars over the assessed value," McCarthy said.

"Very reasonable. Being close to The Ranch and all . . ."

"Especially in light of what it might be resold for," McCarthy said, ending the thought for him.

"Or developed for."

"I plan never to be there to see that happen."

"You're thinking of moving then?"

"If certain legal proceedings go my way. Yes."

They fell silent. McCarthy could tell the gears were turning inside Crawford's mind, already conniving to do the deal.

"You'll hear from me," Crawford said.

"I would expect so," McCarthy said. "And soon."

When Crawford had left, McCarthy found himself studying the black flecks in the tabletop. It had been easier than he thought and that's what sickened him. What had brought him here? Cynicism? No, that was too easy. Awareness? Maybe that was what spawned the cynicism. Whatever it was, the cumulative effect was to crush the last bit of his belief that there were commonly held standards of right and wrong. He knew now that he was finished as an investigative reporter, as a reporter of any kind. He couldn't stand back and observe anymore. He was involved.

There was just this last story to get. He would see it through to the end. He owed News that much.

The House of Bile . . .

"This is Connie."
　　　"I know a motel on State Street."
　　　"Is that a fact?"

"It is. And I know that in a half an hour there will be a brown leather satchel on the bed in Room 11-B."

"And what will be in that satchel?"

"Three peacock feathers and a silver-sequined mask."

Neil Harpster smeared the phone against his ear, waiting anxiously for Mills's marvelously perverted mind to turn the four inanimate objects into a carnal fantasy capable of off-setting the dread that had enveloped him the past thirty-six hours. Every ninety minutes since leaving LaFontaine's wake he'd received phone calls from Margaret Savage. Here in the office. At home. Lydia calling him in from the garden, demanding to know who his lover was. He, warding off her attacks with the three-pronged weeding fork, pleading, telling her it was all a campaign of persecution to keep him from getting the promotion he deserved. Then going back out into the garden to find the azaleas chopped to bits, the shredded leaves arranged on the dark soil in a letter "Z." He desperately needed to escape on the exotic landscape of Connie's body.

The line was silent.

"I said, three peacock feathers and a silver-sequined mask."

"Doesn't do anything for me," Mills replied.

"What?"

"Boring."

"You and me with three peacock feathers and a silver-sequined mask—boring?"

"That's what I said."

His ears rang. Cold sweat broke out in his briefs. Harpster tugged his tie open and looked out through his Glasshole. She had her perfect backside to him. Exactly the way he wanted it. But naked and in their squalid motel. "We . . . we could be inventive. Maybe pretend we were circus stars. Yes, that's it: acrobats!"

No response.

"Or . . . or Harlequins. I'll pick up some black-and-white makeup on the way?"

"Sorry."

Beyond Mills, on the far side of the newsroom, Harpster saw something that put him over the edge: Savage had arrived in skintight stirrup pants, matching tank top, gold pumps, a hundred-dollar hairdo, and a foot-high stack of books. Savage turned his way, oblivious to the uproar her appearance was causing, and winked knowingly.

Harpster cried into the phone, "You've got to come with me, Connie. You don't have a choice!"

"Are you saying you'd force me to go to Room 11 B in the motel on State Street?"

"If I have to, yes," Harpster growled. "You owe me. I've given you everything. Your career. Everything. I need this and you'll comply."

"Oh, thank you, Neil," Mills purred.

Harpster sighed with relief. If she wanted to play rough, why didn't she just say so? "That's my girl. See you there in twenty minutes?"

Mills turned her chair around to face the glass. She held a cassette recorder and the phone. Between the two was a thin black wire. "You'll be served papers sometime later today," she said, her tone frigid. "This little conversation will be icing on the cake."

"What papers? What icing?"

"Sex harassment lawsuit, Neil. I've done your bidding for too long. It's payback time."

The Assistant Managing Editor for Form and Content went slack-jawed. The image of a weedy vegetable garden overcame him. He was a carrot. Bobbie Anne Pace had him by the top leaves. She was yanking.

"Margaret, what is the meaning of this?" the Assistant Managing Editor for News and Information demanded.

"Meaning of what?" Savage cooed.

Pace tilted her head so the rest of the newsroom couldn't hear what she was saying. She thumbed at the dozen romance novels that littered Savage's desk. She nudged her Birkenstocks against the columnist's new pumps. "The books, the shoes, the pants, the . . . oh dear . . . Margaret you're a redhead!"

"Auburn head," Savage corrected. "The cellophane treatment gives my natural brunette the auburn highlights."

"A protest, that's it, isn't it? This is some form of protest against the way women are made slaves to the cosmetic and fashion industries. Am I right?"

"A protest?" Savage replied. "I prefer celebration. A celebration of my awakening."

"Awakening to what?"

Savage puckered her lips. She whispered, "My femininity. My passionate femininity. And the man I love."

"Man? What man?"

"Why Neil of course. What other man could there be?"

Pace's stomach reeled. She fought for control.

"Not Neil, Margaret," she pleaded. "Anybody but Neil. You're forgetting what we've fought for, everything we've fought for."

Savage stared right past her toward the glassholeman of her dreams.

In one last reckless attempt, Pace leaned forward and yelped like a puppy.

"It won't work," Savage said. "There's only one pack animal I'm interested in now."

An hour later, just before the morning meeting, Claudette X stared at the ceiling and prayed, "Lord, I never asked you for much, 'cause I didn't figure I'd ever get it. That's just how it was being Afro in America. Now I'm asking. No, I'm begging. Spare me the nightmare I fear is about to become reality."

The heated aura of an end time had been spinning in the newsroom since the word of News's death had reached the city desk five days before, building in tighter, more concentric circles with each passing moment. She'd come to work this morning to find Pace wandering toward Lobotomy Lane making hound dog noises. In the daily story budget file, Margaret Savage indicated she was writing a column examining the lessons society could learn from romance novels. Neil Harpster had closed the blinds to his office and taken his phone off his hook. Ed Tower had disappeared just as they had a computer breakdown during transmission of the next five days of comic strips. Kent Jackson said his behind-the-scenes-at-the-Portillo-campaign piece was a bust; they had denied him access the last week. Isabel Perez was acting the prima donna, refusing to write up any more political hate Faxes until she was done with the Barnes story, which admittedly had legs and deserved the great play it was getting.

But the corker was Stanley Geld. He had arrived at his desk this morning in drab olive cotton top and bottom, shaved head, no earring. Like a Marine prepared for battle.

About the only people adhering to *The Post* status quo were Connor Lawlor, working hard in his office; the Zombie, flailing at his keyboard; the Stepford Editors, scrolling through boilerplate copy; and Abby Blitzer and Augustus Croon, hanging out in front of their police scanner.

Claudette X didn't allow herself to look over toward News's old desk or to McCarthy's. For a reason she didn't understand or didn't want to, that part of the newsroom represented a sledgehammer that threatened to break down the glass walls of the house of bile that was now *The Post*.

She glanced at the wall clock and groaned. Ten-thirty.

"Let's meet, people," Geld said.

The Stepford Editors rose and shuffled toward the conference room. The door to Harpster's Glasshole opened. He tottered out, by turns lurching and reeling between the desks, as if he'd been kicked in the testicles. From the opposite side of the room Pace stumbled from her office, dabbing at her eyes with a tissue.

Claudette X raised her hands toward the ceiling Holy Roller style. "I tell you I'm begging. I'm begging!"

The phone rang. She snatched it from the cradle. "Post, city desk."

"She's gonna kill him!" an elderly woman yelled.

"Kill who, ma'am?"

"That little boy. She's got her little boy and she's threatening to kill him. They have the cops all over my roof and they got the whole street shut off. Haven't you heard? Gail Howe, she lives with that artist fellow. She's gonna kill that boy."

Claudette X scribbled the address, thanked the woman, and hung up. She lumbered toward Croon and Blitzer. "You got anything on a SWAT operation, something involving a little boy?"

Croon shook his head. "Nothing. But we've been listening on the main channel, maybe they've gone alternate."

"Little boy?" Blitzer asked.

"Mom threatening to kill him. Lives with some artist at 3407 Palm View. Go."

Croon slung cameras and lens bags around his neck. Blitzer remained seated.

"Abby, I said there's a tragedy going on."

Blitzer's shoulders trembled. "I'm not feeling well. Maybe I came back too fast, you know? Maybe I need another day."

The executive assistant city editor drew on a heretofore untapped reservoir of fury. "This is a daily newspaper and that's news happening now. You're the tragedy expert. You're here. You go!"

The tiny reporter took on a crazed expression. Claudette X took a step backward, afraid Blitzer might bite. Croon knelt and said, "Abby? We'll go together, all right?"

Blitzer's eyes spun. Then they dulled. She nodded, took Croon's hand, and walked.

For a long time, Claudette X stood frozen. This had never happened. Never! She had been scared of that little woman. No, she had been goddamned petrified. *I'm losing it,* she thought to herself. *I'm going down.*

"Claudette?" Geld called from the conference room. "Hurry up, please, it's time."

She turned to find Geld chomping on an unlit cigar. John Wayne ready to storm the beaches in a World War II movie. It was all a dream. Just a bad dream. She took her seat at the conference table, aware, but not panicking at the sensation that a strange liquid streamed into her lungs. It was good, actually. This was what they said about drowning, wasn't it? After those first couple of breaths you enjoy the narcosis of the deep?

After Geld had dispensed with the perfunctory chores, including a brief mention of the unfolding tragedy Croon and Blitzer had gone off to cover, he smiled and turned the meeting over to Harpster, who was hunched over his end of the table.

"My wife is suffering side effects from taking sedatives to control her rage at the vandalism being done to her garden," he began in a tone that reminded Claudette X of Boris Karloff on a bad day. "I myself have slept outside nearly every night for two weeks. My neighbors have formed a garden watch society. It's all they talk about. I want to know why we haven't published a story."

At the other end of the table, Pace arched her eyebrows and sighed audibly. "The gardening problems of a bourgeois neighborhood hardly make for real news, Neil. I mean, my god, it's not like people's pets are disappearing."

Harpster glared at her. "The story's been written, hasn't it?"

"Been in the can for a week," Geld announced.

"Then why hasn't it run?" Harpster demanded.

"My call," Pace said. "There were more pressing stories."

"Your call! Who are you to make that kind of decision?"

"The Assistant Managing Editor for News and Information!"

"I'm the Assistant Managing Editor for Form and Content!"

Pace leaned forward over the table. "What exactly does that mean, other than the fact that you get paid more because you're a man?"

The Stepford Editors shrank, their irises thickening to the consistency of soda bottle bottoms. Claudette X pushed back to avoid being caught in the cross fire. Geld pressed forward, his attention darting from one end of the table to the other like a rabid fan at a hard court tennis match.

"Paid more?" Harpster stood now. "Damn right I'm paid more. I deserve more, not because I'm a man, but because I'm a pro. I've got credentials! You! You're a goddamned fashion bimbo who rode her way into her job on the back of a hairy-legged he/she who can't write! And when that wasn't enough, somehow you convinced my secretary to sue me for sex harassment!"

Like a platoon on a parade ground, the Stepford Editors snapped about-face and gave him the collective flinty eye. Sex harassment? This guy's career just went poof! They shifted their attention to Pace. She still mattered.

"A bimbo!" Pace whined. "Neil called me a bimbo! You're all witnesses."

Geld shook his head in disbelief.

Pace got her second wind, hissing, "You demeaned that girl, you and your filthy lunchtime rendezvous. I was the one who freed her from your lecherous grasp. You're finished, Harpster! I will be taking Ed Tower's job!"

Ed Tower's job? Several of the Stepford Editors wondered if they should take to their knees before this shooting star editress whose career had unfathomable velocity.

Harpster's expression turned cockeyed. Claudette X had witnessed that sort of facial cast only once before, the day Geld learned that Pace had been given the job he'd long coveted. For a split second she wondered if Harpster would break into a crazed dance for lust lost and potential thwarted.

Harpster choked on his spittle. "I'm not the only one who's going down. I've got your nutcase columnist making seven obscene phone calls to me on tape. I'm suing you and her for causing me and my wife severe mental anguish."

Harpster stood and pointed at Geld. "Look under her fingernails! I can see dirt from here. My gut tells me Bobbie Anne shitcanned the cactus-napping story because either she or her deviate friend is the plant assassin! She's been trying to drive me nuts so she can take Ed's place. I'll prove it. Connor will believe me!"

The cigar flopped from Geld's mouth. This was better than he'd ever imagined. Yet even the dancing city editor could not have predicted what happened next. The veins at Pace's temples stood out like worms after a heavy rain. White flecks of phlegm appeared at the corners of her mouth. She leapt onto the table, a clog held high.

"You turned my best friend into a hormonal mess!" she screamed. "Now you shall feel my wrath!"

Pace bared her canines, howled, and tore past the giant outstretched hand of Claudette X, which had reflexively

reached for the editor's ankle. A Dutch shoe rotated downward with furious intent. Harpster flipped back out of his
chair. They fell onto a pile of yesterday's editions. Harpster
cowered from the blows. Pace swung and barked and swung
again.

Everyone in the room played the part of perfect objective
observer. Except for Claudette X, who'd seen enough street
brawls to understand that a clog was as deadly as a black-
jack. She dove across the table. She hauled a sweating, cursing Pace off Harpster and threw her into the corner and
ordered her to "SIT!"

Confronted with a true Alpha bitch, Pace's fury evaporated. She slid meekly to the floor and fought the urge to roll
over on her back and expose her belly.

Claudette X bent over Harpster. Blood trickled from a
gash on his forehead. The smell of urine filled the air. He'd
pissed his tropical wool pants. She gripped him by the collar, jerked him to his feet, and sent him to the men's room.
Harpster waddled out in silence.

Claudette X waited until he was gone, looked at Pace,
and pointed to the door. "Now you go get yourself cleaned
up, too." Cowering, Pace slunk through the door.

Claudette smiled. This was more like it: To keep the
nightmares at bay you kept the fury high.

Geld! She clenched her fists, turned, and immediately felt
the liquid surge into her lungs all over again. The entire
cadre of Stepford Editors stood at attention, their eyes as
translucent as fine Waterford, gazing in adoration at the city
editor. Geld returned to them a snappy salute.

Mrs. Van Gogh . . .

"What's going on, Abby?" Croon asked once they were out on the freeway.

"What's always going on with us, Croon?" Blitzer said. "The wretchedness of remorse. A total reversal of fortune. Or calamity. Or exceptional suffering. Anything that appeals strongly to common human sympathy and pity."

"No, Abby, I mean with you."

"Take your pick."

"You going to let me in on what's been eating at you the past few weeks or not?"

"This is our exit," Blitzer said.

Croon cut across three lanes and roared up the ramp right into the 3200 block of Palm View Avenue. Two blocks east they saw the black SWAT van and a police barricade.

The second Croon had the car parked, Blitzer was out, moving in the direction of the barrier. Croon jogged after her. He grabbed her by the shoulder. "Before we go up there, you tell me what . . ."

The reporter spun and twisted out from under the photographer's grasp. "Stay out of my business and let me do my job! Okay?"

Croon bit down hard on his back molars, a trick he'd learned at SEAL school to control his anger when he was being chewed out by a superior officer. He looked through her as if she wasn't there. "Sure, Abby, I'll do that."

Blitzer hesitated, unsure of Croon's sudden detached tone. "Good, then. Everything will be fine, then."

"Abby, let's just get this tragedy and get it over with. Maybe for good."

"What's that mean?"

"I think it's time for us to search for catastrophe on our own."

Croon brushed by her. Blitzer watched him jog up to one of the crowd control cops and show him his press badge. The officer nodded. Croon disappeared into the melee beyond the barrier.

Blitzer was seized by an excited phobic reaction, half-intellectual, half-sensory, that she had been here before. That comforted her and terrified her at the same time. Yet she noticed that she was walking now as if she had no choice in the matter, one foot after the other, faster with each step toward the cop who controlled the street.

He glanced at her press pass. "Go on in, but stay in back of the second line up there. This one's a barbarian."

In one motion she had her notebook and pen out and ducked under the line searching for the root of the crisis at hand. She saw Lieutenant Conrad, the SWAT team leader, standing at the rear of the black SWAT truck and homed in for the details.

"Hello, Conrad," she said.

"Hey, Blitzer, long time no see."

"No animals held hostage this time?"

"Just a ten-year-old little boy. So you can consider this operation preapproved by the SPCA as well as the Humane Society, thank you."

"What do we got?"

"Just a second." He held a finger to the headset he wore and spoke into a microphone. He turned to a black male in his late thirties dressed in a trench coat who held a portable phone. Conrad whispered. "We have a free field of fire from the roof of 3405."

"Not yet," the hostage negotiator mouthed. He turned away and resumed his murmurs of assurance, conciliation, and goodwill.

"Conrad?" Blitzer said.

The SWAT lieutenant pushed the microphone away from his mouth. "Gail Howe, forty-one. Makes her living as a free-lance graphic designer. Neighbors say she's been supporting a Stephen Bernstein, struggling artist . . . painter I think . . . and his son the past eight years. Kid's name is Isaac, aged ten. Bernstein supposedly hit it big, a New York show, loads of recognition, promise of money. And, as the story goes, Bernstein told Howe he and Isaac were moving out about a week ago."

"So he basically sucked her dry until his boat came in."

"It's a shitty world, but she didn't have to take it out on the kid."

Blitzer didn't want to hear what was already coming out of Conrad's mouth.

"As far as we can tell Howe's been taking antidepressants ever since Bernstein dropped the bomb. Busbar, some drug the FDA just pulled off the market. Turns out they have a nasty hallucinatory side effect if you double them up."

"That's enough," Blitzer said. "I can't take this anymore."

She began to walk away.

"She cut the kid's ear off," Conrad called after her. "She's threatening to take the other if Bernstein doesn't come back to her."

Blitzer stopped. She saw the face of a little boy peering out from the pages of a newspaper, a perfect little ten-year-old boy with a gap in his front teeth and sandy blond hair and a shy smile. She felt the unmistakable, seductive, evil craving for Jack Daniel's slip over her like a shroud.

The hostage negotiator yelled to Conrad. The SWAT lieutenant bellowed into the microphone. The flat crack of the .270 sniper's rifle came to her as if over a telephone line marred by static. She moved toward the noise, the way one will move toward something familiar in a foreign place. She noticed an opening in the phalanx of police officers and wandered through. Two paramedics rushed toward her, carrying a gurney. A little boy cried and bled on the gurney. Blitzer followed him toward the flashing red ambulance, turning finally at an insistent bumping from behind and calls for her to get out of the way.

A woman on this gurney. Strapped down. Red sunset on her right shoulder. Her tongue not acting normal, hanging out the side. And Blitzer sobbing now, pleaded with the woman "How could you do it to him? How could you do that to a little boy?"

And the woman, dazed by the gunshot and the rush of events, lolled her rag doll head to see the little reporter. "Didn't you know?" she slurred. "I'm Mrs. Van Gogh!"

Blitzer barely remembered striking the woman, let alone Croon grabbing her from behind while she flailed and cried and demanded the right to put the bitch out of her misery.

It was almost an hour until the kaleidoscopic perceptions gathered into a whole and she knew that she was in Croon's arms and they were on somebody's front lawn down the street from where Gail Howe had mutilated her boyfriend's son.

Blitzer raised her head to Croon.

"I was drunk," she whispered. "I was at a bar for happy hour one night after work and I refused to let my fiancé drive me home. When he wasn't looking I skipped out the back and got behind the wheel. I don't remember hitting the boy, not really, just a thump on the way home. I thought he was a pothole."

"Abby, I didn't . . ."

She pressed her fingers to his lips. "You have a right to know. His name was Dennis Carter. He was ten and wanted to be a movie director. He had a video camera that he took with him everywhere he went. They found it near him.

"I saw the story in the paper the next day. A tragic hit-and-run. They said he was wearing a red shirt when he was hit. I went to the garage to head for work. Hung over as usual. I saw the shred of a red shirt stuck in the corner of my car near the headlight."

"You never told anyone?"

"I was too afraid," Blitzer said. "Too afraid that they wouldn't punish me enough for taking that little boy's life. So I got sober and decided to punish myself every day by getting a job where I had to confront tragedy on a never-ending basis. Only harsh reality became a drug like any other. I got hooked on it, Croon, and it masked what I had done and wouldn't let me go until it started to eat me."

Blitzer shivered in the heat. Croon tightened his grip on her.

"I'm tired of tragedy. I was tired of it before News died, but I just couldn't stop. I feel like Dennis Carter's this monkey on my back. I need to tell his mother what I did to him before I get hooked on something more narcotic than tragedy that'll sedate me to where it doesn't matter if she knows or not."

Croon stroked her hair. "I'll go with you, Abby."

"Why would you do that, Croon?"

"Because I don't think you'll ever think it didn't matter. It's always going to be there to hurt you. That's what personal tragedy is, a painful mystery that's never solved."

"How do I live then?" Blitzer whispered.

"You get hooked on something that helps even the weakest people in the most tragic of circumstances to survive."

"What's that?"

"Love."

When she looked up at him he was crying. She cried, too, and smiled at the same time.

"I think I could do that, Augustus Croon. One day at a time."

He Died Smiling . . .

At the same time, McCarthy was sweltering in the heat outside the Los Angeles County Jail, waiting to see Shirley Barfield, the hooker who'd gone with Gentry to one of Tiger's parties.

He'd been here nearly two hours, waiting, while other members of the motley visitor's group had already been allowed the enter. The deputy in charge of visits had made it clear she considered reporters scum lower than child pornographers, crack whores, and criminal defense attorneys. He was about to go plead with her again, when she called out his name.

A second deputy, square-jawed and muscular, accompanied him to a room divided by partitions of bulletproof glass. A brooding guard sat inside an elevated glass box at the center of the room. "You got booth seven," the deputy growled.

He walked down the row looking for the hooker who had been to one of Tiger's parties. Shirley Barfield, a.k.a. Anne Carris, was already seated on her side of booth seven, already making an evaluation, a street survivor appraising him as predator or prey.

Peroxide blond, pouting lips, a pert nose, and brown searching eyes. Mid-twenties. Even in the baggy jail clothes, McCarthy could tell her body was long. Her breasts were high and large. She shifted so her bearing altered from streetwise to erotic promise. She'd probably used it a thousand times on a thousand strange men.

"What do you want with me, lover?" she asked. Her voice rolled, a husky blend of velvet and too many cigarettes.

"My name's McCarthy. I'm a reporter with *The Post.*"

In an instant the pose of hooker to street john vanished. Panic seized her and diminished her to the point of child before the fall.

Before she could get up, McCarthy blurted, "Those two cops didn't kill Gentry. It had to do with Tiger's Escort, didn't it? Please, I believe my best friend was killed because of this."

Barfield slumped in the chair. "I'm scared," she whispered.

"That's why you have to tell me," McCarthy said. "You'll be safer if someone else knows. It's protection."

He forced himself to soften his face and open his eyes wide and kind, projecting the persona of the caring social worker. Barfield wavered, the child and the whore doing battle. The whore won, but barely. "What's in it for me?" she asked.

"I can talk to the cops. I know the homicide detective in charge of this case."

The second laugh was heartless. "Fisk? You're in the dark, aren't you?"

McCarthy stammered, "What are you talking about?"

"He knew Carol Alice, used her just like he used me. Like he used a lot of the girls on the Boulevard."

McCarthy's thoughts lurched back to Fisk in his office, Fisk angry when he said he didn't believe Blanca and Patrick were the killers. And Gentry! *This goes up much higher than street cops.*

"Tell me about Fisk."

"I asked you before, what's in it for me?"

"I've got $125 in my wallet. I'll bring you more."

Barfield leaned back in her chair. "It's a start."

McCarthy drew out his notebook. "Let's go then. How did Fisk use Gentry?"

"She was his informant, just like me," Barfield said.

"That was back about a year, year and a half ago, when Fisk was working Internal Affairs before homicide."

McCarthy interrupted her. "Fisk has never worked IA. He couldn't. He had his own problems ten years ago."

Barfield tossed her thick hair back over one shoulder. "Maybe not officially, but that's what he was doing. He told me he was working directly for the chief of police on sensitive internal matters."

"No offense, but why would someone like Fisk spill to you?"

She drew a fingernail along the lapel of her jail shirt so the shadow of her heavy breasts appeared. "Some men, especially short ones, need to prove themselves to women."

"He slept with you?"

"Fucked is a better description. Fucked Carol Alice, too, I'd think. Once a week I'd meet him to turn over what I had on who was up and who was down on the streets. Bad boys or good guys, he didn't care as long as I was giving him dirt and some of the nicey."

"So he was investigating the sex for protection scheme on the Boulevard . . ."

"At the same time he was screwing me and Gentry."

That's why Fisk was so quick to seize on Dusk's story. It cleared the books and shut the door before his role in the sex scandal could be discovered. McCarthy asked, "How do you know he had the same relationship with Gentry?"

"She told me."

"And that's why you don't think Patrick and Blanca killed her?"

"No," she snorted. "Different stuff."

McCarthy stayed silent until he could see her getting antsy for him to say something reassuring, to tell the child inside once again that it was okay to tattletale. "Don't you think it's time you told someone all that you know?"

"You're really going to help me?" she said in a voice that was almost sweet.

"I said I would."

She looked at her fingernails for a long time, then adjusted her bra strap. "There was a party back in February or March sometime, I can't exactly remember. Before then I'd done a few tricks for Tiger's just like Carol Alice, only she was more a regular, I think."

"Who ran Tiger's?"

"I don't know. I called a number and a woman talked to me a long time, said Carol had spoken highly of me. Asked about my prior employment. I lied and said I worked the upscale hotels near the beach. I got hired. They called me when they needed me."

"All right. What about the party?"

"I didn't get a call for that one, just Carol coming up to me midweek and asking was I available for a special event that Saturday night? The deal was for the maximum, fifteen hundred dollars."

"Where was it held?"

Barfield waved her hand. "Somewhere up north of the city on this swank estate. A limo picked us up around five in the afternoon. Pulled up to a gate, then up a steep driveway. The house was one story, white, and had a big patio, a pool, and a Jacuzzi. We were up on a hill because I could see the city lights below us. Besides the five gals in our limo, there were six or seven other ladies I'd never seen before already inside."

"Nothing else about the estate?"

"Hey, it wasn't like I was there to take inventory. The place looked like someone very rich owned it."

"Okay. How many people at this party?"

"With the gals from the second limo, probably twelve pros. And fifteen, twenty men, typical johns—forties and older."

McCarthy flipped a page in his notebook. "Go on."

"We went in and mingled like we were told to by this woman, Dee."

"Describe her."

"About my height I'd guess. Five-eight, five-nine. In her forties. Pretty, sort of silver blond hair. Dressed to kill."

McCarthy stopped writing. "Was there a guy with her, this Dee?"

"Not right then, but later, yeah. But I'm getting to that. So we went in and played the party hostesses, telling them what studs they all were, having a few drinks. The guy who latched onto me's name was Dickie. Early fifties, balding, kind of tubby. He was a medical equipment salesman or something. Anyway, by about ten, people were swimming nude in the pool and in the Jacuzzi. It was getting kind of crazy."

Barfield stopped and chewed on her lip. McCarthy said, "Where was Gentry?"

"That's the thing," she went on. "I'm busy with Dickie and another couple in the Jacuzzi. I look over my man's shoulder. She's heading inside with this older guy in white tennis shorts. A half an hour later my randy boy's getting his second wind when bang, out of the house comes Dee. She's in a black silk robe now, moving fast. She's going from scene to scene, voice low, saying there'd been an accident that could *prove embarrassing*. Everybody starts going for their clothes."

McCarthy was writing as fast as he could to keep up. "What kind of accident?"

"Give me a second here, will you?" Barfield pouted. "Dee walks away and old Dickie's freaking 'cause he can't have any more of my nicey. He's asking me do I want to go to a hotel? But I'm not seeing Carol and I'm getting real nervous, cause I wasn't leaving without her and I told Dickie so. I got in my clothes and headed for the house."

Her expression sobered. "I get inside the house and it's like you read about. Paintings on the wall. Designer furniture. Huge living room with a floor-to-ceiling window overlooking the city. Only there's one strange thing."

"What's that?"

"Sinks in every room. Like they have in doctor's offices, you know, with those high kind of curved faucets and the paddle things to turn the water on and off?"

"Burkhardt," McCarthy murmured.

"Who's that?"

"Just someone I've been thinking about a lot." He refused to show excitement until he'd heard the whole tale.

He could tell she didn't believe him, but she didn't press the issue and continued. "I was looking at this one sink—built in to the wall of the library with nice fixtures—when I heard a bunch of voices, including Carol's down one end of a hall.

"Carol started screaming, so I ran down the hall. There's this pale guy with a ponytail in red boxer shorts. He's got Carol pinned by the throat against the wall. Her man's on the bed, belly-up, naked, with this silly smirk on his face. He ain't breathin'."

McCarthy's jaw hung slack. "Gentry used to boast that she fucked a guy to death."

Barfield pressed her tongue against her bottom teeth. "No lie, lover."

A female deputy came up behind Barfield and signaled that they had three minutes.

"Finish it," he said when the deputy had left.

"Okay. Mr. Ponytail sees me and stops choking her. She's coughing, telling him it was only a joke. I figure she made a crack about the dead dude only he didn't think it was funny. Ponytail tells me to get the hell out. I told him I wasn't leaving without Carol. He stares at me like I'm a dog or something and makes a move toward me, but I pull out the can of pepper gas I always carry and he stops. He thinks about it for a second, then gives me a cat grin, throws her dress and bag at her, and tells us to go."

"And you go?"

"You bet we do. Outside the driveway is nuts, with these

old guys jumping into BMWs and Mercedes and limos. Carol, she's laughing like it was all a ride at Disneyland."

McCarthy jumped in. "The choker, did he have a mole over his lip?"

Barfield thought about it for a second. "Yeah, he could have. But it all happened so quick, I can't say for sure."

"But you'd recognize him if you saw him again?"

"I think so. But there's more to the story."

"Hurry up. We're almost out of time."

Barfield turned to her left and held up a finger to the deputy who was approaching now. "Please, just one more minute."

The deputy crossed her arms, but nodded.

She whispered, "Me and Carol were the last to be dropped off that night. As soon as the last girl was out, she starts laughing again. And I tell her it's not too cool to be laughing about a john croaking under you. I believe in ghosts, you know? She pulls out a little cassette recorder from a side pocket of her bag and tells me the joke, 'the cosmic joke,' as she put it, is who got a phone call after her man died."

McCarthy squirmed in his chair. "Who?"

"She didn't say. But she sure had whoever it was recorded. She kept singing that song about 'having a ticket to paradise.' Couple of months later she bought that condo."

The deputy was back. She put her hand on Barfield's shoulder. Barfield grimaced, then looked at McCarthy and rubbed her thumb and finger together. His legs had melted at the rush of these disclosures. He steadied himself enough to stand and smiled weakly at the woman and the deputy. He pointed to the guard station.

The guard gave him an envelope into which he stuffed all the cash he had in his wallet. He passed it through the iron drawer. She drew the lever down, opening the drawer again. Inside was an envelope from Barfield. In the room on the other side of the guard's bulletproof cubicle, the hooker mouthed a plea "open it."

The piece of paper inside read "DON'T USE MY NAME. I TRUSTED YOU. I'M SCARED. MORE $$ SOON?"

McCarthy glanced at her and nodded. He walked unsteadily to the door and down the gallery through the gate past the obnoxious deputy. One part of his mind was already sorting the awful facts into story form, seeing the gaping holes still to be filled. Gentry had been blackmailing Burkhardt and whoever else was on the other end of the telephone over the death of one of the boys at the sex shindig. The odds-on favorite for the corpse had to be Burkhardt's banker, Bobby Carlton.

The challenge was to place Carlton at a party that everyone would swear had never happened. And, of course, to figure out just who had been called and how they got Carlton's body to The Ranch Country Club. Lurking at the periphery was the question of how News had figured it out and who had killed him for his knowledge.

He'd do whatever it took now to figure it all out. He'd lied to Shirley Barfield. He would use her name in the story. She didn't matter to him. She was information, not a person. She would hate him and he didn't care. He tried to tell himself he was doing this for a greater good. Self-deception fled with the memory of himself proposing a bribe to the husband of a superior court judge. He didn't know who he was or what he stood for anymore.

Before he got in the car for the long drive south, McCarthy stuck two fingers down his throat and vomited. There were no humans involved. No humans involved in this story anymore.

An Exotic Minority
Hire . . .

T he next morning, Isabel Perez fondled the con-
traband sniffable badge through her red silk
blouse while admiring the front page of this
morning's *Post*. Her fifth A-1 piece in a week, a humdinger
based on a leak she'd gotten from a regional staffer with the
Environmental Protection Agency detailing a broadening of
the federal probe into night dumping by candidate Barnes's
high-tech company.

On a common day this would be occasion for the home
run trot around the newsroom bases gathering kudos from
editors and reporters, blatantly drubbing Kent Jackson's
nose in the knowledge he'd been one-upped again. These
trips were necessary to keep the career trajectory steep and
the fragile ego in its proper distended state.

But today was no common news day of twisted events,
contorted civic platitudes, and grandstanding promises
never to be kept. Cyclone winds had blown inside *The Post*
these past twenty-four hours.

Connor Lawlor and Ed Tower had gusted into the after-
math of the brawl between Bobbie Anne Pace and Neil
Harpster, demoting the former back to fashion bimbo and
the latter to a cubicle at the rear of the room from which it
was rumored he would edit the food and garden news pending the outcome of the sex harassment lawsuit.

Margaret Savage had been ordered to write her farewell
column on the Metro page. She'd been given the society
beat in recognition of the sudden and decisive dulling of her

point of view not to mention her newfound love of frippery, mock cashmere, and Ralph Lauren at discount.

Fearing her litigious bent and in acknowledgment of her Stanford education, Lawlor had assigned Connie Mills to work for Tower managing the Swingo game and any other game of chance her fecund, if deviate, imagination might devise.

And then there was the Zombie. He'd showed up to work wearing a Hawaiian lei around his neck. A weird smile was pasted across his lips and he'd turned his desk to face the cubicle where Harpster toiled in exile.

No doubt about it, Perez thought, the old hierarchy of Lobotomites had toppled. The fast-trackers derailed. Now the question was: whose ass was best smooched to assure an unchecked ascent to the strata of the sniffable?

Stanley Geld had been given the responsibilities of the former Assistant Managing Editor for News and Information and the Assistant Managing Editor for Form and Content. The wags in the room were calling him the Assistant Managing Wizard for Machiavellian Alchemy. In hushed tones in private, of course. No need to screw up the future with an objective, public assessment.

At this very moment, Geld had his spit-shined combat boots up on the desk in Pace's old Glasshole. He sported aviator sunglasses and waved an unlit cigar over his head while blaring into a phone with all the fire and pig lust of a Hollywood agent.

Claudette X now occupied Geld's old spot. She'd been offered Harpster's Glasshole, but strangely turned it down. Perez's lightning-quick news analysis? Claudette X lacked true upper-level newspaper leadership qualities. Still, she was a woman to be feared. Especially because she could not be ass-kissed.

It was rumored that the carrot of investigative editor had been dangled in front of McCarthy's nose, but *The Post*'s premier gumshoe had not made an appearance in the news-room in several days.

Which brought the consummate careerist back to herself. There was no doubt that she'd supplanted Kent Jackson as Big Foot political reporter. Jackson was coasting these days, a member of the vast political journalism stockyard, feeding contentedly and without follow-up on fax fodder, position papers, and news releases.

Perez knew that more bovine reporters would be ecstatic at this turn of events. But she understood that even with this promotion she was nothing more than a big fish in a small pond. In the greater stream of the news business she was no closer to becoming an odor-producing, agenda-setting re-porter than she had been four months ago.

She got her credit card folder from her purse. A good binge and purge would quell the current inferiority com-plex. She glanced at the clock. Ten minutes to noon. She'd saunter off for a quick buying spree and be back by one, able to survive to deadline with the anticipation of a little sinsemilla and evening fashion show with her mannequins.

The phone rang. She snatched it from its cradle.

"Post. Perez."

"Isabel Perez?" A man's voice with an assured East Coast accent.

"Speaking."

"Phelps Harrison. A.M.E. Human Resources. *The Wall Street Journal.*"

"Yeah, right. Who is this?"

The man laughed in a hale manner that struck Perez as somewhat forced. "I get that all the time," he said. "This really is Phelps Harrison."

"Good God," Perez said, immediately annoyed at her re-action. She smacked her forehead with the butt of her palm to calm herself. "What can I do for you, Mr. Harrison?"

"Ms. Perez," Harrison began. "We, at the *Journal* I mean, have been terribly impressed by your work of late.

Breaking Barnesgate and all. And we asked around a bit and, to be honest, we're attracted also, well, by your, um, background and your . . . er . . . how do I put this? . . . lifestyle."

"Excuse me?"

"Getting me to qualify," Harrison stammered. "Good reporting instincts. Okay, Ms. Perez, I won't beat around the bush here. Of late the *Journal* has been criticized for its rather limited, Eurodollar outlook, and we're looking to broaden it."

Perez's heart beat wildly. "With a Hispanic . . ."

"Lesbian perspective," Harrison finished the thought for her.

"Bisexual," she corrected.

"Oh, right, bisexual," Harrison coughed. He coughed again. "Now the position we have open is on the editorial page. Are you wed to the reporting side of the business?"

Perez swallowed and fought off the impulse to shout *No! Whatever you want! Whatever it takes!* She played for broke. "Depends on what the job entails."

"General editorial writing at first and, within a year, as we see how you get along, signed editorials offering your, er, unique viewpoint on politics, social trends, issues of the day. You get the picture."

"I do," Perez croaked.

Her temples roared. She was having trouble breathing. Black dots appeared before her eyes. She realized with horror that in her attempt to retain composure she'd twisted the chain of the stolen *Washington Post* amulet so tight around her neck that she'd almost choked herself into unconsciousness. She untwisted the chain and let the blood flow back to her brain.

"Ms. Perez? Are you there?"

"Yes," she gasped. "Yes, I'm here."

"Well? Does the position interest you?"

"One question. Do your editorial writers go to national political conventions?"

"You'd eventually be based in our Washington bureau, so I'd imagine so."

"I'd get a badge on a chain? A badge that says *The Wall Street Journal?*"

"Absolutely."

Perez sat up straight to savor the moment. She imagined at her feet a rainbow of career possibility arcing up at an impossibly steep angle into the journalistic ionosphere. She flared her nostrils at a dreamy wind. She inhaled slowly, sweetly, swearing to herself that even now there was the un-mistakable pheremonal scent of agenda-setting power wafting up from between her damp breasts.

"Well, then, Mr. Harrison," she purred, "you've got yourself an exotic minority hire!"

Full Disclosure? . . .

Meanwhile, oblivious to the status inversions occurring inside *The Post*, McCarthy leaned on the public counter inside the coroner's office, a low-ceilinged, cream-colored affair tinged by the faint but troubling odor of chemicals. He was studying the complete autopsy report on Robert S. Carlton III under the watchful eye of Dr. Nicholai Trush, a Ukranian expatriate and one of the city's deputy assistant medical examiners.

"Sperm and vaginal secretions in his pubic hair," McCarthy said. "You didn't think that was unusual for someone who was supposed to have had a heart attack on a tennis court?"

Trush, an almost-skeletal man in his late fifties, chain-smoked unfiltered Pall Malls. He tongued a smoke ring into the air. "I note it, did I not?" he said.

"But you didn't include it in the conclusions."

"No need. Carlton dies of heart attack brought on by heat from playing the tennis."

"I have reason to believe Carlton died while having sex."

"With who? Ball girl? Maybe linesbaby?" Trush guffawed at his joke.

When he saw McCarthy's dark countenance he stopped. "Look, McCarthy, for all I know, he has sex before the tennis. He was found on court at night. Alone. I write that he has these secretions on him. As far as I am concerned he dies because he's a fatty bank president who thinks he a nocturnal Andre Agassi. Case closed."

Seeing he'd get no more out of Trush, McCarthy got a copy of the autopsy report and drove downtown to the courthouse. His nerves were raw. Sleep hadn't come at all last night, after the way he'd lied to Shirley Barfield, after the late call he'd received from Judge Crawford's husband concerning their arrangement.

Crawford's message was clear-cut: "You've got a deal. List your property exclusively, no multiples, with a small Realtor. I'll be in touch."

Karen Rivers had called shortly afterward. Part of him had wanted to go to her, to take refuge in her arms if only for a little while. Instead he'd been abrupt, told her he wasn't feeling well and would call later in the week. He knew it had been a cold thing to do, but his focus had become so narrow that any romantic side trip was unacceptable.

He'd gone to the hallway outside the children's rooms afterward and watched them sleep to give him the strength to finish what he'd begun. Now, as he headed to the clerk of the court's office to find Carlton's probate documents, he wondered if the lying and the posturing would ever become easy.

According to the documents, the late bank president had a net worth of $11.6 million, most of it in stock and real estate holdings. There was also an art collection, a coin collection, and an ample investment portfolio of mutual funds, bonds, and commodities.

McCarthy found the appendix that itemized the real estate investments. The first two pages were routine: an accounting of Carlton's primary residence north of the city and vacation homes in Oregon and Montana as well as a condo at an Idaho ski resort and a partial share in a hotel in Cozumel. Given Carlton's financial stature, nothing shocking.

Halfway down the third page he came across a listing that broke sweat on his wrists: a four-acre parcel on Lake Mead in Nevada. Page four turned the spigot: Carlton had three-quarters of a million sunk into a Texas partnership known as Suburbia, Ltd.

This story was taking on shitkicker dimensions.

The image of News hovered before him as he took the stairs two at a time back to street level. He got angrier and more respectful of LaFontaine's reporting instincts with every jump; somehow that crazy bastard had gotten onto this. Somehow, if Perkins wasn't lying, it had got him killed. McCarthy stopped on the sidewalk outside the courthouse amid the crowd of legal dogs and swine, the sued and suers, the scum and the victims.

A thought bloomed. He tried to deny the attraction, but couldn't. It was the journalistic grail, the unspoken dream of all those who sit before computer terminals in grubby newsrooms. The annual April accolade. The singular laurel of heavyweight status. The dimensions of the story were there: corruption, murder, cover-up, exposure, murder to cover it up again. No doubt about it. McCarthy was working Pulitzer terrain.

* * *

A knot of papers choked his newsroom mailbox. He tugged the lot out and moved cautiously to his desk. He thought about the obvious sanitizing of LaFontaine's files. If there was a leak inside *The Post*, he didn't want to tip his hand by appearing in any way exuberant. That may have been what got News killed. He should avoid the newsroom completely. But he needed one more look at LaFontaine's files and, depending on what the mail held, access to the paper's computers.

McCarthy slipped by the Zombie, whose hands rested dead still on his keyboard. He eased into his chair unnoticed by the rest of the reporters and editors, many of whom were gathered about Isabel Perez.

McCarthy rifled through the mail. In the middle of the stack lay a thick yellowed report from the U.S. Justice Department. Date: May 1963. This had to be the report News had noted on the back of his Burkhardt file. How the hell had this gotten in his mailbox? He glanced up at the newsroom. Nothing unusual. He opened the report.

It detailed the findings of the federal probe into corruption surrounding the old Jennings administration, including a recommendation to indict the former mayor on charges of bribery, kickbacks and tax evasion. The report also noted the jailing of Lawlor, the editor's refusal to name his sources, and his subsequent physical injuries. It noted that several inmates suggested that jail guards were part of the attack in which Lawlor's leg had been broken. The incidents were described as examples of Jennings's widespread abuse of power.

Deep inside the report he found a dog-eared page. On it, a list of people the Justice Department had brought before federal grand juries during the investigation. Fresh pencil underlined the names Coughlin Burkhardt, T. Lawrence Leslie, and Ricardo Portillo.

"What's the point, News?" McCarthy muttered. "Trujillo told you they all went back that far."

He thought about it some more, looked at the list again, not finding Carlton's name as he'd wished, then closed the report, confused. He turned the document over and found a name and an address: Pablo Ramirez, 111 Carbine Dr.

Why had News been so interested in this guy? McCarthy tossed it off when no explanation offered itself, put the report in his briefcase for future reference, and returned his attention to the remaining stack of papers.

A three-page fax from Austin. He closed his eyes and said a silent prayer. He turned the cover sheet over and read. Countryside Ltd. and Cityscape Ltd. were partnerships organized two years ago "to engage in business, including, but not limited to the purchase and development of real estate ventures." Each partnership had three shareholders, all unidentified. The listed general partner on all of them was M. L. Crisp, offices at 99 Hawthorn Way, Suite L., Houston, Texas.

McCarthy jiggled his knees under his desk. He knew that Chief Leslie was one of the partners in Countryside. And Mayor Portillo an investor in Cityscape. That left two other partners in each case to discover. Something else there tugged at his memory, but he couldn't place it. He set the documents aside and pressed on.

The next Fax report was thicker. Blurry photocopies of the quit-claims, transfers, deeds, and liens surrounding acreage on Lake Mead. Both Leslie and Portillo had purchased their land—contiguous, according to the subdivision map the paralegal had smartly thought to include—in May three years ago. They each had mortgages from the same Nevada bank. The seller: Sandstorm Development Corporation, offices at 1190 Pierce Way, Suite 3B, Las Vegas.

Even without requesting the information, McCarthy's instincts said that Carlton's land on Lake Mead was also bought from Sandstorm and that his partnership in Suburbia, Ltd. was linked to one M.L. Crisp of Houston. But what did it mean?

McCarthy closed his eyes, breathed deep, and let his mind wander, free-associating possible links among the jumble of data that had assaulted him the last five months. Scared whores and slain whores and dead bankers and murdered reporters lay nude on the shoulder of a highway paved with public documents. Bouncing fast over the ragged potholes on the road, he kept glimpsing something in the blur of his peripheral vision. An address. A name. LaFontaine's chart!

McCarthy had the bottom drawer of his desk open in a flash, tearing through the files he'd stowed two days before, back through the interviews, until he found it—News' carefully constructed diagram of the dummy companies that made up Sloan Burkhardt's Blue Coast Partners Inc. Max L. Crisp, address 1190 Pierce Way, Suite 3B, Las Vegas, was the agent and sole director of Flower, Stone, Tree, River, and Tressor, Inc.

"Holy shit!" he whispered to himself. "There's the link. I've almost got it!"

There was no denying the interlocking nature of the various partnerships, land deals and corporations within the documents before him. The mayor and chief of police were financially involved with a real estate tycoon who'd just landed the biggest waterfront development deal in Southern California, a deal that had to be okayed by the mayor and the city council. For all McCarthy knew, Portillo and Leslie had interests in one of the corporate shells behind Blue Coast. Maybe those Texas shells owned the Nevada shells!

His instincts said Carlton had had a role in all this, too. It was possible the mayor and his police chief were involved in the cover-up of the banker's death—at a sex party no less!—and the subsequent slaying of a blackmailing street whore. But why exactly?

Then his instincts took over. The campaign. Gentry was

killed because of the governor's campaign. He still didn't know why, but he was certain it was true. He told himself to compose, to affect a wearied disinterest. He got up and ambled across the room to intercept Perez as she made for the door, credit card billfold held smartly in hand.

Perez spied him and said, "No need for congratulations, Gid. I'm kind of worn-out from the attention I've been getting."

"Congratulations?"

"Can't you smell it? *The Wall Street Journal.* I've been hired!"

News was right. The world was ending. He managed to say, "It couldn't have happened to a more deserving person."

She pecked him on the cheek. "Thank you, dear," she said. "It will happen for you, too, someday. You're a fine reporter. We'll have to do lunch before I depart."

"Do lunch? Uh, right. Say, would you mind if I ran something through that campaign database you were building a while back?"

Perez laughed brightly. "It's incomplete, I never had time to finish putting in all the records, but you can do whatever you want. I don't give a damn about any of it anymore."

She mimicked a deep male voice: "Isabel Perez, you've just been hired by the Daily Diary of the American Dream. What are you going to do next?"

She paused for effect. "I'm going shopping!"

With that she giggled and skipped off toward the elevators.

McCarthy went to Perez's desk and brought up the database on her screen. It was divided into several fields of reference, including contributor's name, corporate affiliation, address, amount of contribution, candidate's name, and whether the money was given during the primary or general phase of the election process.

He sorted by name asking for Robert S. Carlton III. Two

hits. McCarthy broadened the fields and fingered the enter button. Carlton had given the maximum to Portillo in the primary and the general election for a total of $5,000. The date of the later contribution was March 24. Two days after he was found dead.

McCarthy predicted a pattern. He narrowed the field to date only and asked for all contributions received by Portillo on March 24. He struck enter and grinned wildly when a list of fourteen names, thirteen of them male, blipped onto the screen. He knew some of the men by reputation, all of them local political and financial big-swinging dicks. Eighth on the list, a man named Dickie Hatch, corporate affiliation: Transverse Medical Systems—Shirley Barfield's Jacuzzi partner. Ninth on the list, Sloan Burkhardt. And right behind him, the only female, Diane Tressor.

It was a textbook example of "bundling." The individual or organization sponsoring a fund-raiser acts as a middleman to the campaign, gathering all the checks, then bundling them together for delivery. Though the coordinator of the fund-raiser goes on record as giving only the limit, members of the campaign remember that the person was the gatherer of as much as twenty or one hundred times the limit. An effective loophole for gaining influence while remaining within the campaign finance laws.

Despite Carlton's death at the perverse fund-raiser, Burkhardt had been unable to resist bundling the checks and delivering them to Mayor Portillo. McCarthy printed the screen, then quit out of the database and returned to his desk.

He sat very still for several minutes, organizing the various themes within the information he'd uncovered in the last twenty-four hours until the story moved logically in his mind.

Two o'clock now. He studied the pace inside the newsroom. He wanted to talk to Lawlor alone, to spring the story on him without interference from any subeditor. Especially, one suspicious subeditor. That meant deadline, when all attention would be diverted away from the largest Glasshole in the room.

Setting the Trap . . .

"Got a minute?" McCarthy asked.

Connor Lawlor twisted away from his computer terminal. His normal wind- and sun-polished complexion had turned sallow. He had raccoon eyes. He had lost weight.

"Not another disaster, I hope," Lawlor said. "I can't take another crisis for at least a month after that fiasco with Pace and Harpster yesterday."

"Just the opposite," McCarthy said.

The editor pointed over the reporter's shoulder, taking in the newsroom with one sweeping motion.

"Goddamned business has gone birdie. Used to be you expected eccentrics, even supported them for the good of the paper. A corkscrew mind has a way of uncorking things people want to keep sealed away. Now reporters and editors got agendas, personal and professional. No one out there just loves to tell a good story. It's like a bunch of certified public accountants, image consultants, public interest groups and corporate strategists got together and sent their spear-carriers into the newspaper business. Inside they decided to throw an orgy. Only they're all impotent or frigid."

He picked something off the end of his tongue and flicked it away. "Enough of the ravings of an embittered old man. What's up?"

"May I close the door? I think there's a leak inside."

Lawlor made a dismissive gesture. "Of course, there's a

leak inside. This is a business of blabbermouths. Nothing that's news can stay in here for long."

"No, I mean a serious leak, concerning the biggest story I've ever been onto."

The bushy gray eyebrows gathered together at the bridge of the editor's nose. "Shut the door. Then out with it."

McCarthy closed the door and took a seat. He started with the documents that described the interlocking corporate structure of Sloan Burkhardt's Blue Coast Partners, all of them linked to Max L. Crisp of Las Vegas, Nevada.

Thunderheads formed on Lawlor's face. "I told you to lay off Burkhardt."

"Prentice and I worked on this after hours. I've got it cold."

Lawlor rubbed at his eyebrow in annoyance, then signaled him to continue. McCarthy took the editor through LaFontaine's discovery that Coughlin Burkhardt had Fernando Trujillo seal the prostitute beating case against Sloan Burkhardt with the help of Chief T. Lawrence Leslie.

That got the editor's interest. Lawlor sat forward and drew a legal pad and pen toward him. "You're sure Leslie was there?"

"Outside Trujillo's office. The lawyer swears it."

"On the record?"

"No. It's a sealed case, remember? He can't talk officially."

"Okay. We'll get around it. Where do Burkhardt and Leslie fit together?"

"And Ricardo Portillo. But I'm getting to that. Just hear me out."

"The mayor?" Now Lawlor was all business. "Keep going."

McCarthy pressed on, taking Lawlor through Dusk's telling him that another hooker feared that Gentry had been killed for reasons other than finking on Patrick and Blanca, the phone call he received from LaFontaine just before he died as well as Brad Perkins's assertion that he found News dying when he got to the condominium.

"You believe this guy Perkins?"

"He makes a good point," McCarthy said. "The place was in a shambles—remember?—someone went through his files. Why would he do that if this was a crime of passion?"

"Money. Information. I can probably think of a dozen reasons."

"Perkins swears he had enough money. And his life secrets are hardly news."

A clerk came to the door, knocked, and poked his head in.

"Not now," Lawlor growled without looking up."

"Please, sir, there's a question on . . ."

"I said, not now!" Lawlor roared. The kid scurried away. Lawlor pointed a finger at McCarthy. "Continue."

McCarthy gave the editor an account of the various people who'd told him that Gentry had boasted of screwing a john to death. Lawlor rolled his eyes, but McCarthy pressed on without giving him a chance to interrupt. He explained how he'd gone to the L.A. County Jail and how Shirley Barfield gave him the story of a heart attack at a sex party. He repeated Barfield's description of Gentry's glee at having taped an incriminating conversation.

Lawlor took his cane in hand at that point. It no longer had the dull finish McCarthy remembered. It appeared newly varnished. The editor stood up, leaned on the cane, and paced behind his desk. "She's on the record?"

McCarthy thought of Barfield's plea for protection, gritted his teeth, and nodded.

"But no names. She gave no names."

"Just the guy Dickie. But I know who he is. Who they all are."

Lawlor stopped and turned. "How?"

McCarthy allowed himself a grin. "Campaign finance records."

"You're kidding."

"Nope. It was a fund-raiser of some sort. They all wrote checks the same night last March. Burkhardt couldn't resist bundling the checks and delivering them himself."

Lawlor tossed his head like he'd been hit with a left hook. He leaned over the cane for support. "Then who's the dead guy?"

"Robert S. Carlton III. Died the twenty-fourth, same night the checks were written. He wrote one, too."

"Jesus Christ! I thought it was a heart attack playing tennis?"

"That's the official story," McCarthy said, pulling a piece of paper from a folder he had on his lap. "I pulled his autopsy report. The coroner found semen and vaginal fluids in his pubic hair."

Lawlor picked up the report, read it, and tossed it back on the desk top. He took his seat, leaning his cane against the credenza. "So what do you think happened?"

The hum of the good story. The exhilarating buzz of breakthrough knowledge. McCarthy could see Lawlor sizzling on it as he laid out the rest of his booty, the investments by Portillo and Leslie in the raw acreage on Lake Mead and the mysterious real estate limited partnerships in Texas, all with links to Max L. Crisp.

Lawlor flipped back a page on his legal pad. "That's the Las Vegas attorney you said controls the five limited partnerships . . ."

"That make up Burkhardt's Blue Coast Partners," McCarthy jumped in.

Lawlor was silent for a long moment. "All right, interpret it. Frame the story for me. Better yet, frame it for our readers."

"Starting as far back as the end of the Jennings adminis-

tration thirty years ago, Leslie, Portillo, and Coughlin Burkhardt formed an alliance for political purposes."

Lawlor nodded. "Coughlin was Portillo's first big-name
supporter."

"Right. And Leslie and Portillo worked the Jennings corruption probe, during which I figure they made their contact with Coughlin. Yes?"

Lawlor's nod was noncommittal. "Maybe yes, maybe no.
Coughlin was a big fish back then. Leslie and Ricardo were
on the periphery of the investigation. Mostly gofers."

"But they were involved."

Lawlor scratched his chin. "Yeah, but they weren't central players."

"The point is that they formed relations with the old
man. Now jump forward twenty-five years. Leslie's long
since strengthened his ties to Coughlin by making sure a sex
crime case against his son gets buried. Coughlin dies.
Sloan's on his own, looking to build the kind of signature
project that will allow him to escape his father's shadow."

"And Portillo's in a position to help him get the land to
build the project?"

McCarthy held a finger in the air for emphasis. "Yes, at
the same time the mayor is in a position of need. He has
dreams of being governor. Sloan, through his business contacts, can raise loads of money. To make the relationship
even tighter, Sloan makes sure Ricardo and Leslie benefit
financially."

"You're losing me."

McCarthy tore through the documents on his lap until he
found the ones he wanted. He handed them across the desk.
"Five years ago the mayor was comfortable, but hardly
well-off. Today he has land in Nevada and serious cash in a
Texas real estate partnership that I believe is linked to Cote
D'Azure through Crisp. Leslie was cut into Cote D'Azure
for past favors. And if my gut is right, Carlton got a chunk,

too. Probably in violation of fiduciary rules governing lenders."

Lawlor hesitated, then pointed to LaFontaine's diagram of Blue Coast Partners. "You've accounted for only three of the partners. Who's the fourth?"

"I don't know," McCarthy said. "Maybe Burkhardt threw in a legitimate investor as a wild card."

Lawlor leaned back in his chair again and looked at the ceiling. "What about Gentry?"

"I'm winging it here," McCarthy admitted. "My guess is when Carlton croaked there was a telephone call from Burkhardt to somebody powerful, probably Leslie. Gentry picked up the phone in another room and taped it. Leslie comes out to fix things and Carlton's body is conveniently found on the court at the country club. Everything's hunkydory until Gentry calls Burkhardt or Leslie or whoever and plays her tape. She blackmails until they decide she's too much of a risk."

"And they kill her."

"And dump her out in the desert to make her look like another of the working girls done in by our serial murder."

"Who's the killer?"

"Take your pick."

The clerk, pale as a flounder, knocked on the door again. Lawlor gritted his teeth, looked at his watch. "Give me five minutes to take care of this."

McCarthy gathered up the various documents from Lawlor's desk and put them back into his folder. This was the second time today he'd been through every facet of the conspiracy. He was drained by the exercise, a fatigue amplified by the fact that during the afternoon he'd listed the acreage at the back of his property with a Realtor.

The woman, smelling quick cash in the air when he mentioned that the property abutted The Ranch, had fallen all over herself trying to set up a time to come out and appraise the property. When he'd told her he already had an asking price in mind and wrote it down for her, she almost cried. At a phone booth outside the Realtor's office, he'd made a quick call to Crawford's office, instructing the judge's husband to wait twenty-four hours before contacting the woman.

The foot race of circumstance and twist in the plots of his personal and professional lives were taking their toll. He was exhausted. He wondered if he had the stamina for the final sprint of reporting just prior to publication of a major investigation.

Lawlor hobbled in behind him and shut the door. He went to the window and looked over at *The Beacon*. "You think Prentice got onto this and got himself killed?"

"I think it's a distinct possibility."

"What did he know?"

"Everything I did up until the stuff about Leslie and Portillo's real estate holdings. But we were out of contact for almost a day before he died. I think he figured it out some other way."

Behind the editor's back one hand kneaded the other. The quiet went on and on, and McCarthy's attention wavered and once again he found his gaze drawn to the Pulitzer. He studied every etched line, torn in two directions by the knowledge that even as he poised on the verge of reporting triumph he was embroiled in a bribery scheme.

"It's within your reach," Lawlor said, pointing to the plaque.

"I know."

"You've got a lot of work to do."

"I know."

"This could be the story that saves *The Post*, kills *The Beacon*, and ends this war."

"I know."

"Are you up to it?" Lawlor was watching him closely now.

McCarthy remembered News sprawled on the bedroom

rug. "Yes, but this has to stay between you and me. As I said, I think there's a leak inside the newsroom."

"Who?"

McCarthy shifted uncomfortably in his chair. This was not going to be easy. "Maybe it would be better if I described two incidents that took place after News's death."

He laid out the conversations with Ed Tower at the Slotman's during LaFontaine's wake and then again after his jailhouse interview with Perkins. He took a deep breath and told Lawlor about his belief about News's computer and hard files being sanitized.

"Someone inside had to have done it," McCarthy concluded.

Lawlor's mouth hung slightly open. He stared at the reporter for a long time, then down at the pad of paper. He glanced over at Tower's empty office. "I don't believe it."

"I'm not saying it is Ed," McCarthy said. "It could be anybody in here with a working knowledge of the computers. The point is that this story is as volatile as I've ever seen and someone in here is very interested in what News and I were working on."

Lawlor's attention again shot to Tower's empty office and back. "What's his motivation?"

"He's big on the social circuit, a member of Burkhardt's Lollipop Kids—I know you are, too—but he's in there tight. And it's no secret that he's a big fan of the mayor," McCarthy said. "But to be honest, I haven't wholly figured out his angle."

Lawlor bristled. "You're asking me to withhold a story like this from a man I've known and trusted for more than three decades?"

McCarthy swallowed, regaining confidence, now that the worst of it was told. "It's not something I do lightly. But for the sake of the story, yes, I am."

Lawlor remained quiet for a long time, rubbing his thumb across his eyebrow. "Okay," he said finally. "Because of your suspicions, which I do not believe, this story will stay between the two of us until we are ready to print."

McCarthy nodded.

Lawlor went on, "Now. I'm going to advise you to do something against the conventional wisdom. Under ordinary circumstances I'd tell you to hit the peripheral players first, Burkhardt, this Tressor woman, the medical equipment entrepreneur. You know how it works, they begin to panic, the players get nervous, waiting for your call. Ordinarily, a sound strategy. But the stakes are too high here. If you make those kinds of calls, the story will begin to echo, and you could lose it."

McCarthy saw the logic in what the editor was saying. "So who do I go to first?"

"Here's how it's going to work," Lawlor said. "You're going to check out a laptop computer to begin framing the story. I don't want it on the main system. An hour from now, when the newsroom calms down and clears out, you're going to get Leslie's and Portillo's private phone numbers from Kent Jackson's Rolodex. You're going to set up a meeting in a public place tomorrow, preferably late afternoon. You tell them we're about to publish a story of grave consequence to the campaign that requires their comment and you tell them that I'm the editor. You tell them nothing more than that."

"What if they balk?"

"If you're right and LaFontaine was onto this earlier, they won't. They'll try to see what you know, especially because they'll know that I know what you know."

"Photographer? Do I take Croon with me?"

Lawlor shook his head. "If you request him, you'll start a paper trail in here. And if there is a leak, that could be enough to tip them off."

"What if I just have him tag along free-lance, no formal, documented request that would leave a paper trail in here?"

Lawlor thought a moment. "Okay, do it. But have him

shoot from somewhere far away with telephoto. I don't want his presence to louse up the ambush. And do not tell him what this is all about."

"Done."

"Good. Go get the laptop and start writing."

On Deep Background . . .

he next morning McCarthy sat at his kitchen table with the phone in front of him. The hairs on his arms tingled as if narrow-bodied, delicate winged insects were slapping him, and he realized that this was déjà vu; on a summer vacation in Oregon several years earlier, McCarthy had been surrounded and touched by clouds of orange monarch butterflies migrating over the Mt. Hood glacier.

While certain entomologists would have thought the memory sensual, the tingling only served to increase McCarthy's anxiety. Croon was scheduled to meet him at 3:00 P.M. in *The Post* parking lot. McCarthy had assured the photographer he'd be done by 6:00 P.M. so he and Blitzer could make their flight to Philadelphia for vacation.

Estelle was at the grocery store. Carlos and Miriam at school.

He'd talked to the mayor a half hour ago. Reluctantly Portillo had agreed to meet at a picnic area near the Alta Bay Marina at three-thirty. Chief Leslie proved more difficult. His phone had been busy for nearly fifteen minutes, leading McCarthy to believe Portillo had called him immediately. When he reached the chief, Leslie had demanded to know the thrust of the story before agreeing to the interview. But McCarthy held firm to Lawlor's instructions and in the end Leslie had agreed to same time, same place.

The odds stood in McCarthy's favor. But he could not quell the jitters, the tunnel vision, and the cotton mouth, wondering if he had the stuff to take them all down.

He listened to the quiet of the house. McCarthy remembered this stillness from long ago, from before Tina, a stillness he'd grown to hate. He got up and wandered, finding himself in front of her portrait on his dresser. He hadn't allowed himself to pore over her features—the almond eyes, the strong cheekbones, the intelligent smile—in many weeks. He did so now and was frightened to find that he didn't have the normal urge to cry.

"I thought it would never happen, but I guess I'm losing you," he whispered.

And at that an awareness of motivation swept through him and he confessed: "I've been invoking your memory a lot lately to do things I'm not very proud of. I've done this more for myself than anyone else, even the kids. I guess I have this idea that I can make the world understandable if I just make it right for me."

The admission took him to a deeper level of confusion. Better to dwell on pragmatic concerns. Four and a half hours until the interviews. Lawlor would wait at the office for the remaining pieces of the puzzle.

The phone rang. It was his Realtor, informing him of interest in his property. A well-connected developer. They'd come to inspect the property during the early afternoon. McCarthy agreed and hung up. The phone rang again. This time it was Isabel Perez. Arlene Troy had called her, fishing for information on what he was meeting Portillo about.

"As chief political reporter, even though I'm a short-timer, I'd like to know what's going on," Perez demanded.

Goddamn it, McCarthy mouthed. It's out. How did these things always seem to find the sieve hole? He stalled, then saw one possible escape route.

"It's personal."

"Personal?"

"And I can't say any more than that." He hung up.

The air in the room seemed to condense and squeeze his chest. The phone rang again. He needed to get out of here, to move, before this story swallowed him whole.

He gathered up all his files and the laptop. He threw the lot in the passenger seat of the Escort, came around, and climbed in the driver's side. The Justice Department report fell to the floor. A direction out of the aimless nervous energy that had enveloped him. He picked up the document, flipped it over, and found the address LaFontaine had scrawled on the back.

One-eleven Carbine Drive was a long, low building at the back of a cul-de-sac hard by the Mexican border. A brass plaque on the door read "Aztec Import/Export." McCarthy entered into an air-conditioned reception area. Expensive photographs of the Mexican pyramids hung on the wall. He introduced himself to the receptionist. He didn't have an appointment, but he'd appreciate ten minutes of Mr. Ramirez's time.

No argument. A pleasant "Be Seated." He couldn't sit. Movement was the only thing that kept the jitters away.

"Mr. McCarthy?" a velvety tenor voice called to him. To any audience, Pablo Ramirez would have been the star. Tall, a smooth, handsome face, steel gray hair slicked back at the temples. An expensively cut navy suit, freshly pressed white cotton shirt, red tie. A guileless smile. A firm handshake.

"It isn't so often I receive two reporters in one month," Ramirez said. He put his hand on McCarthy's shoulder and pressed him back through the door into a hallway with deep green carpets and beyond to an office tastefully decorated in heavy wooden pieces.

"Prentice LaFontaine came to see you a couple of weeks ago?" McCarthy began.

"I assumed you were he when the receptionist said a reporter was here to see me."

Ramirez was smiling. He didn't know.

McCarthy cleared his throat. "Mr. Ramirez, Prentice was murdered the evening after he talked with you."

The smile dissolved. There was a slow collapse in Ramirez's posture. "I was leaving for Mexico City the afternoon after we spoke. I just got back. I didn't know. I'm so sorry. Have they caught . . . ?"

"There's been an arrest. His lover."

"I'm sorry," he said again. The vibrant man who had greeted McCarthy in the hall was gone. "I am always confused in the presence of violent death. My brother, Jamie, who raised me, committed suicide. But, of course, you know that."

"Uh, no, sir. Why would I?"

"That's why Prentice came to see me. Among other things."

"If you don't mind me asking, Mr. Ramirez, what exactly did you two talk about?"

At that, the vigorous intelligence returned to Ramirez's face. "Do you think our conversation is somehow? . . . I thought you said they arrested his lover?"

"I did. But there's a lot of unanswered questions. He was my friend and I'm trying to tie up some loose ends by figuring out what he was doing that day."

"I can tell you he spent noon to two o'clock here in this office, talking about my brother and our current mayor."

"I need to hear it, too."

Ramirez nodded. "The greater community, Latino and otherwise, treat Ricardo Portillo like a savior. I know better. He's an opportunistic, ruthless bastard. He's as corrupt as anything you saw thirty years ago in this town. Only he's smart. He uses attorneys and bankers and other business connections instead of thugs and bagmen."

"You have proof?"

"Let's say I had reason to make Ricardo Portillo a personal project. Every time he made a move or made a personal financial disclosure I made sure I got a copy and followed it up. He's had his hand in several shaky deals over the years."

"You knew about his land in Lake Mead and the investment in Texas?"

"Then you found the papers I gave LaFontaine?"

"No, sir, I didn't. They've disappeared. I found that connection on my own."

Ramirez seemed surprised at that. "Some of it I didn't understand, but your friend saw a name . . ."

"Max Crisp, I'll bet."

"Yes, LaFontaine said he was an attorney in Las Vegas who was connected to Sloan Burkhardt, another mud crawler."

McCarthy sat back, stunned. News had it all. What had he done with it to get him killed? "You said there were other shaky deals."

"At least a half dozen," Ramirez said.

"Why didn't you expose him, call the papers with what you had?"

The older man's lips turned beaklike. "I wanted Ricardo to rise up so high that when I pushed no one would be able to save him."

"Why?"

"Because he all but pushed my brother off a ledge thirty years ago."

Ramirez told him how his father, who had started the import/export business, died in the early 1950s. His mother succumbed to lung cancer when he was twelve, leaving the boy in the care of Jaime and his uncle, Leandro, who took over the business. Jaime was smart, graduated from college and then law school, and was recruited to work in Jennings's office in 1957.

"People talked glowingly of my brother," Ramirez recalled. "There was faith that he would be a great man."

Jaime's first job for Jennings was as a staff assistant. Within a year, however, the mayor realized how bright the young lawyer was and promoted him to a senior staff position overseeing intergovernmental affairs. About that time the stories of kickback schemes involving Concrete & Construction began to appear in *The Post* and the district attorney launched his first investigation.

"Portillo was part of the probe, not on the front lines, but behind the scenes, that's how he works," Ramirez said. "They'd feed him the investigative reports and he'd come up with interpretations. I guess you'd call him the analyst."

Despite the allegations of corruption, Ramirez said his brother never saw it personally. Jaime remained loyal to Jennings throughout the following two years of local and state probes, throughout the constant barrage from the various city newspapers, most notably *The Post*. Ramirez's uncle Leandro died of a stroke in September 1962, leaving the import business and properties on both sides of the border to the boys.

"About that same time I remember Jaime telling me it was time to get out, that he'd decided that Jennings was indeed a crook and that working there any longer would hurt his reputation," Ramirez said, his voice hoarser now. "But he wanted to give Jennings the benefit of not resigning before the election."

A week later, *The Post* ran stories that linked Jennings to Raphael Quintana, at the time the most notorious gangster in northern Mexico. Quintana was reputed to control prostitution, narcotics, and gambling operations south of the border. The stories centered on a building in Tijuana that investigative sources maintained was used by the Quintanas as a brothel and a way station for heroin mules. The building had been owned by the late Leandro Ramirez and now Jaime and Pablo.

"The stories quoted an internal district attorney's document that indicated that the investigation was focusing on whether money had gone into the Jennings campaign from the Mexican narcotics trade," Ramirez said "The other papers in town picked up the story and Jaime's face was on all the front pages. He was crushed."

"Was it true?"

"No!" Ramirez said. "Some second cousin of Quintana rented two apartments in one of our buildings and may have been running whores there. But he was a small-timer.

"The Justice Department's report, which accompanied the federal indictments said, and I'm quoting here, 'While there is no doubt of pervasive corruption within the Jennings administration, there is no strong evidence to substantiate reports that Jennings or his staff were in any way linked to the Quintana narcotics organization.' "

"You think Portillo was behind the story?" McCarthy asked.

Ramirez nodded. "He had to be. Portillo was four years younger, a nobody slaving in the D.A.'s office. It was common knowledge that he resented my brother's position and status. Who knows, maybe he saw Jaime as a potential political opponent one day and wanted to get him out of the way."

"So Portillo leaked the story to the papers . . ."

"And my brother jumped."

The Ambush Interview . . .

It seemed fitting to McCarthy that the showdown would occur along the bleached shores of Coughlin Burkhardt's Alta Bay Park. Here vacationers jet-skied and sailed on the turquoise water while their beached brethren cavorted half-naked, toting the obligatory beer can and Frisbee, oblivious to the cesspool of betrayal, corruption, and innuendo on which the park was built.

The place had once been a swamp. Coughlin Burkhardt had used dried sewage as landfill to create several of the famous islands in the massive recreational development. On particularly hot days with the right west–east breeze, the fetid odor threatened to turn the holiday beer belly queasy. McCarthy grinned at the irony.

He glanced down at the tape recorder and the notebook and two pens by his side. Somewhere behind him, Augustus Croon was setting up. His orders were to take pictures of whoever McCarthy talked to. No need to know the story.

Ramirez had spent the last hour of their conversation taking McCarthy over the ground he'd first explored with LaFontaine, showing him documents that he alleged showed further examples of behind-the-scenes dirty dealings by Mayor Ricardo Portillo. Most of them concerned development of other downtown properties. Several detailed undisclosed free trips the mayor had taken with citizens who stood to benefit from his influence. All of these incidents blurred through an avalanche of paper subterfuge.

Too much to digest and corroborate for tomorrow's story, McCarthy thought. Certainly fodder for the page-one barrage he expected to launch over the coming weeks. The mayor and the police chief were class-A felons, perhaps accessories to murder, though the defense attorneys who would soon swoop into the action were likely to keep that appellation at bay through years of appeal.

No matter. McCarthy would get what he was here for—the meal, once tasted, that a reporter never forgets and forever hungers for: The Mike Wallace Special, the subtle, not-quite-smoky, venison flavor that fills the mouth when the bad guy flinches that first time, flinches because he knows he's put his head in a snare, anticipating the cutting wire loop, soon to be wild game for the table.

In the past McCarthy had enjoyed his share of such repasts. Today he predicted a four-course banquet: the police chief, the candidate for governor, the sadistic real estate developer, and interior designer/madam. Reporters across the country, maybe even Mike Wallace himself, would soon grind their jaws on the bones he planned to leave by the table.

The autumn sun sneaked beneath the umbrella of the palm tree and caught him square in the face. He saw the two men, one short, one tall, approach the picnic area opposite the small marina as backlit silhouettes.

"Dinnertime," McCarthy murmured. He got to his feet, calmly brushed the grass from his pants, and walked at a brisk pace directly west into the brilliant sun.

It wasn't until he was thirty feet away that he realized the scenario he'd envisioned had been bent, a prismatic distortion that cast the story in a whole new light.

"You couldn't leave fucking well enough alone, could you?" asked Lt. Jerry Fisk.

Sloan Burkhardt perched on the picnic table. He patted his hand with a fresh Wash N'Dry, like a crane preening its feathers. "The strumpet wasn't worth the effort," the developer said.

"We're being watched and photographed," McCarthy

said, sliding to one side so Croon could get them all in frame.

"Of course we are," Fisk said, waving. "I scouted the perimeter before coming in. Anyway, we mean no physical harm."

"Tell that to Prentice LaFontaine."

"The queer's demise?" Burkhardt snickered. "Not our industry at all."

Fisk said, "Not to say we weren't sort of happy at the event."

"A meddlesome queer," Burkhardt observed. "The worst kind."

"And I suppose you'll tell me the bomb . . ."

"Coincidence, too," Fisk said. "That's the problem with you reporters, a couple of random violent acts in the same quarters, instantly you're thinking the grassy knoll and the Texas Book Depository."

"I think it's an institutional weakness, the predilection for conspiracy theories," Burkhardt said, making a strange wheezing noise that McCarthy realized was his laugh.

Fisk went on, "I admit after the bombing I was on Maalox figuring we'd have a Don Bolles reenactment here with a hundred national reporters crawling all over the place. But no one showed up. Guess the intrepid old days of all for one in the journalism business are history."

McCarthy ignored the baiting. "I came to speak to your boss and your candidate."

"Too busy to be bothered," Fisk replied. "Got a campaign to run, you know."

"Then I'll just have to print my story of sex, blackmail, political corruption, and police complicity without their comment," McCarthy said. He started up the hill.

"Judge Crawford sends her regards," Fisk called after him. "So does her husband."

Burkhardt added, "That's prime land you got out there behind your place. I took a tour earlier this afternoon with your Realtor. Fits my three criteria—Location, location, location. Maybe I'll make an offer."

McCarthy didn't think he'd be able to turn. The blows had come too fast. When he managed to get himself around, Fisk and Burkhardt were backlit again, threatening shadows. Laughter and wheezing poured from the darkness.

"At the death of your sweet friend, we surmised you might turn zealot in your hunt," Burkhardt said. "The lieutenant's been tailing you since the funeral."

"Didn't take much to figure out what you were up to," Fisk stated. "The judge is sort of jelly-kneed when it comes to her reputation. Only a year away from retirement, you know. The husband's even weaker."

"Stellar investigative scribe bribes superior court judge, tsk, tsk, what a headline!" Burkhardt said.

"It's their word against mine," McCarthy said defiantly.

"Their word alone would probably do it," Fisk said. "But we didn't take chances."

From his pocket Fisk pulled out a microcassette deck like the one McCarthy held in his hand. The homicide detective flicked it on. Voices blared. McCarthy and Crawford on the phone last night ironing out the details of their illicit deal.

"You fucking sons of bitches," McCarthy said.

Fisk's grin was like a hammock. "By the way, thanks for that miserable ride through the smog to the L.A. County Jail the other day. I was wondering where little sweet Shirl had hidden herself."

"You evil dwarf."

Fisk chuckled. "Evil dwarf! C'mon, McCarthy, I got the upper hand here. You're not gonna get me to go off. Not for your photographer, anyway."

"So play your hand, Rumpelstiltskin."

Fisk's laugh choked off. He glared at the reporter, then gestured to Burkhardt, who said: "Your debauched narrative, if you want any chance at retaining custody of your beloved late fiancée's children, is now spiked. That's the operative term, isn't it?"

"That's what it's called," McCarthy said. "But I can't spike it. The editor of the paper's running this show."

"So you told the chief and the mayor," Burkhardt said.

"So here's the plan," Fisk said, "We provide you with documented explanations you can take to your editor to show it's no story. At least not the story you want to tell."

"And in return?"

"We ensure that the honorable Evelyn Crawford names you ward of the brats," Burkhardt said. "Of course, there will be a succession of delays before she makes the conclusive resolution, say six to eight months' worth, during which time you'll resign from the paper, depart the environs, and obtain office in a less strenuous line of affairs."

"If I don't?"

"You will," Fisk assured him. "The thought of nasty daddy with the defenseless little boy and girl will make sure of that."

"Not to mention the threat of incarceration for attempted judicial coercion," added Burkhardt. "In which case the promise of you seeing the fruit of your lover's loins ever again would be next to nil. You being a convict and all."

McCarthy suffered an alloyed response to the threats, a dull metallic blend of humiliation and claustrophobia that he realized were bars. For a fleeting instant he fancied himself the stoic martyr in the tradition of Hollywood storytelling, willing to sacrifice all for the sake of outing the truth. Jimmy Stewart on the floor of the Senate railing against political greed came to mind. Up in the press gallery, however, he saw Carlos and Miriam peering down at him.

"Face it, pal," Fisk said, when he didn't reply. "You're fucked."

McCarthy was too demoralized to do anything but nod in agreement.

"Thrilled to transact commerce with you!" Burkhardt said, smartly flicking a piece of lint off his blazer. "What wisdom may we impart?"

McCarthy was bowed, but his reporting instincts were not broken. For his own sake he wanted to know.

He took several steps forward out of the sun, faced Fisk, and made a thumbing motion at the developer. "Fernando Trujillo paid you ten thousand dollars to stay quiet about this verbally adept psycho's sadistic tendencies, am I right?"

Burkhardt jumped off the picnic table, his lips purpled, pasty hands clenched tight.

McCarthy pointed a finger at him. "I'm no hooker half your size, Sloan," he warned. "Besides, you might get yourself dirty wrestling out here in the great outdoors."

Fisk got between them, his forehead barely reaching the developer's tie. "We're here to answer questions, Mr. Burkhardt, remember?"

The detective turned to McCarthy. "And you're here to listen and leave. No need for disorderly conduct. The game is over."

"I'll ask the questions I want to ask," McCarthy countered. "I don't go gently, even when I've lost."

Fisk smiled again. "Fair enough. As to your question. Off the record. Yeah, sure that was me who got the money."

McCarthy turned to Burkhardt. "Sloan, you called Fisk or T. Lawrence himself when Bobby Carlton died the hard way, didn't you?"

"For the record," Burkhardt snarled. "There was no expiration at my residence. Mr. Carlton and others supportive of the mayor gathered at my house for an engaging cocktail party and buffet that broke up at nine. Mr. Carlton, for reasons I can't fathom, decided that tennis was an intriguing way to expunge the effects of smoked salmon and champagne."

"And everyone at the party, everyone who signed campaign checks that evening will testify to that?" McCarthy asked.

"Most assuredly," Burkhardt said.

"Off the record?" McCarthy asked.

Burkhardt smirked and rubbed his hands together. "The chief was most accommodating and razor-sharp in his thinking. The lieutenant here arrived within an hour to carry out the mission."

"But Gentry managed to get you on tape talking to Leslie?"

"She listened in on the bedroom phone while I spoke from my office."

"How much did she want?"

"That's irrelevant," Fisk broke in.

"Oh, humor me," McCarthy said. "I can't do any harm now."

"Fifty thousand the first time," Burkhardt said. He had his back to McCarthy, rearranging the paper towels he'd been sitting on. "A hundred thousand the second. Two hundred thousand the third. We declined to recompense at the third request for funds."

"Which came after her infamous statement that corruption went much higher than street cops?"

"Don't answer that," Fisk ordered. "You're pissing me off, McCarthy. This has nothing to do with why we're here."

"It has everything to do with why we're here. If I don't know the truth, how can I adequately fashion the lie?"

Fisk studied him a moment. Reluctantly, he said, "Yeah. She was fucking out of control."

"A liability best written off the books," Burkhardt said.

"So you killed her, Lieutenant?"

The detective flushed. "Me? No way."

"But who better to set the crime scene up so it matched the way the other whores had been slain?" McCarthy said.

"Who better to lure her in than the cop she'd acted as informant for, the cop she'd been granting sexual favors to?"

Burkhardt's head twisted around to appraise the homicide detective. "And here I thought I was sole keeper of hellish secrets."

"Shut up, Mr. Burkhardt," Fisk said, evenly. "On the record, off the record, I don't know what you're talking about, McCarthy. The justice system will eventually hold that Officers Patrick and Blanca were guilty of that heinous crime."

"I'm sure it will."

"What else you got?" Fisk demanded. "I've got things to do."

"Whoever killed Gentry didn't find that tape, did they?"

Neither man responded.

"I'll take that as a yes and further suppose that your efforts at recovery at Gentry's apartment and Billy Kemper's place were unsuccessful and the tape remains at large."

They stayed silent.

"That's a problem, isn't it?" McCarthy asked.

Burkhardt broke and sneered at him, "Not if it remains in oblivion. And if it hasn't surfaced now, it's unlikely that it ever will."

"You're becoming a pest, McCarthy," Fisk said. "Now finish up so I can hit the gym before I go home."

McCarthy addressed the developer. "Who are the limited partners behind Blue Coast?"

It seemed that Burkhardt had been waiting the entire time for that question to be thrown. In one fluid motion he opened the black briefcase beside him, retrieved a manila folder, and said. "For your purposes, I think these documents will suffice."

They were copies of contracts marked "confidential" drawn up by Max L. Crisp identifying the various partners as several well-known California financiers known to invest in real estate and two Japanese concerns McCarthy wasn't familiar with.

"I take it that these are bogus," McCarthy said.

"You certainly can't verify their authenticity without a subpoena," Burkhardt said. "And that is beyond the constitutional powers granted the fourth estate."

"Convenient that there's no mention of several Texas limited partnerships also devised by Mr. Crisp."

"Even the bona fide contracts wouldn't show that," Burkhardt said. "Max is a virtuoso of the corporate shell game. It would require excavations in secretary of state filings in sixteen states to unearth the identities behind those partnerships."

"How then do I explain to my editor the coincidence of Mr. Crisp's name on land holdings on Lake Mead, Blue Coast, and those Texas partnerships?" McCarthy asked.

Burkhardt had anticipated that question, too. "The mayor mentioned to me at a political dinner a few years back that he was interested in planning for his retirement. I knew Max was involved in some valuable raw acreage. I made a referral to a trusted business associate, who also happens to be a gifted financial planner. What other investments Max may have recommended to the mayor and his friends, I couldn't say."

"But you do have documents to prove it."

"Of course." He drew out a second sheaf of papers. Filings stamped by the Security and Exchange Commission concerning the Texas partners.

"SEC stamp, impressive."

"An acquaintance inside who owed me," Burkhardt said.

"But this can be double-checked in the documents room in Washington."

"Could be. But won't. The aura of authenticity surrounding an SEC stamp coupled with the notorious laziness of the vast majority in your profession will more than suffice."

The wind changed, blowing the odor of dried feces across the bay. "Anything else?" Fisk asked, wrinkling his nose.

McCarthy's bravura composure faded, replaced by the demoralizing realization that he had maneuvered himself out of the best story of his life. His career was finished. He shook his head wearily. "Nothing else."

"Then remember the deal and get the fuck out of here," Fisk said.

Burkhardt didn't look at him. He was languidly opening a new Wash N'Dry when McCarthy turned to drift up the hill.

The anesthetized, yet hyperaware state the conversation left him in reminded McCarthy of the mushroom trip he'd taken his sophomore year in college. The grass in the late-afternoon turquoise light had Technicolor edges that shimmered. The back of his tongue tasted of foil. His vision was watery, yet his understanding of his situation was lucid and complete. He was amused at the overall feeling. And he almost laughed out loud when he recognized that it might be best termed "an objective point of view." He was a bona fide member of the cult of modern journalism once again.

"You get the story, Gid?" Croon asked. "Shit, that sun made getting the photos hell. Had to fart around with three or four filters to get it to work."

McCarthy was surprised to find that he had made it back to his car.

"No, Croon, I didn't get it. Thought I had the goods and didn't. Sorry for hauling you down here for nothing."

Croon fiddled with a 400-mm lens. "Hey, don't look so goddamned low," he said. "We all chase ghosts sometimes. Part of the game."

"Me more than most." McCarthy opened the car door. He threw the recorder and the notebook inside on the blue vinyl seat. "Do me a favor, knock on Lawlor's door. Tell him the story's a bust. I'll explain tomorrow."

Croon drew off his sunglasses and leaned in the window as McCarthy started the engine. "Where you heading?"

He threw the photographer a shell-shocked grin. "Montana soon. Gonna be a dental floss tycoon."

Old Gossip Never Dies . . .

Over the next few hours McCarthy coursed aimlessly along freeways, over gritty back streets, and through swank seaside developments. As he drove he developed a prescription for surviving in the journalism world in the 1990s: Go with the flow and you'll find yourself at *The Wall Street Journal*. Screw with the Powers That Be and you'll eat shit.

The sun hovered low over the Pacific. He stared at the ocean. And a sobering thought flooded in. Burkhardt had been in his backyard today, maybe seen the children. He raced home.

He slipped through the back gate unnoticed. Estelle rocked on the back porch. Miriam clambered about the swing set. Carlos tossed a baseball at a backstop with elastic strings that sent the ball popping high into the air. McCarthy stood for several minutes in the twilight beside a camellia bush where they couldn't see him, taking solace in the fact that this evening they were normal kids and if he did as directed, they'd be assured some degree of future normalcy.

When the ball struck the elastic net the next time, he ran out and grabbed it from over Carlos's outstretched arms. He picked the boy up and swung him in a big circle before setting him down to do the same thing to Miriam. Estelle got teary when he whispered that in the long run Owens would not receive custody.

"But the judge, I thought . . ." she stopped in mid sentence, deciding it was better not to question Providence. "Mr. Lawlor has been calling here for hours."

"Take the phone off the hook," he said. "I'm in no mood to talk."

McCarthy spent the remaining time before bed with them, going over Carlos's math homework, reading Miriam two books. A father at peace. He thought of Karen Rivers and decided in the long run it was probably for the best to cut it off now. She thought of *The Beacon* as her beginning. He thought of *The Post* as his end.

After he'd tucked them in, McCarthy got into bed. In the darkness he gauged the effect his resignation would have on *The Post*. None, he admitted; there were so few journalism jobs available that a hundred naive kids would come hungering for his slot, hungering for a shot, any shot, not understanding the hard lessons they would have to learn. His position could be filled in a matter of days. The war machine would keep rolling. His secret buried. The story untold.

He couldn't sleep. Voices whirled to him in a maelstrom of mental chatter he couldn't silence: the tabloid witch blathered of twisted circumstance, Charley Owens lied about the past, Diane Tressor whispered of desires unfulfilled, Shirley Barfield pleaded with him to keep her safe, Lawlor lectured him about the crimes of journalism, Fisk and Burkhardt laughed at the notion of fairness, LaFontaine confided some bit of newsroom gossip. All of it spiraled downward, speed and gravity of fact and analysis arcing into a directionless black hole until he lurched out of bed sweating and claustrophobic.

McCarthy got into his clothes. He slipped from the house and backed the car down the driveway, not knowing where he was going. The aimless approach had soothed earlier.

He stopped at a bar and had a double bourbon, which calmed his stomach and stopped the sweats. He left before a second round. Becoming another statistic for Mothers Against Drunk Driving wasn't the answer either.

Another half hour behind the wheel and he found himself

downtown. The city's streets were deserted at one in the morning. Tattered pages of newspaper whipped by the sea wind fluttered and burst up the sidewalks between the skyscrapers. He got out of the car on lower Broadway and walked west.

The security guard in the lobby at *The Post* barely acknowledged his presence. He went upstairs. The newsroom was silent and empty. He sat at his desk before the green glow of his computer tube. The mounds of printed material rising around him were as big as they were the first day he'd reported to work. Only the facts in the information garbage heaps differed.

McCarthy wondered what he'd accomplished in almost two decades of churning out copy. A feeling that he'd been witness to some history. A few stories he regarded as significant. A dozen or more plaques on the wall at home, notice that his peers considered some of his work exemplary.

The sad truth remained, however, that his work had been of fleeting importance and ephemeral interest. He always thought it absurd that book companies published collections of daily journalism. Such work was all too fragmented and transitory to make any enduring sense; the lasting patterns required time and distance to reveal themselves.

"Story of my life," he said out loud. He got up and left.

Outside the wind had gathered force, throwing the grit of the city around him. He walked west again with the gale at his back for several blocks. Ahead a solitary figure in black leather lurched toward him.

"Hello, Gid," Ralph Baker slurred. "Ya missed last call. Slotman pulled the plug on the blues forty-five minutes ago."

"That wasn't where I was heading, Ralph."

"Ah, shit, call me Roy. Roy Orbison," he said, weaving

unsteadily on his feet. "I'm thinking of having my name changed. In memory of News. He named me, right?"

"Right, Ralph, er Roy. Prentice would have thought that was funny."

Baker threw his arm around McCarthy's neck and brought his boozy face close. "I knew you guys used to bet on when I'd spill my coffee, you know. I was more aware of things than you guys thought."

McCarthy felt rotten at the memory. "I'm sure you did, Roy. But it was all in fun."

"Course it was," he said. "I did the same kind of thing twenty years before. Same guy did it to another old fart twenty years before me. You know what that's called?"

"No, what?"

"An institutional memory!" he cried, and pointed to himself. "That's what I am. The things I could tell you!"

"I'll bet you could, Roy."

The old reporter got a bewildered look on his face. He belched. "Roy Orbison, that's me," he sung, horribly off-key. "Only the lonely, do do do do dee dee do.

"Ha! Don't know the lyrics yet. Got to know them before the legal switcheroo. Amazing thing, you know? You get an attorney to change the letters on a few pieces of paper and you got yourself a new identity. It's California! Hell, it's America now, it was just invented out here. No one's interested in substance. Image is all!"

McCarthy smiled in spite of himself. He hadn't heard Baker this worked up in years. "Figure on rounding up some groupies and heading out on tour, Roy?"

The leather-clad wonder scowled. "You can invent yourself, McCarthy. You can concoct things that never happened and say it did. That's the way it works now. Want to go to Congress as a military hero? Write it up in the résumé that you flew in Vietnam even though you barely spent a month at a supply depot in Saigon. Hell, there's a couple of assholes in the House of Representatives . . . the damned

U.S. House of Representatives did it. And you know what?"

McCarthy shook his head.

"Everybody knows. But no one cares. And those dick-wads get reelected year after year. No one gives a shit any-more about the truth. Do you care about the truth, McCarthy?"

McCarthy hesitated. "Yes, I think so."

"Do you really? Does anybody in our business really care what's real and right anymore? Or is it just about spin?"

Baker lurched to one side. McCarthy grabbed him under the armpits. His head lolled. Spittle dripped from the cor-ners of his mouth.

"Look at us, McCarthy," Baker mumbled. "You and me, we're part of a farce that goes way back and no one gives a hoot. The things that I could tell you. . . ."

Baker passed out then, the weight of oblivion buckling his knees, almost dragging McCarthy over onto the sidewalk with him. McCarthy was afraid the old reporter would choke and vomit. He got him upright and dragged him back down the street toward his car. For reasons he couldn't comprehend it seemed more important than anything he'd done in a long, long time to get this poor raving burnout safely home to bed.

He shoved Baker into his car and buckled him into the front seat. He realized he didn't even know where the old reporter lived. He fumbled around inside Baker's black mo-torcycle jacket until he found a wallet. He cringed when he recognized the address on Baker's driver's license as a sin-gle-room occupancy hotel in a seedy neighborhood.

A burly front desk attendant took five dollars from McCarthy to help Baker up the stairs and into his little room. When they had him on his bed, no bigger than a cot really, McCarthy covered him with a blanket.

"I'll stay with him a little while to make sure he's okay," McCarthy said. The attendant shrugged and shut the door.

It was a tiny room. A new reclining chair, an old couch, a battered coffee table, and a stereo with a collection of vinyl jazz and blues albums. A television, a VCR, and a small kitchen table with a red-and-white-checked plastic table-cloth. Two wooden chairs in need of fresh paint. In the closet were four sets of the Roy Orbison wardrobe. On the wall hung a copy of the front page of *The Post* the day after the apocalyptic albino took the pony hostage. The paper had already yellowed and curled at the edges.

A stack of thick brown scrapbooks several feet high occupied the far corner near the window. McCarthy brought several over to the reclining chair and opened them. It was strangely hypnotic to read clips from years gone by: the events that made news, the fashions in the photographs that accompanied the stories, the issues of the day.

McCarthy passed the hours between 2:00 and 5:00 A.M. that way, reading backward in time through Baker's life as a reporter, back through the intermittent dispatches of his last days on rewrite, back to the early eighties, when his production was quicker, his prose tauter. Here a tender portrait of a gang kid who'd extricated himself from the streets, there a series of articles on migrant workers. And earlier still to Baker at the height of his journalistic powers, covering the state government with authority, at Nixon's Western White House and, before that, two years of admirable work out of Saigon, including a number of eyewitness combat accounts from Hue and Khe Sanh.

A fifth scrapbook. The work no longer published in *The Post*, but the defunct *Chronicle*. Court coverage mostly.

In the middle of the book, McCarthy came across a head-line and subbar:

Jennings Aide at Center of Scandal Kills Self
Grisly Jump from City Hall at Rush Hour

He read down through Baker's account, most of it detailing the same facts Pablo Ramirez had recounted to him not twenty-four hours before. He turned the page and was surprised to find a similar headline from *The Post,* this one with a byline by Ed Tower. Lawlor was in jail by then. The facts were essentially repeated, but told tougher, more forceful in their detailing of the alleged link between Quintana and Jaime Ramirez and Harold Jennings. It was typical: in a news war every brigade crows loudest about the breaches it has wrought in the defensive line.

Baker grumbled in his sleep, rolled over, and began to snore loudly. McCarthy kept going. He found dozens of Baker's stories about the Jennings investigations, all of them accompanied by similar accounts written by Tower and earlier by Lawlor. Twice he read one of Baker's stories concerning the fact that only *The Post* reporters had ever claimed to actually have seen the district attorney's report documenting the link between Quintana, Ramirez, and Jennings. The other papers were quoting *The Post* on the report.

The lack of sleep the last forty-eight hours crept up on McCarthy. He nodded into that semiconscious state in which artists say creativity lurks. He wandered in a swirl of shadows and fog. And in the mist he caught sight of a tubby reporter given to flamboyant, bitchy statements. He ran after the ghost. LaFontaine faded and disappeared. A light in the fog now, pinpoint and red. The light moved. It glittered like a kid's sparkler on the Fourth of July. It arced and left orange trailers in the air, faster and faster until at last they connected into a fiery circle that exploded into a ball of phosphorescent brilliance, like the flashbulb of an old news camera.

McCarthy startled awake, rubbing his eyes. He looked about himself. He didn't know whether to leap with joy or sob at what he now understood.

* * *

McCarthy was home at dawn. He took his father's trumpet from its stand near the fireplace, softly slid back the glass door to the back porch, and he and the dog went out. They walked down the old path through the avocado trees. The dew had thrown the tangy scent of sage and a mélange of cinnamon and thyme into the air.

He crawled out onto the stone where his father used to play. Below he could see the vague outline of the home of the Oklahoma natural gas man. He thought about what he would be forced to do later in the day, felt tears again, then choked them down.

He closed his eyes. He listened to sounds of the land waking up, sounds that went back as far as his boyhood. He pressed the trumpet to his lips and blew. The music rolled sweet from the horn, one of his father's favorites, old and yet new under the effort of his lips. The music floated away into the canyon, rolling off the rocks on the far side, echoing back to him like fresh gossip.

The Ghost between the Lines . . .

First edition deadline at *The Post* was 7:00 P.M. McCarthy entered the newsroom at five minutes to five in the afternoon, just as the crescendo of the day's work started to surge. The beat reporters hunched over their keyboards, telephones cradled in their necks, taking the final interviews, pounding out the copy. The line editors frantically examined the stories already in queue for instances of imbalance, incongruity, and editorial aside. And beyond the Glassholes, there on the other side of Broadway, he could make out the same rising energy at *The Beacon.*

He knew he'd probably never witness it again from the same perspective and for a moment he was struck by a profound sadness. As flawed a world as it was, he'd given his life to it and loved it for just this time of day when the pace and pressure compressed, when the competition for story was at its peak, when he knew what others didn't and he was about to spring it on the city.

He shook the melancholy off. No allowances. No pity. Go for the jugular.

McCarthy marched through the maze of desks like an avenging angel. Isabel Perez twirled by in an elegant navy dress. She stopped, made as if to interrogate him, then said. "Oh, who cares what you're up to. Do what you want. It doesn't matter anymore."

"No it doesn't, does it," McCarthy said.

The Zombie stopped typing as he passed. The flaring orbs of the living dead followed his every move. Claudette X called out to him, asking if he could make a few calls on deadline. McCarthy shook his head and kept moving toward Lobotomy Lane.

Ed Tower and Stanley Geld were having an argument about story placement inside Tower's office. McCarthy made a mental note of Tower's position as he strode past the open door to the easternmost glasshole, the floor of which was raised by two inches.

McCarthy entered without knocking and shut the door. Lawlor stood immediately.

"Where the hell have you been?" the editor demanded. "I've been trying to get in touch with you since Croon came back yesterday."

"I figured," McCarthy said.

"I hold the first edition for an hour and you tell me 'I

figured,' " Lawlor cried. "This is a daily newspaper, McCarthy!"

"C'mon, Connor, you knew we weren't going with that story this morning or any morning," McCarthy said. His tone was serrated.

Lawlor hesitated. "I don't know what you're talking about."

"It was right there in front of me the whole time," McCarthy said. "But it wasn't until I stopped thinking like Gideon McCarthy and adopted Prentice LaFontaine's perspective that I figured it out."

The editor threw up his hands. "Now you've totally lost me."

"Okay, I'll be pithy: Famous editor knows about political corruption tied to sex scandal but covers it up. I feared a leak in here, but I always figured it was Ed. Never you. Never *The Post*'s icon of virtue."

McCarthy expected an explosion. Instead, Lawlor laughed softly and shook his head. "I should have listened to that voice that said 'Get him out of here' when you pulled that plagiarism stunt last spring. I tried to tell myself it wasn't the first sign of the reporter in burnout, the first thin line in the crack-up. Now here it is, the completed web of paranoia spread out on the glass. Maybe I should move you to rewrite or obituaries."

"I've got the facts," McCarthy said.

"This I've got to hear."

"You weren't there at Burkhardt's the night Carlton died," McCarthy began.

"I should say not. I was at a fund-raiser for the Museum of Fine Arts."

"I know. I checked the library. We printed a photo of you having cocktails with some local luminaries on the society page."

"At least you still do some reporting," Lawlor said.

"But after you got home, you got a phone call, a panicked call from the mayor."

"Red pencil time," the editor interrupted. "That's what's called an unsubstantiated leap of logic in this business, McCarthy. You have some kind of telephone company document to back that up?"

"I wouldn't use it in the printed story. But for the sake of narrative continuity in my oral history, I'm including it for you."

"The addled mind develops elaborate explanations. Keep going, you're on a roll."

"I figure Mayor Portillo didn't know about the shenanigans planned at Burkhardt's fund-raiser until Carlton died. But he realized the dire implications of an event like that coming to light. So he immediately touched base with his very private spin doctor."

"Me?" Lawlor said, incredulously.

"You," McCarthy said. "Pete Taylor was on night cops when Carlton died. He'd written a much bigger piece about the death, noting discrepancies in the official story. He talked with the night manager at the tennis club who'd been by that practice court ten minutes before Carlton was found. It was empty. And the security guard who discovered the body received an anonymous tip about Carlton's location. Pete says you ordered the piece hacked and buried."

"The second page of the Metro section is not buried."

"That story deserved page one play—financial mover and shaker dies mysteriously, except we didn't even mention *mysteriously*, did we?"

Lawlor's expression turned hard. "Nice piece of fiction," he said. "But I haven't heard anything that connects me to any of this."

McCarthy reached inside his sport coat and drew out a sheaf of papers. "A wonderful thing about lawyers. They tend to file documents pertaining to the same project the same day. So I asked a paralegal to pull out every document

Max Crisp filed in Nevada on the day he filed for Portillo and Leslie. There you were."

He tossed the papers on the desk. "You bought land on Lake Mead the same day as Portillo, Carlton, and Leslie. Your divorce records from five years ago show you're a limited partner in a Texas real estate venture, which I believe that with enough digging I could bring full circle into one of the partnerships in Burkhardt's Blue Coast organization."

Lawlor looked through McCarthy as if he wasn't there.

"It gets better," McCarthy said. "This morning I had a researcher at the SEC in Washington take a close look at the debentures *The Post* floated two years ago when we were in trouble. A substantial portion was underwritten by Carlton Bank through a New York firm. And my sources say that Burkhardt purchased a significant volume of the bonds, which means he has influence in here. Connection enough?"

"It proves nothing," Lawlor snapped.

"But it raises questions the *Columbia Journalism Review* would have a field day with. And raising enough questions is all it takes these days for the press to destroy a reputation. But you've known that for decades, haven't you?"

"I don't know what you're talking about," Lawlor said again. But McCarthy caught the slightest quiver in his hands.

"Let's go back, shall we? deep background to a time when a largely untested reporter gets onto the biggest story of his life," McCarthy went on. "It begins with a tip that a construction company owned by the mayor's family has been making kickbacks in return for lucrative public projects. The reporter works hard and ethically and documents several instances where money changed hands in return for contracts.

"The first story appears and the district attorney, who has been looking for a weak link in the mayor's organization, opens up an investigation. Because you broke the story, you have the upper hand when it comes to getting scoops and information. And to your credit, you work day and night."

Crevice lines of concentration appeared on Lawlor's forehead. "I didn't take a day off for more than two years."

McCarthy nodded. "Those stories were hard-fought-for, beautiful examples of what investigative reporting should be. I went through just about every one this morning and you were ahead of the government professionals at least two dozen times."

"We're not in the business of just reporting the news," Lawlor said as if from a distance. "A good newspaper makes news."

"You made big news. And if my own understanding of how wrapped up you can get in a story is any guideline, you got to the point where you felt an almost-religious need to expose Jennings, to bring him down."

"He was a walking cesspool," Lawlor stated flatly.

"As thoroughly corrupt as they come," McCarthy agreed. "But the voters didn't care, even in the face of all you'd uncovered. They reelected him. You felt betrayed."

Lawlor did not respond. But McCarthy knew he'd struck the raw nerve under the scarred-over tissue.

"When I stole those quotes last spring you lectured me about the minor crimes in journalism," McCarthy pressed on. "You said you can tape someone without telling them you're making a recording. You can let the opposition beat you on a story you knew about first, but failed to write. You could name a source you promised would remain anonymous, something you went to jail rather than do.

"But you said the worst crime you can commit in this business is to take someone else's work and call it your own. You called plagiarism 'the intellectual equivalent of armed robbery.' "

Lawlor nodded warily.

"I never thought about that metaphor closely until last night," McCarthy said. "Armed robbery isn't the worst crime there is. Murder is. And libel—making up a story and publishing it as the truth—is about as close as you can get to verbally murdering someone, isn't it?"

"I made nothing up," Lawlor said. "Jennings was corrupt."

"It's funny how year upon year of repeating a story to yourself makes it almost true," McCarthy said. "But I've read the Justice Department report. There was no evidence to support your story that the mayor was tied to Quintana through Jaime Ramirez."

"There were investigative documents," Lawlor said. "I quoted from them."

"The wonderful official document." McCarthy laughed derisively. "We reporters love them, don't we? An authentic government document says Mr. X has engaged in questionable business practices so we dutifully print it and scald the man's reputation without pausing to question, really question, if there were ulterior motives behind that piece of paper. Why? Usually we don't have time. But it's also that questioning is hard and it makes a story harder to tell. Better to jump on the *hard fact* of the allegation and, of course, put the poor man's attorney's protests in paragraph seven and tell ourselves we've been jolly well balanced."

McCarthy pointed at the editor. "Here's what I think happened. You were crushed when Jennings got reelected, even after all your stories. So were Portillo and Leslie, your two prime sources, the men with access to whatever information you needed. Add to the mix the man any investigative reporter worth a damn is going to start milking in a situation like this, the man who hates Jennings most, Coughlin Burkhardt."

The editor's thick eyebrows twitched.

"I figured you all decided that if Jennings was going to be driven from office you needed to bring in the big guns, Bobby Kennedy's boys," McCarthy said. "What better angle than the Quintanas, who had ties to the New Orleans mob?

"So Portillo and Leslie cooked a document based on the innocuous fact that Jaime Ramirez had inherited a piece of property frequented by a nobody at the outer edge of the Quintana organization. Official document in hand to show your editors, you did some sleuthing and discovered a series of anonymous sources who would back up the document's findings. Only there were no anonymous sources. It was all bullshit."

"Fuck you, McCarthy," Lawlor seethed. "Jennings was corrupt and he had to be brought down."

"What about Jaime Ramirez?" McCarthy asked. "You destroyed an innocent man for your own personal gain."

A wave of pain crossed the editor's face. "I did it for the good of the city!"

"The ends justify the means?"

"You're damn right it does. I was sick when Jaime jumped. But look around you. When Jennings was in control this was a cow town with a bunch of military bases and the promise of greatness. Now it's one of the finest cities in this country, a place people from all over the world come to study as an example of progressive urban development."

"But they don't get the real story, do they?" McCarthy demanded. "The real story is that to get these buildings up, pockets have to be padded. Face it, Connor, this is just another big city with an even bigger crook at the helm."

Lawlor shrugged. "You get to my age, you realize that sometimes you have to overlook minor transgressions for the larger benefits."

"Like your illustrious career?"

"I've stayed true to the ideals of this profession."

"You hypocrite. The entire story on which you built your career was fabricated!"

"No, it wasn't. Just Ramirez."

McCarthy gestured at the mementos on the editor's credenza. "But that was the integral piece, wasn't it? Because of it you got hauled before a judge, who compelled you to reveal your sources. You refused, not because of some goddamned reporter's right under the First Amendment to the Constitution, but because the sources didn't exist. You went to jail. You were lionized by the national press as some kind of journalism saint. They gave you the Pulitzer Prize!"

"I deserved it."

"You faked it!" McCarthy yelled, not caring that heads were probably turning in the outer room trying to figure out what the two were arguing about. "You faked a story to win the Pulitzer."

Lawlor's skin turned beet red. "I was no Janet Cooke crafting the entire world of a five-year-old heroin addict for *The Washington Post*!"

"You were worse! You were this close to getting it the right way and you decided to cut corners and tell yourself you were doing it for the benefit of mankind. Bullshit! You were doing it for the benefit of Connor Lawlor. And you sucked Ed Tower into it. Ed Tower idolized you and because of it he wouldn't dig deep enough to see you for what you were: a fraud."

"Who are you to talk to me about cutting corners for the greater good?" Lawlor snarled. "You figured out you weren't going to get Tina's kids by working the system, so you decided to bribe a judge. The ends justified the means. Face it, McCarthy, you're just like me."

"Maybe I am," McCarthy said softly. "Maybe that's the problem with this entire business. We set ourselves up as watchdogs over government, business, society. But who's watching the watchdog?"

McCarthy waved his hand at the newsroom. "I could take you out there and document every shortcoming we take delight in exposing on the front page. We've got sports reporters who gamble on the teams they cover. You don't see them being banned like Peter Rose. We've got writers with drug and alcohol problems. You don't see them chronicled in the gossip columns like Liz Taylor. We've got pundits with agendas as glaring and as biased as the Reverend Al Sharpton. We've got editors as conniving and as mad for power as Oliver North, but we ignore it, shrug it off. Almost every tough reporter turns tongue-tied or apologist when asked to explain the culture inside hard news."

"We're journalists. We aren't public figures!" Lawlor seethed.

"The hell we aren't," McCarthy responded. "We put our names, our bylines, under our stories. Stories where we filter and mold an understandable reality for our readers. That's as big a public responsibility as any. Because by shaping reality, we're playing God. And who the hell are we to play God?"

"I don't know about you, McCarthy. But I've never played God."

"No? You decide what goes in the newspaper every day. You decided thirty years ago that Harold Jennings should be thrown out of office, so you played fast and loose with the facts and ended up causing an innocent man's suicide. I always wondered why *The Post* never achieved greatness, why it was such a twisted, screwed-up place to work. Now I know. Because the moral center, you, was rotten."

Lawlor grinned and then laughed. "Nice speech, McCarthy. Too bad no one will get to hear it. You open your mouth and the kids are gone, so why don't you get out of my newsroom before I have you thrown out."

Now it was McCarthy's turn to laugh. "You know, if all you had done was fake the Pulitzer, I'd probably turn around and walk right now. The newspaper business is doomed anyhow. What's the difference if this is exposed?

"But you did more than fake the Pulitzer, Connor. You were frightened when Prentice and I started looking at this story, not because of what it could do to your buddies, but because of what it could do to you. So you started tracking us by breaking into our computer files. And when Prentice, the gossip master, figured out that there were no anonymous sources and no truth behind *The Post*'s one Pulitzer, you killed him."

At that the editor's entire body turned tense, like a snake about to strike. "You'll never prove that."

"Yes, I will," McCarthy said. "You deleted his files the day he died. But what you forgot was that we have a backup disk in the computer room."

"I didn't forget," Lawlor said. "I deleted that, too."

"I know," McCarthy said. "Two days after you killed him, you called and asked to have that day's disk loaded on the mainframe so you could review the files. The computer guys keep a record of those requests."

McCarthy took two steps and picked up the editor's famous cane and weighed it in his hands. "I imagine if the police were to scrape away the new varnish on this old shillelagh, they'd find a smattering of Prentice's blood in the wood, enough to put you away for life."

Lawlor's voice was viperous now. "That's a story that will never be told. As I said, your kids depend on you."

"You didn't think I was going to let you get away with killing News, my best friend, did you?" McCarthy asked. "This morning I called Charley Owens's mother in Denver and told her what a scumbag her son is. I told her the kids deserved a grandmother in their lives. We cut a deal and then I arranged to sell my land and give the money to Owens in return for his dropping the custody suit. The necessary documents were filed a half hour ago."

Lawlor shifted in his chair. He opened the top drawer of his desk. "There's still the tape of you talking about the bribe with Crawford's husband."

"True, but no money ever changed hands. I'll take my chances with a conspiracy charge."

Suddenly there was a very small revolver in Lawlor's

hand. "I don't think I can allow this to become public. It would mean the end of *The Post.*"

McCarthy stared at the gun, incredulous. "What are you going to do, shoot me in the middle of the newsroom?"

Lawlor shook his head. "No, outside somewhere. Here's the story: I was tipped that you tried to bribe Judge Crawford. I confronted you with it and told you your career here was finished. Because I loved you like a son, I wanted to get you out of the newsroom before you could embarrass yourself, to get you outside where I could suggest counseling. But you attacked me out there on the street. I have a license to carry a concealed weapon. It was self-defense. A tragedy."

"No one will believe that."

"I'll take my chances." Lawlor kept the gun low and motioned to the cane. "Lean that against the desk please."

McCarthy did as he was told. Lawlor got his blue blazer on. He took a silver letter opener and handed it to McCarthy.

"Good, now put that in your pocket," Lawlor said.

"My weapon?"

"Yes. You'll manage to stab me once before I shoot you down."

Lawlor put his hand with the gun in his right pocket and picked up the briarthorn cane. "We're going to take a walk out of here, real calm, real collected. If you open your mouth or make a move, I'll shoot you dead and claim you were insane in here. I was trying to get you out of the newsroom before you hurt someone. Now move."

McCarthy turned. Lawlor came up close behind him and nudged the reporter forward. "Open the door. Smile."

And then they were out in the newsroom. Several of the Stepford Editors who'd heard the muffled shouts emanating from the editor-in-chief's office looked up, but seeing the cheerful expressions on the two men's faces, they returned to their computers.

Geld approached from his Glasshole. "Connor, I have a question about . . ."

"I'm sure you can make that decision on your own, Stanley," Lawlor said briskly. "That's why I promoted you. Gideon and I are off to the Slotman's for a drink to finish hashing out a story he's been working on."

"Decision?" Geld said. "Sure, I can do that."

"Good man," Lawlor said.

McCarthy kept moving, mouthing to the various reporters who looked up at him: "Help me. Help me please."

But they were too engrossed in deadline to pay any attention. He stopped as two editors arguing about the fine points of one of yesterday's headlines passed. Lawlor bumped up against McCarthy's back with the muzzle of the little gun and he pushed on.

They continued through the newsroom and had passed by McCarthy's desk, almost to the door that led to the elevators, when the blow came. It was a spinning roundhouse Shotokan karate kick perfected on thousands of boards and hapless sparring partners that caught Lawlor flush in the rib cage. Bones snapped. The editor crumpled in his tracks.

Before McCarthy knew what had happened, the Zombie had the gun in his hand and was holding it to Lawlor's head.

The living dead reporter looked up at McCarthy, his irises the inner core of a nuclear reactor, and broke the decade of self-enforced silence, "I've suspected he was wrong for years. Go write it."

From all corners of the newsroom, editors and reporters surrounded them.

"Let me go!" Lawlor screamed. "They're both madmen. McCarthy threatened to kill me in there. Stein's obviously part of it."

Ed Tower took two steps toward the Zombie, who altered the angle of the gun slightly to stop the editor's advance.

"Gideon?" Claudette X asked.

"He faked the Pulitzer Prize thirty years ago," McCarthy said. "He knew about a huge sex scandal involving Burkhardt and the mayor and Gentry. He covered it up. News figured it all out and he killed him for it."

"Lies!" Lawlor screamed. "McCarthy's a plagiarist, a disgraced reporter! I won the Pulitzer! They'll believe me, not you!"

McCarthy's smile was cruel as he knelt before the editor. "No, they'll believe me."

He unbuttoned his shirt to reveal a running cassette recorder taped to his chest. "I've got you."

Lawlor struggled with the terror of a trapped animal, but the Zombie's viselike grip held him prone. "I won't let you write it! This is my paper! *The Post* is my paper and I control what goes in it!"

"But you don't control *The Beacon*," McCarthy said.

Behind him Karen Rivers appeared. He popped the tape and handed the guts of the story to the opposition.

"Sometimes," McCarthy said, "minor crimes, even in journalism, can be committed for the greater good."

WHETHER IT'S A CRIME OF PASSION
OR
A COLD-BLOODED MURDER—
PINNACLE'S GOT THE TRUE STORY!

CRUEL SACRIFICE (884, $4.99)
by Aphrodite Jones

This is a tragic tale of twisted love, insane jealousy, occultism and sadistic ritual killing in small-town America . . . and of the young innocent who paid the ultimate price. One freezing night five teenage girls crowded into a car. By the end of the night, only four of them were alive. One of the most savage crimes in the history of Indiana, the four accused murderers were all girls under the age of eighteen.

BLOOD MONEY (773, $4.99)
by Clifford L. Linedecker

One winter day in Trail Creek, Indiana, seventy-four-year-old Elaine Witte left a Christmas party—and was never heard from again. Local authorities became suspicious when her widowed daughter-in-law, Hilma, and Hilma's two sons gave conflicting stories about her disappearance . . . then fled town. Driven by her insane greed for Witte's social security checks, Hilma convinced her teenage son to kill his own grandmother with a crossbow, and then feed her body parts to their dogs!

CONTRACT KILLER (788, $4.99)
by William Hoffman and Lake Headley

He knows where Jimmy Hoffa is buried—and who killed him. He knows who pulled the trigger on Joey Gallo. And now, Donald "Tony the Greek" Frankos—pimp, heroin dealer, loan shark and hit man for the mob—breaks his thirty year oath of silence and tells all. His incredible story reads like a who's who of the Mafia in America. Frankos has killed dozens of people in cold blood for thousands of dollars!

X-RATED (780, $4.99)
by David McCumber

Brothers Jim and Artie Mitchell were the undisputed porn kings of America. Multi-millionaires after such mega-hit flicks as BEHIND THE GREEN DOOR, theirs was a blood bond that survived battles with the mob and the Meese Commission, bitter divorces, and mind-numbing addictions. But their world exploded in tragedy when seemingly mild-mannered Jim gunned down his younger brother in cold blood. This is a riveting tale of a modern day Cain and Abel!